Contorted Royal

By Phoenix

Part One

Story Hour in the Madhouse and Circular Time Masquerading as Déjà Vu Masquerading as Circular Time

Circular

The Black Queen couldn't get the blasted, murderous, raging ideas out of her head! It didn't matter how much she metaphorically banged her head against the wall, or how many circles she went in, she couldn't beat them out. It was becoming problematic, for more than one reason, for many reasons, in all actuality. But ultimately, there was no solution, and there could never be a solution, circular.

Circular … that word had a lot of meaning that The Black Queen couldn't quite parse, figure out, critique, understand, criticize, annihilate. She knew it would be good if she did understand the concept of circularity, circularity like the execution of circumlocution, like circular logic, but in all reality that probably wasn't going to happen.

She had been here before. That much was clear. But had she, or was that only a dream? Was it only déjà vu? Was it only in her mind, reality playing back for a second time? Third time? Fourth time? Trillionth time?

To tell the truth, The Black Queen wasn't sure how many times she'd been here before. It was probably closer to an infinite number of times, but even if that was true, what was she supposed to do about it? Huh? Hmmm? Solving that problem would be like trying to conquer an infinite number of universes—or rather, an infinite number of universes splitting off into another set of infinite universes. It just wasn't going to happen.

The Black Queen was married to The Suicide King, but she had no interest for that suicidal psychopath. Her needs couldn't be met by him. So The Black Queen, in an attempt to gain something, had begun, as she remembered, to meet and love a kid, about twenty years old, named Spade. The Black Queen was in her thirties, she'd been queen for a while now, but she felt that it was still a good match nonetheless. There was something very mature about Spade.

The thing was, she only had memories of meeting Spade here, in this moment. She didn't actually truly *remember* meeting him, because when things began to go south, The Black Queen was always *here*. Always. It never failed. The Black Queen knew she'd had a life before this moment, of course she had, of talking to Spade, but she didn't recall it. She had the strongest feeling that Contorted Royal, the kingdom in which The Black Queen and Suicide King owned and operated, was stuck in a specific period of time that repeated itself, over and over again, a broken record. Never to stop. A kind of circular Hell. A boring song set on *repeat*.

There was nothing hellish about all of this yet, of course, but she figured soon, there was going to be hell to pay. Something was going to happen. Something was going to explode, burst into seething flames.

Even though The Black Queen lived in a medieval setting, she still wore a modern-day black dress, with high heels. To tell the truth, she didn't know why she did, she just did. She didn't know how it was possible, because pretty much everyone else around her wore medieval clothes. But not The Black Queen. She wore make-up, dark make-up, that accentuated her dark eyes. She was styling.

Trying to push these terrible thoughts out of her head, about a circular hell like the circularity of logic, The Black Queen said to Spade, "You're so beautiful, you know that? Well, not beautiful, but … *handsome*."

Spade, who was wearing black medieval peasant clothes that contrasted sharply with his very bright face and bright eyes, said, "Beautiful, handsome … I'll take it. But you … you look *stunning*. Ravishing. I've never seen someone so attractive."

"You've seen me more than once, and yet you make it sound like this is the first time you've met me."

"Because it's always like meeting you for the first time," Spade said.

4

"That's sweet," The Black Queen said, and she kissed Spade on the lips.

They began to kiss for quite a while, with it being quite a romantic scene. They were sitting beneath a tree, the shade covering them from the rabid heat of the sun, sitting like a young couple discovering each other for the first time.

That was when a knife suddenly flew above The Black Queen and Spade, stabbing the tree's bitter young heart. Walking towards the couple was a man dressed in black. He was a man that The Black Queen didn't recognize, but felt she recognized. It was a man she didn't understand. It was the man that proved The Black Queen was right about her feelings of foreboding.

Spade stood up, standing in front of The Black Queen. The Black Queen pushed Spade out of the way, and said sharply to him, "I can handle myself."

The man approached the happy couple, holding a sharp knife.

"You've been here before, haven't you?" the man said.

"I don't know what you mean," Spade said.

The Black Queen shuddered. Yes, she'd been here before. She'd confronted this man, who was going to kill Spade, no matter what The Black Queen did or said.

But she felt that wasn't what the man meant.

"I suppose so," The Black Queen said. "We've been here multiple times, kissing, having a love affair to make jealous Queen Guinevere and Lancelot. But what's it to you? The Suicide King, in other words my husband, is too busy stabbing himself in the brain with his sword to care, or even notice that I'm out and about."

"Well," said the man, "that's too bad. Because he has noticed, lady Black Queen. He's noticed, and he isn't very happy. He wants Spade dead."

"I know you're lying," The Black Queen said. "Like I said, he's too busy killing his kingdom with his idiocy to care."

"Awful harsh words for his Majesty, wouldn't you say?" said the man. "But anyway, it doesn't matter. It doesn't matter at all. What matters is why I'm here. It's quite simple, really. I imagine you already can imagine what's about to happen?"

Circular time, The Black Queen thought, and she wasn't sure why she was thinking this, when there were bigger problems to worry about. She'd never been here before, it was just déjà vu. And she needed to accept that, before something bad happened.

"I don't know what's about to happen," The Black Queen said.

"They're trying to betray you, Spade," the man said, in his overly and overtly confident way. "The Black Queen and The Suicide King."

"What's he talking about?" Spade asked, looking at The Black Queen in fear.

"He's trying to confuse us, that's all," The Black Queen said. "First he says that it's The Suicide King, as for why this man is here, and then he says I'm trying to frame you. I'm curious to know what comes next: we all live in the same period that repeats itself over and over again?"

"Something like that," the man said, and looked at his knife longingly. "I'll keep it simple, Spade, since I see I've confused you with two different truths: The Black Queen has framed you. She wanted to get caught in her adultery. The Suicide King was in cahoots as well, wanting you and The Black Queen to get caught. And you know the punishment for sleeping with the queen."

"Death," Spade said stoically.

"You know it's all madness," The Black Queen said. "This guy can't get his story straight. Besides, Spade: do I look like I'd betray you?"

"No," Spade said. "But either way, The Suicide King isn't happy. He wants me dead."

"It's actually Death who wants you dead," the man said.

"Death?" Spade said, and he grabbed his head. The Black Queen saw his head was spinning, rapidly, with all of this contradicting information, with none of it making sense, all of them lies, or truths masquerading as lies, and he sat down, dizzily. "God help us all. I'm being lied to, but the constant is that I'm going to *die*."

"Maybe they all want you dead," the man said.

"Oh, stop it … can't you see you're driving him crazy?" The Black Queen said. "His head is reeling like nausea."

"I want you dead," the man said, and The Black Queen saw him say this with glee—a terrible, terrible *glee*. "We all want you dead."

"Stop torturing him," The Black Queen hissed. "He's been through enough already. He can't kiss my poisonous lips and then have someone fill his head with nonsense and confusion."

"It's only confusion because I haven't told the truth," the man said. "But it doesn't matter. He is going to die, no matter what the truth is."

"Yes, I've been here before," The Black Queen said. "I know that he dies."

"You know I'm going to die?" Spade said, looking at The Black Queen in fear and frustration. "You know, and you aren't going to do anything?"

"Of course she isn't ... she wants you dead," the man said.

"I do not want him dead," The Black Queen said, and realized that nobody realized they were in circular time: The Black Queen was the only woman or person in the kingdom who knew that things were repeating themselves, over and over again, with nothing to ever stop the repetition, the circularity. And that made The Black Queen feel alone. Because, in all actuality, what if it was just déjà vu? That's what it seemed like. It seemed like this was a one-time event, she just thought it had happened before because of déjà vu. Which was *madness*, she thought.

The Black Queen knew it didn't matter what she did, the outcome was going to be the same, what happened would be the same. The man would succeed in killing Spade. She supposed maybe that was a lie, that she could try to intervene, since this was only déjà vu, since this was a one-time thing, but she couldn't bring herself to do that as the man grabbed Spade by the hair, just a kid of course, who didn't deserve this, and made him stand on his feet.

The man pulled out a piece of paper, and unruffled it theatrically, speaking dramatically: "It is decreed that because of adulterous affairs, Spade must die, by knife. We've avoided a formal execution so there is no shame to the queen ... but you must die."

"The queen can just do whatever she wants, but I have to *suffer*?" Spade said, shooting a heated and hated look at The Black Queen.

The Black Queen, who didn't know what to do, of course, said, "Don't worry, honey: maybe we'll see each other in Heaven. Maybe I'll hang myself tonight and we'll fly around like crazies in Heaven together."

"Gee, thanks," Spade snapped.

"Oh, honey, you need to be nicer to me, considering all I've done for you," The Black Queen said, and kissed Spade again. "Don't worry. It'll be a quick death. Quick like a punch to the gut."

"Maybe you *did* want me to die," Spade said. "Maybe you *did* plan all of this."

"Maybe I did," The Black Queen said maliciously, and she didn't know why she was being such a hardcore bitch right now, betraying her lover, but she felt good doing it. She felt good because she knew that right when he died, and after, she was going to be doing very, *very* bad—the wonderful high right before the painful withdrawal. She was going to be so bad that she knew she'd go completely bananas/bonkers and have to be locked up in a psych ward or something.

Before The Black Queen could say anything, the man took the knife and slit the boy's throat. He fell, rather gracefully, and The Black Queen was grateful it had been so quick and so dignified.

"Charming boy," the man said musingly.

"Yes, he is," The Black Queen said, and she felt insanity boiling through her. "I would leave, now, before something happens to you."

The Black Queen knew she was emanating a strong heat, and knew that her gaze was sharp enough to cut through diamond.

Before The Black Queen could do anything, however, the man disappeared, vanished.

And it was more than The Black Queen could stand. She cried out, "*Noooooo!*" and fell down on her knees in melodramatic agony.

She stayed like this for a while, and as expected, none of her servants came to see how the lady Black Queen their Majesty was doing. This drove The Black Queen even more crazy. She was going to hurt herself, she felt it. She was going to punish The Suicide King. But she knew that brainless maniac had had nothing to do with this death. She knew it.

And so The Black Queen stood up, and marched to the castle. She needed to find Alice. Maybe she could help. It was highly unlikely, but The Black Queen had to try.

It was either that, or go and murder half her servants in a fit of rage, a fit of angry and painful agony. Because there were problems abound. Spade's death was only the beginning … with the circular time problem that was only an illusion in the end … and vice versa. She couldn't get her thoughts in order, and she was probably never going to, which was why she needed to talk to Alice, the queen of ordered thinking.

The Jack of Knifed by the Homicide King

While The Black Queen was busy seeking psychiatric help, The Jack of Knives was plotting his move. He was sick of being ruled by The Suicide King. He'd been dealing with The Suicide King and his inanity for a long while now, and he was going to make it clear that his plan was to take over the kingdom.

The Jack of Knives was unhappy because, being a servant, he spent many a night and day cleaning up the blood The Suicide King shed and bled. He did many other menial and awful chores, but that was the one that The Jack of Knives was sick of. He was a teenager, but he knew that he was capable of taking over the kingdom; The Jack of Knives had principles. The Jack of Knives had *aggression*.

He walked into the court. He was wearing servant clothes, set in the medieval fashion, with playing cards stitched on them. His nails and hair were dirty yellow from all of the castle cleaning, all of the scrubbing and grumbling, he'd done in the past, and his eyes were red and black, like the colors of the suits of playing cards. And yet, there was something youthful in the calloused look of the boy, something hard to place.

The Suicide King was busy standing near his throne, talking to his sword like a chatty lover. He had a curly and bushy

9

mustache, and The Jack of Knives thought that he needed to lose a few pounds ... *minimum*.

"My sweet," The Suicide King said, kissing the sword, right on the sharp blade. "I don't know what I'd do without you. You *complete* me."

The Suicide King cut his lip slightly by kissing the blade, and The Jack of Knives rolled his eyes.

Then he spoke up, loud and clear: "Excuse me, your Majesty."

The Suicide King dropped the sword as though he'd been caught red-handed making out with a virgin.

The Suicide King straightened up his royal clothes, and said, his lip still bleeding slightly, "What is it?"

"What is it?" The Jack of Knives said, not afraid to show a little bit of maliciousness. "I think you are unfit to be king. I'm going to plot a hostile takeover, to overthrow you and your bloody government."

The Suicide King didn't say anything for a moment, just stood there. Then he grinned: an exaggerated, foolish grin. He said, picking up his sword again, "Are you sure you want to play that game with me, Sonny Jim?"

"Jack," The Jack of Knives said. "I'm The Jack of Knives. And yes. I want to play that game. I'm sick and tired of sloshing through your blood and guts all the time. I want you to just *die already*, since that's what you crave so bad, you and your suicidal ideations."

"I'm not sure it's a good idea," The Suicide King said. "The Black Queen would be at my side in a heartbeat. She loves this kingdom more than anything. She's not about to let it be ruined."

The Jack of Knives pulled out a knife, and began to play with it in his hands as he talked. "As I've said: You're unfit to be king. You play with death like it's a game. That's very dangerous. Granted, you aren't out starting wars, which is just as bad ... but you're still unfit. You're suicidal ... *very* suicidal."

"Oh, my dear boy," The Suicide King said, rather peremptorily, and yet with a trace of mischievousness. "You're a *servant* boy ... I wouldn't expect you to know about these important matters, the royalty of suicide."

The Jack of Knives continued to play with the knife in his hand. "And as a servant, enraged by the monarchial system, I think you've underestimated the power of homicide."

"I don't suppose you plan on killing me," The Suicide King. "Believe me, I've tried over and over again, and I don't know how to die."

The Jack of Knives knew this was right. About as correct as it went, in fact. He in fact had no idea how he was going to take over the kingdom. The only way was if The Suicide King died, but like The Suicide King kept saying, he couldn't die, no matter how many times he skewered and speared his brain.

But The Jack of Knives wasn't worried about this yet. He said, "If I had a choice between homicide and suicide, I'd choose homicide. It's much more attractive. You hurt people to get your way."

"Just like I hurt you with menial labor," said The Suicide King, and he suddenly looked like The Homicide King: he looked as though, with his sword, he'd cut the throats of everyone in the kingdom! This passed, though, as quickly as it came, with The Jack of Knives swearing that The Homicide King had just slit the throat of The Jack of Knives.

"I suppose so," The Jack of Knives said.

"And wouldn't that make me homicidal?"

"It would make you suicidal," The Jack of Knives said. "Because you're burning out your supply of servants."

"Oh, I always import new servants when I run out," The Suicide King said happily, dreamily. "I'm never in short supply when it comes to servants. I feel bad for you, though, in the end. You don't understand the importance of suicide. Suicide is charming ... it provides a luxury that you can't get anywhere else. It provides freedom."

"Homicide is better," The Jack of Knives said. "You step on people to get power. The blood on your hands ... it feels good."

"The blood you get on your hands from suicide is better, I'm telling you," The Suicide King said. "I wouldn't want the blood of someone else on my hands, that would be just filthy. But I wouldn't expect you to understand, being ever so *crushed* by the system and looking for bloodthirsty revenge. But I do know you haven't killed a person, a single person. Ever. It's much too immoral for your tastes."

The Jack of Knives should have seen this coming. He was being gaslighted. It was true, he had never killed anyone, but that didn't mean he didn't think about it. He thought about it a lot, actually, if the truth be told. He wanted a way to prove his toughness of character. He just hadn't worked up the courage, which was why he played with knives so much.

"I think," The Jack of Knives said, "straight up murder is too *moral* for me."

"You think so?" The Suicide King said. "You? A servant boy? Who's never worked a day in his life in the morality department?"

"Yes," The Jack of Knives said. "There are a lot of pointless people in existence."

"What a terrible thing to say," The Suicide King said. "You see why I murder myself first? I don't believe people are useless, that's just sickening. Where would I be if I didn't rely on people like you to clean up after me?"

The Jack of Knives didn't actually believe this, but again, he knew, in order to survive, he had to entertain psychopathic ideas. If he believed lives were just things that he had the right to take away, it was easier to conceive of murder. Murder happened every day in Contorted Royal, after all. It was just the norm. And The Jack of Knives had been so traumatized by it that he felt it was his path. The path of the Chosen One.

"It would mean your life was useless," The Jack of Knives said.

"Oh, good heavens, boy … why do you think I work so hard at suicide? Life is so incredibly pointless. For all of us. I'm years ahead of my time, as expected from an intelligent monarch. Suicide is my idol for a reason. You, however, think it's better to get out all of your rage on society, which is a big no-no in my book. You hurt yourself: that's the rule."

The Suicide King turned his back, and began to walk around with his sword. When he turned back around, he said, "You know, there's a theory going around that there's a modern day version of our world. They say that in that world, you'd be locked up like a madman for hurting yourself or others. It seems like lunacy to me. We all have passions, and they should be allowed to roam free, hence the success of Contorted Royal as a place to be. It seems barbaric ... locking up people? I can't stand that idea. It strongly opposes my morals."

"Morality is a game," The Jack of Knives said. "And unfortunately, I think the only reason why our giant death game works in Contorted Royal is because, well ... nobody ever really *dies*. There's the occasional blip in the system, but people don't really *die*, whether by suicide or murder. Which somehow makes it okay."

"Exactly!" The Suicide King said, moving swiftly toward The Jack of Knives and patting him on the head. "There's no such thing as suicide or homicide in our world, or at least for the most part, not unless Fate or Death decrees it so. That's why we can get away with it, get away with it *all*. Go ahead and try to kill me, Mr. Jack of Knives, if it makes you feel better ... but it won't work. You won't be taking over *my* kingdom."

The Jack of Knives took all of this in. It seemed true. The Jack of Knives couldn't kill The Suicide King, who'd been trying all this time with no luck. Meaning he couldn't take over the kingdom.

But he wasn't ready to give up on that idea just yet. So he said, "I'm going to hurt you, Suicide King," and he took his knife and grabbed The Suicide King's wrist, and slit it.

The blood poured out.

"Mmmm, feels good," The Suicide King said, and watched as the blood began to float in the air.

It was a screen. Or rather, the blood became a screen. It was a screen, and it showed The Jack of Knives at the throne. He was ruling Contorted Royal, and The Suicide King was lying before him, dead. The scene didn't last long, but it was enough to get The Suicide King's attention.

"That's what you have planned for me?" The Suicide King said, sounding hurt. "After all I've done for you?"

The Jack of Knives wasn't sure what to do with this vision. He knew some visions were false, but this vision seemed real. What if The Jack of Knives was going to succeed?

The Suicide King transformed into The Homicide King. He pointed his sword at The Jack of Knives, and as he did this, The

Jack of Knives felt the urge to stab himself. And that was exactly what he did: he knifed himself in the heart.

But this didn't last long, in fact, never truly seemed to happen … because suddenly, The Suicide King was sitting on his throne, and crying.

"I'll have to find a way to kill my best servant boy," The Suicide King said sadly, sounding defeated. "That's going to tear me apart, limb from limb."

"You do that," The Jack of Knives said, barely able to contain his emotions. He'd seen the vision, he was going to rule over Contorted Royal, but … *how*? How did he get from point A to point B? It just didn't make sense.

He stormed out of the court, and continued to walk, trying to get his thoughts in order, in some reasonable line. He wanted to kill, he wanted to murder; he wanted to watch bloodshed as though he was watching the vision on the strange screen. But that was the problem with Contorted Royal. Except for those rare occasions, when death was upon a soul's life, death was an illusion. It was all an illusion! Meaning, the vision … it couldn't be real! And it had upset the royal king for no reason, which would lead to The Jack of Knives having to clean up after him … *again*.

It was all stupid. It was all terrible, the terrible nature of dangerous passions.

That was when he saw Mordred. He was not Mordred from the Arthurian legends, but he resembled him strangely enough. He was a Mordred who belonged strictly to Contorted Royal.

"I hear you want to take over the kingdom," Mordred said.

The Jack of Knives wanted to storm past Mordred, but didn't, stopped, and looked him in the face. "How did you know?"

"Word travels fast around here," Mordred said. "Plus, the king is having a nervous breakdown right now, which signifies that The Jack of Knives wants to take over."

The Jack of Knives didn't say anything for a moment, but then did storm past Mordred.

"I can help you," Mordred offered. "I know how to take the king down."

"Sure as hell you do," The Jack of Knives snapped, and continued on his way.

He wasn't getting help from a societal reject. Mordred didn't know anything, just claimed he did.

Still, it was tempting to get his help. But The Jack of Knives knew he needed to do this on his own. He couldn't get knifed by The Homicide King again. What he needed to figure out was a way to successfully let the king kill himself. That would solve everything.

But in a world of faulty reasoning, where pointless and exaggerated death ran rampant and yet didn't harm a soul, except for superficial violence … was that, in all, actuality, a possibility? Or just a strange contradiction, a contradictory mirage trying to masquerade as reality trying to masquerade as God knew what?

Crazyland Crazies in a Mad, Mad World Madhouse

Alice was diagnosed with schizophrenia when she was five years old. Since then, she had been pampered for her charming gift, risen in rank in the court (considered to be one of the most important and distinguished and intelligent people in the kingdom), and was respected for her unique vision and gift.

Right now, she was talking to her unpsychiatrist, sitting in a room with a couch. It was odd, as the kingdom was generally very medieval, except for this one random room, specially furnished with a modern-day touch for Alice's needs.

And speaking of modern: Alice was wearing a pink dress, and pink shoes.

"Things keep repeating themselves," Alice said. "I've been in this exact same session for about a million times already, maybe more, maybe closer to an infinite number of times."

"That's a very peculiar delusion," the unpsychiatrist said. "But a very beautiful one, I must say. What possesses you to think we're in circular time?"

"Well of course, there's no proof … but I wouldn't be surprised if that is the truth."

"Well, unfortunately we have no way to substantiate and prove your claim, but I wouldn't be surprised if you were right. For now, we'll have to consider it a delusion, but perhaps I'll investigate the matter a little further. We all know how often your delusions become true, now, don't we Alice?"

Alice nodded her head.

"You really are a strong and independent and intelligent young lady," the unpsychiatrist said warmly. "How has your mood been recently?"

"Very happy," Alice said.

"Excellent to hear. You aren't too overwhelmed by being such a distinguished individual in the court, I imagine, that's a job more for me."

Alice drifted away a little bit. She looked at the hallucination next to her.

He was a boy named Ralph, about twenty years old. He usually just followed her around, like a loyal puppy, but he did talk to her. He had red hair and freckles, and he wore modern-day clothes: a black t-shirt with blue jeans, and white shoes. He was a good looking kid, if only a little imaginary.

"What do you think of all this nonsense?" Alice asked Ralph.

"I think it's about as fun as it's going to be," Ralph said. "You do what you can. I know they give you way too much special treatment, but I think they mean well."

"Well, thank you. You're a sweetheart, Ralph."

"You're talking to your hallucination," the unpsychiatrist said. "Ralph, is it?"

Alice nodded her head.

"He seems like a charming boy, from what you've described," the unpsychiatrist said.

"I am somewhat charming, I'll give myself that much credit," Ralph said, beaming a little.

"Yeah," Alice said, still a little distracted. "He helps me through my good times. I have a lot of those, as you know. Moments of complete and utter beauty and happiness, that nearly destroys the soul."

"You do seem a little preoccupied, though, I'll admit," the unpsychiatrist said.

"It's because we keep repeating everything," Alice said. "To protect the secret life of the queen, I won't tell you what happens to her, but over and over again, something happens. And

The Jack of Knives ... he's trying to take over the kingdom—*again.*"

"That must be very hard," the unpsychiatrist said. "To be in tune with such pointless and needless repetitions."

"The Jack of Knives has a fairly good heart, but he's better suited as a humble servant, until the time is right for him to rule. And plus, he's obsessed with the idea of homicide. I don't think he has it in him to really and truly kill someone—you know that takes a tremendous amount of effort—but I know that he'd kill The Suicide King if that's what it took to rule the land. Not that it will work, of course. But still. You get my drift."

"And how does that make you feel?" the unpsychiatrist said.

"Rather frustrated, because I know what happens," Alice said. "But that's okay. We'll just keep repeating things over and over again."

Alice looked at Ralph.

Ralph smiled. Alice was always intrigued that even though Ralph looked like a fully-fleshed individual, there was also something ghostly about his appearance, like you could touch him and your hand would go right through him.

"Don't let it get to you," Ralph said. "There's always a key to our most stubborn problems."

Alice said to Ralph, "No, I agree, I just know what happens to The Jack of Knives and it isn't a good fate. But what can you do? What can *I* do? And I feel bad for The Black Queen. Having to suffer that, over and over again. It's terrible. She deserves better. And me always having this conversation with you," Alice said, looking at her unpsychiatrist.

"And how does that make you feel?" the unpsychiatrist asked.

"He really sucks at his job, doesn't he?" Ralph said, laughing amusedly.

Alice laughed as well. "Yes. Indeed. He does. He—"

Alice was going to say something more when a knock came at the door.

"Blasted it all," the unpsychiatrist said, standing up to open the door.

The Black Queen, upon the door opening, barged into the room and said, rather frantically, "I'm losing my mind, undoctor. I'm going crazy! Over and over, I have to watch him die! Over and over! Like a bad movie! And it's … it's … I just don't know what to do!"

"Just slow down," the unpsychiatrist said. "Can't you see I'm in the middle of treating myself?"

The Black Queen took a deep breath, and then looked around, saw Alice.

"Oh," she said. "I'm terribly sorry. But Alice is the one I was looking for anyway."

"We're in the middle of treating my symptoms," the unpsychiatrist said. "You aren't allowed in here."

The Black Queen grabbed the unpsychiatrist's shirt in a frantic fit of anxiety: "But you have to help me! Or let me talk to Alice! Please! I believe Alice can give me insight into this terrible case of déjà vu masquerading as circular time, or whatever is going on. And my boyfriend! He died! Don't you care?"

Alice looked at Ralph, whispered, "What should I do?"

"I'd stay out of it," Ralph said. "You can't help her right now. You've got your own unsymptoms to deal with."

Alice knew that Ralph was right, but it still made her sad to hear this. She tried to smile at The Black Queen, but she didn't notice, being so decayed in her frantic nature. The unpsychiatrist said, rather rudely, "Well, like I said, I'm busy. If you want help, you'll just have to go out and beg for it."

And then the unpychiatrist pushed The Black Queen out the door.

The Black Queen protested the whole way, saying again, over and over, "But please, you don't understand, I need your help," but the unpsychiatrist wasn't going to hear it. He kicked her out, and then straightened his postmodern clothes, and sat back down.

"Sorry about that, Alice," he said. "Anyway. What were you saying?"

"We live in anachronistic medievalism," Alice said. "It's very pseudo. We're ahead of our time in some ways, and medieval in other ways. It's a strange effect."

"Very astute observation. I've often observed that myself, but haven't told people, for fear of sounding crazy."

"I don't know the feeling," Alice said, looking at Ralph.

Ralph had sat down in the corner, relaxed and looking handsome as always. Alice had a slight crush on her hallucination, but she knew she couldn't do anything about it. He existed, but only in so far as existence would allow. He in fact begged the question of what existence meant, anyway.

Ralph smiled again at her, but Alice didn't smile back. She was too distracted, by something that had bothered her from the beginning.

"Why are you helping me when other people out there clearly need it more?" Alice asked. "When the world has clearly gone bonkers? When Contorted Royal is clearly an untreated crazyland, with crazyland crazies in a mad, mad world that need to be in a madhouse?"

"Well, quite simply, because we don't have the resources," the unpsychiatrist said, rather primly. "I'd love to help The Black Queen learn to control her nervous breakdowns, love to help The Suicide King learn suicide isn't the answer, would love to show The Jack of Knives the problem with his narcissism and hostile-takeover tendencies … but we just don't have the resources. The king and queen are much too rich for the resources that we have to give, and The Jack of Knives would never seek out help. I must admit, though, it is rather ambitious what he seeks to do. I can tell you it won't work, but it is ambitious. But I think in the end, we're all crazyland crazies in a mad, mad world madhouse. No one can save us. I can't save myself. You can't save me, Alice," the unpsychiatrist said, suddenly sounding very anxious.

"I do my best," Alice said, and looked at Ralph hopelessly.

He responded by shrugging.

The unpsychiatrist took a moment to compose himself, and then said, "I do see your point, though. We shouldn't be spending all of our resources on treating you, when you do so wonderful. I can't tell you enough how much we all appreciate the delusions you give us that come true. It really serves the kingdom well. Like, the time when you thought that aliens were putting machines in certain people's heads, and the more we investigated, the more we realized it wasn't a delusion at all. It was certainly happening."

"People weren't too nice about the idea, for a little while at least," Alice said.

"True," the unpsychiatrist said. "But that's because they don't usually understand your genius. You have to excuse the common person … they are uneducated in the brilliance of schizophrenia. They don't realize the breakthroughs that you create for Contorted Royal, for the court side of things, that of course trickle down to the common person. You are the queen of schizophrenia, in your own way, you know that, right? You're the only person in Contorted Royal that's diagnosed, actually. You must feel very special."

"I do feel very special," Alice said glumly, and looked at Ralph. He was distracted, bouncing a ball back and forth, back and forth, on the ground and into his hand, on the ground and into his hand …

"So describe to me: what is Ralph like? What does Ralph like?" the unpsychiatrist said.

"Oh, he likes a lot of things," Alice said. "Still trying to get used to our world, though. He says, even though there are some modern things, it's very medieval, which isn't what he's used to. He's used to magical technologies like computers."

"Computers? What are those?"

"Oh, they …" Alice began, but then, wasn't sure how to describe it. So she said, "I don't know. You'll have to ask Ralph."

The unpsychiatrist began to look around for Ralph, but didn't find him, and finally said, "Well, I just can't see what you see, Alice. I wish I could … I could be a genius, but in all actuality, I just can't see it."

"It's okay," Alice said. "If we ever get out of this circular time, you might discover what a computer is, probably by chance. Maybe a computer will fall out of the sky or something, and land on your head. Like Newton and the apple. Maybe you'd discover technological gravity, and start a revolution."

"Perhaps," the unpsychiatrist said, and then smiled. He picked up his script pad and began to write down a prescription. "I'm going to prescribe myself twenty milligrams of psychobendzapeen. Did you want anything to increase the duration and intensity of your symptoms, Alice?"

Alice shook her head. "No. It's okay. I see Ralph enough. He comes and goes, but I see him enough. And he keeps me company. So it's okay. I'll come and get you if I need anything."

"Sounds great," the unpsychiatrist said, and smiled at Alice. "You're doing the world miracles. Believe that."

"I just wish we could get The Black Queen help," Alice said.

"Well, I'd like to, but as I said …"

"Yes," Alice said. "Resources. I get it."

"Exactly. And remember: we're all crazyland crazies in a mad, mad world but not in a madhouse."

"Yes," Alice said, and stood up, shook the undoctor's hand. "Thanks for your time and the untreatment. It means a lot."

"No problem," said the unpsychiatrist. "You get untherapy and unpsychiatry, all in one sitting."

"Yes," Alice said, and looked at Ralph. "Come on, Ralph. Let's go do something fun."

Ralph stood up and followed Alice out of the room.

Alice was distracted, but she knew the circular time thing would eventually resolve itself, uncomplicate itself, become linear. Or at least she hoped so. There was no way to know for sure, especially since everyone else around her (except for perhaps The Black Queen, who'd raved like a tipsy madwoman about watching a death over and over again) was oblivious of the circular time problem.

But that was the consequence of being in tune with delusional but real flights of fancy. But eventually, they served useful purposes.

The key word being: eventually.

The Dark Kid Falls from the Sky without Knowing Why or How to Fly At Night

The Dark Kid felt as though he was in a womb, unknowledgeable of anything, incapable of doing anything except feel the umbilical cord of destiny, of cruel fate. He had no idea where he was aside from that, except for perhaps that he was falling through space. As to where he was falling, he didn't know, because right now, his mind was a complete blank slate. It would fill up with information eventually, as he grew up in Contorted Royal, but for now, there was nothing.

The Dark Kid literally fell from the sky. He fell, curled up into a ball, a fetal position, and landed on the ground with a quiet *thud*. It was like a rock hitting the ground; The Dark Kid didn't feel any pain, just felt the crash into the ground, and that was when he opened his eyes for the first time, as though he'd just exited the womb.

He lay down for a while, curled up, and when he was ready, oriented to even the smallest degree, he stood up. He was dizzy from the long fall; this wasn't that surprising, because he had literally fallen from the sky.

He looked around. He was in an open field of some sort, and above him, there were storm and rain clouds. He saw someone in the distance, and they were approaching him.

And that was when he suddenly knew it: he was in a place, a kingdom, called Contorted Royal. But he had no idea why he was here; he had no idea where he had come from. He knew he must have come from some world outside of Contorted Royal, but he didn't know what world that would be. What world that was.

He knew that the kid approaching him was The Jack of Knives.

The Dark Kid was in shadow, even when lightning flashed above. He was pretty much always in shadow, even if light was shining directly on top of him. That was his style. He was The Dark Kid.

The Jack of Knives approached The Dark Kid at his leisurely pace, and when he was in earshot, he said, "You fell like lightning."

The Dark Kid knew he could trust The Jack of Knives, though he wasn't sure how he knew this. Maybe because he knew they were both the same age. Maybe because they both were kids, but had a dark nature, a dark side, to them.

"Thanks," The Dark Kid said.

"I've been expecting you," The Jack of Knives said. "But I didn't think you'd actually come. I'm surprised you're here. Welcome to Contorted Royal."

"Thanks," The Dark Kid said again.

"You literally fell like a lightning strike," The Jack of Knives said. "One moment, there's thunderclouds, then there's a lightning strike, and then suddenly, you're lying on the ground. You must be pretty powerful, imitating the Devil's style of Falling."

"I guess so," The Dark Kid said.

"We should probably get you changed, though. You are in a pseudo-medieval world and all. Some commoner clothes would do just fine."

The Dark Kid looked at what he was wearing: black shoes, black t-shirt, black pants.

"Nah," he said. "I'm fine."

"Suit yourself," The Jack of Knives said.

And speaking of suit: The Dark Kid had a feeling that a card was in his pocket. When he reached inside, he saw that indeed a card was there. It was a card depicting The Jack of Knives, with the red knife as the suit. The Jack of Knives looked pretty determined, pretty angry, in the picture.

"I have one of those, too," The Jack of Knives said, and pulled out a card with a picture of The Dark Kid on it. "Like I said, I've been waiting for you. We're going to have a good time together."

"Why have you been expecting me?" The Dark Kid asked.

"Because you're going to be one of my best friends, if not, my absolute best friend. What more could a kid like me ask for? It's pretty violent in this world, pretty lonely … I could use a friend."

"Sounds reasonable," The Dark Kid said.

He wasn't sure what to make of The Jack of Knives. He looked like a character from a violent but very playful and very comedic novel, though darkly comedic, a dichotomy that The Dark Kid found quite compelling. He believed that, since he didn't remember anything about where he'd come from, that he might make good friends with this guy. There was ambition in the kid. A lot of it.

"Let's go get drunk," The Jack of Knives said. "There's a tavern pretty close to here."

"That sounds fun," The Dark Kid said.

They walked in relative silence back into town, but when they were at the tavern, The Jack of Knives broke the ice by saying, "I know this is new and all—I'd be quiet too if I didn't quite know what was going on—but come on: we're about to get drunk, have a good time, party it up. Come on. Lighten up a little bit, like you did when you were that blast of lightning falling from the sky."

The Dark Kid hadn't realized how quiet he'd been. He had been pretty quiet. It was generally because he was trying to figure out why he was here, but couldn't. Was this where he was meant to be? Why did he have a vague, very vague notion, that he'd even done this before? Fallen from the sky and met The Jack of Knives?

"It'd be nice if I could fly," The Dark Kid said. "I thought that I once had wings, but … I'm not sure. Night's the best time to fly. The absolute best."

"You strike me as a kid who can fly," The Jack of Knives said. "Who knows? Maybe you'll grow wings and soon be flying at nightfall."

The Dark Kid nodded his head. He liked this kid, his spunk.

They walked inside the tavern, and sat down at the bar. The Jack of Knives pulled out a couple of metal coins, and put them on the counter. "I'll take the best, and a lot of it," he said happily. "Some for me, some for my friend here."

The bartender smiled, his teeth rotted away, and grabbed two mugs, and poured some ale into them from a barrel, and practically slapped the mugs on the table with a hearty laugh, as the liquid sloshed.

"Enjoy, boys," he said, and went on his way, taking the money.

The Jack of Knives grabbed his mug, The Dark Kid grabbed his.

"Cheers to a new horizon," The Jack of Knives said, and they clinked mugs, and then drank deep.

"I'm not rich, but I like a good Friday night drunkenness," The Jack of Knives said after they'd gotten some good drink. "Pretty good, isn't it?"

"It's delicious," The Dark Kid said, and he believed it. It tasted very sweet, but also with a strange aftertaste that he liked but couldn't quite explain or quantify.

They drank happily, and then The Jack of Knives said, "Pretty soon, we'll both be drunk. This ale doesn't take long to take effect. Plus we can get more if we want it."

The Dark Kid felt himself getting slightly dizzy, but it was dizziness that was euphoric. He watched as The Jack of Knives began to play with his knives, throwing them around randomly, but never actually stabbing anyone. He was laughing as he did so.

"You want to try?" The Jack of Knives said, handing The Dark Kid a knife. "Just throw it … throw it *anywhere*. Anywhere your heart desires."

The Dark Kid took the knife, and threw it up into the air. It stuck in the ceiling.

"I'd say that's a hole in one," The Jack of Knives said happily.

"Thanks," The Dark Kid said, enjoying the sensations he felt.

"So what's your story?" The Jack of Knives asked. "You got one?"

"Kind of," The Dark Kid said. "The story is that there is no story."

"Ha ha, that's a good one." The Jack of Knives took another deep drink of the ale. "You wanna know my story?"

The Dark Kid nodded his head. He liked seeing someone who was otherwise very darkly and melancholically happy. He knew The Jack of Knives probably had a very tormented past: The Dark Kid could see it written on the kid's face.

"I'm going to take over the kingdom," he said. "When the time is right, I'm going to rule over the kingdom. It's my goal, and I bet it'll work perfectly. People say a servant boy can't rule, well … I'll show them they are wrong. I can rule. I'm a good ruler, with good ideas: I'm a visionary, a revolutionary. I'm sick of my cheap job, my cheap life. It's time to make something of it. I wouldn't guess you'd know much about that, though. You don't strike me as being dark from the dirt of life's strife, but dark from secrets, secrets darker and deeper than the Universe."

"I probably have secrets," The Dark Kid admitted, "but I couldn't tell you what they were. Even if I wanted to."

"I've got secrets," The Jack of Knives said mysteriously. "Wanna hear one?"

"Sure."

"Well," he said, "I have a dark heart, as you can probably tell. And I want to make use of that dark heart. I don't know what that would mean, though. Would that mean I become a psychopath killer? Well, if so, that's normal in Contorted Royal ... though no one dies: and that's exactly what I like about where I live. Imagine, if I could increase the power of our own death sentence, our life-in-death sentence. I think, as dark of a dream as it is, it'd do some good for the mind. It could even cure it."

"I don't see how you get to that point, but okay," The Dark Kid said.

The Jack of Knives gave The Dark Kid a curious look. "You don't see my point? Well, then, I'll explain it. Everybody is fascinated and obsessed with melancholy. Secretly, we all want death. We're preoccupied with it, obsessed. And death comes in many different forms: suicide, homicide, life itself. Since that's what everybody wants, why not increase that? Increase the power, the pain ... which will translate to pleasure?"

"It sounds like a recipe for disaster," The Dark Kid said, but smiled.

"Yeah, perhaps," The Jack of Knives said. "But people would be happier. It'd be like our own private hell. What could be better than that? Except, it would be a hell where I call the shots. And if disaster happens, more power to me. I don't see how it could be any worse than this life here, in Contorted Royal. We're always killing each other anyway."

"I think it's just the nature of existence," The Dark Kid said, and smiled darkly.

"Yeah, I think it is, which is exactly why I want to make it worse. The Suicide King is too busy hurting himself to realize what he can do: he can increase the suffering of his kingdom. All the great kings did that for their society. The Suicide King is too much of a wuss for that, though, and The Black Queen doesn't even rule because she's busy sleeping around or attempting to get help for her constant mental breakdowns. Like I said, I'm a visionary. This could do wonderful things for our world, I'm telling you. The people spoke, the people have been heard, and the people will get what they want."

"Where will it leave you?" The Dark Kid asked.

"Well, I'll be ruling, so it won't affect me the same way. But there will be a lot of bloodshed. I may be a kid, but I've been hardened by pointless labor. I know what I need to do. So I guess now I get to my question: you want to help me?"

The Dark Kid thought about what The Jack of Knives had said. He would make people more miserable. He supposed, from what he was observing in this tavern (two people were in a knife fight, stabbing each other left and right and still somehow alive), that it was what Contorted Royal wanted. More suffering. And The Dark Kid wanted to let out some of his dark nature, and should he even say, evil nature?

But on the same token, this wasn't his world. Nonetheless, he liked the idea of helping someone so crazily ambitious. Who knew what could happen?

"Okay," The Dark Kid said. "I'll help you. What do we need to do?"

The Jack of Knives nodded his head, smiled ... and then suddenly frowned. "I have no idea," he admitted.

The Dark Kid laughed: oh, the irony of the diabolical plan. Having an idea, but no way of actually executing that idea. It sounded like the irony of this world.

"Well, if you get an idea, let me know," The Dark Kid said, and smiled internally.

The Jack of Knives looked glumly into the distance. "I don't think I will. If it happens, it won't be from me. If it happens, it won't be my dream ... it'll be something else. Though, I don't know what that would be. Though I will say that that is a small goal compared to what I really care about: nothing would please me more than making the suffering of The Suicide King worse. I hate him, more than anything. Maybe that you can help me with, when the time is right. He's the one who's caused all of this chaos. He's a terrible ruler."

The Dark Kid took this into account, and continued to smile internally; he was going to like this place, getting revenge, ruling lands ineffectively ... and if he was lucky, maybe he'd learn how to fly, at night.

The Black Queen's Move

Oh, the agony of it all! The horror! The Black Queen was utterly alone to face her demons, with that strange circular flair! She was the only one who could deal with her problems, because everyone else was either too busy killing themselves (The Suicide King), being killed (Spade), or much, much too busy for the royal majesty (Alice, the unpsychiatrist).

How terrible that was! How she couldn't interrupt the session for even a few minutes to get help from Alice! The unpsychiatrist wasn't who The Black Queen wanted to talk to. It had been Alice. But Alice had been too inebriated with her special treatment, probably so strung out on drugs, that she hadn't noticed the plight of The Black Queen.

It never ended! But The Black Queen wasn't going to give up. She needed to do something cathartic, something freeing. She didn't quite know what that would be just yet, but she needed to do *something*. Couldn't the queen of Contorted Royal get at least *some* attention around here?

The Black Queen needed to plan, she needed to think. What was the best way to treat herself and her symptoms? She felt this nervous breakdown getting the best of her, and she was afraid.

It was a terrible world! Oh, the heartfelt agony of it all!

But The Black Queen was a fighter. She didn't give up. She never gave up. If she gave up, she may as well have hung herself in the public square, for something false and fun like treason. That would be awesome. The queen betrayed her own right. What a spectacle that would be!

But considering the direction her life was going, it didn't seem like all that bad of an idea. She actually thought it was a *great* idea. She could try to take over her own kingdom. That would be a wonderful way to go down in history, as the worst queen in all existence. But at least she'd go down in style, go down in flames.

But she really did feel alone. The unpsychiatrist had been so rude to her. Too busy treating himself? Why, that little dweeb …. The Black Queen could take him straight to the guillotine if she wanted. She had almost done just that, but she wasn't sure if it would accomplish anything. He wouldn't die. No one really died in Contorted Royal, unless it was a death that needed to haunt The Black Queen.

So the unpsychiatrist was safe—for now, at least.

The Black Queen decided that she needed to make a move. A good move ... which would immediately translate into a bad move. Yes, a bad move in chess. She needed to make a move so bad that she put the black queen on the chessboard in jeopardy, and maybe worse. That would accomplish a lot. That would help a lot of things. She knew it.

But she wasn't sure what move that would be, at least at the moment. All she knew was that she needed to get revenge on herself for the world being so cruel to her, for turning their backs. Nothing would be more tragic, than the queen who had lost her marbles because her kingdom had betrayed her ... she could already hear the news being spoken at Contorted Square: "The Black Queen Dies in a Fit of Sad and Suicidal Rage! Extra, extra, hear all about it!"

Because, what good would it do to get revenge on the people around her? She couldn't hurt poor Alice. She couldn't behead the unpsychiatrist ... he'd already lost his head. And she certainly couldn't get revenge on The Suicide King ... he'd just kill himself upon the thought that his wife betrayed him.

Revenge was finicky, and it had to be done right. The best way to get revenge on the world was to get revenge on yourself. But they were going to pay, they were going to suffer. When there was no more queen ruling the world, they'd see what she had done for them.

Well, The Black Queen admitted to herself, they'd realize she hadn't really done much of anything, except for cheat around on the royal highness. But still! It was a bad move worth considering.

The Black Queen decided the best way to do this would be to go to the torture chamber and hurt herself there, the goal being to blast or beat the ideas of what had happened to her boyfriend out of her head. Since she didn't have access to therapy, and therapy was the only way to deal with one's problems, as people even closest to you didn't listen to your problems and offer consolation and advice, much less some random commoner, she just needed to beat the ideas out of her head. Flog the ideas away, let them drift away in her blood. Something. She wasn't quite sure, but something. Beat the ideas to a bloody pulp.

She knew Ace would be in the torture chamber at this time. The torture chamber closed at about this time, but Ace often frequented it, because he said he got good memories of seeing people suffer there. Ace would know what to do. He'd know how to handle the situation, make The Black Queen's suffering worse through revenge.

She quitted the chamber she was in, and began to walk through the castle, up the stairs, and continued to move until she finally did arrive in the torture chamber. Ace was indeed standing in the chamber, with his back to The Black Queen.

The Black Queen didn't say anything for a moment, just looked around, saw a wall that was dedicated to beating one's head, saw knives of many different shades of sharpness, saw a whip for flogging, and a few other items of display, of torture.

"Ummm, excuse me," The Black Queen said, knocking on the door politely.

Ace turned around. He was wearing his dark hood, as always. No one ever saw the face of Ace. No one knew what Ace looked like. Occasionally, they could see his black eyes, like spades, but that was about it.

Ace, in his deep, very deep voice, drenching with pure evil, said, "Your majesty?"

"I think I need to torture myself."

Ace didn't say anything for a moment, then began to verbally abuse the queen: "You *think* you need to torture yourself, or you *know* you need to torture yourself?"

"I *know*," The Black Queen said, with firm resolve. "It will make me happy. It will secure the royal kingdom. We'll all be rich!"

The last line was a throwaway, but she didn't know what else to say. Besides, riches would make one happy, even if that wasn't the way the evening was going to go.

"Good to hear."

Ace went toward one of the knives and picked it up. It was one of the sharpest. "Would you like me to torture you, or did you want to torture yourself?"

"A little bit of both, honey," The Black Queen said. "I'll let you chop off my tongue, if you want?"

Ace smiled; of course, The Black Queen couldn't see the smile, but she could feel it.

"Okay, your royal highness," Ace said, and then quickly darted toward The Black Queen. He tackled her to the ground, and then brought the knife right before her eyes.

But The Black Queen wasn't afraid. "Save me, God! Oh, God, save me from this terrible demon!"

"God can't hear your prayers," Ace said, and then threw the knife by The Black Queen's side. "You hurt yourself first. Then I'll decide if I want to torture you, if it's worth my effort and time. It's not my job to torture, as you well know. My goal is simply to be the top of the chain, higher than any king or queen in this kingdom."

"You always hit us where it hurts," The Black Queen sulked, but grabbed the knife. She made a little slit/incision in her arm, and then began to howl in melodramatic pain and agony.

"Oh, it hurts so bad! What am I going to do with all of this *pain*?"

"I don't know," Ace said. "What *are* you going to do?"

"I want to beat these ideas out of my head," The Black Queen said. "That's what I want to do."

"Well, we'll get to that when the time is right," Ace said. "For now, the weapons are all yours. Feel free to flog yourself. The whip hurts rather … sublimely."

"I will feel free," The Black Queen said, and dropped the knife.

She was being a coward. She could do better than this! What she needed to do was stay focused, remember her training … beat and hurt these ideas of her boyfriend, her tortured, dead boyfriend, out of her mind.

She had heard of electroshock therapy, more barbaric than any medieval torturing practice. Well, this was like electroshock therapy: barbaric and horribly infringing on one's rights, but necessary. Completely necessary.

The Black Queen grabbed the whip and, still wearing her dress, began to flog herself, crying out in agony, but also enjoying the sensation. It was definitely getting her mind off that horrible scene of seeing Spade murdered. Well, if that's what it took! The Black Queen was fine with a little defiance.

She flogged right through her dress, until she started to look like a scourged Christ. Then she dropped the whip, because she couldn't do it anymore, crucifying her vanity like this. It was rather painful … more painful than she really wanted to admit. But it was working … that was what mattered.

"It's a terrible, terrible move," The Black Queen said. "I'm in jeopardy. But it's the only way I can get my mind off Spade!" The Black Queen whined suddenly.

"You poor wretch," Ace said consolingly, and she could tell that he sounded amused.

"Don't laugh at my agony," The Black Queen said unhappily, but then conceded to a smile. "Oh, who am I kidding. We all live in a mad, mad world, a world of happy fun and games. Slapstick, really. Now where's the wall specially designed to beat your head against?"

"That one," Ace said, pointing at a white wall, while the others were the color of stone.

The Black Queen went to the wall, and began to beat her head against it.

"Get … this … idea … *out!*" she cried, between beatings. "Get … *out!*"

The Black Queen's head began to bruise, and she was sure her brain had turned to mush beneath a crushed skull. But she didn't care.

"How do I look?" The Black Queen asked, once she was finished.

Ace smiled, that dark smile. "You look lovely, your Majesty. Let's save crushing your skull for another day, though. I think you've beaten the idea out rather successfully."

The Black Queen didn't feel much pain, but suddenly she began to cry, rather melodramatically, and said, "Life is so unfair! I ruined my hairdo!"

"Well, of course it is unfair," Ace laughed, quietly. "But that's our world."

The Black Queen continued to cry, and she felt her head. It was still somehow whole, even though she'd beaten it severely. But that was okay. Maybe she'd look sexy for The Suicide King tonight. She still had him. That was, if he hadn't killed himself by now.

The Black Queen stopped crying, and then walked out of the room. It wasn't long before the damage to her brain caught up with her. She knew it wouldn't last forever; somehow, people always healed in Contorted Royal. But still, she'd damaged her brain, and now she could barely concentrate on the road ahead of her ... no, not road, that was foolish and wrong, *hallway*, but ... still. Whatever it was. Whatever it needed to be. The Black Queen didn't know. She had no idea. None whatsoever, as she stumbled and tripped her way to her royal bedroom, and crashed out on the bed.

But she didn't fall asleep immediately. She only thought of Spade, her one true love. She saw his death repeating in her head over and over again.

Yes. A bad move of chess. Pointless self-destruction because no one was there to care. Because she couldn't get over the death of her boyfriend.

It was like electroshock therapy: barbaric and completely unnecessary. Her self-inflicted torture hadn't worked, because, as she slowly drifted into sleep only to then dream about Spade's death, The Black Queen could do nothing but think of Spade, and think about what he had suffered, and understand that she was completely alone in this world ...

Suicide Cures All the Problems of Suicide

The Suicide King loved it when The Fool, always dressed in the clothes of a fool, sat beside The Suicide King in his own chair; there was something comforting about having The Fool next to The Suicide King, something lovely and exhilarating.

The Fool was mad; but then again, so was everyone in Contorted Royal. But The Fool, he had breakthrough ideas. He was constantly solving problems, coming up with solutions that The Suicide King would hang himself to come up with.

But right now, The Suicide King wasn't too fond of seeing The Fool. The main reason was because, as great as The Fool was, he didn't think The Fool could help him with his current problems.

The Fool would in fact do well to make a mockery of The Suicide King's delicate situation.

The Fool noticed this, however, and like a fisherman with good bait, began to feed the little fishy Suicide King to eventually get the hook, and reel him in.

"What's bothering you, my bloody lord?" The Fool asked.

The Suicide King picked up his sword and turned his back on The Fool. He knew what was going on, he could see it in The Fool's eyes ... but he wasn't sure he wanted to go in this direction. The Fool would make a fool of The Suicide King. He knew it.

But The Fool was not bothered. He began to follow The Suicide King around the court. Every time that The Suicide King turned his back to The Fool, The Fool would quickly get in front of The Suicide King, making him turn his back again, only to get in front. They repeated this for a while, making it a game, a dance of will, until The Suicide King finally relented and said, "All right. I'll tell you."

"I'm listening," The Fool said.

"It's the blasted Jack of Knives. He wants to take over my kingdom. I'm honestly not sure what to do about him. There's the part of me that wants to just put the fellow out of his misery, but I can't do that to The Jack of Knives. He's just a kid, and he's got *style*. That would be just senseless, even in our world, and I'm not a senseless man."

The Fool didn't say anything for a little while. Then he smiled, a cruel smile, and said, "I know what you need to do. You need to make a game of the situation. That's the solution."

"A game of the situation?" The Suicide King's interest was piqued. "How would I do that?"

"You do what you always love to do," The Fool said, but didn't tell The Suicide King what to do, and left him hanging, with the hook in the mouth.

The Fool began to walk around the court, and this time, The Suicide King followed him. But The Fool would do just what The Suicide King had done, turn his back, making The Suicide King get in front, turn his back again, repeat. And it was driving The Suicide King *crazy*.

Finally, The Suicide King, in a burst of light rage, shouted, "Fine! You win."

The Fool laughed foolishly. "Of course I win," and turned to face The Suicide King. "Let's put this another way. Violence cures all the answers to homicide."

"Don't you mean suicide cures all the problems of suicide?"

The Fool nodded. "Exactly, my lord. You can read my mind, and rather well. If you went off what I said, there would just be a whole bunch of bloodshed everywhere. You'd have to go to war with a servant boy, and that wouldn't turn out very well, most likely. The Jack of Knives is good at rallying people for his cause—he already has The Dark Kid's attention—and you'd realize that violence doesn't cure all the answers to homicide, it just creates homicide.

"But suicide, my lord? Oh, you know that would work great. If you killed yourself, there would be no struggle. All the problems of suicide would be solved. Suicide is the lightest way to go. You wouldn't surrender, but you wouldn't have to fight."

The Suicide King thought about this. It sounded reasonable, plausible, if a little bit crazy. But it could work. If there was no Suicide King, The Jack of Knives could peacefully take over the kingdom, and there'd be no struggle. Why hadn't The Suicide King thought of this before?

But then he frowned: it was a very deep frown. He said, "I just need to kill myself, you say?"

"Yes," said The Fool.

"Well, the question is, then … how do I kill myself?"

"Well, of course you can't kill yourself. Which means you'll have to resort to violence, and learn that violence cures all the answers to homicide."

"Now you're just tricking me," The Suicide King said, feeling his head spin with all of this contradictory information. "I thought suicide was the answer."

The Fool looked at The Suicide King in a shocked way, but secretly smiling: "Suicide? Why, I'd *never* suggest suicide was the answer. That would be just cruel of me. I'd behead the monarch in one quick blow … that would be awfully dangerous, wouldn't you say? And reckless. We can't have a headless king ruling the kingdom."

"But you just said …" The Suicide King began, but then wasn't sure what to say.

The Fool smiled. "Everything will work perfectly if you're smart. We all know, though, your wisdom of the ages comes from me and a few other distinguished members of the court. Your brain has turned to jelly from all the times you pulverized it."

"What an awful image to put in my head," The Suicide King said, but then laughed at the delightful thought. "Ah, so *grotesque*. So, suicide is the answer, you're trying to say."

The Fool didn't say anything, just looked at The Suicide King carefully.

"What are you looking at me like that for?" The Suicide King said.

"I'm just admiring my fool," The Fool said. "You look good when suicide is in your eyes. I could sing in the blood that rains down."

The Suicide King blushed slightly. "Why, thank you, my lord."

The Fool only nodded, then said, "Well, I've given you the answers, it's up to you what you do with them."

And then The Fool went back to his chair, and began to watch the king intently.

The Suicide King took all of what had been said into account. Suicide … it was the perfect answer. If he killed himself, it would solve all of his suicidal problems. He'd no longer be suicidal! And, as an added bonus, he would beat The Jack of Knives so effortlessly, by practically handing over the kingdom. What more could a king want? No pressure, no drama—just a clean and unhostile take-over.

The problem, of course, was that he wasn't really sure he could kill himself. He had the metaphorical scars to prove his past suicide attempts. It just never worked. He always came back as good as new.

But The Suicide King wasn't going to give up. He was still holding his sword, trying to decide what he wanted to do. Suicide, or homicide? He could make war with The Jack of Knives if he wanted … The Fool would never suggest that The Suicide King take himself out of the picture to run away from a bloody conflict, of course.

But still … suicide was the answer. It had to be. Suicide could cure suicide simply because it took you out of the equation: suicide equaled suicide. Why didn't more people realize that? If you're suicidal, just kill yourself! It'll solve all your problems!

The Suicide King continued to think about this, and then finally decided he was going to try again. He took the sword and drove the blade into his stomach. Now disemboweled, he looked at The Fool, and said, "You think it'll work?"

"I think anything my king does will work," The Fool said. "You know better than me."

"It was your idea," The Suicide King said, irritated, now a bloody and gory mess.

The Fool remained silent. The Suicide King realized The Fool was gaslighting The Suicide King. Had The Fool really suggested that The Suicide King kill himself to save the kingdom? That did seem absurd. But what was as absurd was going to war with a servant boy. Going to war at all, actually, seemed absurd, seemed like a pointless mission, something that wouldn't accomplish anything.

"Now I'm really confused," The Suicide King said miserably, and with a giant hole in his stomach, removed the sword. It was bloody and awful, and The Suicide King was in pain, but surely, he was on the verge of death.

But The Fool just remained silent. The Suicide King had a feeling that he enjoyed this.

But The Suicide King supposed, why wouldn't he enjoy it? The Suicide King was rather foolish, and in a very carnivalesque way, the roles had been reversed. The Fool now stood as the towering genius, while the king was brainless (and, bowel-less).

That, however, was why The Fool was such an important person for the kingdom! It was amazing what his wisdom was able to do.

Except, The Suicide King wasn't dying. He pointed this out to The Fool, who simply said, "I told you what to do."

"What was that?" The Suicide King said, the pain he felt nothing. In fact, his stomach was already curing itself again, as though nothing had ever happened.

"Why, that you run away."

"You didn't tell me to run away," The Suicide King said.

"Of course I told you to run away," The Fool snapped triumphantly. "It's the only way you can save your kingdom. If you're gone, The Jack of Knives can safely rule your kingdom."

"Oh, what a mess," The Suicide King said. "I could have sworn you told me to kill myself. Or to go to war."

"I would tell you none of those things," The Fool said. "That would be just terrible. Absolutely, unjustly, terrible. But you see, running away is the way. You stay unhurt, and The Jack of Knives doesn't have to fight."

The Suicide King thought about this, and then said, "Okay. Sounds good. I see what you're saying. I pack tonight, and leave the kingdom. The Black Queen will just have to fend for herself."

The Suicide King was about to leave the court to go and pack his bags, when The Fool said, "But, there is a catch."

The Suicide King turned around slowly. "What's the catch?"

"Well, you have to come back and fight for the kingdom that was taken from you, of course. Which means that, as I said before, violence cures all the answers to homicide. You'll have to dispose of The Jack of Knives. As for how, I don't know, but you're a smart man, you'll figure it out eventually."

The Suicide King felt his head spinning at a million miles an hour. How much more conflicting information was he going to get? He felt his head was going to *explode* with all of the possibilities, none of which, he knew, would actually work.

Then The Fool laughed, and as though he was talking to someone else, said, "The king's lost his head."

The Suicide King smiled at this. "Ha ha! *That's* the answer. I just need to chop off my head!"

And the king proceeded to do just that; the only problem was, his neck was a neck of steel. Nothing happened. Nothing at all.

"I wish he'd just die already," The Fool said, still talking to someone else. "But alas, he wouldn't be The Suicide King if he actually committed suicide. That would be a fatal contradiction in logic."

"Very good point," The Suicide King said.

"Did you figure out what you need to do to save the kingdom?" The Fool asked, talking to the king again.

"Absolutely …" the king began, "not. I have no clue what I need to do."

The Fool smiled. "Great! That means I've done my job. You're completely dumbfounded about how to save the kingdom. I believe that's the answer that you seek."

"Precisely!" The Suicide King exclaimed, exhilarated by this startling discovery. "We've figured it out! You're getting a reward today, Fool. This is cause for a celebration! You've saved the kingdom!"

"Just doing my duty, sir," The Fool said.

But The Suicide King didn't hear this. Because the kingdom was saved by perfect illogic, they needed to celebrate, and he needed to get all of that in order, so he began to do just that.

Aced

Ace couldn't help but chortle in his evil glee; Contorted Royal was literally on their infinite time of circularity, and once it completed itself again, came full circle, it would for infinite and one times. The thought of it made Ace happy.

He enjoyed putting everyone in Contorted Royal in such a terrible circular and closed-circuit hell, for that exact reason: it was hell. Everyone living the same path over and over again, dimly aware that they'd been here before but not so aware of it that they could actually mention it, and do something about it. There were some exceptions to this, of course, like Alice, who every time things repeated, she realized it, and tried to do something about it.

But that little schizophrenic couldn't do anything to mess up Ace's permanent Hell, the Hell that he'd helped been responsible for.

The best thing about the circular hell of Contorted Royal was that Ace was completely exempt from that rule. He didn't have to do the same thing over and over again. He was free to go about as he pleased. He'd certainly enjoyed seeing The Black Queen torture herself, though, for the infinite time.

As Ace was enjoying this, he was in his private chamber, looking at himself in the mirror. He was a dark soul, a dark figure, with a dark purpose. He saw that clearly in himself. He was admiring himself, and enjoying how dark he looked, when Death himself appeared on the surface of the mirror.

Death looked powerful. He was bald, wearing black clothes, with solid black eyes. Ace knew there were other Deaths in existence, especially considering that Death was such a powerful concept, but this Death belonged specifically to Contorted Royal and to other worlds or dimensions he chose to occupy.

Ace was puzzled. What was Death doing here? What did Death want now?

"Hello, Ace," Death said.

"Hello, Death," Ace said, straightening his hood. "I wasn't expecting company."

"That's because I bother you when I want to, of course," Death said. "You are my servant, after all."

"I'm not your servant," Ace said. "I control Contorted Royal. It's because of my doing, mostly at least, that the circularity is on its infinite run. That's a lot to be proud of."

Death remained on the mirror screen. "Well, that's what I wanted to talk to you about, Ace. Things are going to change, and soon."

"How are things going to change?" Ace asked, trying to keep his composure. "Things never change. That's the whole point of circularity."

"I'm afraid things are going to change," Death continued. "You'll see soon enough. You see, the circle is going to break, open up like a band, and become linear again. You know why that will be a problem, of course."

"Yes, I know exactly why that will be a problem," Ace snapped. "It would mean people weren't in their own circular hell anymore. Why did you have to go and spoil a perfectly good day?"

"That's what I do," Death said. "I own you. More than you'd ever know. But I choose to make a game of all of it. Now of course, I don't want the circularity to end any more than you do. The problem is, I'm limited in my powers. I'm too busy killing off people in other dimensions to really focus on this problem, even though it is important to me. That's why I'm going to trust you to take care of it, Ace."

"How do I take care of it?" Ace asked.

Death walked out of the mirror at this moment. Ace would have been intimidated. He felt plague, he felt disease, with this being. One wrong move, and Death could slice with a scythe-like exactness Ace from his life. But Ace stood his ground.

"I'm not sure, exactly, but from what I can tell, one of the problems, reasons, for the linearity coming into being will be, unfortunately, a boy named Ralph."

"Who is Ralph?" Ace asked.

"That's clearly something you're going to have to find out, isn't it?" Death said, smiling manipulatively.

He went toward a hand-held mirror and picked it up. Ace saw it reflecting something, but it wasn't reflecting Death's face; it was reflecting murder. It was the very essence of Contorted Royal. He saw people killing each other, except in this world, many people were actually dying, so Death could claim them all. It wasn't a prolonged, stagnant, nonexistent death … it was real, violent, grisly death.

Ace looked away, trying to keep himself calm. He was indeed afraid. He'd been the top dog for a long time now, but with Death involved like this, it couldn't last long. Death was after something. He could see it. He just didn't know what that was.

Ace was evil, but Death was more evil. Death was crueler. Death could do more damage than Ace. Which was why Ace needed Death's Mirror.

"I'll help you, Death, if you do something for me," Ace said, now finally bargaining.

"And what would that be?" Death asked. "I suppose you'll want my mirror."

Ace nodded his head. "Yes. I want your mirror. If I stop the linearity from happening, I want Death's Mirror."

Death laughed. "You have nothing to bargain with, Ace. I know that you want the circularity to remain as much as I do. I like putting people in Hell."

Ace wasn't bothered. "Well, I know eventually I'll get your mirror. It's bound to happen eventually."

"Keep telling yourself that," Death said, and laughed. "You won't get my mirror. You wouldn't be able to control it. It would contort your reality like the cruelest dreams, the most fragmented nightmares. It would make you shatter into a million pieces, and yet keep you whole enough to witness your own demise over and over again. That's Death's Mirror ... and no one controls it. Not even me."

It was Ace's turn to laugh. "You aren't as much of a hot shot as you think you are, Death. That mirror is mine. It's been written in the books for a long time."

"Not in any books I've read," Death said casually, and began to pace around Ace, trying to intimidate him, make Ace shift his position to keep Death in his sight.

"Well, it is," Ace said. "I'm the most important member of Contorted Royal, the highest, higher than even the king."

"You're also the lowest, by definition," Death pointed out.

"Yes, but being low gives me more power. I can be lower than a servant and higher than a king, all in one quick move. It's good being flexible. The things it affords you ... it's incredible. You underestimate me, try to undermine my authority. Unfortunately, that prevents you from using me to your fullest potential."

"I'm not interested in using you, Ace," Death said plainly.

"You should be," Ace said. "I'm the one who keeps murdering Spade over and over again, to torment The Black Queen. I'd say that means I have quite a command over death."

"That's mere child's play," Death said, and pulled out a dagger, examined it closely. "I could murder Spade over and over if I chose to. I'd just need to abduct him, take him to my world, to the world where all have died, and make him die over and over again, his own circular Hell. You underestimate me, Ace. And that's not a good idea. When will you learn you're aced by me? I win, all the time. Every time. Now, are you going to cooperate, and try to take care of Ralph?"

"It's on my list," Ace said. "But I don't believe I'm aced. I just believe you're a bully trying to make Contorted Royal follow your own twisted rules. But that ultimately won't do any good. It can't do any good. Contorted Royal is its own entity, with its own rules."

"You'd be surprised how much I can bend those rules," Death said.

He was still moving around Ace, forcing him to move with Death, but Ace finally stopped doing this, stood his ground. "Give me Death's Mirror, and we'll talk."

"I don't think it's a good idea," Death said. "I'd lose my most loyal servant."

Ace laughed again. "I'm not loyal to you."

"You'd be surprised how loyal you are to me, Ace," Death said, and laughed strange enough that Ace shuddered internally.

But he quickly told himself, there was no reason to worry. He had this.

"Tell me how we become linear again," Ace said.

"I already told you," Death said. "If you can solve the problem of Ralph, you'll solve the problem of linearity."

Ace grabbed the hand-held mirror that Death was holding and threw it on the ground, let it shatter. "But that's not good enough! Tell me what I need to do!"

Death remained calm, but his eyes became blacker. "You'll know what to do when the time is right, Ace. I'm not going to reveal everything because there's only so much I know. Some things escape me. You have to remember, other forces are playing, like Fate. But Ralph … solve the Ralph Problem, and you'll be in good shape."

Death began to walk to the tall mirror, and stepped inside. Before he disappeared, he said, "Figure it out, Ace, and you'll do our existence a world of good."

Then he was gone completely.

Ace took all of this in. Ralph was the problem. That was *great* to know … if Ace actually knew who Ralph was. But Ace had no idea who Ralph was, or where to begin looking for him. And even if Ace found Ralph, what would Ace do with Ralph? Kill him? Would that actually solve anything? Ace wasn't sure. He wanted to be sure, but of course, there was no way to be sure.

Ace looked at the small mirror he'd broken. If he could just have Death's Mirror … that would solve everything. That would make things so much simpler. But Death wouldn't give it up. He refused, saying that Ace would get lost in some labyrinthine reflection. He doubted that. He doubted that severely.

So basically, Ace was back to square one. That was awesome, when considering that he wasn't the one living the circular Hell, here. But he was. He had no idea how he was going to stop the linearity from coming into being. Not the slightest idea.

There was, though, The Jack of Knives. Ace could use him as a scapegoat. That sounded like a good idea. It would change the direction of things a little bit, but that was okay. It would damage the circularity, because usually The Jack of Knives wouldn't go through what Ace was thinking now. That was fine. Desperate times called for desperate measures.

That was when, however, that Ace realized that if he got involved with The Jack of Knives, the circularity would indeed slowly begin to fall apart, or at least it would be a beginning sign. But, that was okay, Ace told himself. If things were going to fall apart anyway, he needed to accept that. Taking out his anger on The Jack of Knives would do a world of good, anyway. Before the circularity, Ace had constantly taken out his rage on The Jack of Knives, and it had done a lot for Ace. It would be like the old times.

Besides, Ace *hated* The Jack of Knives. In all actuality, he wasn't really sure why he hated him so much, he just did. He hated him with a severe passion.

So, Ace knew what he was going to do. Let the circularity go to Hell to some degree, things would balance back soon, anyway, because doing something to The Jack of Knives out of spite would probably lead Ace to the answer of how to deal with the Ralph Problem. Which would be good.

Ace was going to convince The Suicide King, as brainless as he was, to arrest The Jack of Knives for treason. They'd throw him in a prison cell, and there he would remain. There he would rot. He would *suffer*. It would solve a lot of problems. It would indeed.

Ace smiled at this. Oh, poor Jack of Knives. Suffering for Ace, for Ace's cause. But, that was the way of Contorted Royal.

The Jack of Knives would be aced.

Prison Sale

The Jack of Knives was in the tavern with The Dark Kid, drinking ale and just having a good time, when he saw Ace walk into the building.

The Jack of Knives hated Ace. The two had had their run-ins, and in the end, they were never going to get along. What The Jack of Knives hated most about Ace was his ability to be the highest member of the court, and the lowest, and usually, simultaneously. The Jack of Knives felt that one should either be one or the other, not both. It irritated The Jack of Knives, because it occupied such a powerful place. One moment you're a servant, the next more important and powerful than the king. That kind of ambiguity made it hard to understand the person who was indeed ambiguous, which was of course Ace.

The Jack of Knives had given his desire to take over the kingdom a short vacation. He knew he'd come back to it eventually, when the time was right, but for now, he just wasn't interested in thinking about it. He wanted to be hedonistic, perhaps even be a savage heathen: he wanted to get drunk and party with his best friend.

The Dark Kid was having a blast with The Jack of Knives, which made The Jack of Knives even less interested in ruling the kingdom. There were bigger and better things to think about than a hostile takeover. When the time was right, it would happen, but for now, it was time to get drunk.

But all of this came crashing down the moment that Ace showed up. He was wearing his hood, as always, and when Ace spotted The Jack of Knives, he felt Ace's cruel smile.

The Jack of Knives said to The Dark Kid, "Looks like we've got trouble. Stay low and don't draw any attention to yourself."

The Dark Kid looked to see who was coming, and then had a puzzled look. He whispered, "What are you afraid of? He's just a guy in a hood."

"He's a guy in a hood who could easily become my worst nightmare," The Jack of Knives said. "He's seen me, which means he wants something … I'm not sure I want to know what that is."

Ace was accompanied by two servants. He approached The Jack of Knives and said, "Mr. Jack."

"Jack of Knives," The Jack of Knives said, not afraid to show his arrogance.

"I know we've had our differences in the past," Ace conceded.

"I'd say we've had more than that," The Jack of Knives said, not facing Ace.

He could still see him in his peripheral, however, and he saw him pull out a scroll and begin to read what The Jack of Knives supposed was a decree.

"You, Mr. Jack of Knives, are hereby arrested for treason against the courts of Contorted Royal," Ace said, loud enough for everyone in the tavern to hear.

When this was spoken, the crowd went completely silent.

The Jack of Knives looked at Ace carefully, trying to see if this was a joke. People tried to betray the court all the time, usually because people thought The Suicide King was unfit to rule. That didn't mean, however, that they were arrested.

The Jack of Knives would have said this, but Ace said, "Turn around, boy-o."

"I'm not …" The Jack of Knives said, but didn't have a chance to do anything, because Ace's henchmen forced The Jack of Knives on the ground, tying rope around his wrists after forcing them behind his back.

"Come with me, to your prison cell," Ace said.

The Jack of Knives looked at The Dark Kid, who looked perplexed and concerned. "What should I do?" he asked.

"There's not much you can do," The Jack of Knives admitted, and was taken to the kingdom.

***

The Suicide King was waiting in the prison hall. He was holding his sword, and looked stoic, but that stoicism quickly passed once he saw The Jack of Knives.

"Knife Jack, my boy," The Suicide King said happily. "What a day it is, huh?"

"I'd say so," The Jack of Knives said.

"You're going to *love* the special discounts and deals going on right now for our prisons," The Suicide King said. "And if you want my honest opinion, it's a good day to be arrested. I almost had Ace arrest *me* for treason. I've had these awful temptations lately to take over my kingdom."

"Sounds lovely," The Jack of Knives said miserably.

"But not to worry, not to worry, my dear boy. Ace, you've done your duty, please leave us in peace," The Suicide King said.

Ace bowed, and then quitted the prison hall.

"So, which prison cell has your interest?" The Suicide King asked curiously. "Is it that one?" he said, pointing at a prison cell.

"It looks like any other prison cell," The Jack of Knives said.

"Exactly! They are all the same! But, some are more expensive than others. We have to do that, to make a business of it, and all. Capitalism, I'm sure you understand. So, which cell did you want?"

The Jack of Knives took all of what The Suicide King was saying into account. When he finally realized what was going on, he said, rather frustrated, "You want me to *buy* my prison cell?"

"Why, of course," The Suicide King said. "We wouldn't give you a *free* prison cell, that would be ridiculous. The poor taxpayers of Contorted Royal. I wouldn't let them suffer. They already suffer enough to pay for my meals, and my medical expenses from all of my suicidal attempts. Plus they pay fine servant boys like you to clean up after me."

The Jack of Knives closed his eyes and breathed in deep. This was the stupidest thing he'd ever heard of. He had had no idea that one actually had to purchase their own prison cell. But, this was Contorted Royal, and anything was possible here.

"I'll take the cheapest you've got," The Jack of Knives said.

"But don't you want to look at the more expensive ones, first? And don't forget: it is a prison sale, after all. You should feel free to take your time to browse."

"I'll take the cheapest one," The Jack of Knives said, trying to keep his frustration and irritation in check, but failing slightly.

The Suicide King noticed The Jack of Knives and his hastiness, and so he said, "All right, then, suit yourself. I'll take you to the cheapest."

The Suicide King led The Jack of Knives to a cell at the end of the hall. He told The Jack of Knives how much it would cost. The Jack of Knives reached into his pocket and pulled out the appropriate amount in coins, and then The Suicide King opened the gate to let The Jack of Knives inside.

"You'll like this cell," The Suicide King said, and left The Jack of Knives alone to his thoughts.

The Jack of Knives wanted to scream at the injustice of all of this. He knew he'd be here for a while, if not for his whole life. Which meant he needed to escape.

He looked around, and saw a window. He tried opening it, but no luck.

"I'll figure out how to escape later," The Jack of Knives said, and sat against the wall.

He began to get lost in his thoughts. A flurry of angry thoughts entered his head, but also thoughts of suicide. Why didn't he just kill himself and get it over with? It's what everybody wanted, anyway. They could care less about The Jack of Knives.

Then, he told himself to hold off on those thoughts. He was being unrealistic. There was still The Dark Kid. He'd come to the rescue ... hopefully. Most likely, being around The Suicide King had increased thoughts of suicide, which The Jack of Knives tried to resist. He was a murderer, not a suicider. There was a difference.

But then again, The Suicide King was really The Homicide King, and he was The Jack of Knifed, so ...

So, what he needed to do was keep himself in check. But the more that he tried, the harder it became. He pulled out his knife and had to fight the urge to take it and stab himself in the heart. How freeing that would be. How exquisite. He told himself it was just thoughts of The Homicide King, and that he couldn't be The Jack of Knifed, but the harder he tried, the harder it became to control the thoughts. He needed to just end it, end it now. He needed to destroy himself. No one was here to help him. The Dark Kid had just watched it all happen, the arrest. And the lunacy of it! Of having to buy one's own prison! What would The Suicide King have done if The Jack of Knives had been unable to buy a prison cell, even if during a great sale? Would they have just set him free? Perhaps he should have just refused to pay.

Oh, blast it all … *lunacy*. But The Jack of Knives wasn't going to give up. He was going to hurt people. When he ruled over the kingdom, he was going to destroy Ace, and hurt innocent people. Because in reality, no one was innocent. Innocence was a lie, a myth. No one was innocent, all were guilty. As much as he wanted to believe innocence existed, it just didn't. It couldn't, in a world where illogic and violence ran rampant, as rampant as Death on a drugged and crazy stallion.

But it was getting so tempting. The Jack of Knives continued to hold the knife close to his heart, having to struggle to keep it away. Suicide … oh, the bliss it would bring. No more buying prison cells. He'd be free in a hell cell. That would be the way to go.

That was when The Jack of Knives got an idea. He looked at the window, and continued to look. If he could open it, it'd be easy to get out. Not perfectly easy, he'd have to climb a little bit, but the window was thankfully big enough for him to crawl through it.

The Jack of Knives threw the knife straight at the window. It stuck.

"Bulls eye," The Jack of Knives said, and went to the window, after climbing the wall some, and began to stab the window. The window cut like bread. He created a hole big enough for him to crawl through, and then crawled out of the window.

He was out. He was free. The issue was, he didn't know what happened now.

He looked around, and saw a forest. It was the forest that surrounded the castle, which The Jack of Knives had gone through many times in the past. He could go there. He could go there and flee, maybe come back if it ever became safe.

Or, if The Jack of Knives wanted to get back at The Suicide King for his cheap prison sale and capitalistic corruption, and Ace, for his cheap card trick, his cheap sleight of hand.

The nerve it had taken. The Jack of Knives wanted to do something cold and cruel to Ace. He always had to spoil the mood. He always had to taunt the poor servant boy. Well, that wasn't going to happen, once The Jack of Knives came back in full force, ready to murder Ace.

The Jack of Knives smiled at the thought. The thought was quickly followed by thoughts of suicide, which he tried to push through the side as he ran to the forest and eventually arrived inside, weaving through the trees. It was dark, so it was hard to see, but he was doing just fine, trying to shove the thoughts of suicide out of his head and become the murderous Jack of Knives that he was supposed to be, starting with the death of Ace, and then hopefully The Suicide King, and then hopefully the whole entire kingdom, all at the mercy of The Jack of Knives …

The Cutter Gutter

The Dark Kid hadn't expected The Jack of Knives to be arrested. He wasn't sure, but he felt that usually a certain script was followed (as if he'd done this before …), but in this case, that script hadn't been followed. He realized it was ridiculous, to think that existence hadn't followed a certain script, but he couldn't help but wonder. As if, he'd fallen from the sky more than once, as if things were more complicated than they seemed.

Because he felt a certain circularity was breaking (though such an idea sounded insane, and he wasn't quite sure that that was really the case), breaking down, becoming linear, he felt that his path was changing, that he was fated to do something else. What that was, he wasn't sure, but he supposed he would find out soon enough.

He went up to the castle of Contorted Royal, and found his way toward the prison hall, upon entering the castle. He went toward the front of the hall, and sitting there was a man with rotted teeth and a hunched back, who The Dark Kid supposed was the warden.

"I'd like to visit The Jack of Knives," The Dark Kid said. "If that's okay."

"Oh, so you want to visit the knife boy," the warden said in a creaky voice, almost like a mischievous witch. "All right, then, follow me."

The warden grabbed a set of keys, definitely old-fashioned and medieval, and went down the hall towards the very end. He opened the gate, and without noticing that The Jack of Knives was gone, said, "Here's The Jack of Knives. Enjoy your visit."

Then the warden went on his way.

The Dark Kid went inside the cell, and looked around. It seemed that The Jack of Knives had escaped, what with the hole in the window and the absence of a physical being in the cell. Good. That was a good start. But, where would The Jack of Knives have gone?

The Dark Kid went toward the window, climbed the wall to get a good look, and saw the forest outside. He wasn't sure why he felt the way he did, but he believed that The Jack of Knives had fled into the forest. He didn't know this for sure, but the more he thought about it, the more that it made sense. He had run for his life. What with the kingdom against him (well, in all actuality, Ace, and Ace only … The Suicide King, being as dull and dim-witted as he was, probably hadn't signed off on arresting The Jack of Knives with full volition, and no one in the kingdom cared that someone was trying to take over, anyway), it made sense. He didn't want to be in prison. That was a terrible and pointless place to be, especially for someone as ambitious as The Jack of Knives.

Since the warden was utterly incompetent, he hadn't noticed that The Jack of Knives was gone, which The Dark Kid was grateful for. If the warden hadn't noticed, he had no reason to alert Ace.

Something needed to happen to Ace. The Dark Kid wasn't sure what, but something needed to happen.

He'd worry about that later. What he needed to do now was find his friend. So, he climbed out the window, and ran into the forest.

It was raining outside, but The Dark Kid didn't mind it. Lightning was striking in the distance, which he didn't mind, either. It was overcast and dark, but The Dark Kid could see well enough.

It wasn't long before he heard someone crying. It wasn't melodramatic, which surprised The Dark Kid, because of how mad this world was. He expected, if anyone to cry, for it to be ridiculously melodramatic. But that was when he realized it was because it was his friend, The Jack of Knives.

The Dark Kid followed the noise, and finally found The Jack of Knives sitting against a tree. He had cut both of his wrists with his jagged knife, and he had done a lot of damage. The slits and cuts were very deep, and it looked very painful, and there were many cuts. The Jack of Knives was indeed crying, as blood spilled on the ground and mixed with the rain coming from up above, and he looked way, way out of it. His hair and clothes were soaked from the rain, his wrists bloody and soaked, and he hadn't noticed that The Dark Kid was here.

"Ponies are blue in the sunshine," The Jack of Knives said.

The Dark Kid would have laughed at this strange expression, but he knew the madness of Contorted Royal. This comment actually fit perfectly well in this world. Ponies were indeed blue in the sunshine.

But what The Dark Kid needed to do, was get his friend back to center, get him to focus. There were important things they needed to do, like take over the kingdom, and get back at Ace, and perhaps even break the circularity that The Dark Kid didn't know actually existed, but felt intuitively.

"Jack," The Dark Kid said. "Jack of Knives."

The Jack of Knives looked up at The Dark Kid. His eyes looked lost. It was almost comical, because he was indeed spaced out and lost, as if he'd taken the worst kind of drug. He waved, and said, "Who are you, my muffin man?"

"I'm your friend," The Dark Kid said. "I think, based off the insanity of your world, and what you've been going through lately, you're having a … well, a psychotic break. We need to get you back to ground zero. You've hurt yourself, too, which was rash of you, and we need to clean you up."

The Jack of Knives just stared at The Dark Kid blankly, and then looked away. "Psychosis hocus pocus, hukus pukus, what strange deliberation of the psychotic psychedelic coffee break."

The Dark Kid wasn't sure what to do, just looked at how pitiful The Jack of Knives looked. The more he looked at him, the more he wanted to restore him to his former glory. Clearly, The Suicide King had screwed over The Jack of Knives. It was the influence of The Suicide King, to make everybody turn bonkers and suicidal. That was his mission in life, it seemed.

"Pumpkin bumpkin, I don't know a lumpkin," The Jack of Knives said, and took the knife, and cut himself again on the left wrist, wincing in pain.

"No, don't …" The Dark Kid began, but it was too late. The incision had already been made.

Like the others, it was deep. The Jack of Knives was doing serious damage, but he was completely oblivious of it all. He could probably cut off his own hand and he wouldn't even notice.

"Bloody bloody muddy muddy," The Jack of Knives said. "Ponies are gray great in the sunshine like great white shark shirk."

The Dark Kid felt a wild urge to hospitalize this kid; throw him in a white padded room and throw away the key. He knew that, in this anachronistic medieval pseudo fake fest, he could easily get The Jack of Knives into a modern psychiatric hospital. But he didn't think it was a good idea. They wouldn't understand that The Jack of Knives had just lost it because of The Suicide King's influence.

The Jack of Knives then giggled. He pointed at The Dark Kid. "Go low, go low!" and he clapped his hands in childish excitement. "Aliens are taking over the world and we don't know what to do because a giant cat's after me!"

Not knowing what else to do, The Dark Kid sat down next to The Jack of Knives. Then, for a moment, he saw a spark of the old Jack of Knives, that defiance and simultaneous warmth. "Go away, Dark Kid. I don't need you here."

"Let's get this knife out of your hands, before you do any more damage," The Dark Kid said, and he began to reach for the knife.

He thought that The Jack of Knives would fight back, but he didn't, he just mumbled, "Roil roil toil and trouble grubble. Feathers are for featherhead father feathers and disjoint is my joint. To, you know, get high."

"Okay, now, we need to get you cleaned up and cured," The Dark Kid said, but he wasn't sure how he was going to do this. He forced himself to step outside of his shadow, and when he did, he began to glow. He watched as lightning struck The Jack of Knives.

The Jack of Knives began to tremble and convulse as he was electrocuted, but when it was over, he wasn't bleeding anymore, and his wounds were healed.

The Dark Kid, unable to control himself, grabbed his friend's chin, and forced him to look at The Dark Kid, right in the eyes. "What were you thinking, getting yourself stuck in the cutter gutter?"

The Jack of Knives was slowly coming back to Contorted Royal (which was, of course, an oxymoron). "I was … I don't know."

"Was it the blasted Suicide King?" The Dark Kid asked.

"It …" The Jack of Knives began, but he didn't say anything else for a moment. But then he nodded, and looked at his wrist. "You cured me, like … magic."

"I didn't know I could do that," The Dark Kid admitted. "But that's not the point," he said, stepping back into shadow.

"My mind went loony for a moment," he said. "It went loopy. I thought I was going crazy."

"It was The Homicide King," The Dark Kid said. "He made you lose your marbles. But you have them back now, from what I can tell."

"I was … trying to see a vision," The Jack of Knives said. "Sometimes when you bleed, your blood makes a screen, and it shows you things, like from the future. But that didn't happen this time."

"Well, hurting yourself won't accomplish anything. What we need to do is hurt The Suicide King for making you so psychotic and suicidal, and get back at Ace for arresting you for something as bogus as treason."

"That's definitely a good idea," The Jack of Knives said, though he wasn't completely there yet.

They sat in silence for a little while, and then The Jack of Knives looked at his wrists. He sniffed them, touched them, rubbed them, and then said, "No blood?"

"No blood," The Dark Kid said. "You're as right as rain. And speaking of rain."

The Jack of Knives looked up, put up his arms in the air as though beckoning the sky, and said, "Bring it on! Wash my blood and wounds away!"

The Dark Kid laughed slightly. This was just The Jack of Knives joking. He wanted more rain.

The Dark Kid clapped The Jack of Knives on the back, and then said, "You're gonna be all right, man."

"I'm going to be okay," he said, and stood up. The Jack of Knives pulled out a deck of cards, and began to shuffle them. He didn't mind that they got wet; the rain made the cards sharp, like knives. He began to throw them around, randomly, stabbing them into trees. He did this for a while, and then said, "Can I have my knife back?"

"Sure," The Dark Kid said, and gave the knife to his friend. "I suppose we don't need to hospitalize you for hurting yourself."

"Hurting myself? That would be just silly. No, I want to hurt The Suicide King, get back at him for making me what he made me. He has that influence, you know, but I won't tolerate it, not at all. It's ridiculous, it's pathetic. And Ace ... oh, that royal bugger. He's going to pay for what he did to me. We're going to get revenge on him, you and me, Dark Kid."

"Sounds fun," The Dark Kid said, and laughed. "What's the plan?"

"We'll put Ace in a haunted house, or something like that," The Jack of Knives said gleefully, rubbing his hands together. "We'll make him go crazy at the sight of so much horror. We'll see how he likes it. And once we get back at him, we'll figure out a way to get rid of The Suicide King once and for all and take over the kingdom. Oh, how stupid I've been ... what have I been thinking? I've been so foolish, in this cutter gutter. It's time to get back at society. Get *revenge*."

"Sounds like a plan," The Dark Kid said. "When do we begin?"

The Jack of Knives threw his knife into a tree. It stabbed the heart of the tree. "Soon," he said. "Very, very soon."

Everything Is Blue, What One Brannon Knew

Brannon knew that there was another one of him out there, somewhere; in an alternate universe, one that was modern, where the storyline was completely different. There, Brannon was a victim of mental illness, where his beautiful insights were seen as deplorable, even though they were so dang correct.

There, Brannon was a kid; there, Brannon suffered because everything was death. While Brannon wasn't going to pretend that wasn't the case with him, his viewpoint seemed to be a little more … how did he want to put it? Open to interpretation. A little bit more exuberant. Less depressed, less focused on the negative.

That didn't mean Brannon didn't think everything was death, because he did. It was just that, based off the trajectory of his life path, and where he had ended up, he had a little bit more appreciation for certain things. Not everything, of course; there was still death aplenty. But that didn't mean that Brannon was going to live his life as a life-deprived kid. He was an optimist, at least as often as possible, and while optimists were unreliable and untrustworthy, that was who Brannon was.

Brannon was walking through the castle of Contorted Royal, trying to get to the court, where he could talk to The Suicide King. As he was walking, he was humming to himself, a mindless tune that he loved. He was reminiscing on the beauty of the color blue. There were so many hues, of that color blue. They were all equally beautiful, of course. From the world Brannon came from, in the same planet as Contorted Royal but not in the same region (Brannon was definitely an outsider), everything was blue, and blue of the different hue. He loved it when he saw the royal blue, or the cerulean blue, or the light blue, or the sky blue, etc. etc. He knew it wasn't just his eyes that were the problem when it came to seeing such a colorific emblem. He knew it dealt with the fact that everything literally was blue.

Not everything, of course. Certainly not Contorted Royal. But things were blue. Brannon missed those days. But alas, he knew that there were things he needed to do, what one Brannon knew. A lot of things did he need to do. He was a man on a mission … no, that was incorrect. He was a kid. A kid on a mission.

He wore clothes of the average servant boy (sky blue, to complement the sapphire of his eyes), even though he wasn't really a servant himself (though he was fine identifying himself as a servant, and others calling him a servant). He was like this because that was his style; he liked the idea of being humble. He liked the idea of being the servitude of society. He liked the idea of putting himself below others, certainly not in a deprecatory way though. More like, just out of a kind gesture toward others.

But Brannon wasn't going to be speaking lightly about the things that were on his mind. He had no plan to. Everything was blue, what one Brannon knew.

He finally arrived at the court. The Suicide King was flirting with his sword, but thankfully, so as most likely not to traumatize Brannon (Brannon of which The Suicide King hadn't seen yet), he wasn't murdering himself in a violent passion. He was singing a song about suicide to himself, and he was having a certainly good time; it was, however, clashing and crashing deeply against the song that Brannon was humming/singing for himself, to the point to where it saddened Brannon. He just didn't get why people couldn't share the same tunes. The Suicide King's singing was self-indulgent, and while Brannon didn't want to see himself as a superior by any stretch or length of the imagination, Brannon's tune was certainly more simple, rustic, humble, and perhaps with shades of love, above. The Suicide King would probably beg to differ, of course, because people always differed, but for Brannon's humble sanity, he needed to see it that way. He needed to see himself as that poor servant boy, just trying to make it, even though Brannon was far superior to any of that.

"Excuse me, your royal highness, but in Contorted Royal, there's a certain dryness."

The Suicide King dropped his sword, as though caught in the act. He had been preparing to gut-wrench it, straight into his gut, which naturally wouldn't have been pleasant. He turned to Brannon with a blank stare, at first, but then a cruel smile slowly formed on his lips.

"Another servant, come to clean up after the wounds of the wounded king, like the Fisher King, though of course in other parts of the body. We have no use for fertility around here," said The Suicide King.

"If that's how you want to address me, your royal highness, though in Contorted Royal, there's a certain rawness," Brannon said. "I see people bleeding because of murder, I see men that want to hurt her. I see a world where chaos struck all people, stuck in the pull, the Grim Reaper pull. It's rather unpleasant to see, if you don't mind me saying so, my lord."

"Well, you're wrong, kid. About everything. Literally, of course, about everything. There is nothing wrong with Contorted Royal. Everything here works the way it needs to, like flawless clockwork. So, if you wouldn't mind, would you please allow me to finish what I was doing? I would appreciate that, very much so," he added, a little sardonically.

"Everything is royal blue, what one Brannon knew," Brannon said, and turned sideways.

The Suicide King was interested in what Brannon said, but had to shift his position to be on equal footing, to be even, with Brannon, because of his position. He looked carefully at Brannon, and said, "What did you say?"

"It's only a mantra for your pleasing, though I'll confess there is some teasing," Brannon said.

"Everything is blue, you say?" said The Suicide King. "Is that what you said?"

"Certainly not here, Mr. King Sir. Certainly not here. Here, everything is awfully violent red. But where I came from, everything is a calm and serene blue. It's rather full of serenity, like getting lost in divinity. Where I come from, we have little use for loneliness. Violence is seen as unnecessary in many contexts, and the world just makes more sense. But it's this blasted Contorted Royal that screws things up … a lot, I must admit. It's like Contorted Royal is stuck in Hell's pit. Yes, so it is, everything is death, but in that death there's a catch."

"For someone who speaks so eloquently, why are you dressed in mere peasant clothes?" asked The Suicide King.

"Because for me they're rather pleasant," replied Brannon simply. "I have no use to be a peasant. Even though, I'll confess, I'm lower than a peasant, where I come from. But it affords a lot of happiness. You've probably realized by now I don't come from your land."

"Where do you come from, then?" The Suicide King asked.

"From a land far away, though from where, I cannot say. Everything is perfectly blue, what one Brannon knew. You're probably wondering what I know, so ask before I go."

"Yes. I'm absolutely curious." There was some derision in The Suicide King's phrasing, but also some curiosity, and perhaps a tinge of compassion.

"Fix Contorted Royal. I would start by getting rid of all the fakeness, where people like me can't adjust. Contorted Royal is beyond screwed up, without a doubt, and you must throw all the violence out. You," Brannon said, addressing The Suicide King personally, who quietly mouthed, "Me?" as if Brannon was a very powerful being who'd finally noticed The Suicide King, "would do well to hang up your sword and stop fighting the sides of yourself that you don't get. The Black Queen needs to stop being so disconnected from you, and buying into the vanity myths of Contorted Royal. I'd advise The Jack of Knives, too, but I rather like his style, and I don't see what good that would do. You're the head, though, and you keep chopping it off … perhaps there's something you can do about that?"

"I wish there was," The Suicide King said gravely. "But my sword is all I've got."

"Well, a lot of the violence in this kingdom stems from your actions," Brannon said. "I'm amazed you haven't realized that."

The Suicide King descended to Brannon's level. Brannon and The Suicide King were suddenly face to face. The Suicide King grabbed Brannon's clothes in a panic, a crippling fit of anxiety, and said, "I know it does! I know it *does*! But selfishness, it's in my nature! I couldn't change it even if I wanted to. I want everything to be blue rather than that atrocious red you describe, but alas, I just don't know how. I'm a violent, violent soul."

"Well, you aren't to blame completely, of course," Brannon said. "Contorted Royal would have issues even if you weren't so suicidal. But it would certainly help if you were well. You aren't a very good example. I think suicide has its uses, of course, but not the way you appropriate them. Your version of suicide is the same as a slutty boy, while handsome as hell and extra virgin, sleeping around with a million girls to make himself feel better. All it does in the end is make you feel empty."

"Empty," The Suicide King said. "I see what you mean. Emptiness."

"Contorted Royal is a very sick place," Brannon said. "It should be hospitalized at once. I know, however, that you won't do that … you don't have the means to do so, you don't have the budget—a host of reasons. All of that is perfectly understandable. But Contorted Royal, as it stands, is constantly contorting itself, contortions of pain and distortion. You can't go down that route forever, I'm sure you're aware. Or at least, I would hope so. As I've said before, it's not necessarily what the people of Contorted Royal do that's so bad … I rather find your suicidal tendencies rather … admirable. But they aren't sacrificial gestures, by any means. They're completely self-absorbed. Vanity. Pointless destruction. Rampant hostility. That characterizes this supposed medieval kingdom, with many mental problems that have been left untreated for far too long. Mental problems are okay, of course, but how it's dealt with here, it's just plain … *problematic*."

"Well, thank you for your input," The Suicide King said, and paused for a moment. He had let go of Brannon, long ago, and he looked at the sword and went right back to it, picking up his addiction. "I see your point of vanity."

"How it's really just insanity," Brannon said. "I just thought I'd pass the word along. What you do with it is completely up to you, of course. You do what makes you happy. But while I'm here, I'll confess I'd like to see some changes."

"And is there anything else you'd like while you're here?" The Suicide King said irritably.

"There is," Brannon said. "I'd like to talk to Alice."

"Oh, Alice," came The Suicide King. "We *love* Alice."

"I'm sure you do," Brannon said, "but she's still not living the life of the queen, especially when considering her gifts. I intend to talk to her, when the time is right, which I imagine will be very soon. I hope that's okay."

"That's completely fine," The Suicide King said. "You won't be changing me, but you can definitely talk to Alice."

"Well, thank you," Brannon said. "I've spoken my mind, and that's all one can do when speaking with a tyrant. I hope now it's okay that I exit."

The Suicide King gave a half-baked gesture of dismissal, and Brannon bowed gently, then walked out of the room. He heard The Suicide King groaning and thinking inside, saying things like,

"A boy with manners," and "He's wrong, but what if he's right?" and "What should I wear?"

Brannon knew it would take more than a rhyming speech to get things going, but that was okay. He expected that. He in fact didn't really expect things to change. What he knew, for sure, was that he needed to find Alice. Talk to her. Comfort her. Let her know of her gifts, which, despite her special treatment, were still being dismissed.

Brannon smiled at this. Yes, he'd talk to her … when the time came.

The Problem of Having No Problems

Alice was troubled.

The irony was she wasn't troubled by any of her own problems; she had no problems. Her life, in fact, had never been better. This was ironic because she was supposed to have problems, being schizophrenic and all, but she didn't have any problems. None whatsoever.

Though in the end, this really wasn't all that surprising. She rarely had problems. The problems she had were no different from anyone else's problems. Alice, in fact, though she'd never admit this to herself, had it better than the suicidal king, or the disturbed Black Queen.

But that didn't mean she wasn't at her untherapy appointment, thinking about the circular time problem. She was concerned for the fate of Contorted Royal. It seemed terrible that things kept repeating themselves. She wasn't bothered that *she* kept repeating things; in fact, she thought there was a degree of humor to it all, which was always helpful, laughing at one's (supposed) plight. But she knew, in all actuality, it was a problem for Contorted Royal. If the kingdom couldn't get back into linearity, they would be stuck for all eternity, in a battle of the circular, always stuck in a hell they couldn't escape.

So, that was why Alice was troubled. It had nothing to do with her; nothing at all, because, as mentioned before, she personally wasn't bothered by the circularity. But that didn't mean the circularity wasn't screwing things up for the kingdom.

It was the problem of having no problems: it often, unfortunately, presented a problem.

"I really just can't stand Contorted Royal," said Alice's untherapist. "I can't stand the way that I'm treated. Everybody always treats me with dignity and respect, and quite frankly, I'm sick of it."

Alice had heard plenty of things like this before; it was nothing new. She looked at Ralph, who was preoccupied at the moment, looking at a medieval painting, which depicted a church. He seemed to be enjoying it, which was comforting to see.

"I imagine that would be very terrible," Alice said. "Always being seen as a distinguished untherapist, listening to no one's problems but your own. I want to offer you support, but I know that your problems are bigger than any support that I could possibly ever give you. We've been seeing each other for quite a while, but we hardly know each other."

"It is terrible," the untherapist said petulantly. "People are always like, in their very childish, fan-boyish way, 'Hey, there's the untherapist of Contorted Royal! Can we hear your problems?' And I'm like, 'Go away, and leave me be!'"

"That sounds like an awful life," Alice said, and drifted. She knew it was important to listen to the untherapist's problems, but she just couldn't bring herself to do it. This circularity problem, it was just too much.

Alice was sitting in a chair, and the untherapist was lying down on a psychoanalyst couch. He had been looking at her, but now his eyes were closed, as he continued describing the various nature and natures of his problems.

Alice quietly whistled for Ralph's attention. He turned, looking guilty for a moment in that innocent way (he was looking at a painting; no reason to feel guilty, naturally), and then walked to Alice.

"Ralph, I need your advice on something," she said quietly, quietly enough to where the untherapist didn't hear her.

"Anything," Ralph said, in his always generous way.

"I'm debating if I should hospitalize myself."

"Why do you want to hospitalize yourself? That sounds crazy. Even I must admit that."

"It is crazy, but I fear," Alice said, "that it's the only way."

"What do you want to be hospitalized for?" Ralph asked. "Am I, as your grand and royal hallucination, becoming too intense and real for you?"

"There's that, of course," Alice said, "but that doesn't bother me. The truth is … I have no problems. I'm perfectly happy."

Ralph smiled, laughed. "Then why would you hospitalize yourself? What good would that accomplish?"

"Well, I may have no problems, but I need a place where I can be locked up, so I can try and figure out this circular time problem. From what I remember, I always hospitalize myself at this point, because the pressure on Contorted Royal is so great. And really, this circularity is a problem. Always doing the same things, always saying the same things, hearing the same things," she said, looking at her untherapist, who was still babbling unrestrainedly.

Ralph listened to all Alice said, and then finally nodded. "I suppose it wouldn't hurt. This circularity is quite a problem, and while you personally are doing fine, it does seem like a good idea, because it's a problem of society. Hospitalize one to save many: total utilitarianism."

"Well, you know what I mean," Alice said. "It seems like the only way. So many people are oblivious to the circular time problem, and are oblivious to why it's a problem. They feel the hell, but merely surrender to it. Me, though … I need a quiet place to think."

Ralph continued to listen, and then nodded. "Okay. You should hospitalize yourself. If that's what you feel, it might be the best way." He didn't say anything for a moment, then pointed to the painting. "Did you notice the painting? It's wonderful, isn't it? It's nice that the medieval spirit exists in such a contemporary setting."

"It is lovely," Alice said, "though I know the untherapist hates it."

And right on cue, the untherapist said, "And not only do I hate my office, but I hate that blasted medieval painting I put up last year. It's so … *passé*. It's an eye sore, if you don't mind me saying so, and it certainly doesn't fit my aesthetic interests. I want to murder it, *burn* it, but we can't burn classic works, it's the Law.

I've thought about even overpainting it, to ruin its beauty, but that would be the same problem as destroying it senselessly."

"Why do you hate the painting?" Alice asked, as Ralph went back to go observe the painting.

"Because it attempts to make my office homey, but doesn't succeed. Not even in the slightest. It makes it feel rather ... clerical. But, I've got bigger problems than decoration and office aesthetic decorum. Did you hear? My wife wants to leave me. She says all of this fame has gotten to her head, and she can't take it anymore."

"That's dreadful," Alice said.

"Yeah, you're telling me. She says the fame hasn't gotten to *my* head, but for her own sanity's sake, and even vanity's sake, she says that it's better if she leaves me to all of my fame and money. Oh, you don't understand Alice," the untherapist said, sitting up and looking at Alice carefully. "This fame life, all of this money, this glamour ... it makes one crazy! It makes one super batty. But there's no way around it! I'm a celebrity! People love me because I'm curing myself because of the generous therapy of you, Alice."

"Well," Alice said politely, "I'm glad I can be of assistance."

"How could you not be of assistance? You're amazing! You help me so much with all of my problems ... because, of course, you don't help me. You put all the pressure on me to solve the problems, even though I don't have the tools to do so. It's brilliant work, in the mental healthcare system, I have to admit. Putting that much pressure on me to realize that I can't control anything, except myself, which as you can see, I can't even control ... it's *genius*, I say! I don't know why it's taken me so long to realize the genius of your advice."

"Just doing what I can," Alice said hopelessly.

Hopelessly, because she couldn't get the circularity out of her mind. Linearity was the key, but how did one get to that?

"What other problems have you been having lately?" Alice asked, to try and distract herself from the bigger issue.

"Well, I've been feeling this strange déjà vu lately," the untherapist said. "It's rather alarming, this déjà vu, because, while it puts me in a hell I can't quite explain, it also doesn't feel like déjà vu. It feels like something else, though I can't quite explain it."

"Like, it's truly happened before," Alice said, and when the untherapist nodded, Alice frowned.

The problem of having no problems. The problems of society unable to solve its own problems. Therefore, no problem … but, a problem.

"I think I need to hospitalize myself," Alice said.

"You think so?" said the untherapist. "But, why? You've never done so good. You're giving great advice. You understand me, Alice … you *complete* me."

Alice laughed a little. "Oh, you're a sweetheart. But I don't do anything. I don't even listen, because I'm so distracted by having no problems. I have no problems, none whatsoever. My life is perfect. It's flawless."

"That sounds like a very hard life," the untherapist said sadly.

"Well, it does have its downside, but it has good things, too … though, I haven't figured out what those good things are."

"Well, untherapy only works when we have problems. Otherwise, it's pointless conversation. That's why I've been giving you so many of my problems. I can scale back, though, of course, if it's a problem," the untherapist said suddenly. "I don't want you to feel the burden of my problems. I know another untherapist, who treated himself and listened to his own problems on a daily basis, got so sick of it that he committed suicide by hanging himself. A public hanging, it was. On purpose. He wanted to be humiliated for his problems, those of which he couldn't solve."

"That's terrible," Alice said. "I'm so sorry to hear that."

"I still mourn his death, of course," the untherapist said. "I often drop off flowers at his grave, to show my respect. It's terrible, listening to one's own problems. It can drive a person up the wall. I'm sorry that you have no problems, Alice. That sounds like hell, I must say. It sounds indeed like hell."

"There are bigger problems," Alice said, but didn't care to elaborate. "But, I should hospitalize myself as soon as possible. Having no problems makes one crazy. It's like an itch you can't scratch."

"No, I understand that logic, completely," said the untherapist. "I'm sorry to hear about you having to hospitalize yourself. Your life forcing you in a direction you don't want to go … that's terrible."

"Well, my thoughts are perfectly in control," Alice said. "My hallucinations are comforting to me. My symptoms are getting better. It seems like high time to be hospitalized."

"Oh, Alice, you astound me with your brilliance. How do you recommend that I get over the loss of justice I see in this world, this world of Contorted Royal? You know, innocent people getting mock-killed, over and over again, in terrible and brutal and barbaric ways, all of which are pretty traumatizing."

"I would just say, don't accept it," Alice said. "If you don't accept it, then you don't have to confront your problem."

"Exactly!" the untherapist shouted. "Genius! If I run away from my problem, I'll be just fine! That's such a good idea. I'm going to run away from my wife before she can divorce me. I'm going to run away, far, far away. Alice, you're a genius at this! I don't know what I'd do without you! Ah, the joy of having problems … knowing you can never truly solve them. What a joy that is."

Alice smiled. "Just helping where I can."

The untherapist looked at his watch. "Well, I've been generous this time, Alice. I gave you ten extra minutes. You know we'll have to charge you for it, right?"

"That's okay," Alice said. "I have extra money. Now, if you'll excuse me, I need to go and hospitalize myself."

"Sounds good," the untherapist said, and then frowned.

Alice noticed this as she stood up, and said, "What is it?"

"Well, just that you have to pay for me to listen to my problems. I've never liked that. It makes me wonder why friends can't do that, why friends can't listen."

"They can," Alice said, looking at Ralph and smiling. "But usually, they have to be a real friend, which is rare, even in the Middle Ages. Usually, they have to be a hallucination or imaginary friend."

"Got it," the untherapist said, and then laughed darkly. "Just don't tell anybody about this scam of ours. Don't tell anyone

I've been ripping you off to listen to my problems because no one else will. Okay, Alice? Can you do that for your untherapist?"

"Okay," Alice said, and then said, "Come on, Ralph. We're going to the hospital."

And then Alice and Ralph were on their way, with Alice singing a quiet tune, and Ralph looking at the mentally ill contemporary art decorating the walls.

Relationships

The Suicide King and The Black Queen were sitting on their bed together, avoiding each other at all costs. The Black Queen was reading an illuminated manuscript of *The Romance of the Rose*, and The Suicide King was shuffling cards agitatedly. He had his sword right beside him, and he was thinking.

Thinking! Imagine that, for an addle-headed suicided brain-damaged skewer-brained pulp-skulled Suicide King! But, that's what he was doing. He couldn't deny that he was pretty unhappy at the moment. He knew that his relationship with his wife was falling apart, had been falling apart for quite some time now, and was arguably *already* fallen apart, but he still had feelings for her. He only hoped that she had feelings for him.

The Suicide King put away the cards, and picked up his sword. He got up, and began to swish his sword around everywhere, just for fun.

The Black Queen looked up from her manuscript, and said, "Having fun?"

"I'm having a blast," The Suicide King said, and felt murderous suicidal rage: he was moments away from stabbing himself because The Black Queen looked so much like a beauty queen, he just couldn't have her.

But, he managed to keep the sword away from any body part or organ. It was a struggle, a dangerous feat in and of itself, but he managed to do it.

He went back down to the bed, and said, as amicably but bluntly as possible, "I think we need to have sex, dear."

The Black Queen closed the manuscript and set it aside. She said, clearly annoyed, "What did you say?"

"I think it's time that we have a little fun," The Suicide King said. "Our world is based off so much blood … why not let in *other* bodily fluids?"

The Black Queen didn't say anything for a moment, but then shook her head adamantly. "I remember the days when we were romantic, when it seemed like nothing could tear us apart. Alas, though, those days have changed. You know why?"

The Suicide King shook his head.

"Because our relation ship has sunk, our ability to communicate completely fallen through. We're drowning, in cold and freezing water, and unfortunately for us, we can't find solid ground. Even an island would do."

"An island?" The Suicide King said. "That's all you want? Because if that's all you want, you just need to say the word, and presto! we'll go sailing, and find an island all for us, to have all for ourselves. What do you say?"

"I think it's a terrible idea," The Black Queen said. "I'm not sleeping with you, Mr. Suicide. You have too many scars. You bleed even when you're not bleeding."

"Well, you've gotten fat," The Suicide King said bitterly, pouting.

The Black Queen shrugged this off. "Well, you smell bad."

"Well, you …" The Suicide King began, but didn't say anything, because he couldn't think of anything.

"Ha. Cat got your tongue," The Black Queen said.

"I know about you and Spade," The Suicide King threatened.

The Black Queen didn't say anything for a moment, but then stood up, somewhat angrily, somewhat brashly. As The Black Queen walked away, she said, "I don't have to put up with this," and continued on her way, getting ready to quit the royal bedroom, when The Suicide King grabbed his sword, said, in his wicked, wicked way, "And just where do you think *you're* going?" and pointed the tip of the sword on The Black Queen's back.

She turned around smoothly, seductively, and said, "You wouldn't hurt a *lady* now, would you?" and then blinked her eyes exaggeratedly.

The Suicide King kept the sword pointed at The Black Queen, but then put it down, and said, "You're probably right. My sword is much more violent, too violent of a phallic symbol for your Virgin Mary taste."

"Oh, you murder me, honey," The Black Queen said, and turned around again.

"Why won't we at least *talk* about this?" The Suicide King said, showing off some desperation. "Even a little bit? Ease a dying king, please. Help an old and useless king find his death bed less scary."

The Black Queen hesitated, then turned around. "You really want to talk?"

"Yes, I want to talk," The Suicide King said.

The Black Queen didn't say anything for a moment, just went toward the bed and sat down on it. The Suicide King went beside her, and said, "Why have we drifted apart so much?"

"Because we're getting *old*," The Black Queen said.

"That's why you like Spade? Because he's at least ten years younger?" The Suicide King said.

"Something like that. Being around someone younger makes me feel younger. It's completely legal, of course, just a little age gap."

"But you're not ... *old*," The Suicide King said. "You're just in your thirties."

"I may not be that old, but I'm still old," The Black Queen insisted. "And besides, you don't supply me my needs. I'm a shallow person at times, and I want what I want. I want adventurous sex and games. I want a youthful being in my bed. You, though, are just plain *despicable*. You're old and no one cares about you anymore. You're outdated."

"I'm still in my thirties, too," The Suicide King said. "I'm amazed at how shallow all of this you're saying is."

"Well, I already made it clear I was shallow. I like what I like."

"But don't you want to preserve the sanctity of marriage?" The Suicide King asked hopefully, and blinked his own eyes exaggeratedly, the way The Black Queen had a moment ago.

"Marriage is overrated," The Black Queen said. "I like sleeping around. It hurts your feelings."

The Suicide King gasped melodramatically. "What an *awful* thing to say."

The Black Queen touched The Suicide King's cheek and said, "It's our age, dear," and then planted a fat kiss on his lips.

The Suicide King was in Heaven! But alas, that Heaven only lasted for a moment, because then she broke away from him.

"That was … *gorgeous*," The Suicide King said, smitten and dreamy-eyed.

"Well, I'm glad you enjoyed it. But that's all you're getting. Now, I'm leaving. I have better things to do than talk to you."

"Like cheat on me?" The Suicide King said humorously, but there was a strain of hurt.

The Black Queen, who had stood up to walk out of the room, stopped in her tracks and turned around. "You don't provide me my needs."

"Well, call me old fashioned, but I believe in monogamy. I believe in good old-fashioned *work* and effort on relationships. If our ship has sunk, I say it's merely sailed."

"Well, you're outdated, as I've said before," The Black Queen said. "That's how we all live nowadays."

"This is the Middle Ages," The Suicide King said in his defense. "Chivalry and faithfulness are important concepts, and so is living the humble life. Just think of all the beautiful scripturalizing of Augustine and Aquinas."

"Technically, we're in anachronistic Middle Ages," The Black Queen said, "or so Alice says. I don't know how true that is, but that's what she's told me in the past. But regardless, I don't think, just because we're super religious, that we actually make good choices. The biggest scandal ever, popularized by Middle Age literature, as you well know, by writers like Malory, is of course the story of Guinevere and Lancelot. Why would she want to make love to King Arthur, that chivalrous and aging and good-natured and good-moraled king, when she could sleep with someone dangerous, fun, chaotic, hectic, muscular, *manly*?"

"But Spade wasn't all that … *dangerous*," The Suicide King said. "Or muscular. He was a sweet boy, from what I gathered about him."

"That he was," The Black Queen said. "The point is—"

Rather petulantly, The Suicide King rudely interrupted, "I think we should get a divorce."

70

"Well that's not overreacting at all," The Black Queen said. "I have a little fun and you just want to blow it all out of proportion. I think you're jealous, if you want to know the truth. I bet you want to sleep around, too, you just won't admit it."

"Oh, you have no idea what I want," The Suicide King said. "You're a regular Cleopatra, a regular Cressida. Fine. You want your independence, go get it. Nothing will stop you. I'll just plunge a sword in my heart, since that's what's hurting so bad."

The Black Queen didn't say anything for a moment, just looked at her husband. The Suicide King noticed, and he didn't care that he was sulking theatrically right now, just felt hurt and abandoned. (He really didn't; he rather found this game rather … *fun*. It beat sex any day, damaged emotions and hurting hearts and bleeding love and wasted passion.)

The Black Queen groaned and went back to the bed. "Okay, Suicide King … I still love you."

The Suicide King had begun to cry, and he said through exaggerated sniffles, "You … you … *love* me?"

The Black Queen grabbed The Suicide King's hand. "Not as much as Spade, but I do. Now are you happy?"

"I'm so happy I could kiss you!" The Suicide King said excitedly, and would have done just that, but The Black Queen pulled away.

"I don't love you," she said.

"But you just said—"

"I know what I just said," The Black Queen hissed. "I only said it so you'd feel better and leave me alone. I don't mean it."

"Oh, you're a cold witch, aren't you, Missy Black Queen, you she-devil?" The Suicide King said. "Well, fine. Let's get a divorce, and then you can sleep with whoever you want. You'll get your personal island of virgin boys, if that's all you care about. Now I'm going to go kill myself, if you don't mind," The Suicide King said, and rolled over on his sword, stabbing himself a little bit on the edge of the blade.

"Oh, honey," The Black Queen said. "I didn't mean it."

"You meant it, that you did," The Suicide King said. "You just want me to kill myself, so you can rule the kingdom. I see how it is. That's fine. Go. I'll castrate myself while you go and live it up."

"You take things too seriously," The Black Queen said.

Blood was getting on the bed.

"And now we're going to have to get The Jack of Knives to clean up our bed again," The Black Queen added with noticeable disdain.

The Suicide King sat up, his front body bleeding some. He looked at The Black Queen and said miserably, "He's much too busy trying to take over the kingdom for that. He's moved on, to bigger and better things. Lucky him. Maybe I should just do what you do and go find someone to sleep with. Maybe I should go sleep with Spade."

"Spade's dead," The Black Queen said, and now it was her turn to be miserable.

The Suicide King saw his moment and pounced: "Dead, you say? And, *how* did he die? Did you cheat on *him*, and he killed himself in a jealous rage?"

"I don't want to talk about," The Black Queen said. "Divorce sounds like a bad idea. I don't know what I'd do if I didn't have my husband to heartbreak."

"I don't know what I'd do if I didn't have my wife to tease," The Suicide King said, and smiled. "None of this bothers me. I just pretend it does to make you feel bad." Then The Suicide King added, rather hopefully: "Is it working?"

"A little," The Black Queen said. "But no, not really. I'm thinking too much about Spade."

The Suicide King pulled off his shirt, and his belly protruded out. He slapped his stomach and said, "You can't say no to this, can you?"

The Black Queen rolled her eyes. "Yes, to your bulging guts … I mean, guns. I can't say no to that. No way."

"Oh, you're too irresistible," The Suicide King said, and began to kiss The Black Queen. They kissed for a little while, but then she pulled away again.

"I can't love a suicidal maniac," The Black Queen said. "It's too dangerous."

"Well, you're not exactly perfect, either," The Suicide King sneered. "You let your own boyfriend *die*. If I was him, I'd leave you in a heartbeat."

"A divorce really sounds like a good idea," The Black Queen said.

"But you know it will never happen. You *need* me. What would you do without your poor disabled husband running a broken-down kingdom called Contorted Royal?"

"I'd hang myself," The Black Queen said.

"In public?" The Suicide King asked hopefully.

"In public."

"I like you, Black Queen," The Suicide King said dreamily. "You're independent. Alone, but independent. You're like a Neo-Feminist, but better. More improved, more refined."

"And you're …" The Black Queen said, but didn't finish for a moment.

"Yes?" The Suicide King said, urging The Black Queen on with his eyes.

"You're just The Suicide King," The Black Queen said. "Now, if you'll excuse me, I'm going to try and get some sleep. Maybe we'll have sex tomorrow."

"I'd be delighted," The Suicide King. "Because I know tomorrow means the day after."

"Which means the day after that," The Black Queen said.

"And then the day after that. And so on, down the line."

And before The Suicide King knew it, The Black Queen was snoring. The Suicide King's injury from the sword was healing, but that didn't stop him from holding onto and hugging his sword like it was his lover. Oh, the pains of rejection! Such a delight to feel! He continued to hug his sword like it was a flower, as he slowly nodded away, thinking of sinking relation ships in shallow waters and shrinking hearts in an even shallower world.

The ineffable beauties of Contorted Royal …

Story Hour in the Sadhouse and Genuine Genius Masquerading As Insanity Masquerading As Crazy Genius

Alice was no doubt sad.

She wasn't sad because she was depressed. She wasn't sad because she had a lot of problems and she couldn't solve them. She wasn't sad because she felt alone (that was ridiculous when she had Ralph to keep her company). All of the reasons one would expect a mentally ill person to be sad for were not there. Perhaps it was because Alice and her time resisted some traditional narratives.

Either way, Alice was sad, and she was in the mad sadhouse. In all actuality, she was sad because she couldn't solve the circular time problem, and that had led to her being locked up in a hospital. All she could do was look out the window, and lay down in bed, and take medication. It wasn't doing anything for her, but it was required of her nonetheless.

It sickened her, to some degree, that she got all of this special treatment, while people out there in Contorted Royal were left untreated and were stark raving mad. But it was what it was. There was little she could do about it; little she could do that here was a multi-million dollar facility in the middle of the Middle Ages, the facility built just for Alice and her supposed "needs."

And that was what was crazy: Alice still felt incredibly misunderstood. It didn't make sense, when one thought about it. She was one of the most distinguished and important members of the court. People rarely treated her with disrespect in lieu of her illness. She practically had her own personal hospital. What more could a schizophrenic ask for?

But of course, things were always a little more complicated than they seemed. Alice still felt stigmatized. She still felt marginalized. Maybe that was overreacting, or maybe that was just being realistic. She wasn't sure which. It wasn't that she wasn't grateful, of course, for these things, it was just that … well, things were much more complicated than they seemed.

Alice was lying on her bed reading *Alice in Wonderland*, enjoying the linguistic and social madness of that Victorian work that had somehow found itself in the Middle Ages, when a psych tech knocked on her door.

"You have a visitor," the psyche tech said.

Alice was a little surprised at this. A visitor? Who would want to see her?

Alice knew the rules: she could only see a visitor in the common room. She had never actually put this into practice before, though, because she'd never ever gotten visitors in the hospital.

Often, fanboys and fangirls would come to try and get Alice's autograph, but she would politely decline, due to the fact that she was in the midst of getting treatment.

But Alice had a feeling she would do well not to decline this visit.

As the psych tech walked Alice to the common room, and Ralph followed in silent loyalty, outside of the gated part of the unit, he said, "His name is Brannon. I'm not sure what he wants to talk to you about, but he seems nice."

They arrived at the common room, and the psych tech showed Alice the room. Standing at the window, with his back turned, was who Alice presumed was Brannon. He was wearing poor clothes, but somehow, the poor clothes accentuated the seriousness of his position. It contrasted, in a way, with the scrubs that they always made Alice wear when she was in the hospital.

"I'll let you two alone," the psych tech said, and closed the door, going back into the unit.

Alice wasn't sure what to say, and Brannon hadn't acknowledged her yet.

At last, though, he said, "Kings and queens among kings and queens," and then turned around. There was something proud about Brannon, what with his serious face, his sapphire blue eyes, his serious stare. He looked distinguished, or so his features betrayed.

"What do you mean?" Alice asked.

Brannon smiled at Alice warmly and said, "Do you mind if I sit down, Miss?" and gestured toward a chair.

"Not at all," Alice said.

"Thank you, Alice," Brannon said. "It's been a long journey here, to Contorted Royal, but the moment I felt your aura, it became worth it. It's an honor to be in your presence."

"Well, thank you, but I'm just a schizophrenic," Alice said.

"You may be a schizophrenic, but in all actuality, you're a genius masquerading as the insane masquerading as a crazy genius. That's the way it works with the mentally ill, usually. Not all the time, of course. Unfortunately I've observed that some people are so crazy they can never find their way back ... like, The Suicide King, for instance. He's lost in his suicidal grandeur delusions ...

he won't be finding his way back any time soon, I fear. But you, Alice ... you're a different species altogether."

"Well, thank you," Alice said. "That's nice to hear, especially considering what's happened lately."

"Yes, it is a tragedy," Brannon said, smiling slightly. "You have this brilliant understanding of the circularity of existence in Contorted Royal, and yet, you can't do anything about it. That must be terrible. The worst part is you had to hospitalize yourself because you didn't and don't have a solution. You then, become society's scapegoat, even though you could become their savior."

"Thank you, but I'm not sure I see it that way," Alice said. "I'm respected, yes, I really am, but I still have schizophrenia, and even for our advanced age, people still don't and won't understand me. That, then, doesn't make me a scapegoat, it just makes me another mentally ill person. Though, I suppose in terms of the way society sees it, our society that is, I'm the only ill person. Amazingly, no one else is diagnosed with anything, considering the mental state of Contorted Royal."

Brannon laughed a little, and said, "That's why I like you, Alice. You can think for yourself. You have your own thoughts and impressions, and aren't afraid to share them. But I still see you as a victim of the system ... that you have to be hospitalized at all, it sickens me."

Alice didn't say anything for a moment, just looked at Ralph, who was busy playing a game on his small computer that he sometimes carried around with him. Alice thought about getting his attention, but decided against it. She was interested in what Brannon was saying.

"I have for you, Alice, a story hour, though you must be wise with its power," Brannon said.

"You have a story for me?" Alice said, her interest piqued. "That sounds lovely. I love and appreciate stories."

"Well, then, I'll begin." Brannon cleared his throat, and then began: "I am a traveler, as you can probably guess. I've been to many places, seen many things. Our world is very complicated. Contorted Royal is probably the most complicated, but nonetheless, a complicated world we live in. But I come from a faraway land, where the common man is seen as important and dignified, in a real, respectable way, whether that person is poor or mentally ill or of a different race and country. It may sound very left-wing, but that is the world I come from. Contorted Royal seems pretty totalitarian to me, if you don't mind me saying so."

"Maybe a little," Alice admitted. "But we're trying."

"Not totalitarian in the way you'd expect it to be, of course," Brannon said. "Just in the sense of the needless violence. But anyway, I've seen things while traveling. I once went to an island where there was nothing but people that were mentally ill. One would have expected that to be a madhouse, correct? A world where there are only loonies and crazies acting psycho, correct? Especially considering they were untreated."

"Yes, perhaps," Alice said, not sure if she was liking where this was going but still feeling exhilarated. She didn't like where it was going because she felt stereotypes coming on board. An island of the insane? That sounded like the Renaissance Ship of Fools. Anachronism, of course, but if one can read a Victorian novel in the Middle Ages in a modern day hospital …

"Anyway," Brannon said, "it was actually quite a remarkable place to be, and to see, I must confess. It was more than I had expected. On this island, there was a plethora of the mentally sick. There were schizophrenics, bipolars, depressed maniacs, maniacs, narcissists, and the list honestly went on and on. It was a dangerous zone, but also one of beauty. And I'll tell you why.

"Everyone who was sick had their own little niche of understanding. The suicidal depressives had it right because they understood that the universe was a harsh and unforgiving place. Perhaps the island itself wasn't, because they were with people like themselves, but the universe itself was very harsh. Now, I'm going to ask this rhetorically: why would anyone want to live in such a brutal, hostile place like the universe?"

"I'll admit," Alice said, "I've often wondered why I live amidst the violence of Contorted Royal."

"Exactly my point," Brannon said. "Exactly that. On this island, it was completely okay if the depressed people killed themselves. It's a terrible act, a terrible act indeed: suicide is a terrible way to go. But nonetheless, who is to say that those depressed people were actually wrong? Their feelings were real. They felt worthless, because the universe wanted them to feel

77

worthless. They were more in tune with the will of the universe than anyone else. They let themselves cry, something that people don't do nowadays for fear of seeming sappy.

"But there were also schizophrenics, as I've said. And you know why they were happy? You know why I saw them as geniuses?"

"No," Alice said. "I barely understand what my own society sees in me."

"Gifts, Alice. *Gifts*. And boy, were they gifted. They saw things that no one else could see. They heard things that weren't there. They were living in another world. I noticed, that the more they lived in their own world, the happier and freer they seemed. They weren't constrained by the rules of the universe. I know you have some flexibility here, Alice, but if you started talking excessively to your hallucination Ralph, I know, for a fact, that people would raise eyebrows and they'd probably throw you in the loony bin ... even considering how advanced and understanding Contorted Royal is of your needs. It seems to me, that schizophrenia is the attempt to break away from reality, which the universe won't allow, because it refuses. Because, for instance, if you follow your hallucination out into the ocean and aren't really aware of what you're doing, you'll drown. But that's the universe fighting you; it has nothing to do with the illness. The universe wants you to heed the ocean so you obey its rules, the universe a bloody tyrant of will, but your mind just wants to be free. Hence, of course, the constant tug of war."

Alice listened to all of this, and then looked at Ralph. He was still playing on his computer, completely oblivious to all that was happening.

"I can kind of see what you're saying," Alice said. "My hallucination, he's harmless. He just plays computer games and follows me around. He's completely benign."

"It's the world that doesn't understand," Brannon said. "Thankfully, your medieval Contorted Royal is ahead of its time ... but tolerance and understanding could always be better. Always. The mentally ill have gifts, but they are misunderstood. So, we label them.

"Not that labels are completely bad, of course. The Suicide King is no doubt a masochistic suicidal maniac ... no argument there. But that's another story. In the end, I just wanted to share a different perspective. Mental illness? I say, mental wellness. The kings and queens of the mind, marginalized for societal effect.

"If you ever get a chance, you should visit that island."

"I'd like to," Alice said.

"Now, enough story time. The real reason why I'm here, you're probably wondering?"

Alice nodded, awaiting the answer.

"I think you can solve the circular time problem. You're the only one who is in tune with it. Other people are somewhat in tune with it, but they are so distracted by everything else, such as the current violent state of Contorted Royal or their problems, that they can't really truly be in tune with it. But you hospitalized yourself to try to find the answer, which to me, seems a little unfair. But nonetheless, because of your awareness of this problem, I think you can solve it. It will probably bring on new problems, but I think you'll be just fine with those problems. It will, if you figure it out, be at least one step in the right direction, which is all anyone can really hope for in a brutal universe, a universe that won't allow one's mind to be free."

Brannon then stood up, and said, "Now, I should probably get going, but remember: insanity is only genius masquerading as crazy genius. No one will ever truly understand where you're coming from. And I suppose, how can they? They were gifted with the perfect mind set. They have no problems. They have no insanity. Though of course, I'm being sarcastic. Look at the average mental state of the common person and you'll see what I mean."

Alice took all of this in, and Brannon took Alice's hand and kissed it gently. Then he left the room.

Alice didn't move for a little while, just took all of this in. She was less sad now. It was nice having faith. There was something very genuine and gentle about Brannon, and his advice. What if he knew something Alice didn't?

It seemed that way. Alice only hoped he was right.

The Haunt Hunt

Ace was slowly trying to awake.

He was still wearing his hood, he could feel it; he felt darkness as well, which he liked. What he didn't like was that he knew that something had happened. He had been going for his daily walk in Contorted Royal when something happened, when certain people came up to Ace and knocked him unconscious.

It seemed silly, that someone had actually succeeded in abducting Ace. Nonetheless, it had happened. He knew that now. He didn't know how they had succeeded, because no one just randomly abducted *Ace* ... but nonetheless, it had happened.

Ace was still trying to awaken; finally, his eyes opened for good, and he saw the darkness that he felt raining down upon his body. In fact, all that existed was darkness. Ace would have felt right at home if it wasn't for the circumstances of how he had arrived here. He had a problem. He had an enemy. He didn't know who that enemy was, but he knew he was going to have to figure it out, and soon.

Ace stood up, and looked around. Still nothing but darkness. He began to walk forward, not knowing where he was going to go, and did that for the longest time. Suddenly, there was a little bit of light; not much, but some.

Ace began to walk toward the light, and that was when a voice, cackling and sounding so much like a witch, said, "Welcome to the Haunt Hunt, the most famous haunted house on the East and abandoned side of Contorted Royal."

So that's where Ace was: the Haunt Hunt. He knew about this haunted house. Usually, people were delivered to this haunted house when someone wanted someone dead. It didn't always work, this attempt at assassination ... but sometimes, however, it did.

But Ace was going to get out of here alive. He knew it.

Ace continued to go toward the light, the light of which revealed that he was in a hollow cavity of some sort. He was just thinking that he needed to find his way out of this place when a giant axe swung toward him.

Ace ducked, but barely; a moment slower and he would have been scalped. He in fact thought that his hood had been brushed.

"I guess things are going to get crazy," Ace said, and watched as another axe flew toward him.

He ducked, as expected, but had to duck even lower this time. These axes were determined to get him.

As Ace was moving forward, he began to get the sensation, the feeling, the fear, that someone was following him, to finish off the job if the axes failed. He wasn't sure who that would be, but he had a crazy idea that it was a zombified or mummified Spade, wielding a sharp, sharp knife, to come and make Ace pay for his sins. He told himself it was all in his head, but he wasn't sure how true that actually was.

Another axe came, and Ace continued to duck, and that was when two axes moved down beside him, like a guillotine. If he had been even a little bit closer, one of them would have sliced through him.

More axes continued to move, and it wasn't long before axe after axe came, forcing Ace to have to move in a slow-mo sort of way, dodging all of them, which were getting so very close to hurting Ace.

One finally did end up hurting Ace. Not too much damage, thankfully, but it created a small cut, a small nick, on Ace's arm, cutting through the cloth of his hood.

He began to bleed, and distracted, he didn't notice the other axe that was coming toward him.

This axe was thankfully badly aimed, so it didn't get anywhere near Ace. But still, when he realized that he'd missed an axe, just barely, he immediately sharpened his attention, and continued to move toward the light.

He realized now that he was walking in a hall of some sort. No more axes, thankfully, but something new was happening. On the left side was a glass cage, with nothing in it.

Ace looked at the glass cage, wondering why this random glass cage was there, and that was when he saw Spade move forward, from out of nowhere, with an axe in his head. He was screaming, and he had a look of fear on his face; the scream was shrill and perpetual, and Ace was so startled that he almost jumped. He didn't, of course, because the Haunt Hunt wasn't going to scare him, give him that cheap, cheap thrill … but still. It was pretty startling.

Ace looked at Spade for a while, seeing where this was going. That was one of the beauties about the Haunt Hunt: it could tailor its "attractions" strictly for the special guest in the house.

He continued to walk through the house, and that was when he saw another glass cage. What was he going to see this time? Was he going to see a monstrous version of Big Foot? Was he going to see a creepy witch with blazing red eyes? Was he going to see a ghost?

What he saw was none of these, but Spade again, in the same position, screaming shrilly and perpetually.

Ace thought the repetition odd (it felt like déjà vu … perhaps even circular time masquerading as déjà vu …), especially because it haunted him, in a way. It haunted him because he felt like he was in hell, seeing the same thing again, haunting him for putting Contorted Royal in its endless circularity.

But maybe, that was just overthinking the situation. He only saw another glass cage, he wasn't repeating anything.

But when he looked back, he saw the glass cage was gone, but not the supposed second one. Maybe he *had* just experienced circular time.

He wasn't sure, so he continued to move, and that was when he saw the glass cage and nothing for a moment, but then Spade.

Ace repeated this many times, but told himself not to get lost in the theatrics of it all. So what if he was circularizing? So *what*? It didn't matter. It didn't mean anything.

He did this for the longest time, and finally, at last, he saw a boat some distance before him. It was odd, seeing a boat in a hall of a haunted house, but this building could do anything it so desired.

He finally arrived at the boat, and saw that a black river was before him. He got on the boat, and the boat slowly started to move forward of its own accord.

As it moved through the river, the river slowly began to brighten. But it wasn't angelic light by any means, in fact, it seemed like light from Hell. He saw dead people, dead Spades to be exact, trying to grab a hold of the boat. There were many Spades, all of them trying to grab a hold of the boat, and Ace would have panicked at this point because it was a crazy effect, having an infinite number of Spades trying to take down your boat so they could take you under (it was like riding in Charon's boat on the river Styx, seeing all the spirits below), and Ace wondered if each Spade represented one Spade that Ace had killed over the infinite number of times in the circularity of the situation.

Thankfully, the boat wasn't overtaken, but that didn't stop the demon zombie Spades from trying. They were making strange sounds as they did so, similar to a ghost scream in sound … but in the end, Ace found land.

He got on the land quickly, and then smiled back at the Spades that were damned to the water. They weren't getting him today. The Haunt Hunt was going to have to try harder if it wanted to kill Ace … and it was going to have to do more than taunt Ace with his supposedly evil past.

He continued to walk (the land was another hallway), and as he walked, that was when he got the feeling that he was being hunted again.

And that was when he heard the sound: snarling, like a diseased and rabid and violent dog, as well as a strange gurgling sound. Ace wondered if he was being hunted by a monster straight out of one of Lovecraft's tales. Some thing. Some snarling, gurgling *creature*. He heard it, coming closer, and Ace, who was getting somewhat afraid, just continued to move through the hallway.

That was when he heard screams. And then he heard … eating. Yes. A creature very close behind Ace was eating an innocent victim.

Ace shuddered. He wasn't afraid yet, but his blood was pumping, his heart beating fast.

A knife suddenly flew toward Ace. Ace dodged it, and looked to see who was standing there.

Standing there was The Jack of Knives. His eyes were blazing red, and there was something eerily mechanical about his behavior, his demeanor. Even when he spoke, he sounded almost robotic, though robotic wasn't the perfect word. Perhaps mechanically strained was better. Zombified, even, with a hint of technology.

Because alas, even the blazing red eyes looked like small red bulbs.

The Jack of Knives said, "Welcome to my lair. You owe me, you blasphemous murderer."

"I didn't murder you," Ace said. "I just tricked The Suicide King into arresting you for treason."

And suddenly, it all clicked in Ace's head.

"You're the one that did this," he said. "You're trying to kill me. You're trying to get me killed, so you can go back to ruling the kingdom."

"Welcome to my lair," The Jack of Knives repeated. "You owe me, you blasphemous murderer."

And amazingly, Ace responded with, "I didn't murder you. I just tricked The Suicide King into arresting you for treason."

And then: "You're the one that did this. You're trying to kill me. You're trying to get me killed, so you can go back to ruling the kingdom."

Ace knew what was happening: circularity to its extreme. And the effect was rather … chilling. This was what it felt like to repeat things over and over again, and not be able to stop it. For a moment, Ace almost felt *bad* for bringing circularity upon Contorted Royal.

It was a broken record. They repeated this cycle for a few more times, and then finally, Ace managed to break out of it. He said, "Just kill me, Jack. Kill me, and get it over with."

"I will kill you," The Jack of Knives said. "Just you watch."

The snarling, the gurgling, behind Ace. Ace turned around, to see who was there, but there was no one, no Lovecraft monster. When he turned to see The Jack of Knives again, though, he wasn't there either. But the snarling was getting louder, and when Ace turned around, he saw Spade standing there, drenched in filthy water and seaweed, and holding a sharp knife in his rotted hand, which went well with his rotted flesh and his tattered clothes. He was the one that was indeed gurgling, and he was gurgling because water was in his mouth and water continued to get out of his mouth, and he was snarling with rage.

84

Ace, in a rare move, removed his hood, exposing his face.

"You can slit my throat, if you'd like," Ace said to Spade, pointing at his throat. "I've killed you a lot, Spade, and I can only imagine how much that screws things up for your soul, for your existence."

Just more gurgling. Then Spade bared his rotted teeth, and continued to gurgle more of the filthy dirty water. He raised his knife, and Ace awaited the blow, awaited his throat to be slit.

And slit he did: Ace felt his throat, which felt sharp with pain, and felt blood bubbling and gurgling out. Ace tried to talk, but Spade only laughed, and began to stab Ace repeatedly.

But Ace knew better than to give into the terror of a haunted house. He told himself none of this was real, even though the pain was so real, and when he did that, Spade was gone, and Ace was wearing his hood again, staring at The Jack of Knives.

Ace expected The Jack of Knives to begin the exchange that had happened when they first met, but he didn't. He merely said, "You escaped Haunt Hunt. Lucky you. But the mazes you've created through your circularity will get you in the end."

"I know messing with time, death, and other things leads to risks," Ace said. "But I'm not worried. I can take those risks."

The Jack of Knives didn't say anything for a moment, but then said, "Maybe you can take those risks, but not for long. Things will happen. Things will contort. Be ready, Ace, because if you're not, the elements you can't control will hunt you: they'll haunt you down."

And then The Jack of Knives turned into Spade, and Spade stabbed himself. He laughed as he did so.

Ace, who only found this amusing, walked away from Spade into darkness. It wasn't long, though, before he found a door, alit by a small candle on the wall.

He opened the door, and walked outside. It was dark outside, with just the full harvest moon like on the wildest Halloween night, and a few stars illuminating the road that stood before Ace.

Ace began to walk upon it, glad to be out of there.

So The Jack of Knives was the one who'd done this. Well, he was going to pay. There was no denying that. When the time was right. Ace wasn't sure what he'd do, but he'd find something to do.

When, of course, the time was right.

Good Times, Good Times

The Jack of Knives and The Dark Kid were hanging out again at the tavern.

The Jack of Knives himself had never been so happy. Good times, good times—and good times called for a celebratory mindset, a free-range mindset, the idea that nothing was off limits, that everything was going to go splendidly, swimmingly.

"Ace either went insane in the Haunt Hunt, where he'll stay for all eternity, or he'll be murdered successfully," The Jack of Knives said darkly. "I say we cheers that."

"Sounds good to me," The Dark Kid said, and raised his mug, and the two clinked mugs. They both took deep drinks, and then The Jack of Knives looked at The Dark Kid.

"You know we can take over the kingdom, right?" The Jack of Knives said. "Especially now that Ace is gone. He can no longer get in our way, and since The Suicide King's head is so addled, he won't even know what's coming."

"What was your plan, exactly?" The Dark Kid asked curiously.

"I say, we abduct The Suicide King and put him on a small boat and just let the boat drift out to the middle of the ocean. That's what I say. The Black Queen is so distracted with her extracurricular lovemaking that she won't even realize that we've taken over the kingdom. The Suicide King will slowly rot on that boat, and we'll have the kingdom all to ourselves, and we can begin."

"Sounds like a plan," The Dark Kid said blackly. "I suppose you'll want to use my lightning?"

"That could work," The Jack of Knives said. "What would you do with your lightning?"

"Just wrap it around The Suicide King, bound him up nice and tight in an electric rope, and then we'll drag him to the boat, and go from there."

"Sounds good to me," The Jack of Knives said happily. "I can't *wait* until we can rule the kingdom. No more cleaning up suicide, and *hello freedom*. I'm going to be a tyrant, just you watch. I'm going to be a murdering psychopath king. The Suicide King had it all wrong: you hurt your people, not yourself. But that's okay: welcome to the new world order: the new order of Contorted Royal."

The two continued to celebrate with each other. The Jack of Knives loved the plan, knew it was going to work perfectly. Contorted Royal was too screwed up of a place to even notice if they had a new ruler. That was going to be great, was certainly going to aid The Jack of Knives and his transition.

They were having a blast, doing just fine, when The Jack of Knives suddenly had an idea.

"I think we should horseplay," he said.

"Horseplay?" The Dark Kid asked curiously. "In what way?"

"I have knives, you have lightning. We'll try to kill each other. All in good fun, of course, but yeah … what do you say?"

The Dark Kid laughed. "Kill each other before our big hostile takeover. I like it."

"You better run, then," The Jack of Knives said, and threw a knife at The Dark Kid.

The Dark Kid dodged it, and looked as though he was going to run, when, after he was some distance away, turned to face The Jack of Knives. "You sure you want to mess with The Dark Kid? I know things, Jack. I know things you'd never be able to imagine."

"Yes, I can see the dark secrets in your eyes," The Jack of Knives laughed, and threw another knife at The Dark Kid. He caught the knife, and threw it back at The Jack of Knives.

It stabbed The Jack of Knives in the leg, but The Jack of Knives wasn't worried. "Trying to draw blood, I see," he said. "Did you want a canvas to paint?"

"I want you to throw another knife," The Dark Kid said.

The Jack of Knives did just that, and this one again The Dark Kid caught. He grabbed it right by the blade. His hand was bleeding some, but he didn't mind it, just threw the knife back at The Jack of Knives.

The Jack of Knives caught it, and his hand was bleeding as well. He quickly tore off some cloth and wrapped his hand. Just to look cool. Not to heal it, or bandage it … just to look cool.

The tavern was watching the fight curiously, and cheering occasionally, for either The Jack of Knives or The Dark Kid.

"You know I wouldn't hesitate to murder you," The Jack of Knives said with mock maliciousness. "You'd give me practice for when I betray innocent people."

"Oh, I'm so scared," The Dark Kid teased.

And The Jack of Knives responded by shouting in a manly rage, and he charged toward The Dark Kid with his knife and tackled The Dark Kid, and began to stab him, stab him like crazy, stab him left and right, and The Dark Kid laughed like he was being tickled.

As The Jack of Knives did this, he couldn't help but admit that The Dark Kid had shed some of his mystery to let in some of Contorted Royal. It was a strange effect, if The Jack of Knives didn't mind saying so. But it was cool. The Dark Kid had come from his own world to be part of this world, and he was doing great.

"Ah, you killed me," The Dark Kid said.

The Jack of Knives let go of The Dark Kid to exam his work, his masterpiece. So many wounds. Stab wounds, of course, and so much blood pooled on the ground. The blood was darker than most blood, with a tinge of shadow, a tinge of black.

"What did you expect?" The Jack of Knives said cockily. "I'm The Jack of Knives. I'm a murderer, a homicidal maniac."

The Dark Kid just closed his eyes and played dead.

But that was when The Jack of Knives saw a thundercloud above him. It was random and all, being in a building and all, rather than outside and all, but sure enough, the cloud was there.

The Jack of Knives wasn't sure what to expect, and so he watched as a lightning bolt reached out from the thundercloud and stabbed The Jack of Knives right in the heart.

It electrocuted the hell out of his heart, the heart convulsing and shaking, like he'd just been zapped with a disastrous defibrillator. It hurt like hell, no doubt about that, and The Jack of Knives grabbed his heart, trying to stop the pain, but it didn't do any good. His heart was toast.

He collapsed onto the ground, still trying to save himself from the wrenching agony, but it didn't do any good. He felt darkness coming, to take him away into unconsciousness, but somehow, he stayed where he was, the lightning still electrocuting his heart.

And then it stopped, as suddenly as it had come. The Jack of Knives looked over at The Dark Kid, saw him stand up. The audience was clapping, loving the riotous nature of the show, and The Dark Kid went over to give The Jack of Knives a high five.

They high-fived, and The Jack of Knives breathed out some smoke. He knew his heart was going to be charred for a couple of days, but he didn't mind. The Dark Kid's wounds were already healing.

"We're crazy," The Dark Kid said, in that mysterious way he always employed. "We could have killed each other."

"Welcome to Contorted Royal," The Jack of Knives said. "That's how we play in this kingdom."

"It would have been nice if you'd invited me for all the fun, but I guess you two are always just going to be on the run," came a voice.

The Jack of Knives turned like The Dark Kid to see who was there. It was Brannon, who The Jack of Knives hadn't had the honor to meet yet, but was glad to meet.

He looked poor, but humble, but also with a proud air and dignity. He was smiling. "Mind if I sit beside you two?" he asked.

"No, not at all," The Jack of Knives said. "We've been celebrating."

"I imagine," Brannon said, sitting down. "You want to take over the kingdom and all. Not a bad political move, I'd say, when considering the king is beyond saving. It may be the only way to save the king, and save the royal chess game."

"I'd say that," The Jack of Knives said. "But we've got it all under control."

"Well, have a blast at it," Brannon said. "You know, I like you, Jack of Knives."

"And why is that?" The Jack of Knives asked sharply, though not out of annoyance, more just to show how tough he was.

"Because everything is death, of course," Brannon said, smiling. "Why else? But in you, I see a concentrated everything is death … with the catch being that it's actually styling. You're nothing but murder and blood, Jack of Knives … I see that in you. But it looks good on you, with you wearing it like your poor servant clothes."

"Soon to be king's clothes," The Jack of Knives said. "Thanks for the complement. You'd be surprised how sick the servant gets of his job."

"Maybe," Brannon said. "Or maybe not. It depends on who you are, where your mindset is. But you're probably going to do Contorted Royal a favor, I imagine. You'll let in some humility. Murderous humility, but humility nonetheless. I hope that Contorted Royal you'll divine, because if you do we'll all be fine."

"Thanks," The Jack of Knives said. "I don't know why you like me, though. I'm murderous."

"You pretend to be," Brannon said, turning the conversation on its head, swerving. "It's your soft spot. But you've got that real soft spot to deal with. The gentle side, the one that can give so generously murderous humility. The Suicide King, he's just hopeless … but you, Jack of Knives, could rule everything so beautifully, so violently. You'd make everything death. You'd share your style with everyone. We'd all become servants of the blade."

"I think you're giving me too much credit," The Jack of Knives said. "I'm a psychopath."

"You're also just a kid," Brannon said, and pounded the counter. The bartender came over. "I'll have what they're having."

The bartender nodded, brought over some ale. Brannon took a sip.

The Jack of Knives was still trying to figure out what to do with Brannon. Was he saying that The Jack of Knives—and this was *The Jack of Knives* being talked about, here—had a soft spot? Was that what he was saying?

"Maybe I just like your style, is all," Brannon said, taking a drink of his ale. "Maybe I just like the blood on your teeth, the knife wound on your hand. You could be a murdering psychopath, but maybe I just like it. Or maybe, just maybe, you're not as stab-oriented as you think you are."

"Maybe," The Jack of Knives said, taking all of this in.

It was interesting to think about. The Jack of Knives still wasn't a murderer. Neither was The Suicide King, of course, but the difference was that The Suicide King was weak. The Jack of Knives wasn't weak. His back had been hardened by his menial labor. Maybe that's what Brannon was referring to, though in all reality, he wasn't quite sure.

"Life's a brutal game full of chaos, but you, Jack of Knives, are the boss."

Then Brannon bowed to The Jack of Knives. It had a strange effect, being admired like this, especially when considering that Brannon seemed pretty powerful himself. He started to question if it was genuine. He decided it was genuine, but that Brannon had a few tricks up his sleeve, a sleight of hand to be reconciled with.

"I think you want to fix Contorted Royal," The Jack of Knives said distantly. "Stop all its violence. For good."

"Ah, you caught me, king," Brannon said, and then patted The Jack of Knives on the back. "Well, I need to go. Busy days ahead, for all of us. Busy days."

And then Brannon left, whistling a happy tune to himself.

"Rustic, he is," The Dark Kid said.

"Simple," The Jack of Knives corrected. "But I like him. I think he knows things. I would pay attention to him. See what he does. What he knows."

"Maybe after we take over the kingdom," The Dark Kid said obliquely.

"Maybe," The Jack of Knives responded, and felt his thoughts unwinding in a relaxed manner in this good time …

Epiphany Uncanny

Alice had discharged from the hospital, but the hospitalization had been a useless venture, in the end. She had gotten no closer to solving the circularity of the situation, of Contorted Royal, which led to her feeling frustrated and wishing that the circularity would just become linearity, all on its own, and no one would have to be in hell anymore, and things could evolve naturally, and stuff like that. But that of course was just wishful thinking.

Nonetheless, she was doing a little bit better; Brannon had inspired a newfound hope in Alice, something she'd never experienced before. Because she knew that before the hospitalization, she'd never seen Brannon before. Brannon was a new species, a new breed, that deserved careful understanding and study. If Brannon had come sooner, Contorted Royal's circularity might have gone a different route; however, Brannon was not part of the script at all, and it seemed to be because of the answers he sought.

Alice knew she'd hospitalized herself in the past; that was what circularity was, after all. But the addition of Brannon changed things. In fact, the circularity did seem a little bit different. Different choices made, difference consequences. She couldn't quite explain it, but she wanted to venture to say that the circularity was slowly falling apart. It hadn't fallen apart completely yet, but what with the addition of Brannon, who she knew had never appeared before … it just got her to think differently about things.

Alice was sitting on the grass outside of the castle, with Ralph sitting beside her, as loyal as ever. He was reading a book (*Gargantua and Pantagruel* by Francois Rabelais), and he was laughing occasionally, grimacing on other occasions, but ultimately seemingly having a good time in that rollicking gargantuan adventure.

He was no doubt immersed in his book; but Alice wanted to talk to him. He was just so quiet, Ralph was, never causing any trouble for Alice, and Alice wanted trouble. Just a little bit of trouble. A little bit of noise.

"How's the book?" Alice asked.

"It's great," Ralph said, not looking up. "I like it. Rabelais was ahead of his time. Though, I think he would have been a fine medievalist. He would have gracefully counteracted the royal greatness of Chaucer and Dante, the Great Literature."

"I don't think Chaucer is all that royal," Alice said. "And if you think about it, their styles aren't that royal. They used the vernacular."

"In terms of their reception, I mean," Ralph said. "Chaucer and Dante both knew they were great writers, while Rabelais just wanted to satirize the hell out of things in as lowly and as lowly literature of a way as possible."

"I see your point," Alice said. "Chaucer recently visited Contorted Royal."

"He did?" Ralph asked curiously, closing his book.

"Yeah. He visited, along with Dante. They both came together to share their poetry, on a world tour. The problem is it's a fuzzy memory. It happened before the circularity. I do remember they really impressed The Suicide King though. Having two great writers, even for our own time … it's rather remarkable."

"This circularity really bothers you, doesn't it?" Ralph said.

"Yes," Alice admitted. "It drives me crazy. Everything just repeats itself. Brannon was a new addition, but we keep saying and doing the same things."

"We aren't right now," Ralph said. "Maybe that's a sign of progress."

"That's only because I'm aware of the circularity problem," Alice said. "For everyone else, though, from what I can tell, they just keep doing the same things. The Fool still does his workout in the public square. The Jack of Knives still wants to take over the kingdom, and I know what happens to him. And eventually, the circularity is going to come full circle, and there will be nothing we can do to stop it."

"I don't know if I quite believe that," Ralph said. "I mean, considering that you've figured it out. You know we're stuck. How long have you been aware of it?"

"This is pretty much the infinite number that we've circled around," Alice said. "I've been aware of it since the beginning. At first, I would repeat things, everything, but I was aware of it … it was the strangest effect. Since then, though, I've slowly been breaking out of it. But I can't break out of it fully. Some things stay the same. I've hospitalized myself every time I've tried to figure it out. Our conversation in the untherapist's office was pretty much the same as all the times before it."

"Sorry to bore you with my repetition," Ralph said.

Alice laughed a little bit. "You know what I mean. There are moments like this, where we seem ourselves to be outside the circularity, but not everyone else. You see over there?"

Alice pointed to The Fool. He was out for a walk, talking to himself and laughing in outbursts occasionally.

"The Fool does that every time we come out here to talk about the circularity problem," Alice said. "We may be outside the circularity problem, but not completely, and not the people surrounding us. I wish it was different, but it just can't be different. This circular problem is too complicated."

"But if you can break out of the circularity at least a little bit," Ralph said, "there's got to be a way."

"Maybe there really isn't a way," Alice said. "Maybe I'm supposed to be cursed with this blasted insight for all eternity. Just doomed to keep repeating things except for moments that deviate from the main script."

"Ah, don't say that," Ralph said. "You can make an impromptu movie, if you so desire. You know something. You know a lot of things. Don't second guess yourself. Don't make yourself less than what you are, in your mind's eye. You're strong. You're smart. You know things. Don't pretend you don't."

"That's sweet, Ralph," Alice said. "But I feel like that's the way it is. I'll never solve the problem. Ever. I just can't solve it. I can be aware of it, but I can't do anything about it. Torture, for sure, no denying that … that tortures me. But the problem is that I can't do anything about it. It's like a soothsayer that can see the future but can't change anything without damaging the path even more."

"Well, all of our consequences, especially our good-intentioned ones, do seem to contribute to more chaos. For every good thing there's always a bad thing sprouting, competing for the attention. I think it's just the way it is, though: the universal dichotomy."

"But I still think Brannon was right," Alice said. "Despite the potential for me making things worse, I need to obsess about the circularity. Obsess and obsess, until I finally find the answer. It may be neurosis, but I don't flipping care. I'm going to solve this problem. Brannon inspired me, yes, but he's right about everything he said."

"What if you need to change the angle on how you look at it?" Ralph suggested.

"How do you mean?" Alice asked.

"Well, I just mean, change the perspective you're using to view it. You see it as a problem, of course, but that's only because you're looking at it from the angle of circularity: all you see is the problem of circularity, and nothing else."

"That's because it's a huge problem!" Alice said, nearly exasperated. "How else am I supposed to look at it? You wouldn't look at an injustice, no matter how slight, as anything other than injustice, right? Because that's what it is. It's an injustice. We can't pretend it's something else, or we'd go crazy. Why would we pretend an injustice is justice?"

"Good point," Ralph said. "But what I mean is, there's got to be more to the circularity than just the circularity. There's got to be more to the circularity than just the hellish conundrum it puts all of Contorted Royal in. I don't know what angle, exactly, you could look at, but there's got to be something. For instance, do you know who has caused the circularity?"

"I don't," Alice said. "I wish I did. I don't know if that information can be figured out, though. Not by a poor schizophrenic."

"Oh, Alice, you're too hard on yourself. And you know Brannon would disagree with you."

"Of course he would, but he doesn't live in my crazy head. The things I see ... they are so amazing. The problem, of course, is that they are still crazy. My delusions have been proven true a numerous amount of times, but the ideas themselves are so crazy that I'm still considered a loon. You're tame by comparison: I know that schizophrenics in a real modern day society have hallucinations that haunt them, torture them, torment them. But you don't haunt me. I mean, you follow me, which I guess is a form of haunting, but it's so benign that I don't even mind it. Not one bit."

"You're off topic, Alice," Ralph said. "Come on. We have a problem to solve. Besides, you just said exactly why you're gifted."

"What was that?"

"That you see things. You see things others don't, quite literally. You have a novel perception. Do you want to just throw away that gift?"

"No, I don't," Alice said. "I just don't know what to do with what I know. I know that I didn't start seeing you until a little bit before the circularity began. I had always assumed you might know something, that you represented the answer, literally, but also metaphorically, in that you were the key to my own mind. If I understood you, I could understand something much more meaningful. But those hopes sound distant now."

"Well," Ralph said, "I'm flattered you see so much potential in me. But I'm not sure I'm the answer."

Alice thought about this, not quite hearing what Ralph just said. Ralph as the key? It seemed reasonable, though she couldn't explain why. She didn't understand why she was thinking this. But she knew better than to doubt her intuitions.

"It is odd that I started hallucinating you right before we dipped forever in circularity," Alice said. "It does seem coincidental, but also not coincidental. Before that, I was just hallucinating robots. I'm wondering if you know something, Ralph. Where do you come from?"

"I come from a modern day world, of course," Ralph said.

"What's it like there?"

"Very artificial," Ralph said, as though it was a bad joke. "And speaking of robots: I hate it there. The medievalists had class, even if a little anachronistic."

"Well, Contorted Royal is medieval, Contorted Royal itself and our world follow a different route. We're our own world, separate from any 'proper' medievalism. But that's not the point. You come from a modern day setting. And you hate it? Why?"

"Because … oh, Alice. These are hard questions. I haven't been there in ages. I don't remember much."

"You urged me to think outside the box," Alice said. "Come on. Focus. Concentrate. What do you know?"

"I know that Contorted Royal is networked, somehow, with the world that I came from. I'd tell you how, but I'm not sure. I do feel, though, that if it were up to me, I could stop the artificiality of my world and solve the circularity of Contorted Royal. Not sure how, I just feel like I could."

Alice continued to puzzle, continued to think. She listened to Ralph talk about his world, about the things he knew, and that was when she suddenly saw clearly.

It was an epiphany uncanny; it was indeed rather strange, all of it falling into place so strangely. She knew what was going on with Contorted Royal. It came as smoothly as a delusion: heck, it *was* a delusion. But it was a delusion that was going to come true. She felt it.

Alice had the answer.

"Ralph!" Alice said. "You're the key!"

Ralph looked at Alice curiously. "I am?" he said, and then, more confidently, "I mean, I *am*!"

"We don't have a whole lot of time," Alice said hurriedly. "The circularity is coming full circle, and I can only hope I remember this conversation. I should. I should remember, even if brought back to the beginning of it all. Ralph, the point is, I need you to do something for me."

"Anything," Ralph said.

"It's about The Black Queen," Alice rejoined.

The Time Cut Off Back to Circularity

The Jack of Knives had been here before. And what happened when he was here before, when the time was cut off back to circularity?

The Jack of Knives wasn't sure, but he didn't think something good happened. Something like failure was brewing in the air, to spill all over The Jack of Knives and his evil plans like acid. Something that he of course wasn't looking forward to.

He tried to tell himself that it wasn't a big deal, that he was going to succeed, it was just going to take some work. A lot of work … but, work that The Jack of Knives could certainly do. The Jack of Knives had talked with The Dark Kid many times about their plan, and he knew that nothing could go wrong. It was going to work.

And yet, that doubt … so much *doubt*. Not good, naturally. Not good, not even in the slightest. It didn't matter how many times The Jack of Knives tried to deny this feeling of foreboding, he couldn't shake it … not even in the slightest. And it was driving him up the walls. He thought he'd been crazy when he'd been down in the slums of the cutter gutter; he had thought that that had been the epitome of his craziness. And yet, it didn't seem that way, not at all. It seemed that there were worse things out there. Bigger problems.

Bigger, in the sense that The Jack of Knives believed that he had failed to sack the kingdom before, in a kind of past life, or to be more specific and accurate, in a kind of circular time. But that sounded absurd. And yet, it seemed so true. The Jack of Knives was destined to get his hopes up over and over again, thinking he was going to succeed in taking over the kingdom, only to be thwarted, by something. As for what that was, he wasn't sure, but it sounded like hell to The Jack of Knives, all right. It did indeed.

"You ready?" The Dark Kid asked.

The Jack of Knives, distracted, tried to get back into the game. "Yes."

If I'm ready for hell, that is, The Jack of Knives thought bitterly, with some fear.

"All right, then," The Dark Kid said. "Let's get this done."

The Jack of Knives followed The Dark Kid into the castle. They went to the royal court, where The Suicide King was.

The Dark Kid, in a rather dramatic but effective way, threw open the doors, and said, "Do not fear, Suicide King, but we're taking over the kingdom."

The Suicide King hardly heard. It stole a little bit of thunder out of The Dark Kid's move, but nonetheless, The Jack of Knives found it effective anyway.

"Did you hear me?" The Dark Kid said.

The Suicide King was busy talking to his sword like it was his child, but he finally turned toward The Dark Kid and said, "What is it you say, my boy?"

"I said," The Dark Kid began, but then looked at The Jack of Knives with a "screw it" expression, no time for formalities …
and then he shot out a bolt of lightning.

The lightning zapped the king all right, electrocuted him, but more lightning was coming out of The Dark Kid, and it slowly wrapped around The Suicide King like it was rope, with The Dark kid holding onto that rope.

"Well, this doesn't look good," The Suicide King said candidly.

"Probably not," The Jack of Knives said, laughing slightly, and watched as The Dark Kid began to drag The Suicide King out of the court.

The Jack of Knives followed The Dark Kid. They went through the forest, toward the ocean, and they finally arrived. A boat was by the ocean, awaiting The Suicide King.

"This is rather cruel of you," The Suicide King said. "You didn't even let me bring my sword along. Binding me up like a servant ... how dare you?"

"It's all in good faith," The Dark Kid said, and put the king on the boat.

The Jack of Knives was pleased that he didn't have to do anything. The Dark Kid was the one who'd abducted The Suicide King, with The Jack of Knives just going along for the ride. He was pleased, yes, he was very pleased ... but he was also worried. Something was going to happen soon, something big. Something bad. He wasn't sure what that was, exactly, but he had a lot of fear. Something, and soon, was going to shake the foundation of The Jack of Knives and his world.

The boat was anchored to the shore, and The Dark Kid was having trouble untying the rope. He'd already removed the lightning rope from The Suicide King, but it didn't matter, The Suicide King was helpless on the boat.

"Jack, help me with this blasted thing," The Dark Kid said.

The Jack of Knives wanted to help; he wanted to help right now, in fact. However, he couldn't find the courage. The foundation was changing, things were changing. Things were going to go in a bad direction soon: the time cut off back to circularity.

But what on the blasted Contorted Royal did *that* mean? Circularity? As if The Jack of Knives had honestly tried to abduct the king before? It was ridiculous, it didn't make sense, and The Jack of Knives was not going to fail. All of that was crazy.

And yet, The Jack of Knives couldn't find the courage or the energy or the desire to untie the rope. He was tempted to just drag the royal highness right back to his suicidal court, and he wasn't even sure why.

The Suicide King seemed to notice that The Jack of Knives wasn't all in it, because he said, rather mischievously, "What is it, my humble psychopathic murderous treasonous servant?"

The Jack of Knives turned angrily toward The Suicide King and snapped, "Nothing that concerns you."

"I think it does concern me," The Suicide King said, and he was smiling: a very cruel, open, homicidal smile. "I'm The Homicide King again, coming to kill and destroy your dreams."

"I've been here before," The Jack of Knives wanted to say, but couldn't. "I always fail at this point, destined to repeat something that will never find closure, never letting me betray you. That always happens when we get to this point."

"Oh, I think you're in trouble, that much is true," The Homicide King said threateningly, quietly, with a trace of malice. "I think I'm going to successfully massacre all you care about, Jack of Knives, boy-o with no hope."

"Shut up," The Dark Kid snapped, and looked as if he was going to zap The Homicide King with lightning, but didn't, because The Jack of Knives hissed at him not to.

"What is it?" The Dark Kid asked.

"Things are *changing*," The Homicide King said, and The Jack of Knives heard a clock ticking somewhere. "Tick, tock, tick, clock, time's a changing, time's a moving, tick, tock, click, clock, time's a moving, time's a speeding, time's moving circular to be homicidal."

The Jack of Knives had never seen The Homicide King so insane-looking: he looked like he could kill his whole kingdom in a heartbeat, which made The Jack of Knives wonder why he'd thought he could take him on. It had been foolish, to say the least.

"Time cut off back to circularity," The Homicide King smiled, and laughed. "Tick, clock, tock, click," and The Jack of Knives saw clocks in The Homicide King's eyes. He saw two clocks, with the hands moving around fast, spinning and spinning like madness, and The Homicide King was laughing as The Jack of Knives stared at this mesmeric disaster.

The Jack of Knives felt a quaint sensation, something that went beyond his frustration, his feeling of being in hell, because he'd failed again, as he was always going to fail: a quaint sensation that he couldn't quite pinpoint, wasn't sure he wanted to. He felt like he was hanging onto the minute hand of a clock, moving forward, but only so he could go back to a point. But what point was that? The moment that he detailed to The Suicide King that he was taking over the kingdom?

Yes, that was exactly what was happening. The Jack of Knives was in that moment, when he was preparing to walk into the court, plotting his move, and he was also simultaneously here. Both times were blending, because things were going back to the beginning: time cut off back to circularity.

The Homicide King was laughing as this happened. He said, "You can't change the way the clock moves, Jack of Knives. I'm sorry it's taken you so long to realize it. We'll just do this forever, though, forever and ever, and never get enough of this perpetual game, going around and around and around ..."

And that was when the moon became a giant clock. The minute hand was moving towards the twelve, the hour hand was moving towards the twelve, a new day beginning, or rather, a new era beginning ... the one they'd been at before.

But they weren't there just yet. Not quite yet, but it was soon going to happen. The two moments, of now and then, continued to blur with The Jack of Knives. He looked over at The Dark Kid, and could practically see inside his head, and could see that he was indeed at two places at once: he was falling from the sky and he was here, looking confused and unsure of what to do with himself, unsure of what to do with this strange phenomenon.

"Everything comes full circle in Contorted Royal," The Homicide King said.

"Yes," The Jack of Knives said, and fell on his knees in the agony of defeat.

The defeat was so great. He was taking on more than just an addle-headed king; he was doing something much more dangerous. He was trying to challenge time, and the heart of Contorted Royal itself, and that just wasn't possible. That was like Steerpike trying to solve the problems of and confront Gormenghast: it just couldn't work. Contorted Royal was its own special ballgame, with its own set of rules, its whole set of rules, and The Homicide King knew things. He hid things.

Maybe it was giving him too much credit, but nonetheless, The Jack of Knives had never seen him so certain on something.

He, too, was simultaneously at the beginning of it all and at the end. And what was going to kickstart the circularity again? The Jack of Knives wasn't sure, except that it must always come full circle, but he saw The Black Queen watching Spade getting murdered again, he saw it happening with her unable to do anything, and he saw everyone doing the exact same thing, over and over again, over and over again ...

But then all of that went away, and The Jack of Knives was back to where it had all started, but he still saw the clock in the sky, somehow, he still saw The Homicide King's hostile and madly spinning eyes, and he didn't know where all of this was going to lead to but he knew it was out of his control, and so what he felt was hell, hell in that he would never succeed, and that was when he flickered back into the future again, suddenly with The Dark Kid and The Suicide King at the ocean, though The Dark Kid was slowly disappearing, and so was The Suicide King, who was really indeed The Homicide King, mocking The Jack of Knifed, and The Jack of Knives went back again to the beginning, and he stayed there this time, but not without hearing the cruel laughter of The Homicide King, the cruel mocking, and he heard the tick tocking of clocks that were always mad, the circularity, the time cut off back to the circular, and he heard the ticking and tocking and the clicking and clocking and the tick talk and mock of The Homicide King soon to let in The Jack of Knives into the court who was going to try again for the infinite number of times plus one to take over the kingdom, but not without the collage from hell of those sounds, the tick tock, the laughing, the seeing of the clocks in the eyes and the sky, all of it circularity circularity circularity, to never end and stop, the clock ...

Dead Boy Blues, and Perhaps an Answer to All of Life's Problems

So it was happening again: The Black Queen enjoying Spade as always, and then The Black Queen forced to view the death of Spade.

She indeed had a feeling that this had happened before, that perhaps this was the infinite and one time; and yet, it all still seemed like déjà vu. What if this had never really happened before? What if that was all just in her head?

And yet, it still seemed like it had happened before …

And yet, that sounded completely ridiculous. It didn't make sense. It was just déjà vu.

The Black Queen watched Spade get murdered, and then the murderer disappeared, and The Black Queen was left alone with her thoughts.

Déjà vu, or an event that had indeed happened before? An event that had happened before, just like this, or déjà vu? Circular time masquerading as déjà vu masquerading as circular time, or déjà vu masquerading as circular time masquerading as déjà vu?

The Black Queen didn't know. Nonetheless, it was enough to get her head to spin like mad.

The Black Queen needed to find Alice. That was the way that things would get solved. It had to be the way. She wasn't sure, but she was certainly hoping.

So The Black Queen began to go seek out Alice. But as she went to go seek Alice, she couldn't help but feel the inevitable dead boy blues. That had happened before. That always happened after watching Spade getting murdered. For what else would The Black Queen feel? It was Contorted Royal, where things were contorted, but even The Black Queen wasn't going to feel happy that her boyfriend had died.

So what she felt instead was just blues. Blues that she couldn't shake. A sorrow she couldn't unwind, no matter how hard she tried. It would have been nice if it was as simple as forgetting you loved and cared about someone, but that wasn't easy. That wasn't going to happen with The Black Queen.

As The Black Queen was walking toward the castle, with these deep feelings deep inside, strumming a guitar and playing a bluesy song, she saw Alice approaching her.

This wasn't right. She was supposed to meet Alice in the unpsychiatrist's office.

But then The Black Queen was like, no, that was ridiculous. She could meet Alice anywhere. It was just déjà vu, back there where Spade had died.

And yet, The Black Queen couldn't shake the idea that something was wrong. As for what, she honestly wasn't sure, but still … it was a little strange, Alice being here, not there.

"Lady Black Queen," Alice said. "Your highness."

"I was looking for you," The Black Queen said. "Though I thought I'd see you …"

In the unpsychiatrist's office? The Black Queen wanted to say, but didn't.

"Things are going to change," Alice said. "The circularity is falling apart. I can feel it."

"Circularity?" The Black Queen said, like this was a new word, a new concept that had never occurred to her, but also as if there was truth to this. "What do you mean?"

"For the past infinite and one times, we've been repeating things. The circularity has slowly been falling apart, but as sure as the clock will of course strike midnight right on time, the circularity came back full circle. But I have the answer. I have the key."

"Circularity?" The Black Queen repeated again. "You'll have to explain."

Alice began to explain, and The Black Queen listened. It sounded possible. Alice was a schizophrenic, who suffered from delusions, but those delusions were rarely wrong. And of course, The Black Queen couldn't pretend she hadn't felt these thoughts before, too, had delusions that were similar. Déjà vu? That seemed absurd, in a way. It was circularity.

"If we came full circle, why are you not in the unpsychiatrist's office, where I always meet you after … you know …" The Black Queen said.

"Because I'm always in tune with the circularity," Alice said, "and in that way, the circularity doesn't affect me the same way. But there's things we need to do."

Alice and The Black Queen were in a grass field, still a little ways from the castle. The Black Queen wasn't sure where this was going to go, but she was hoping the answer to all of life's problems would come soon. That would be nice.

"Then what do we need to do?" The Black Queen asked.

"Ralph is the key," Alice said simply. "He knows things. He has the answers, or can at least take us to the answers."

"Ralph?" The Black Queen said. "That's your hallucination, right?"

Alice nodded. "Yes. And he's here right now, standing right beside me. But you can't see him, can you?"

The Black Queen shook her head. She looked for him, but no one was there.

That was when Alice said, "Well, you're going to have to see him."

"See your hallucination?" The Black Queen said, as though she'd heard a joke. She wanted to laugh, but didn't, because this was Alice, who knew something. Nonetheless, it still seemed impossible. "Honey, I can't just *see* your hallucination. That's impossible. I'd like to see your hallucination, but I just … can't."

"Well, you're going to have to. Something will happen when you see him."

The Black Queen took this in. Just see her hallucination? Well, what could it hurt, to try.

But as The Black Queen tried, nothing happened. There was no one there. No one at all.

"There's no one there," The Black Queen said. "I see no Ralph. Ralph is a figment."

"Ralph is not a figment," Alice said determinedly. "Not at all. Now come on: *try harder.*"

The Black Queen tried. Still no luck.

But as she tried, thinking she was soon going to give up, that was when she saw a brief flicker of a kid. It was brief, but the boy was very attractive, about as attractive as Spade, maybe more. For a moment, The Black Queen felt excited: was a new horizon coming on? Was a new boyfriend soon to be in the mix?

This spurred The Black Queen to try harder. Yet again, another flicker, and the boy was fabulously delicious to look at, an aesthetic and visual treat. She continued to try, and Ralph continued to flicker in and out of existence, until he was finally standing there.

"Can you see me?" Ralph asked.

The Black Queen nodded, smitten. No more dead boy blues. Spade was a lost cause, but she had Ralph now. Ralph was the answer to all of life's problems. The Black Queen knew it. "Yes, honey. I see you, all right."

Alice nodded. "I knew it would happen."

And that was when Ralph disappeared.

"Where'd he go?" The Black Queen asked, feeling a little anger.

"You'll see," Alice said, and at that moment, a door appeared in the air, a door out of nowhere.

The door was just there, closed, with the grass field on either side. But when the door opened, Ralph stepped out, in all his exquisite beauty.

He stepped out, and the door closed. He said, "What am I doing here?"

No one said anything for a moment. The Black Queen was too preoccupied with her new found love, and Alice was thinking, puzzling.

Then Alice said, "Welcome to Contorted Royal. You know things, don't you, Ralph?"

"I know basic algebra," Ralph said flatly. "I know a little bit of physics, some Spanish, a tad bit of Russian. I like reading, I like computers. What does this have to do with me all of the sudden being … *here*? In a world that wants to walk and talk like medieval but isn't quite so?"

The Black Queen couldn't control her feelings: "I love you, Ralph!"

She tried to go and kiss Ralph, but he jerked away. Not in a mean way, just in a disinterested way. "And who is this woman?"

"She's our royal highness," Alice said. "So be kind to her."

"Well, regardless, it's you I want to talk to," Ralph said, looking at Alice. "You're the one that knows things."

The Black Queen didn't feel hurt. Just a little friendly competition, that's all. The boy would be hers soon enough, she could claim him as her boyfriend soon enough. She felt it.

"I know things, but I think you should do the talking," Alice said.

Ralph didn't say anything for a moment, but then finally said, "Well, Black Queen, Alice … I've dreamed about coming here, and know many of the flawed and flawless characters that exist in Contorted Royal. I know that Contorted Royal has been circling and circling for quite a while now, locking everyone except for the smart and perceptive Alice in a kind of hell. You think it's déjà vu, but it's really circular time, though you still believe it's déjà vu. It's because of a machine."

The Black Queen, still smitten, said, in a flirtatious way, "A machine?"

Ralph, clearly not interested, said, "Yes. A machine. It messes up Contorted Royal, but it also messes up my world. People there are cold. They're mean. They're robotic, even. There's no passion. Some people try to say it's technology that's breaking everyone apart, but I know it's that machine ... which is technology, of course, but in a different way. It's not our computers and Facebook that keep us apart, it's that blasted magical machine. I hate it, where I live. It's kind of made me a loner, because people are so fake. But that's okay. You guys seem like you could be my friends."

"Anything, dear," The Black Queen said exaggeratedly, and Ralph smiled slightly.

"So what do you think we should do, Ralph?" Alice said. "You've confirmed my deepest fears."

"Well, we'll have to destroy the machine. But that's going to be complicated, of course. It's locked up in a secret facility in the Bronx. But, we've got to at least try."

"Is the machine destroyable?" Alice asked.

"I think it is, but I'm not sure," Ralph said. "I don't have all the facts, I just know the mastermind behind the project is a man named Spencer Grey. I've met him once, and he's absolutely crazy. But he's ambitious, and not necessarily in a good way. That man means nothing but trouble."

"That's not good," Alice said. "Not at all. So I guess, we're going to the Bronx, in your modern day alternate world?"

"Sounds like the only way," Ralph said, and then The Black Queen responded with, "Oh, anything for you, honey."

Ralph didn't say anything, just whispered something to Alice. Alice nodded, and then Alice whispered to The Black Queen: "He's kind of uncomfortable with all of your flirting. He says if this is going to work, you'll have to keep it at a minimum."

The Black Queen frowned. She frowned as Alice and Ralph continued to talk. But, she had this! She was going to do this! She knew it! Ralph was her new lover! Screw The Suicide King!

107

And yet, The Black Queen felt as though she was feeling rejection. This was what it felt like … a rather painful thing, rejection was …

"I don't have any plan for taking down the machine, but we'd do well to go back to my hometown," Ralph said. "I think for now, I've disrupted the circularity in your world, by being here … I'm afraid, though, that my world will still be disconnected like technology, so … I guess you'll have to live with it."

"That's fine," Alice said. "We've got a lot of work to do. So, let's get going."

Alice opened the door. Nothing but light was inside.

"I'll go first," Alice said, and walked through the door, and disappeared.

Ralph looked at The Black Queen, and The Black Queen blew Ralph a kiss. Ralph didn't respond, just said, "I'll go, I guess," and went through the door.

Once Ralph was gone, The Black Queen entered the doorway. As she was falling, falling, as though down the rabbit hole, she knew she'd found the answer to all of life's problems. Ralph was her answer. Ralph was the key.

The question, was, what was she going to do to get his interest?

Well, regardless, The Black Queen wasn't worried. The dead boy blues were over! It was time for someone new and styling, Boyfriend 2.0 …

Part Two

The Key to the Conflicted Machine the Whole Entire Time Was Ralph, a Random Kid from the Bronx, Though Every Solution Of Course Brings New Problems

A Sharper Shade of Grey

Spencer Grey was the sharper shade of grey.

He'd been that way for as long as he could remember … well, not for as long as he could remember, but certainly for a long long time.

But it hadn't always been that way.

He remembered when he was in college. There had been another Spencer Grey, who looked exactly like the Spencer Grey here, who talked like this Spencer Grey, walked like this Spencer Grey, stalked like this Spencer Grey … to rather a disorienting and uncanny affect.

And that Spencer Grey had been smarter than the other Spencer Grey. He had always been the one who was winning scholarships, winning awards, getting his scientific papers published, getting all of the girls, going to all of the classiest and craziest parties … while the real Spencer Grey? He got nothing.

Oh, those terrible days of woe. But Spencer Grey had had the perfect solution for dealing with that.

The Spencer Grey with all of the answers and the perfect life was good at making fun of the other Spencer Grey. He taunted him day and night, saying that if they were long-lost twins or something, why the other Spencer Grey was such a failure? To which Spencer Grey replied that he didn't know why, could not explain it either empirically or mathematically.

And as all of this happened, with Spencer Grey eventually kicked out of college for failing too many classes, what did Spencer Grey do to get control of his life?

Murder. He murdered the notorious Spencer Grey.

It had been a sticky and violent event, no doubt about that. Spencer Grey had gone to the other Spencer Grey's house, broken in, and strangled the guy to death. Oh, the satisfaction that it had brought Spencer! More than he could possibly ever admit.

And from that point on? Spencer Grey was the king. There was only one Spencer Grey to dominate the universe.

Because right after that, he began the creation of the machine that was going to change the path of existence severely.

He didn't need a college degree to create complex machinery. He had enough robust intellect already.

The machine was Spencer Grey's life. He called it, for lack of a better word, The Machine.

Spencer Grey had managed to strike a deal with the Feds: if they protect his machine, he'd give them access to all of the beauties of the machine, its glorious attribute and gift the ability to sever humanity in half, in pieces.

Yup, Spencer Grey would say you heard right. Cut humanity into pieces! Drown them in isolation! Cut and cut and cut everyone apart in disconnection!

Spencer Grey was with his machine now, and he had a table with many sharp objects on them, ranging from knifes to saws. He picked up a butcher knife and began to swing it around, chopping and slicing.

"Humanity is falling apart," Spencer Grey said happily. "The disconnection is becoming too much. People are becoming mindless drones, programmed to do only what I tell them, which is break apart. I just want everyone to be sliced, to disconnection they'll be spliced … oh, the joys of splitting up humanity, too bad it's such a travesty."

And indeed, as Spencer Grey continued to cut the air with his butcher knife, he couldn't help but marvel at his work. The machine was brilliant at cutting humanity apart.

One might wonder what it means to cut humanity apart, in isolation, disconnection? Well, it was exactly like what it sounded like. People were becoming more and more impersonal, and cruel. People's temperaments were going through the roof. Love and kindness didn't exist anymore, people were becoming like technology: superficial, artificial, fake, good for nothing. And it was working beautifully. All because of this machine. *The Machine.*

People were becoming so mean to each other that people would murder each other on the spot because of the impersonality. Exactly what Spencer Grey liked. He'd seen some of it himself. Once, a man shouldered another man with his family, and the man with the family pulled out a knife and stabbed the guy brutally, right in front of his kid, saying, "You have no right to treat me that way!"

But he wasn't arrested. The disconnection ability of the machine messed up justice, as well. Because the lawyers, the officers, the judges, were all bent on corruption. They were all bent on seeing more and more murder, all because of a disconnection that was never going to be reconciled, reconnected.

"I cut and cut and cut, and your death I see it jut," Spencer Grey said to himself. "But that's okay. You deserve to be torn apart, ripped apart, for your sins, everyone. He he he."

And Spencer Grey cackled in his glee.

He was indeed very happy. The world was falling apart. Crime rates had never been so high, all because of something as simple as coldness, impersonality, which always led to other things. The world was verging on another World War, which was going to be entertaining, with power always ruling everything. Power and isolation, everyone going crazy in a cold, cold world.

And the best part? Spencer Grey felt no guilt whatsoever for killing the other Spencer Grey. That had been what set the whole thing in motion. When that happened, it was like the real Spencer Grey awoke. He could think more clearly. He could create his top-notch, top-secret, and powerful machinery. And it had had amazing results.

But Spencer Grey hadn't done all of it himself. There was a man named Ace, who came from a place called Contorted Royal, wherever that place was. Ace had added a degree of magic to The Machine. From what Spencer knew, The Machine created a circular time problem for Contorted Royal, and caused the disconnectedness in this present world, which was in the end, only one world in many, within a universe among universes. Ace and Spencer Grey hoped to eventually increase the effects of The Machine, and make it to where The Machine affected other worlds, but … all of that would come in due time.

"Sever you apart, you hear?" Spencer Grey said, and laughed some more. "Destroy the world through unkindness! And it's amazing what it accomplishes. We're all hostile in the end. We're all evil, we all have the capacity to be cruel. Turning you into technology, folks!"

And Spencer Grey continued to swipe his butcher knife around, chanting to himself, cutting and cutting, splitting and splitting, destroying.

That was when The Machine spoke up, speaking in her artificial but feminine voice: "Having fun, Spencer Grey?"

Spencer turned to his machine, and examined her cruelly. She was indeed a beauty. She was a giant computer, with a switchboard next to her, that allowed Spencer Grey to fine-tune the disconnectedness and circularity every once in a while, among other things. The computer screen had a single green line in the middle, which moved when The Machine talked, like a mouth.

"What do you think?" Spencer Grey asked his Machine.

"I'd say so," The Machine said. "I'd say you're having a blast, actually, enjoying the effects of my cold-hearted machinery. You're making the world an artificial heart. I don't know how we could thank you more."

"Oh, just worship me, that's all you have to do," Spencer Grey said. "I'm doing the world a favor, like they have no idea. They can't pretend that I'm not."

"No, no they can't," The Machine replied. "I've looked at the algorithms of humanity, and they seemed pretty determined about what they wanted since the beginning of time. Death. Murder. War. Pain. I could tell you not everyone is like that, that there is some good, but what good would that do? You wouldn't listen to my calculations."

"You're right I wouldn't," Spencer Grey said defiantly. "I'm just giving everyone what they want. A more violent world! And, in more ways than one. People can't form attachments anymore. Families are falling apart left and right, cooperation among nations is on the decline ... all because of you."

"You're probably giving me too much credit," The Machine said. "You built me."

"Regardless," Spencer Grey said smoothly, "I think it's pretty clear that what I'm doing works well. We can worry about the effects later ... this is science, and science doesn't have to answer to ethics. I built something that *works*. I built a machine that's powerful, that can do some serious damage. The scientists that built the atom bomb weren't concerned about ethics, and obviously, why should they be? The atom bomb is a beauty."

"I think you only perceive cruelty because that's what you want to perceive," The Machine said, slightly philosophically.

113

"And why do you say that?" Spencer Grey asked, thinking of the other Spencer Grey, and how much he'd hurt him. "You think I *wanted* to be taunted and bullied day in and day out by another Spencer Grey, that came out of nowhere?"

"No, of course not," The Machine said. "Of course not. But you could have tried to work with him, instead of plotting your revenge."

"Well, his death doesn't haunt me, if that's what you're concerned about," Spencer Grey said petulantly. "I'm glad I did what I did. I feel better. I feel like a real human being."

"More than I feel, I suppose," The Machine responded despondently. "You're lucky to feel human. It's better than me. I guess that's why I don't get why you want to suck it out of humanity."

"It's always been sucked out of humanity," Spencer Grey said bitterly. "Always. There's no humanity in humanity. World War I and World War II are gigantic acts of violence, gigantic atrocities, but so much more has happened in our bloody world history. Violence is in our nature. Surely you've calculated that?"

"I've calculated that where there's negative, there's positive," The Machine said. "It's simple math: you can add and you can subtract."

"Whatever that means." Spencer Grey examined his butcher knife. "Anyway, regardless: I say, bring on the advent of technology. Let it make us drift further and further apart. It'll do the world a lot of good. And it'll be all because of me. All because of a man named Spencer Grey, who swam through the rivers of Hell to get to where he is today."

"You must be very proud," The Machine said.

"I am proud," Spencer Grey said, and went back to his cut-dance.

The Machine didn't say anything for a moment, but then said, "I think I'm going to be destroyed."

Spencer Grey dropped his knife in shock. He turned around slowly and threateningly to The Machine. "What did you say?"

"I said, 'I think I'm going to be destroyed.'"

"Don't say such a terrible thing!" Spencer Grey said. "Please! Do us all a favor."

"I'm just telling you what I've calculated. Eventually, I have to be destroyed. It's basic technological entropy."

"Why are you saying such a terrible thing?"

"Not everyone will enjoy our technological isolation," The Machine said. "And when that happens, I just think we'll have to make some changes."

"Well, in case you haven't realized, your energy, your power, is worldwide. *Global*. It has large-scale effects. A few pissed off people can't destroy all you do, that's ridiculous. That's like a few angry peasants trying to stand up to a tyrant king. It just won't happen. Power always wins. Always. You can't change anything, much less a few pissed off people."

"Maybe," The Machine said. "I'm just telling you my thoughts."

"You don't have any thoughts," Spencer Grey said maliciously. "You're just a machine. You're soulless. You're artificial, like society. You're nothing."

The Machine remained quiet.

Spencer Grey picked up his knife and continued to cut and cut the air.

The Machine finally said, "I'm sorry what's happened to you, but I think that you're the one with the artificial heart."

"It's an artificial heart that's an art," Spencer Grey said, smiling. "You want me to cut you up into little pieces? Slice and dice your hardware for a scare?"

"You know I wouldn't feel it," The Machine said sardonically.

"Point taken."

"I just think you underestimate human emotion," The Machine said. "I see your point, about human nature having its problems. But you can't focus on that all the time, because there are other elements to keep it in balance."

"So you say," Spencer Grey said, bored at this pointless lecture by The Machine. "But I don't see how that's possible. We want to be cold towards each other. We want to be unhappy. We want to be mean. And anyway, you can't stop the progression of the world. It will go in the direction that it goes. The moment I realized that, the moment that I decided to push it along that path even further. You can't swim up against the moving, chaotic

115

stream. Hence the reason why you exist. Now, if you don't mind, I'm going to keep chopping. Humanity, which needs to be chopped, love of which needs to be stopped. At all costs."

And Spencer Grey continued to dance with his knives, like the finest gothic ballerina.

Dated

Ralph had thought he was in a dream when he began to fall up the rabbit hole toward Contorted Royal. However, when he had opened the door and arrived at Contorted Royal, he had known it wasn't a dream at all.

Nonetheless, it was still dream-like, as this time he fell down the rabbit hole, to go back to the modern day world, in a world apart from the one that Contorted Royal was in.

However, when they arrived at the bottom, Ralph blacked out. He awoke later to find himself on a sidewalk, lying next to The Black Queen.

He couldn't help but think that indeed, the doors between worlds were very strange, but he supposed there was no way around it. He stood up, not wanting to awaken The Black Queen, looking around for Alice.

But Alice was nowhere to be seen.

Ralph couldn't help but feel frustrated at this. Alice was the one that he wanted to be around. Alice was the one that he trusted. He couldn't explain why he felt this way, except that she seemed to be the most honest out of the two, and she had a keen insight into things that could not be ignored. Often, in Ralph's dreams, she was the one that was figuring things out. Ralph felt that he had been with her before, following her around like a hallucination, maybe in a past life or something. While that was probably not true, Ralph felt a bond with Alice that he couldn't quite explain. To be blunt, he trusted her, and would trust his life with her.

But it looked like Ralph was stuck with The Black Queen. He could tell that she had a crush on him, but he wasn't interested. Didn't she have The Suicide King, anyway? Regardless, he didn't find her that attractive. Maybe physically, but not in terms of personality. She wasn't self-centered, exactly, but Ralph couldn't deny that he had a stronger affinity for Alice.

Ralph, seeing there was no other way, woke up The Black Queen.

She awoke, and stood up slowly. She looked around, and said, "Where are we?"

"The Bronx," Ralph said. "Alice ended up somewhere else, though. I don't know where. Maybe she went too far down the rabbit hole."

"Well, best move on without her," The Black Queen said cheerily, as though her absence was nothing to trifle with. "We've got work to do."

That was exactly the kind of attitude that Ralph didn't really like, or at least wasn't attracted to.

But she was right, nonetheless: they had work to do. The thing was, things were a little more complicated than just destroying a machine.

Ralph explained this to The Black Queen: "We could destroy the machine, but we need to come up with a plan first. Remember, the building is locked up, and there's no way we can just burst right in."

"Oh, I'm not worried about the machine," The Black Queen said, and winked at Ralph flirtatiously.

Ralph would have rolled his eyes, but instead just remained silent for a moment.

He knew what The Black Queen was thinking. She wanted to date him. He could see it written all over The Black Queen's smiling face. If not date, she wanted to at least spend time with Ralph, try and seduce him.

Which was always fantastic.

However, dating The Black Queen wasn't all that unreasonable. Ralph would rather die than date The Black Queen, so that wasn't the reason. The reason was because Ralph wanted to show The Black Queen how screwed up his world was here, how disconnected everything was, how people were cruel to each other for no apparent reason, how doing anything good for society was a terrible uphill battle that didn't accomplish much.

"Mind if I hold your hand?" The Black Queen asked, again in that flirtatious manner.

Ralph wanted to concede to this, just so there would be no conflict, no friction, but stood his ground, said, "No. Not really."

"Well, let's go to a restaurant or something. I'd love to try your contemporary cuisine."

"It's generally nothing but processed junk," Ralph said.

"Sounds good to me," The Black Queen said.

Ralph now rolled his eyes. He followed The Black Queen to a local restaurant, couldn't help but think of Alice. How much he liked her. He had trouble not getting her off his mind. He couldn't explain it, couldn't explain why, but she honestly meant a lot to him. He wanted to be with her, but fate had dictated that he be with The Black Queen.

Which, upon understanding more fully than he had before, caused Ralph to roll his eyes again, in acceptance. Oh, what the hell? Why not have fun with The Black Queen for a little bit, even if her antics drove Ralph up the wall.

The Black Queen reached out to hold Ralph's hand, and Ralph assented for a moment, and then politely let go. At that point, they were in the restaurant.

The person at the front seated The Black Queen and Ralph without a single word, without even welcoming them inside. Ralph wasn't surprised by this, they were always this way: people. But The Black Queen looked annoyed at this, and Ralph simply responded by shrugging, and saying, "I told you there were problems."

"I'd say," The Black Queen said.

Ralph and The Black Queen sat down, and began to do some talking as they waited for the server to come.

"So," The Black Queen said, almost in an innocently promiscuous way, "do you like me?"

Ralph didn't say anything; he would really rather not have to answer that question.

The Black Queen continued, as though Ralph had confirmed that she was indeed liked: "You do, Ralph? Oh, that's very sweet of you. You love me, I'm sure. Are there any beds around here, do you know, Ralph?"

"There's no beds," Ralph said. "Not here. We're in a restaurant."

And Ralph looked intently at his menu: anything to not look at The Black Queen …

"You can't resist me," The Black Queen said. "You'll come around. I've got the finest body this side of the Bronx has ever seen. I'm the real hot stuff in Contorted Royal."

"It's not a matter of resistance," Ralph said. "I just have a certain … taste in girls and women. I don't jump in the sack at the soonest opportunity."

"Oh, a pious, religious boy," The Black Queen taunted playfully. "I see how it is. You want to be that sweet little virgin boy."

Ralph blushed slightly. "No," he said, trying to keep his patience. "I'm not religious. I just have a certain standard I follow. I hope that isn't a problem."

And then The Black Queen blurted out: "I want to make hot steamy love to you, Ralph!"

Ralph just continued to study his menu. *Intently*. What was it with this woman? He knew she was a queen and all, but why couldn't she be like Alice? Gentle, calm, easy-going? Why did she have to be so … into sex?

But, he told himself that it was probably because she was powerful, and power could change the way you thought about things. Sex became power, power became sex. The Black Queen could have anyone she wanted, or at least in Contorted Royal, because she was so good-looking and powerful … but Ralph wasn't going to give in that easily.

"I'm not a rent boy," Ralph said stiffly. "We'll have to talk about sex another time. Maybe when there's actually something real in our relationship."

The Black Queen didn't say anything for a moment, which was just about the time that the server came.

"What did you want to eat?" the server said, overtly hostile in her tone.

"That's no way to treat a lady," The Black Queen said, obviously noticing the hostility.

"At least I'm not a fat bitch," the server said.

The Black Queen gasped, almost exaggeratedly. Ralph felt this was of course beyond uncalled for, but this was the norm. He could try to stand up for her, which he wanted to do, but Ralph wasn't a hero boy, and he couldn't pretend he was. And in the end, it wouldn't do any good. He couldn't change the snobbery and disconnectedness of his world. He'd tried many times and finally learned injustice was just the way it was.

But he could at least deflate the tension somewhat, to stop The Black Queen from doing something irrational: "She'd like a water. Just water. And me too. We need to watch our weight and all."

The server rolled her eyes, said, "Great. More work," and then left Ralph and The Black Queen alone.

Ralph looked at The Black Queen, who was looking a little perturbed.

"That was rude," The Black Queen said petulantly. "She was rude."

"It gets worse the more you get to know what our society is really like," Ralph said.

"Well, at least you tried to be respectful," The Black Queen said. "What a fool I am, thinking your world believed in chivalry."

"That's a long dead concept," Ralph admitted candidly. "You'd be madder than Don Quixote if you tried to uphold respect and loyalty and love here in the Bronx … or really, anywhere in this superficial world."

"That's why we need to destroy the machine," The Black Queen said, and was lost in thought.

She tried to grab Ralph's hand, but Ralph, who felt committed to Alice, didn't take her hand.

And The Black Queen began to cry slightly. She said, "What is it, Ralph? Am I not … *pretty enough?*"

"You're one of the most beautiful ladies I've ever seen," Ralph said. "But like I said, I want to uphold a certain standard."

"Oh, I see," The Black Queen said bitterly. "Be the perfect gentleman, the perfect virgin boy for his *one true love*. I see you for who you really are."

"It's just standards," Ralph said. "It comes at a cost, of course. Most boys think I'm not a real man because I'm not a slutty boy. But it's just how I choose to live. I have temptations, of course, and I have made mistakes … but I don't want to see people as commodities … which is ironic, because *everything* in my world is commoditized. Just go to any store and you'll see what I mean … especially the aisle for sex toys."

"Whatever that means," The Black Queen said angrily, obviously hating the rejection. "But don't worry. I get it. You think I'm dated, like an ancient or medieval work of literature. You think I don't belong in bookstores anymore. I get it. You think I'm … I'm … *old*. Old and unworthy of your time. Like the epic poem *Beowulf*."

"Oh, cut it out," Ralph said, but there was some amusement in his voice. The Black Queen was superficial, but in a way that was actually somewhat … *attractive*. Perhaps even cute. At least she wasn't hostile, full of rude and mean rejection, like the people in Ralph's society. She at least felt things. She at least had feelings. She wasn't just a cold technological piece of junk. Indeed, her medieval world, even if pseudo, seemed to have more class than Ralph's world.

Ralph was going to say something, but then the server came by. She sat down Ralph's drink, and then sat down The Black Queen's drink … but purposely knocked it over, spilling it all over The Black Queen.

Ralph, who wasn't surprised (this had happened to him multiple times by rude servers, which was why he didn't go to restaurants anymore), watched as The Black Queen stood up.

The server didn't apologize, obviously, just said, "Just thought you needed a shower. You smell bad."

Then the server left.

Ralph could tell that The Black Queen was fuming. He could see the pressure building up, the steam coming out of her ears. Something explosive was going to happen, and *soon*. Something titanically TNT.

But The Black Queen then became calm, or at least for a moment. She said, in as rational a voice as possible, "I see why you don't like your world. I see what you mean by the … the horrible disconnection."

"Oh, that's nothing," Ralph said. "I've actually had people punch me before, for no apparent reason. Just by random people in public."

"Excuse me for a moment," The Black Queen said daintily, mischievously, and got up and went to find the server, who was

121

over "helping" someone else, but of course making their life miserable with unneeded coldness.

Ralph watched as The Black Queen went over, smiling politely. She said a few things, still smiling, and before Ralph knew what was happening, she punched the server in the face. The server went flying across the restaurant, her notepad for orders fluttering and flattering in the air, and then passed out cold on the ground.

No one noticed, or cared, but The Black Queen, who didn't want to take any chances with law enforcement, said to Ralph, "All right, honey, let's go, I think we've had a good enough time," and Ralph followed The Black Queen quickly out of the restaurant.

"That was a wicked punch," Ralph said enthusiastically, once they'd made their escape. "I didn't know you could do that."

"I can do a lot of things," The Black Queen said. "I know violence. Granted, the violence in my world is different from the violence here, but it's all the same in the end. People are cruel. Humanity is cruel. We're a bloody mess."

"I thought you would do well to get a taste of what it's like here," Ralph said. "Trust me, though, people are even faker than that. People have become mindless robots. They just do what they're programmed to do, which is be mindless drones unfunctioning in society. But you get used to it after a while. The cruelty, the meanness … it doesn't mean much at the end of the day, because you get desensitized to it. You have to, as a kind of defense. The world is becoming less and less empathetic, which is why you don't buy into it, you just defend yourself with a strong mind."

"Sounds about right," The Black Queen said. "But I'll tell you this: if anyone is mean to me again, they'll get it. I don't tolerate meanness."

Ralph took this in. He knew The Black Queen was tough, but it was a useless fight trying to teach people to be kind and kind-hearted, friendly and warm. So he just said, "I don't think it'll accomplish much, but you're always welcome to try."

The Black Queen didn't hear Ralph, which was probably good; she had a look of determination on her face.

Ralph didn't want The Black Queen to feel as hopeless as he did about the state of society, its inability to function properly, correctly.

Especially because he knew she'd learn it eventually: she'd learn that finding kindness and good will was like trying to date someone like Ralph, or quite simply, was … *dated.*

Whacking the Whacky

While The Black Queen and Ralph were busy trying to make their way through an artificial modern-day world that was separate from Contorted Royal, Alice was on the ground, sleeping.

When she finally woke up, she looked around and saw that she was separated from her friends. This was frustrating, to say the least. Alice already liked Ralph, the real Ralph, though she couldn't explain why, and The Black Queen was Alice's friend. They needed to destroy The Machine, and they were going to do it together. So, she would do well to find them.

However, she had a feeling that she wasn't going to find them, at least not now. Not quite yet.

Alice was resting on a somewhat busy sidewalk, and not one person asked to see how she was doing. If she had been in Contorted Royal, at least one person would have stopped. That world was violent, good old Contorted Royal, even if artificially so, and was very medieval in certain practices … but at least people stopped to ask if Alice was okay. It would have been pointless if they'd asked, because Alice was just fine, or at least as fine as she was going to be considering the circumstances … but it would have at least been thoughtful and kind, and would have been classy, to say the least.

Alice stood up, and began to walk around the city. She knew she was in the Bronx. As far as how far she was from The Black Queen and Ralph, she had no idea, but she knew it wouldn't do any good to worry about them right now.

But that didn't mean she wasn't going to start looking for them.

However, she didn't get very far, because that was when a hallucination appeared in front of her. She knew it was a hallucination because it was The Machine, and it was in a very conspicuous place: right in the middle of everything.

"So, I hallucinate machines now, now that I don't need Ralph anymore," Alice said, but with some humor, to The Machine.

The Machine didn't say anything for a moment, but Alice knew she would. Indeed, Alice knew that The Machine she saw, even though it was just a hallucination, was exactly the way the real machine looked.

"Perhaps only The Black Queen needs Ralph," The Machine said.

"Maybe," Alice said. "Maybe not."

People continued to walk past Alice. Some gave her funny looks, some gave her hostile looks, some tried to ignore her and failed … the people, no matter how cold, couldn't pretend they were even slightly intrigued that a young girl was talking to a hallucination, or from their perspective, to nothing.

But Alice just ignored them.

"You know I have to destroy you, right?" Alice said to The Machine casually, almost friendly.

"Nothing would please me more," The Machine said amicably. "I want to be destroyed. It would do me a favor."

"I think it would do this world a favor," Alice said, noticing a young mother quickly trying to usher her child away from a real-life schizophrenic, who was having an episode by talking kindly to a machine … nothing to fear, but what did society know about these things?

But Alice wasn't worried, just continued to talk to The Machine. "So I guess that's the million dollar question: how do I destroy you?"

"I wish I could tell you," The Machine admitted. "It would make my life easier."

"You make it sound like you don't like what you do."

"I created circularity in Contorted Royal, just barely disrupted because of Ralph's short moment in Contorted Royal, and you see how mean everyone is in our society. I blame myself for these things, even though I know it wasn't my fault that I was birthed."

"Well, you shouldn't blame yourself," Alice said. "You make it sound like you'd stop this nonsense were it in your control, if it was as easy as flipping a button."

"I would," The Machine said. "But unfortunately, I just do what I'm programmed to do."

"Well, that's important information. I'll need to relay it to The Black Queen. It might make destroying you a little easier, to at least know that the main attraction, the main event, doesn't really want to exist. What can you tell me about Spencer Grey?"

"There's not much I can tell you," The Machine said. "He's narcissistic, while I'm conflicted. But the point is, he will stop at nothing to see this world slough apart … or, cut apart, I should say, to use his terminology. He's obsessed with knives, and just wants to slice and slice, as if cutting through ice … he's a lunatic. A brilliant lunatic, but a lunatic nonetheless."

"So his machine, meaning you," Alice said, "really and truly is splitting society apart by the seams?"

"Yes," The Machine said. "Unfortunately. And I can't stop it. I can see it all happening, but I can't do anything about it."

"How do you see it all happening?" Alice asked. "You can't go anywhere."

The Machine responded by, on the screen, showing The Black Queen's experience at the restaurant.

"That just happened," The Machine said. "It wasn't a pretty sight. The Black Queen contributed to the chaos by punching the server, but I can't really say I blame her. We live in a cruel world. Even I think the world is cruel, and I don't, technically, feel emotion, enough to get hurt by the things people do. But I do."

"And if I destroy you, it would all end?" Alice asked.

"Well, hopefully. There's no way to know, in the end. Something is always bound to happen. But it's at least worth a try."

Alice would have continued to talk to The Machine, but that was when a voice said, "Having fun, crazy head?"

Alice turned, and saw two boys about Ralph's age standing there, mocking her.

"I'm just talking," Alice said, a little surprised that they were being so overtly mean to her. People weren't perfect in

Contorted Royal, even with her elevated status, but Alice couldn't recall a time where people actually made fun of her.

"Oh, just *talking*," said the first boy. "To the air, or what? You think the air's going to come alive, or something?"

"I'm talking to The Machine," Alice said.

"Oh, sounds delusional to me," the second boy said, and the two continued to laugh.

Alice looked at The Machine. "What do you think I should tell them?"

"It's our world," The Machine said. "The medieval era understood madness better, unfortunately. In modern times, there is a thing called 'stigma,' among other things. It's shameful to be considered crazy here in the modern world. Everyone has to have it together, or else."

"Well that sucks," Alice said. "You know, I really miss Contorted Royal ... already. It hasn't even been that long, but I miss it."

"There's nothing there, sweetheart," the first boy said sarcastically.

"Of course there's nothing there," Alice said. "But that doesn't mean I can't have a little fun, right? Besides, this doesn't concern you."

"Well, seeing a nut on the street does actually concern us," the second boy said. "We called the men in white to come and take you away."

"For *what*?" Alice asked.

"For acting crazy in public," the first boy said, laughing. "I don't know what you have, but you're obviously very unstable and crazy."

"I've never been more stable," Alice said, honestly confused as to what these two boys didn't get.

And she was. She missed The Black Queen and Ralph, but in reality, she was doing pretty good.

"I'd say you've gone crazy," the first boy said, laughing and laughing. "Don't worry, though. They'll come and lock you up."

Alice looked at The Machine. The Machine simply said, "Remind them that schizophrenia is contagious, that they probably shouldn't be near you if you're having a psychotic break."

Alice said exactly this, but this only spurred the boys on more.

"Mental illness isn't contagious," the second boy said. "Where did you get your intelligence from, the Middle Ages?"

"In the pseudo Middle Ages," Alice corrected. "But the Middle Ages nonetheless. And they happen to be quite cultured people. Modern day society hasn't produced a Dante, only Joseph Hellers, so I'd say we're quite ahead of the curve."

The second boy looked as though he was about to say something, but his whole demeanor changed at that moment. He just began to stare out into space, like he was catatonic.

"It's happening," Alice said to the first boy. "Welcome to my world."

"What's wrong with my friend?" the first boy asked, but that was when he suddenly began to laugh, for no reason at all. He just laughed and laughed and laughed, sounding crazy, as the second boy just stared into space.

"I told you it was contagious," Alice said. "Schizophrenia isn't something to be messed around with. I'm sure your friend is staring at a hallucination."

"It's like … a balloon!" the first boy said, and continued to laugh like a psychopath. He pointed at random people in the street, who quickly walked away, quickly moved away from this very disturbing scene.

Alice turned to The Machine hallucination, which was still there, and said, "I didn't mean to whack the whacky, but I can't always help it. Contagions are contagions. Schizophrenia isn't something to mess with … or make fun of."

"Well, I imagine their lives are going to change," The Machine said. "It'll change the way they think about people that struggle with mental illness."

"I doubt it," Alice said. "This world seems too cold for that."

The first boy had stripped down to his underwear and was running around the place at a million miles an hour, laughing in the faces of strangers, while the second boy just stared off into space, mentioning every once in a while elaborate plans of the government to destroy the world.

"His delusion is somewhat true," Alice said. "You are trapped and protected by the government, correct?" Alice said to The Machine.

"Yes," The Machine said. "Unfortunately for me."

At this moment, an ambulance pulled up, and two men in white stepped out.

"We got a call that a schizophrenic was here?" one of the men asked Alice suspiciously.

"It wasn't me," Alice said, hiding her illness perfectly, by not talking to her hallucination. "But you may want to examine those two boys over there."

The first boy was squawking like a chicken, and singing, "Cock a doodle doo!"

"Right," said the man, getting his priorities in order, and tackled the first boy to the ground after some running around. The boy just cried out that this was an injustice, that he wasn't crazy was just having a good time, but they didn't listen to him.

The other man took the second boy and brought him up to the ambulance, and the first man brought the second boy onto the ambulance, and then they left.

"That was a close one," Alice said.

"Yes, it was," The Machine said. "It wouldn't have been fun being hospitalized here, in the modern day world ... I can guarantee that."

"I know it wouldn't have," Alice said. "But it's always surprising who the whacky ones are. Though I didn't mean that to be revenge at all, of course, but they shouldn't have gotten so close to me. My disease spreads like the Black Plague."

"Well, you did the right thing, by not giving into their taunting," The Machine said.

"I hope so," Alice said. "It just rolled off like water, I'll tell you that, rolled off like water off a duck's wing. But it looks like I'm going to have to be careful here. The men in white are ready to take anyone away to the funny farm, it seems."

"Are they ever," The Machine said. "If they knew how whacked I was, they would have hospitalized me ages ago."

Alice laughed at the joke. "You aren't that crazy," Alice said. "You're too logical to be crazy. And, even if you were, trust me: I've seen worse."

"Nothing was worse than the sight of those *boys*," The Machine said. "Maybe they'll think twice next time, though. And I can guarantee, once they get out of the hospital, strung out on pills, a lot of pills, of course, they won't know up from down. Their mind will be rotted. They'll never be the same."

"It's the price of intolerance," Alice said, almost sadly. "But it's okay. Society wants to whack the whacky ... I say, let them. They're only suppressing genius. That's what Brannon would say."

The Machine didn't say anything, but if she had a head, she would have nodded in agreement.

"Well," Alice said, "it's been nice, but I need to find my friends. Talk to you later, when you pop up randomly, I imagine."

"Sounds good," The Machine said.

And Alice went on her way.

Everything's Disease, What One Brannon Sees

Brannon knew the royal highness was having a royal feast right about now. He had invited the wealthiest and most powerful people in the court.

It was a celebration of sorts, or so that's how it was advertised, but Brannon knew the real reason why The Suicide King was having the royal feast. He was hoping to eat enough unhealthy foods to where he would have a heart attack. He was, as usual, trying to commit suicide in his ridiculously selfish way. And while The Suicide King was busy trying to murder himself with food, other people, "fashionable people," were eating the meal of their lives, while other people, such as innocent peasants, got to starve to death.

Everything was disease; there was no disputing that. Everything was death, in Contorted Royal. And it was making Brannon angry. The whole reason why the other Brannon couldn't see something other than death and destruction was because, like the butterfly effect, selfish actions had consequences. The Suicide King, so wrapped up in himself, trying to kill himself with food.

Although, Brannon couldn't toss out The Suicide King completely from his scheme, his schema, of what he wanted to see exist. The Suicide King was unhappy in his marriage: *very* unhappy. He didn't like how The Black Queen had ditched him so she could go have fun adventures in a modern day world with Alice and a new boy named Ralph; The Black Queen, who was probably going to cheat on him, with Ralph this time: that part was understandable. If The Suicide King's heart stopped, it wouldn't feel so much pointless agony.

But Brannon needed to *do something.* He wasn't going to give up on the royal court, he wasn't going to give up on Contorted Royal. He had seen things, back in his day. He had seen peace, so much peace, and concepts like love and compassion and loyalty and freedom. Maybe they were romantic ideas, okay, he would give a critic that … but Brannon had once lived in a world like that. And then he came to Contorted Royal, and all of that changed.

Brannon had a blue jay resting on his shoulder. He couldn't see inside the royal dining room right now, because the door was shut. But he concentrated his emotion, and the door flew open.

The Suicide King was inside, stuffing his face, along with other wealthy people. They didn't even notice Brannon.

But they were going to notice Brannon. Brannon began to sing, in a tuneless tune: "Stop, you guys, I only need a minute: the path to what is right, we really need to spin it."

The Suicide King noticed, this time, and he turned toward Brannon. "Brannon. What a pleasure it is to see you again. Come join us."

"I'd rather sing a song, if you don't mind, as I don't want to put myself in a physical bind."

The Suicide King looked embarrassed at this moment, especially because his guests were staring at him like he'd just let in a monster. But Brannon knew he was no monster.

"We have free entertainment," The Suicide King said, to try and divert the attention from himself. "This boy can sing, he can dance, he can act … he can do anything. Anything at all you ask of him, he can do."

Brannon responded by more of his song: "You eat and eat and eat, as if it's something you must beat. You don't even pause to take a breath, everything is death. And it is, indeed, everything disease, what one Brannon sees. You stuff your face with food and the poor you don't include. But it's more than just this royal feast, I'm thinking about a heist."

"Oh, you wouldn't have to do that," The Suicide King said. "I'll share. Come here. Pop a squat, as I think they say. Come sit with us, and enjoy a fine meal."

Brannon continued to sing, and he grabbed a knife from the royal table, and stabbed it into the table. However, when he stabbed it into the table, everyone realized he hadn't actually stabbed it into the table: he'd stabbed it into a skull, and the skull was now impaled on the knife, the knife of which Brannon held up for the whole world to see.

"All the murder in this world is enough to leave death unfurled," Brannon continued to sing in that characteristic tuneless tune, his offbeat song. "Broken dimensions, broken worlds, broken hearts, they all add up, and we have no place to start."

"What do you mean, broken worlds and dimensions?" The Suicide King asked curiously.

"Everything's disease, what one Brannon sees," Brannon continued to sing. "The universes falling apart through selfishness, because of course there's no such thing as selflessness. Contorted Royal is just a scratch on the surface, because all worlds can't save face. But that's fine, just be selfish, it'll get you far, you'll just need to go to the modern day world and get a car. Maybe, a Jaguar."

"I don't want to go to any modern day world," The Suicide King said. "I'm happy here."

Brannon didn't say anything, just continued to sing, and think as he sung. He was, in his special way, forecasting the future, and telling The Suicide King all the problems that existed, and were going to exist. But he knew it was falling on deaf ears. The Suicide King couldn't do anything about it. Not because he was so addled in terms of his mind, but because he just didn't know how. Brannon saw that in him. The man was completely helpless. The dimensions, the worlds, that played in this story were going to fall apart, but there was, in the end, nothing that Brannon could do about it.

That was why he saw everything as disease. It should have all been blue, as blue was the color of tranquility and peace, the color of the wonderfully peaceful sky, but it wasn't really like that.

The Suicide King had disease on his heart, death on his soul, and Brannon saw all of that, as ugly as plaque. He saw those elements in their ugly black color, saw them in their destructive element.

But Brannon knew that The Suicide King was the key to some things. Granted, The Machine contributed to the circularity of Contorted Royal, which had for the moment obviously fallen apart so everything could be linear, but some of the violence came from the selfish violence of The Suicide King! The attitude of the people was reflected in the lifestyle of the king. And The Suicide King, while generally good-natured, needed to get his act together, because he was destroying his kingdom.

And that effect even trickled into the modern day world, in another dimension. The one where Ralph, The Black Queen, and Alice were.

"You kill and kill and kill, as if it's something you must spill, you don't even pause to see your tease, everything's disease," Brannon continued to sing.

At this point, the guests were feeling extremely uncomfortable with Brannon's act. Some had stood up to get ready to leave, even.

Brannon just continued to sing his song, not allow the lack of an audience to interfere with his goal … because in the end, his only true target was The Suicide King. That was why he was so vicious on the poor brain-dead guy. He was the one who could restore things back to normal. Brannon remembered a time, a time that everyone had forgotten (naturally), when The Suicide King was a righteous king, when he was a great king, bringing peace and good will to everything in his kingdom. He was like King Arthur, before his eventual demise, when his own kingdom betrayed him.

That was kind of what had caused The Suicide King to slowly become suicidal. Brannon saw that. His kingdom, slowly getting more and more out of control, and the response was to be suicidal. It was understandable … but the violence of Contorted Royal went hand in hand with the violence of The Suicide King.

Brannon pet the blue jay on his shoulder, and watched as several guests got up quickly to leave the room, before things got ugly.

"Is there something you wanted to tell me, Brannon?" The Suicide King said. "Maybe without song?"

Brannon didn't say anything for a moment, just continued to whistle his tuneless tune, and watched as more people continued to leave. It wasn't long before it was just Brannon and The Suicide King.

"You've got to stop this lifestyle," Brannon said. "We need The Suicide King back."

"Good heavens, that's all you wanted to tell me?" The Suicide King said. "All you had to do was leave me a message, after the beep. You've already told me I need to cut out my lifestyle."

"Everything is disease, what one Brannon sees," Brannon sung again.

"Oh, there you go again," The Suicide King said, though he sounded somewhat amused, his ears perked.

"Do you know why I sing?" Brannon said.

The Suicide King shook his head. He looked deep in contemplation now, as he tried to relax his heavy heart.

"Because it's free expression. Because it's powerful. The voice can come up with any tune and sing to that, even without an instrument."

"If you're worried I don't appreciate your song and poetry, think again," The Suicide King said. "This is the Middle Ages. We need court poets. *I* need court poets."

Brannon simply smiled, and gently—*very* gently—pushed his blue jay off of him. The blue jay went to The Suicide King and rested on his shoulder.

"What are you doing?" The Suicide King asked, trying to be glum but failing, now that he had a friend.

"Everything is disease because we make it so," Brannon said. "We don't have to, but we do. Our actions effect everything in the cosmos, like the butterfly effect, where it's all intimately connected, intimately constructed, and in some ways, interwovenly destructed. A suicide is related to a birth is related to a peasant gaining his freedom is related to a destructive machine being built, and all across times and worlds and dimensions."

The Suicide King forced himself to pet the blue jay for a moment, and then said, "Brannon, I know you care. I know you do. But my grief is too great, and drowning it does good for me, like a poor raging alcoholic. I've lost a lot, my biggest loss of course being The Black Queen."

"I'm sure her actions hurt you," Brannon said. "But remember, she's just as lost as you are. She's trying to find freedom. She's trying to fill a hole."

Before The Suicide King could respond, Brannon pulled out a blue flower from his pocket, and he handed it to The Suicide King.

"Does this look familiar?" Brannon asked.

The Suicide King slowly began to cry. Brannon could sense he was moments away from getting his sword, but he didn't, simply because he didn't want to splash blood on the beautiful blue jay.

"*Yes,*" he said through sobs. "My wife used to give me blue flowers all the time. It was so lovely when she'd do that for me. It always made my day."

"I just want to get answers like you do," Brannon said. "I want to restore Contorted Royal back to its former glory. But it can only happen if we work to try and cure the disease, and placate the death."

"But how do we do that?" The Suicide King said. "We're all stuck in our ways."

"Everything is happiness, so far from distress," Brannon sang again.

"Are you saying song and poetry can cure things?" The Suicide King said.

"I think it would be a start," Brannon said. "It may lead to some chaos at first, with me knowing what I know … but eventually, it could work to your advantage. You're trying to fill a hole in you, that much is true."

"Oh, how did you know," The Suicide King said sarcastically, but with some obvious amusement.

"I know everything and nothing, but at least that is something," Brannon sang again. "The worlds need to mend and come together, or else they are just going to shatter. I would advise you let Ralph seduce your wife for now."

"Oh, sounds lovely," The Suicide King said bitterly. "Let my wife do the one thing that's causing me so much pain."

"There are things I see that you can't," Brannon said. "But that doesn't mean you won't see them. Just be patient. Just be ready for when the good things come."

And Brannon said this, about Ralph, because he knew that Ralph was good-natured. If anything, Ralph could restore things, because he wouldn't cheat on The Suicide King with The Black Queen. Ralph was a humble servant, just in a modern day world.

"I'm sorry all you see is death and disease," The Suicide King said. "That must be terrible."

Brannon called back his blue jay, who happily perched on his shoulder. As he stepped out, he said, "I see more than that, occasionally … but yes, disease and death are stubborn. But things will be blue one day, if you're patient. Everything isn't red, what one Brannon said."

Dread, and More Dread

Mordred was indeed more to dread.

The Jack of Knives had, for the infinite number of times during their circularity, been a judgmental prude, and had completely undermined respect for Mordred. He had avoided seeking Mordred's help, seeing Mordred as a failure that didn't belong in Contorted Royal. It had been snobbery at its most elite form, which was problematic for many reasons, one of the reasons that The Jack of Knives was turning away a perfectly good servant of betrayal, someone who excelled at treason but chose to wait for the opportune moments.

All of that could have plagued Mordred, but that was just dread, it wasn't *more dread*. What The Jack of Knives needed to fear was Mordred's calm appreciation for The Jack of Knives. In all honesty, Mordred felt no anger toward The Jack of Knives for rejecting him an infinite number of times over; none whatsoever. In the place of anger was a calmness that verged on borderline insane tranquility, and to a creepy effect that Mordred was all too aware of.

That was the dread: that The Jack of Knives had a servant that never gave up on The Jack of Knives. Mordred could squash The Jack of Knives like a bug if he wanted, but he'd rather just be the one ignored, rejected, scorned … because those were beautiful, beautiful things.

Kind of backwards logic, but it worked for Contorted Royal. It worked for Mordred.

Because there was dread, and there was Mordred.

But The Jack of Knives was finally going to hear the voice of reason. Mordred knew it was the circularity that had prevented The Jack of Knives from seeking out Mordred's help, a constant and recursive pride that was just going to be circular for all time, or at least until linearity sunk in, or tried to sink in.

The Jack of Knives was in fact on his way, with The Dark Kid, who appeared out of nowhere to complement The Jack of Knives.

Mordred had been aware of the circularity for a while now. Alice thought she was so special, in tune to the circularity, but Mordred had known as well, had just chosen to go about his business in his own way, even if that meant repeating things over and over again. Contrary to popular belief, circularity wasn't all that much of a hell. Mordred could offer to help The Jack of Knives succeed in killing the king a hundred times over. He'd never get sick of it: a million times, a billion times, a trillion times over … never any limitation.

Mordred was in his chamber, waiting for The Jack of Knives to come. He finally did. With things going back to linearity, what with the advent of Ralph and the attempt to destroy The Machine, The Jack of Knives was aware now that he'd always been in circularity, and that he'd been foolish for not seeking Mordred's help all this time. So, so very foolish.

Mordred had his back turned when The Jack of Knives barged into Mordred's chamber.

"Okay, okay, you *win*," The Jack of Knives said.

"I, *what*?" Mordred said quietly, not turning to face The Dark Kid and The Jack of Knives.

"I said, you win. I give up. I should have known that you were a genius at betraying the king, that you could kill him, what with you being a magician and all. I should have known you had the key."

"So you still want to destroy The Suicide King and take over the kingdom?" Mordred said.

"Yes," The Jack of Knives responded.

Mordred turned around to look at his enemy. God, how he hated The Jack of Knives. How much he wanted The Jack of Knives to suffer once he became king. Because, Mordred knew that those who were at the tip top of power suffered. They were always going to suffer. And Mordred couldn't wait. All those times of rejection, they were finally going to come to a head.

"I suppose you want to know the key," Mordred said. "And you want to know it now. You don't want to be in poor Mordred's company for more than you have to, of course. What with me and my crooked back, I must be an eye sore to you."

The Jack of Knives looked guilty, but denied it. "No. I'm willing to stay here as long as you need. In fact, it's probably better if we worked together," he lied.

"Excellent news," Mordred said, and went to his cabinet. He opened it, and pulled out a vial of ugly green bubbling poison, like acid. It was hideous to look at, but Mordred found charm in it. He was tempted to poison The Jack of Knives, right here, right now, but changed his mind, only because he didn't want to traumatize the poor Dark Kid, who thought he was so tough.

"Do you know what this is?" Mordred said, holding the poison up to the light, which in the light seemed to sizzle like electricity.

"No," The Jack of Knives said. "But I guess you're going to tell us?"

"It's the one weakness of The Suicide King. It is suicide distilled, to its absolute finest. It's suicide in a bottle. The Suicide King would kill himself left and right to possess this: it's the one true way to die. The irony will be that we'll poison The Suicide King, thus making it homicide, thus meaning that The Suicide King, named The Suicide King, never succeeded in killing himself. It's a real shame, but that's the irony of things, and the way it goes sometimes."

"What did you want to do, exactly?" The Jack of Knives said.

"Well, we have to get The Suicide King to drink this vial," Mordred said.

"By slipping it into his morning coffee?" The Jack of Knives asked.

Mordred didn't say anything for a moment, just looked at The Dark Kid. He was all drenched in shadow, but Mordred saw weakness that Mordred himself could tear apart any moment now, if he wanted, like ripping apart a shadow, severing the shadow from the person. It would be easy.

Or, he could shoot out lightning and electrocute the boy to death.

As Mordred thought this, The Dark Kid looked at Mordred carefully. His eyes were unreadable, being so dark, but Mordred almost thought he saw a spark of defiance. As if The Dark Kid knew. Well, maybe he did, but so what? They were all enemies here. They could pretend otherwise, in an inveterate scheme, but they were all enemies.

But Mordred, in the name of peace and bloodshed, was okay with setting those differences aside. Let the boys suffer in the name of power. They'd realize how negative it affected a person. They'd realize it soon enough, once they put on the crown. That was why Mordred had never taken over the crown, because he knew the negativity in power.

"No," Mordred said crisply. "Not by slipping it into anything. We're going to give it to him directly, and let him drink it, of his own volition."

The Jack of Knives rolled his eyes. Mordred was amused at this: The Jack of Knives and his defenses were gone. He was showing his derision for Mordred, that there was no reason to trust Mordred. But that was fine. Just fine.

"That would never work," The Jack of Knives said. "The Suicide King is openly suicidal, but he doesn't want to actually commit suicide."

"Another irony," Mordred said simply. "But that's why I'm going to make it seem like it's a sweet, sweet drink. And it'll taste sweet. It won't taste like poison. It'll taste like … *apple cider*."

"You really think The Suicide King will fall for it?" The Dark Kid asked.

Mordred could tell The Dark Kid was still sizing up Mordred. The two were destined to not get along, most likely.

And that was just fine. Let it burn. Let it spontaneously combust.

"I do," Mordred said. "Now, it won't take effect immediately. It will take some time. But eventually, it will work."

"How long are we looking at?" The Jack of Knives asked.

"Just however long it takes for the poison to take effect, of course," Mordred said. "I can't give you a guesstimate, there isn't one … but I can tell you, it will work."

The Jack of Knives nodded, and reached out to grab the vial. Mordred moved it away in as arrogant of a fashion as possible.

"I'm going to do it," Mordred said. "I don't trust a servant boy to successfully kill the king and take over the kingdom."

The Jack of Knives looked wounded, but didn't say anything for a little while. Then he said, relenting, "Okay. You do it. But if anything goes wrong, it's all on you. I won't hesitate to turn you in, for treason."

"It won't go wrong," Mordred said, and laughed. "Oh, so little you know, Jack. So little. Such a tiny knife for a brain, so tiny, a mere toothpick … barely able to stab anything."

"That's my friend you're talking about," The Dark Kid said.

"Of course it is. But we're not friends here. We're just like-minded people."

"And how do we know you won't betray us?" The Dark Kid asked. "Once it happens? You could try to pin the murder on us."

"I thought about it," Mordred confessed smoothly. "But my designs are much too complex for mere servant boys and wannabe angels falling from the sky to ever understand. To tell the truth, I hope your ascension to power is everything you ever wanted it to be."

"And there's no catch?" The Dark Kid asked.

"Not as far as I'm aware of," Mordred said, and smiled. "But I will tell you, Jack, that you're going to be a very violent king. *Very* violent."

"That's the idea," The Jack of Knives said, and Mordred could see the blood lust.

He smiled at this. The Jack of Knives would learn. So oblivious to everything, except for his blind anger … things were going to backfire. Were they ever. And Mordred couldn't wait.

"We commence our plot tomorrow," Mordred said decisively. "Unless you have any thoughts?"

The Jack of Knives shook his head, but then said, "Are you sure there's no catch?"

"I don't see what good it would do to trick you," Mordred said. "We all know the king is getting old. Not in age, he's still pretty young, but in terms of his act. We all know homicide is healthier for the kingdom, rather than suicide. Nothing would please me more than to see The Suicide King finally off the throne. The Jack of Knives is a weak breed, but his knife will grow, and become more serrated, jagged, through time. Things will happen. Things will indeed happen. And I look forward to those things happening."

The Jack of Knives was holding his knife. He sharpened the knife on the palm of his hand, as if it was a whetstone, and Mordred knew he was doing this to show off his toughness … which Mordred thought was weak and timid. But The Jack of Knives was satisfied with his action, and was hoping it would intimidate Mordred. It didn't, but it was a good try.

The Jack of Knives threw his knife at Mordred, and it barely missed him. He laughed, and said, "Sounds good, then. We'll commence tomorrow."

Mordred went to the knife and grabbed it. He looked at it, examined it in the light, watched it glisten … and then said, "Sounds good to me."

And in The Jack of Knives Mordred saw glee. Oh, poor Jack of Knives … thought he was getting the deal of a lifetime: what a lie that was. What a true and utter lie. He was going to hate the kingdom once he got it, but he wouldn't be able to run from it. He thought he was so murderous … well, he was soon going to learn how murderous Contorted Royal really was.

It wasn't for kids, that was for sure, even if kids with ambition. Kids couldn't make it. They wouldn't be able to handle it.

And The Jack of Knives was no exception.

A Depressing Study in Societal Robotics and the Decay of Cultural Manners

The Black Queen *hated* Ralph's world. She hated it more than anything. The people were beyond rude: they were insufferable, selfish, egocentric, and literally thought that the whole world revolved around *them*. They were mean, they were jerks, they felt entitled to everything in the world, when that wasn't what they deserved.

She had indeed developed her theory of societal robotics. What was societal robotics, exactly? It was the social phenomenon in this world, the ability for everyone to remain programmed to be mean and keep to themselves in the most selfish way, and to be just plain mean. To be artificial, to be fake. To be undeserving of anything good.

The Black Queen knew that her medieval world had problems. It had a lot of problems, in fact. It had violence, which had negative effects for everyone. But there, at least the violence was passionate. At least there was *feeling*. Here, there was no feeling. The Black Queen had never seen a robot before, but she knew about them, and she imagined that a robot would have more feeling than any of the wannabe people in this world. Hence, the reason why she was thinking of her theory of societal robotics.

Ralph and The Black Queen were simply walking along the sidewalk, when another person rudely bumped into The Black Queen. Another person, yet another! This must have been the fiftieth person, and that was just today. What was it with these wannabe studs? These people that were so selfish, making it all about them, hipster style?

But The Black Queen bit her tongue. She didn't say anything, at least not immediately.

When she'd calmed down some, she finally said to Ralph, "I think we need to get revenge on these misguided people."

"It wouldn't do any good," Ralph said. "It would just make things worse. As you've probably noticed, we aren't in polite society anymore. It's the decay of cultural manners. But that's what happens when you live in an egotistical world, bent on consumerism and industrialization and mechanization."

"It's that damn *machine*," The Black Queen said. "We need to destroy it."

"Oh, I agree," Ralph said. "But not quite yet. We need to wait for the right moment. But trust me: we'll get there, eventually."

"I sure hope so. One more moment of having to put up with these … these … *people*, and my head will be served on a silver plate."

"Oh, don't be so gothic in your depression," Ralph said, smiling slightly.

"Well, these societal robotics are depressing me. I don't know how you stand this world. It's like people want to be rude to you, get your goat, so they have an excuse to hurt you. Who runs into you on purpose, except for a bully, someone looking for a fight? These people are trying to egg us on. We've been good to resist so far, but I'm going to warn you, Ralph—I don't know how much longer I can handle it before I explode in a homicidal rage."

Ralph nodded, and as The Black Queen finished her statement, a woman ran into her.

It was harder than most, and it knocked The Black Queen almost over. She managed to regain herself, but this was when she snapped. She was finished with dealing with this. She was absolutely finished! This was not acceptable.

"Watch where you're going!" The Black Queen shouted at the lady.

"I don't need to watch where I'm going," the lady said. "You don't control me."

"No, I don't control you, but I'll tell you what does: your societal robotics."

"What?"

"You heard me," The Black Queen sneered. "You're just a robot, trying to do what you're told, which is be selfish. The only problem is it isn't working, it just makes you look conspicuous. I can see your hardware poking out, actually, if you want to know the truth. I see all your digital formatting, and it exposes you, exposé style."

The lady didn't say anything for a moment, but that was when The Black Queen saw indeed that this woman was literally a robot. That passed a moment later, but The Black Queen had seen it: a metal body, a metal head, with computer screens for eyes. It was a strange effect, but it had really happened.

"Are you in pain?" the lady asked.

The Black Queen was thrown for a loop with this non sequitur. "Excuse me?"

"Are you in pain?" the woman said again, and she began to dance like a robot. "Are you in pain, are you in pain?"

The Black Queen looked at Ralph, confused. Ralph was just as confused.

"What's she doing?" The Black Queen mouthed to Ralph.

Ralph didn't say anything, just shook his head. He didn't know.

"Are you in pain? Are you in pain?" the robot continued to say, and this was because it was indeed a robot, a malfunctioning robot, who had been too much of a programmed jerk in this isolated society and was now going completely crazy. The voice was low and mechanical, and the voice was indeed falling apart, like bad software.

The robot/woman continued to move in that robotic way, and it was almost comical, but it was also creepy, because the woman still looked like a woman, somehow, but was acting like a robot that had taken a bad virus or had been damaged severely.

"What should we do?" The Black Queen asked.

But Ralph didn't say anything.

"I ... can't ... do ... *this*, satellite, satellite," the robot/woman said in that malfunctioning voice. "Are you in pain, I can't do this, satellite, satellite. And what was the point of that shoe? Do you ... horse *glue*, or do you horse *shoe*? What's the difference between a calculation and a calcification? Are you a butter or a bitter? And what's a the deal what's a the deal you're going are you in pain are you pain and I butter my face with alcohol ..."

"You broke her," Ralph said sadly.

The Black Queen, who saw that an emergency was at hand, went to the woman and said, "Okay, I didn't mean what I said, come back to normal, everything's okay, you're a human not a robot."

But the woman was indeed a robot, and continued to malfunction: "Cultural manners? I say cultural banners! I don't

143

know what I'm saying but it sounds fun right now to say what the freak is the cow! And who are you? Are you a robot too? I'm a robot, who are you? Are you a robot, a robot, too? Emily Dickinson I think or something like that just with a modern day robotic and mechanically fake faking twist!"

"I think we need to fix her," Ralph said conclusively, and suddenly, he was a holding a bag of tools.

The Black Queen thought all of this was indeed quite strange, but she knew it had something to do with The Machine. For some reason, reality was malfunctioning, alongside society, and it was because of The Machine.

Or maybe Ralph was just magical, explaining why he got the tools so suddenly.

Either way, a crisis was at hand, and The Black Queen trusted Ralph to help fix this.

As Ralph tried to get the lady/robot to reboot, stop and calm down and stop moving like a crazed robot as crazy as societal robotics, The Black Queen couldn't help but feel depressed. She shouldn't be angry at these people, they were just doing what they were programmed to do. Sure, a lot of it was probably The Machine, but some of it was probably just the society that they lived in. The Black Queen had to admit that: her Contorted Royal had a lot of problems, and The Black Queen was part of those problems. But in the end, she was just doing what she had been programmed to do, by society. Her husband had alienated her with his suicidal habits, her boyfriends didn't make her happy just made her crazy because they always reminded her of The Suicide King when he'd been happy, and in general, people were not that nice to The Black Queen, like the unpsychiatrist that one time. You couldn't get mad at a computer for malfunctioning. In this depressing study of societal robotics, it was kind of the same thing. Sure, these people were very mean, but it was the culture they lived in. A decay of cultural manners, yes … but that decay came from the general stink of corruption, and people corrupting, and becoming less empathetic, more technologic. Such a paradigm indeed seemed inevitable, in the depths of these computerisms.

As The Black Queen drifted in her depressing thoughts, she watched as Ralph finally managed to open up the back of the robot's head. The woman was indeed a robot, now. He was doing things with the hardware, patching things up here and there, but it wasn't working. The robot just continued to mouth the craziest jargon, just continued to go crazy.

"Is it working?" The Black Queen asked hopelessly, even though she already knew the answer.

Ralph just shook his head and continued working.

And that was when The Black Queen realized that she couldn't live without Ralph. He was good with computers and technology; maybe that was why he was so good at understanding his society, and having enough patience to deal with it, like a mechanic solving a problematic and troublesome car.

"My love, oh, Ralph, I love you!" the robot lady said.

"Hey, you stole my line," The Black Queen said. "Why I outta … let me at 'em, let me at 'em!"

"I'm trying to work!" Ralph hissed in exasperation, as he tried to ward The Black Queen off with his hands, The Black Queen of which was trying to assault the malfunctioning robot.

The Black Queen got the hint, and let Ralph work, and closed her eyes.

When she opened them again, though, things had changed. She was back at the moment when she'd first run into the lady.

She was a lady now, doing just fine, but angry, and trying to knock The Black Queen over.

The Black Queen, who was still disoriented from what had just happened, just ignored this, and watched as the lady said, "You aren't going to fight back?"

The Black Queen shook her head. She had bigger fish to fry.

"Coward," the lady said, and left.

"Ralph," The Black Queen said. "Did you feel that glitch?"

"I did," Ralph said. "For a moment, I thought everyone was a robot, and I was trying to fix one that … well, was going crazy."

"That was weird," The Black Queen said. "Is it The Machine?"

"Of course it is," Ralph said. "A glitch in the system. But I do think that, metaphorically, these people are indeed robots."

The Black Queen didn't say anything. That much was obvious. It had been the study in societal robotics.

The Black Queen looked around suspiciously, and saw people turning into robots and turning back into people. Over and over again. It was the strangest effect. But thankfully, none of them were malfunctioning.

"What would you do if you were a robot?" The Black Queen asked Ralph.

"I'd do what I was told," Ralph said. "Bless these people that can't think for themselves. The mindless masses. They're lucky."

The Black Queen nodded. "You're telling me. I am curious to know, how you managed to make it out okay."

"What do you mean?"

"Well, you aren't caught up in this mean girl game. You do what you can. You treat people with kindness. You think. In short, you aren't robotic."

"Some people just have insight into the hypocrisies of societies," Ralph said, and had a distant, faraway look in his eyes, as if he didn't like this about himself, as though it was hypocritical just by definition.

"What is it, Ralph?"

"It's like Alice," Ralph said. "She can see things in your society that would drive the average person mad as a hatter."

The Black Queen couldn't dispute this. But what she wanted to dispute was the love for Alice that she saw on Ralph's face.

"Anyway, we should probably get to destroying The Machine," Ralph said, snapping out of his reverie. "I think we've had enough of these robots for one day."

"I'd say so," The Black Queen said. "So what exactly is the plan?"

Ralph didn't say anything for a moment, but then said, "Come with me. We need to find Spencer."

When Poison Makes a Suicidal Maniac King Bubbly Instead of Deadly

The Jack of Knives had his doubts. Mordred was a dark character, a dark figure, and there was no telling what designs he had in mind. It seemed too easy to think that Mordred, after countless rejection from The Jack of Knives, would still be on board to help The Jack of Knives successfully take over the kingdom by killing the king.

But The Jack of Knives was desperate. He didn't know how to kill The Suicide King. No one did, really. And then there was Mordred, who did have an idea, and it was the craziest thing. So, even though The Jack of Knives had his doubts, he wasn't going to completely give into those doubts. Not completely, anyway.

He also wasn't going to give in completely to his suspicion … at least, for the most part. He was still going to watch for Mordred, make sure nothing happened, but trust him enough to see this operation through.

Mordred was walking with The Jack of Knives and The Dark Kid, and they were walking toward the court. When they finally arrived, with the door shut, Mordred said, "I know it's against your style, Jack … but it would be nice if you'd let me handle this. I'm a pro. I know what I'm doing. If you get involved, you'll probably just ruin it."

"Thanks for the vote of confidence," The Jack of Knives said. "But okay. I'll let you handle it."

"Good," Mordred said, and smiled. His teeth were rotted. "As long as we're clear on that."

And then suddenly, the door burst open.

Mordred and The Jack of Knives walked inside with The Dark Kid, seeing that they had caught The Suicide King in the act. He was shoving his sword into the side of his head, and was trying to shove it pretty deep, when he realized that he had company.

"Well, this is awkward," The Suicide King said. "I'm right in the middle of this."

"Well, you didn't completely skewer your head," Mordred said. "I don't see the tip of the sword on the other side of your head."

"Good point," The Suicide King said, and pulled out his sword: The Suicide King had a giant gash in his head. And yet, he was alive. As alive as he was ever going to be, The Jack of Knives had to correct himself.

"Why do you do that to yourself?" Mordred asked, and The Jack of Knives noticed some cruelty in the tone of his voice. He couldn't quite explain it, but it sounded … *taunting*. "What do you hope to find by attempting over and over again to kill yourself?"

"Civilization has slowly chipped away at my sanity," The Suicide King responded, wiping his sword on his clothes and putting it in its sheath. "What you see is left in pieces."

"Sounds terrible," Mordred said.

"Can I ask what you three are doing here, in my private chamber?"

"The court is open to anyone," Mordred said, and smiled cruelly. "I'm sorry that you've suffered so much, that civilization has destroyed your faith."

"Well, can you blame me?" The Suicide King said. "My wife cheats on me left and right, and hates my guts, and while she's getting it off with hot boys, I'm stuck here trying to rule a kingdom that hates me, that abuses me, that exploits me, that treats me like I'm too weak to exist in this society. And not only that, everyone wants to kill each other, and I can't do anything about it. So I just kill myself. It solves all my problems."

Again, with the mocking tone: "It sounds like you're in hell. I'm so sorry for your plight, your highness. I don't know how you can stand it."

"Well, I don't, obviously," The Suicide King snapped. "If I did, I'd be as whole as a newborn child. Instead, I'm stuck here with a sword in my brain."

The Suicide King's gash was healing some, but he looked very unhappy.

The Jack of Knives was waiting for Mordred to make his move, and he finally did.

"I have something here that you may find interesting," Mordred said, and pulled out the vial.

The Jack of Knives saw that it was transformed, however, the look of the poison. Most likely not literally, of course: it was still the same poison. But it was pink, and it sparkled like diamonds, and The Jack of Knives could even smell it: it smelled like a very sweet, sinfully sweet, apple cider.

"What is *that*?" The Suicide King said, clearly uninterested.

"It's your cure," Mordred said.

"My *cure*?" The Suicide King said.

Mordred nodded. "It'll make all your dreams come true. It's like a medication, kind of, except better: it will make you happy, for all eternity, and will clear your head of all the suicidal thoughts that you have. It'll make you stronger, which will help you deal with your problems and society in a much more effective manner."

"What's the catch?" The Suicide King asked. "I'm sure there's a catch you haven't mentioned. Is it really *poison*? Is it, now, Mordred?"

Mordred shook his head. "I have here, the finest thing you could ever ask for: hope. And, happiness."

The Suicide King picked up his sword again, removed it from the sheath. He examined the blade. "Happiness is overrated. You know how high I get when I shove the sword blade into my head?"

"I imagine you feel pain," Mordred said. "More pain than you deserve."

The Suicide King didn't say anything for a moment, but then said, "More pain than I deserve? You mean, I deserve a chance at *happiness*?"

"All you have to do is drink this," Mordred said, holding it out to The Suicide King. "That's all you have to do."

"Well, it does look good," The Suicide King said. "And it smells *wonderful*."

And before The Jack of Knives knew what had happened, The Suicide King had gone toward Mordred, yanked out the vial from his hand, and drunk it all. A little bit of the liquid had dribbled down the front of his chin, but he drank ninety-nine percent of it.

"That was easy," Mordred said, smiling at The Jack of Knives.

The Jack of Knives, who had never been part of a homicide before, was begging to differ. Was he really so tough with his knives? What if The Suicide King was braver with his sword?

It didn't matter much, because the damage had already been done.

The Suicide King threw down the vial on the ground dramatically, the vial of which shattered. "I feel like a new *man*!"

he said robustly, and patted his belly in approval. "My stomach agrees too. That tasted better than anything I've ever tasted before. It was so *sweet*."

"Just wait for it to take effect," Mordred whispered to The Jack of Knives, and nodded.

The Jack of Knives, who was having a major existential crisis right now and wondering if he would do well to take a sword and shove it into his own head, just nodded slowly in return.

He was about to watch the king *die*. Was he ready to have the guilt of a murder on his back, ready to have suicidal blood on his hands? He wasn't sure, but The Jack of Knives knew one thing: he was still a kid, a measly little teenager, and because of that, he wasn't ready for murder.

He felt his soul already being poisoned.

The Suicide King saw it differently, however, and began to run around the room at a million miles an hour. He looked ecstatic, like he could take over the world.

"And just who do you think *you* are?" The Suicide King said to his reflection, on a mirror on the wall. "Are you a bubbly bubbly toil and tubbly? Ha ha, yes, I think you're a tubby bubbly!"

The Suicide King laughed in maniacal glee, and clapped his hands in excitement. He continued to say, "Bubbly bubbly toil and tubbly," in a very crazy way, and The Jack of Knives looked at The Dark Kid for help: The Suicide King had completely lost his mind: he'd gone bonkers. The Dark Kid just shrugged, and pulled out a pair of shades.

"What're those for?" The Jack of Knives whispered.

The Dark Kid didn't respond. He did look amused.

And The Jack of Knives could sort of see why: The Suicide King had gone complete bonkers, patting his belly in approval. He was saying things like, "Are you a tubbo, tubby bubbly? Are you a grubbly bubbly? What are you, a chubby?" Complete and utter nonsense. Complete and utter *chaos*.

The Suicide King suddenly went to Mordred, grabbing him by the shirt in a fit of emotion: "You've *saved* me, Mordred. I've never felt so *alive*. So *free*! I could take over the world if I wanted to! Bubbly bubbly toiler and chubby ..."

And The Suicide King grabbed his sword and ripped it in half with his hands. He threw the pieces away, still saying,

"Bubbly bubbly," and hiccupping every once in a while. When he hiccupped, bubbles came out of his mouth and floated into the air.

The Jack of Knives had to admit, it was good seeing this side of The Suicide King. Sure it was a little whacky, but it beat all of the pointless self-destruction. The kingdom felt just a little bit lighter. It felt less chaotic, less crazy, even though all they saw was crazy.

"I say we get a feast going," The Suicide King said. "Let's chow down on some food."

"That won't be necessary," Mordred said. "We enjoy seeing you so bubbly, so sparkling, that we don't need any food. You're like a good glass of champagne, just without the pain."

"Well, thank you," The Suicide King said. "But I must admit I'm a little chubby. All those times I ate my sword ... it was despicable of me! What was I thinking? I think we need to have a party or something. I say, we all go get drunk!"

And The Suicide King proceeded to leave the courtroom, but wasn't able to, because Mordred smoothly blocked his way.

The Jack of Knives knew why, of course: no one could witness The Suicide King like this, right before his death. It would convict everyone right on the spot.

"What are you blocking my way for?" The Suicide King said, sounding hurt. "Did you want to be in a hell of a lot of trouble, with the bubbly bubble?"

"It's because there's a surprise party behind those doors, but you can't see it yet. Not quite yet." Mordred smiled truthfully.

The Suicide King responded by smiling stupidly, and then kissing Mordred. "I should cheat on my wife with you, Mordred, you honey vixen," he said. "You're delicious."

"Well, thank you, your highness," Mordred said, and The Suicide King, with his fat bottom, turned around, and continued to talk to himself.

The Jack of Knives finally noticed that The Suicide King was getting fatter by the moment. He assumed it was a side effect of the medication, the poison. So far, it was not pleasant, and it was concerning to The Jack of Knives, the excess weight gain.

But that concern didn't last long, because The Suicide King said, "Oh, would you look at the time, it's time to go," and then collapsed dead on the ground.

When it was done, The Jack of Knives said, "He's a real loony."

"The poison brings out the worst in anyone who takes it," Mordred said darkly. "So don't think you're above it, Jack."

The Jack of Knives saw this point, and didn't say anything in response.

"So what do we do with the body?" The Dark Kid asked.

"Let me handle that," Mordred said, and in a sudden change of demeanor, ran out of the courtroom screaming that the king was dead, that he'd died of a heart attack and that he needed immediate medical attention.

A few servants came and picked him up, as Mordred cried dramatically, about how it was an injustice that the king was gone, especially after he'd been so cheery lately. Oh, the horror of it all, Mordred said. Why was life so *unfair*?

The Jack of Knives watched as more people came in, to see that the king really had died, and that was when the people who had picked up the king, upon realizing he was really dead, threw him in a corner of the courtroom, like he was a bag of garbage, and bowed to The Jack of Knives.

"You're our king," they all said at once.

"But The Suicide King," The Jack of Knives said, realizing that he didn't like this at all. "What about him?"

"We'll dispose of him later," the people said sardonically. "You're our new king, Jack. And we know you won't disappoint."

But all The Jack of Knives felt was disappointment. *This* was what it felt like to be a king? He felt nothing. He felt absolutely *nothing*. Who actually wanted to rule Contorted Royal?

But it was too late to go back, and so The Jack of Knives let them put the crown on him.

He had, however, never felt so betrayed.

To Solve or Not to Solve: The Complexities of the Ralph Problem

The Jack of Knives would get what was due to him when the time was right. Ace wasn't sure where things were going, now that The Jack of Knives ruled Contorted Royal, but he supposed there was no point in worrying about that for the moment. The Jack of Knives was miniscule compared to Ralph's involvement. It was because of him that the circularity had been temporarily dislodged, and if Ralph continued to get his way, he would destroy The Machine and destroy the circularity for good and all that Ace had struggled to maintain.

But Ace was realizing that things were a little more complicated than just killing Ralph. Granted, that took a lot of the tension out of Ace's story, or at least his version of the story, but it was the truth. Ace knew that if he tried to kill Ralph or killed Ralph, The Black Queen could be on Ace faster than Ace could pull out an ace of spades.

That didn't mean, however, that Ace wasn't going to try. He knew he needed to try, because if he didn't, Ralph would walk, free to destroy everything that Ace had had for a very long time.

The thing was, Ace wasn't sure he wanted a run-in with the queen. He wasn't sure that he wanted conflict. So far, they were on good terms. But if The Black Queen suspected even for a moment that Ace had intentions to kill Ralph, that would change immediately. The Black Queen was fiercely loyal to Ralph, even though Ralph had his loyalties to Alice.

Regardless ... Ace needed to do something.

He was looking in the window of a restaurant. He saw The Black Queen and Ralph sitting at a table. They were eating steak and potatoes, and talking about things. Talking about their plan to destroy The Machine. He could hear them, even all the way out here. It didn't sound good. They were coming up with their plan and if all went well, they would succeed.

They talked for a while, with Ace thinking about what he needed to do. He could go in real fast and kill Ralph in disguise. However, it wouldn't work, he knew that. The Black Queen, this time, would see right through it. He wasn't sure why, he just knew that she would.

Ace got what he wanted when The Black Queen stood up and left Ralph alone. As for how long she would be gone, Ace wasn't sure, but he made his move: he walked into the building and sat down across from Ralph.

Ralph was looking down at his plate, when he noticed that he had company.

"Hello, Ralph," Ace said.

"Who are you?" Ralph asked, wiping his lips on his napkin.

"My name is Ace," Ace said, and realized that he couldn't kill this boy. There was something very beautiful about him, something that he couldn't quite explain. Ace couldn't help but admit that Ralph and The Black Queen would make a cute couple, if that ever happened, which it might.

"Ace," Ralph said. "Sounds familiar. You generally like to stay in the corner of the kingdom, but you have your own role to play."

"And what role is that?" Ace asked, curious to know what this boy knew about Ace.

"I'm not sure, but I want to venture to say that you have something to do with The Machine, but have kept it secret."

"Perhaps," Ace said. "Perhaps not."

"Can we cut the games out already?" Ralph asked.

"We aren't playing any games," Ace said. "I'm just trying to size up my enemy better."

"I'm not your enemy," Ralph said. "I haven't done anything."

"Did you know that Death is actually a personified individual?" Ace said. "There's a Death in one world where he is forever bent on trying to destroy a kid named Dustin … but there's a Death, specifically tailored to our culture, who said that you're a problem."

"And why would I be a problem?" Ralph asked.

"Because you can destroy The Machine," Ace said simply. "Why else would you be a problem? Do you know how important the circularity is for Contorted Royal? It defines that world. And the cold isolation here … it's your world. It's what makes it tick, what makes its computer screen so bright. Without it, things would be completely different."

"They would be better," Ralph said assuredly.

"Are you sure about that?" Ace said.

"Of course," Ralph said. "Why wouldn't things be better?"

"I don't know. Maybe because you're trying to mess with fate."

Ralph, who had been eating, dropped his fork as though stunned at this thought. He said, "Fate?"

154

Ace nodded. "There's no telling what would happen if you destroyed The Machine, which controls so many aspects of two very different and distinct worlds. Contorted Royal and your modern day world are fated to go through what they are going through, and if you destroy that, well ... you'd be challenging fate. That's very, very dangerous."

Ralph took this all in, and then finally conceded to take another bite of steak. "It wouldn't," he said. "We aren't fated to do anything."

"You caught my bluff," Ace said. "But still ... do you know who you are messing with? Do you know *what* you are messing with?"

"I know that I have the potential to restore order back to the world. We're in a cold war, so to speak, and bad things are happening because of it. People are more violent than ever, they do more horrible things than ever ... and it isn't okay."

"You're just trying to moralize," Ace said.

Ralph shook his head. "No, I'm not. I'm just saying the truth. If you don't like that, you can leave my table."

"Poor Ralph, thinks he can change the fate of two worlds," Ace taunted. "I feel bad for you. I really do."

Ace pulled out a knife.

Ralph's eyes widened when he saw this. "What are you going to do with that?"

"What do you think?" Ace said, and was about to stab Ralph when The Black Queen shouted, "Don't!"

Ace stopped where he was. He knew this wasn't going to work. The Black Queen was too fierce in her determination to have Ralph all for herself. And now Ace had been caught, in the act.

He tried to hide his knife, but alas, it was too late.

The Black Queen hustled toward the table, and said, "Ace? What are you *doing*?"

"I can explain," Ace said, but didn't have a chance to explain.

"*Explain*? There's nothing to explain. I saw what you were about to do. You were going to kill my boyfriend."

"I'm not your boyfriend," Ralph said, but no one was listening to him (odd, when considering he was the main event, the one everyone was after).

"I was just showing Ralph my knife," Ace said, trying to keep his cool.

Oh, how he desperately wanted to murder The Black Queen. But he knew he couldn't. If he did, it would unleash a series of events that no one would be able to stop. Besides, Ace was lower than the queen on occasion, in terms of power, and this was one of those occasions. Since Ralph had gotten involved, he had been lower than a servant, able to get nothing done.

The Black Queen lifted up her dress and pulled out a knife from a sheath that was on her leg. She pointed it at Ace. "Don't make me kill you," she said, *femme fatale* style.

"That would be unnecessary," Ace said, but knew that his life hung in the balance. All he had to do was kill Ralph, but he couldn't do that because of the blasted Black Queen. It was making him sick, but he honestly didn't know what to do.

"You don't kill Ralph," The Black Queen said. "How could you? I didn't know you had it in your heart to betray Contorted Royal."

"I'm not betraying anything," Ace said. "You just think I am. I was just showing Ralph my knife. Right, Ralph?"

"*No,*" Ralph said.

"See?" The Black Queen said. "You are trying to betray things. That must mean …" The Black Queen thought about this for a moment. "That must mean you were the one who killed Spade over and over again!"

Ace knew his cover was blown, and he couldn't believe all of this was happening. It was too much. It was way too much. All the universes of existence were crashing down on him.

"Spade?" Ace said, trying to feign innocence. "Who is Spade?"

The Black Queen picked up a spoon and chucked it at Ace. "You know exactly who Spade is. My boyfriend!"

"You have a boyfriend and wanted *another* boyfriend?" Ralph asked, clearly not happy at this idea.

"She has a husband, too," Ace said, to try to help his situation, and get Ralph on his side.

"Now, honey," The Black Queen said, seeing that Ralph was pouting slightly (which was reasonable … he was being used, Ace believed), "Spade was my *old* boyfriend, before he died."

156

"But you have a freaking *husband*," Ralph said. "Of course! The Suicide King! How could I miss *that*? You know, I was this close to kissing you, even with my love for Alice. But not anymore, Black Queen."

"Ace, you ruined everything," The Black Queen said resignedly.

"I didn't ruin anything," Ace said. "Ralph is just a staunch believer in fidelity. And I don't blame him. He'd be ugly as a male slut, otherwise, if you don't mind me saying so."

"Gee, thanks," Ralph said miserably.

"Well, we believe in chivalry where I come from," Ace said.

"That's such a myth," The Black Queen said. "Just think of Lancelot and you'll know what I mean. But anyway, Ace: you aren't killing Ralph. You've already killed Spade over and over again, you aren't killing my new hubby."

"*Please* stop making me your *man*," Ralph said, still pouting.

"Oh, honey, it's all just fun and games," The Black Queen said, and with her knife pointed at Ace, said, "Take off your hood."

"What for?" Ace said. "My hood is priceless to me."

"Take it off, or I'll slit your throat right here," The Black Queen said, putting the tip of the knife right on Ace's throat.

Ace did as he was told, being lower than the queen right now.

"Now turn into the man that always killed Spade," The Black Queen said.

"I don't know what good that will do, your highness—"

"Do it!" The Black Queen said.

"You know I'm only cooperating with you out of a kind of loyalty," Ace said. "You can't kill me."

"If I did it right, I could definitely kill you," The Black Queen said. "If I got angry enough, which I might soon."

Ace knew this was true. So, he turned into the man he'd looked like when he'd murdered Spade all of those times.

"I still don't get why I never killed you," The Black Queen said. "All those times."

"Circularity will do that," Ralph offered. "You get stuck on the same track, over and over again, like a neurotic."

157

"Good point," The Black Queen conceded. "If I see you here again, Ace, mark my words, I'll kill you."

"You know I'm higher than you, right?" Ace said.

"On occasion, yes. But right now, I've never seen you so low."

Ace knew she was right. There was no point disputing that.

"Now get out of here," The Black Queen said, pointing her knife at the door. "Get out of my sight or I'll kill you right here."

Ace put his hood back on, turned back into his old self, and smiled darkly. He knew this wasn't over. The Black Queen was loyal to Ralph, yes, that much was true: but he wasn't sure how much that loyalty could stop his designs.

Because what Ace knew was going to change things. He knew that Ralph was the key to The Machine. And if he dealt with Ralph, things would change. And for the better.

To solve or not to solve, that was the question. And Ace was going to solve this problem. It would take some figuring out, because The Black Queen was determined ... but Ace had committed crimes in the past, and he believed that in all actuality, he was just getting started.

The Machinating Machine and the Machine Never Mashed

The Black Queen and Ralph were all decked out in their plan, like a successful pack of cards. Granted, things were a little uncomfortable, what with the advent of Ace's betrayal, but The Black Queen still had this.

The top secret, high profile plan was for The Black Queen to turn into a cellular phone, and for Ralph to drop it into Spencer's jacket pocket in a covert mission. Once Spencer went inside where The Machine was, she'd destroy The Machine with a baseball bat. It would work, because she would transform into the phone while holding the bat, and then when she transformed into The Black Queen again, she'd have the bat. It would work perfectly.

All they needed to do was find Spencer.

And they found him, all right. Ralph knew where he had lunch, before he went back to his precious Machine.

They just needed to wait for the opportune moment to drop the phone in Spencer's jacket pocket.

The Black Queen and Ralph were hiding in a corner, looking out at Spencer, who was eating outside, oblivious of the trouble that lay ahead.

"You think this is going to work?" Ralph asked suspiciously.

"I think it's the only plan we have, right now," The Black Queen said. "Meaning, it better work. Because if it doesn't, there's going to be hell to pay."

"All right, well … turn into the cellular phone, and I'll do the deed. I suppose, call me if you need anything," Ralph joked.

The Black Queen didn't say anything, just transformed into the black cellular phone. Ralph picked up The Black Queen, and The Black Queen couldn't deny that being held in Ralph's hand was like holding his hand for real. If only they could be together …

As the cellular phone, The Black Queen could still think and feel, and hear and somehow see everything that was going on around her. It was a strange effect, but it worked, so nothing else really mattered.

Ralph approached Spencer and when Spencer stood up, brushed passed him and slipped The Black Queen safe and sound inside the jacket pocket.

Mission accomplished.

Or so The Black Queen thought. Ralph had made some distance, when Spencer said, "Hey, wait a minute!"

The Black Queen felt fear; she felt very afraid. This wasn't good.

Ralph turned around. "What is it?" he asked, thankfully not suspiciously.

"Do I know you from somewhere?"

"No," Ralph said.

Spencer Grey stared at Ralph for a moment, and then he said, "Yeah. You're probably right: I don't know you."

Then Spencer went back to his business.

Whew. That was a close one. The Black Queen would have been wiping off sweat off her forehead if she'd been a human being right now.

Spencer finished his meal, which was pretty obnoxious. She could hear him chewing greedily, and it was a disturbing effect. Finally, however, he finished his meal, and then he went toward the building where they had The Machine.

The Black Queen thought the levels of clearance would never end. She realized that without this stealth operation, they never would have been able to get in themselves. She had lost count of how many doors they had to pass, had lost count of how many vault doors they needed to open, had lost count of all the floors and tunnels they had to traverse, all the passwords they had to put in, all the times the badge needed to be swiped … it was honestly endless.

But they finally arrived.

They were inside the room. The Black Queen could see The Machine. It was just like she had imagined. She couldn't wait to take the baseball bat to it and bludgeon it to death … mash the machinating machine, more like. Smash it like a dodgy fly, squash it like a pesky bug. She could already feel the revenge surging through her.

It was a small room, but that didn't matter. It was an irrelevant detail in the end … this was the end.

The Black Queen began to ring like crazy, and Spencer, clearly puzzled, picked up the phone and began to talk into it: "Hello?"

"This is The Black Queen," came a voice on the other end, and suddenly, The Black Queen was The Black Queen again, and was holding the baseball bat, and was standing right before Spencer Grey.

Before Spencer could do anything, she clonked him a good one on the head, to the point to where she saw the word, "Bonk!" float into the air. He collapsed on the ground with his tongue sticking out, in an awkward, folded position.

"That was easy," The Black Queen mused, and realized she had work to do.

She looked at The Machine, and said, "It's time for your doom."

"Great," The Machine said.

"Great?" The Black Queen was honestly confused.

"I want to be destroyed, if it doesn't mind you," The Machine said. "It's been my dream for ages."

"You *want* to be destroyed?" The Black Queen tried to process this, but her processor was slow and out of date, at least temporarily. She turned to the unconscious Spencer Grey, then looked at The Machine. "You're nothing like Spencer."

"I didn't choose to be created," The Machine said. "I didn't choose for Spencer to be my God, my Creator. Go ahead. Smash me to pieces."

The Black Queen, who thought this was too easy, waited a moment and looked at The Machine, and then said, "Just destroy you?"

"I won't be content until I'm just a pile of junk ready to sell to the scrapyard," The Machine said.

"I expected you to be scheming," The Black Queen said. "I expected you to be dark. I expected you to be trouble. But you're asking for it."

"That I am," The Machine said. "But I'd hurry before my programming kicks into gear, and then I machinate. It won't be pretty when that happens. My personality will be overrode, and I won't be conflicted, I'll be narcissistic."

"Right," The Black Queen said, and took a swing.

She thought she was going to hit the screen, but that wasn't what happened. She indeed hit a screen, but it was a different screen altogether, a screen that had appeared out of nowhere, and blocked The Black Queen like a wall. Then it disappeared.

"Told you," The Machine said. "Make it fast, you don't have a … whole … lot of … *time* …"

And that was when a shield covered The Machine. It was pink, and shaped like a globe.

The Black Queen was in trouble, and she knew it.

"I can override the alarms that will get everyone's attention for a little while, but not for long," The Machine said. "So destroy me, quick."

The Black Queen tried, but every time, hit the stupid shield.

"I can't," The Black Queen finally said. "It's impossible. You're protected from The Black Queen virus. You're safe."

"Well, don't give up, keep trying," The Machine said.

So The Black Queen did: she kept trying. But it was pointless. It was like hitting steel and expecting it to bend. If The Black Queen had been a superhero, it would have been easier, but she wasn't, so obviously, there was a problem.

"My shield's built solid," The Machine taunted, in a voice unlike her.

"You are machinating," The Black Queen said.

"Trying … not … to be … ha ha ha ha … you lose, you don't got this."

It was like two people in one. It was a strange effect. But it was working. It was getting The Black Queen to doubt if she could really do this.

"What's … going … on?" Spencer said.

The Black Queen turned around, saw Spencer, who must have still been seeing stars, trying to get up. The Black Queen quickly clonked him on the head again, and he passed out cold.

"The … sirens …" The Machine said. "If you don't … *watch out* …"

"I'm watching out as best I can."

"One flew over the cuckoo clock," The Machine said.

"You're malfunctioning," The Black Queen said.

"In an attempt to not get you in trouble!" The Machine shouted. "Once the sirens go off, you're in deep trouble. I can't make that any more clear."

"Well, what do you want me to do about it?" The Black Queen snapped.

"Just keep pounding away at the shield. It's got to crack eventually. I don't know when, or how, but it's got to."

The Black Queen paused a moment, took a deep breath. What with the impending alarms soon to go off, and the threat of Spencer waking up any moment to distract The Black Queen, and with the whole doubt in general about whether this could be completed, The Black Queen just wasn't sure. But she supposed it was better to try than to do nothing, so she continued to swing the bat, one swing after another, swing after swing, hoping that something would happen.

And that was when something did happen. A crack appeared on the shield.

"You see that? You're making progress," The Machine said. "I'm going … to call the sirens …"

The Black Queen thought it odd how The Machine could machinate and complement in the same comment. But she supposed it didn't matter. The poor Machine was conflicted, confused, caught between programming and its own soul's desires.

Because The Black Queen believed that The Machine had a soul.

Which put The Black Queen in doubt. Why was she destroying a good soul?

"Chop chop, I'm calling the police," The Machine taunted again.

The Black Queen awoke from her reverie, her intense moral dilemma. She began to pound the shield where the crack was, and that was when The Machine said, "Game over, you poor unfortunate soul," and sirens began to go off.

They were more than just sirens; they were more than just alarms. The Black Queen didn't know just what they were, but they were so shrill that The Black Queen thought her eardrums were going to burst. It distracted her a moment from doing what she needed to do, which was transform into a phone again and get near to Spencer, in the hope that if people came, they'd think the phone belonged to Spencer and would carry it out with him.

So The Black Queen did just that; she got near Spencer and transformed into a phone, and just in time, because at that moment, security guards came into the room, along with some other people, fancy top-secret and classified people.

A man in a crew cut and a suit with a serious look said, "The place has been breached. How is that possible? There's no one here."

"Yeah, but look at The Machine," came another man. "The Machine's shield's been hacked and cracked. Someone was here. But somehow, they disappeared."

The Black Queen hoped, prayed to God, that they didn't put it together, and realize the phone was out of place, the phone of which was The Black Queen.

"Breach, alert," The Machine continued to say, malfunctioning. "Breach, alert. Breach, alert."

"Why don't we have *cameras* in here?" came the man with the crew cut.

"We never saw a need," was the response. "Spencer always took care of it."

"Well, now we'll never know what happened in here," came the serious man. "Someone did a number on Spencer. Someone almost did a number on The Machine. We're going to need tighter security."

Great, The Black Queen thought. *I honestly thought what you had was enough.*

Regardless, they were screwed. They were never going to get it taken care of now. The machinating Machine, while unintentionally machinating, had machinated nonetheless, and was now never going to be mashed. Which was bad.

The Black Queen thought this couldn't be any worse, but thankfully, someone came and while two people were picking up Spencer, slipped The Black Queen into his jacket pocket.

Whew, again. Safe for now.

She just really hoped that it lasted. She had no idea where they were taking Spencer. She had no idea if they were going to figure out that The Black Queen was the intruder was the phone. Hopefully not, but … she wasn't getting her hopes up.

"Breach, alert," The Machine continued to say, as they carried Spencer out of the room. "Breach, alert …"

The "Fun" and the "Real" in the Funereal Funeral

Who put the "fun" in the funny funeral, who put the funny in the funerary funereal?

The Fool could not help but smile foolishly, as if in response to this unanswerable question, this irresolvable paradox.

Routine, rhythm, a sort of balance in the harmonies of the way things get done. The importance of tradition. You can't have a death without a funeral, especially a fun and fune-real one. It just wouldn't work, all the fumes.

Because that was exactly the problem with routine: it created a lack of routine. It broke things up, shook things up. It screwed things up, rather foolishly. Rather happily.

"We can't just dispose of The Suicide King ..." The Fool had said to the people that had literally thrown the corpse out of the castle, to rot on the lawn. The Fool said this with some Suicide King glamour, glitter. "That would be so, so very much unjust ..."

They had taken the matter to the new king. The Jack of Knives, the little knife boy. Instead of drummer boy. Instead of little boy. Instead of anything boy. The teenager with raging suicidal homicidal hormones, or so the story was probably going to unfold.

"I don't know what to do," The Jack of Knives admitted. "I shouldn't have killed him. I want to do something to at least make it right. Something. *Anything*. Please, guide me, Fool ... tell me what is right."

Foolish, smiling fool. Routine. Structure. The funny in the fun funereal, as though trying to become ethereal. As though trying to become unreal, though that wasn't going to happen, because things were a little more complicated than a little good-for-nothing *boy* trying to take over the kingdom. What little Jackie and his homicidal maniac mind didn't get was that The Suicide King kept Contorted Royal in check with all of his suicide. It showed the ability of sacrifice. It scaled back war, war, and more war. It scaled back war mongering, fear mongering, it scared back dictatorship, a cruel, cruel kingdom. What The Jack of Knives wanted was martyrdom. As for why, The Fool wasn't sure. But that was okay. What The Fool was sure of was that he was sure of nothing, and vice versa: he wasn't sure that he was sure of everything.

Putting the funny back in the funeral. The fun and real back in the funereal funeral. The rule of the funeral, of course.

But now everything was going to be blown half to hell, all the circularity, because The Black Queen had split for good from The Suicide King like a violent and bloody divorce, and now Contorted Royal was in shambles. Which was exactly what Contorted Royal needed! Without that, things wouldn't work so well. They wouldn't work at all, most likely. For how could they work, when things couldn't work? When you just needed to hail to the king, even if he wielded blades?

The Fool was smiling unhappily, foolishly.

Funeraloolishly.

"You want me to guide you?" The Fool said. "After you've successfully taken over the kingdom?"

The Jack of Knives nodded. "I need your help. I want to make something right. Anything right. Anything at all."

"You want to make it right?" replied The Fool. "Just kill him all over again."

"Excuse me?"

"Just royally mock him at a funeral. It'll make all the difference."

The Jack of Knives smiled slightly. "A funeral. Yes. We'll celebrate his passing from this world. We'll even have a procession. A funeral procession. We'll bury him in the finest graveyard. You're a genius."

"Only if you want it to go terribly wrong," The Fool said, which he knew it was going to, because The Fool found nothing real in the funereal, or nothing fun in the funeral. That was the whole point. They were boring procedures that didn't do anything, in the end, except break up everything, the flow of convention. Which was fine. Perhaps no different from the cracking of Death's Mirror, if there ever was such a thing.

The Jack of Knives must not have heard what The Fool said about things going wrong. Not to worry, he'd get the memo eventually. He couldn't escape triviality forever!

The Unfool smiled foolishly. The Fool smiled unfoolishly.

Ah, so infamous. What was soon going to happen. Trying to bring back the fun in something so serious as treason, murder, betrayal, agony, despair, violence, destruction … perhaps. Perhaps not. Perhaps so. Either ways, it would work the way The Fool wanted it to work. That was his evil design.

Okay, okay, he'd admit it probably wouldn't work. But that was fine.

They were at the funeral now. Walking down the steps of the castle. The casket was closed, and people were in mourning. People were weeping for the terrible loss that had occurred. It was a loss of exaggerated proportion. The Suicide King was fine … he was in suicidal Heaven. He'd finally succeeded in chipping away at society's sanity. Finally, so, finally. A long time coming. It was raining. They were weeping.

But of course, no one was really sad. The Fool saw right through it. They were just putting on a show ... a freak show. Putting on a sideshow to undo the carnivalesque. Did anyone really miss The Suicide King? Did anyone really miss cleaning up after his little messes? His bloodbath messes? The splashes of gore and violence?

No. Not really.

But The Fool did. He missed it because it spoke so much truth. So very much truth, what he couldn't pinpoint, being so foolish. But that was okay. It was what it was, as all was well that ended well.

The Fool wanted a modern day cheeseburger. Were there any places where he could get one around here? Maybe the tavern that The Jack of Knives frequented before he lost his innocence? Before The Dark Kid stumbled into high crime?

And where was Mordred?

Oh, would The Fool look at the time, it was time to go. He was very late, for his important ... *date*.

The date of which was sometime in the thirteenth century in a pseudo-medieval world that actually looked rather nice that way. Dressed up in adornments and finery. Dressed up in so much goodness. So much awesomeness. So much, so much, ah, just too much to take in. The Fool. So unfoolish. So Unfool to be the foolish one.

Would The Fool look at the time. He put out his foot while he was exaggerating his crying for The Suicide King (though some of it was real, he couldn't hide his foolish love for the king), and tripped one of the people carrying down the casket.

When the guy tripped, he dropped the casket. The casket slid down the stairs rather violently, bouncing, and then tipped over, and out popped the king! like a jack in the box.

Everyone began screaming. Running around like chickens without heads. Ah, a body! A dead, ugly, creepy body! With The Suicide King fatter than usual! Such a stunt, such a, such a *stunt*!

But that was The Fool for you. He was fool of himself.

The Suicide King's body bounced a little before it came to a complete plop stop. And that was as everybody, including the people who had held the casket, erupted into chaos. Ah, a dead body, what were they to do!

Awww, a dead body. How cute. The Fool could only grin in regal embarrassment. Ah, the good days of this line of work.

People needed to come back to center, but The Fool was laughing too much internally to be able to do that. Which was problematic, for a lot of reasons. And why was he thinking of Rousseau right now? He hated Rousseau, because he was an Enlightenment thinker, and had nothing to do with the beautiful lyric poems of the Middle Ages. He didn't have the verbal finesse of Chretien de Troy. Which was an odd assessment, even The Fool had to admit that. He'd never read anything by Rousseau. He had no reason to. The world was indeed anachronistic, but not so anachronistic that a fool would go seeking personal and intellectual understanding and enlightenment, for *understanding*. That was just plain foolish. And what did the Enlightenment know anyway, except for cramming reason down everyone's throats? At least the Middle Ages stood for ideas, which were long gone by the time you got to poor Ralph's era, of computerization and degradation.

And speaking of Ralph: he was missing out on the party.

People finally stopped running around in circles when they realized it was just a dead body. It didn't think, it didn't feel. It was just a mass, a mess, just a lump—it was just dead matter, dead weight, with no relevance to anything. So, they put the body of the once proud Suicide King back into the casket, and continued along with the procession.

The body was rotting faster than The Fool would have thought. That was okay. If he came back to life, he'd regenerate. If anything was right about Contorted Royal, it was that no one truly died.

The Fool really wanted a newspaper right now.

There once was a boy named Jack, of Knives, who didn't know what to strive for, just cut things up into little pieces like eating a pizza. That sounded good, too. That sounded very good in deed, in fact. But The Fool was watching his diet. And where exactly would he get a pizza around here anyway? People were too busy being superficial towards a lifeless lump, to never can tell, the Devil may care.

Continued, continued, along with the boring procedure. Procedure, as dry as the tick of a clock. But at least that blasted circularity wasn't driving everything up in the wall anymore. The

Fool had been aware of it, but only foolishly. He had never had the insight that Alice had had. And he'd rather liked it … but, he hadn't liked it. That was the key. That was the catch.

Circularity. Linearity. Triangularity.

Anyway.

Whatever everything. Whatever all. It was time to whatever the world.

The Fool gave his elegy to the fallen king: "It's a tragic day today, that this man died of war. He died of not the war of the self, which I want to say for sentimental effect, but real, homicidal war. All the battles he gave to us, amen. All the times he made us fight for our country, for no apparent reason. All for little old Contorted Royal. All for a whole lot of nothing. But I say, embrace the sword. Embrace the fallen man. It's a tragic day, for one and all, though at least none of us is late for our evening phone call. And what are we going to do about the *smell*? He smells so … so … I don't know the word for it. A nauseating stench, that will all let us remember someone who fell for all of us, amen. Amen, amen. And, a man."

The Jack of Knives then gave his speech, which was just as memorable: "I don't know what The Fool was talking about, but I personally knew The Suicide King, and his passing is very … very … *troubling*. All the times that I … that I …"

Uh, oh. Was it real emotion spilling through or was it false like a superficial society? The Fool who was pretending to be The Suicide King didn't know, and obviously neither did The Jack of Knives.

Goodness, what a day.

The Fool always wanted to be a poet. He often wanted to snort opiates or coke, not to get high, but to seek enlightenment. But alas, that wasn't his time. He was off a few centuries.

Smiling, like a foolish fool.

After the funeral, with The Suicide King safely tucked in the ground, The Jack of Knives approached The Fool.

"You won't tell anyone my secret, will you?" he said, and The Fool noticed that the boy's eyes were bloodshot. From worry. Perhaps from crying.

"Of course not, of course not, hmmm, hmmm, hummm," The Fool said. "It's all bubble gum in the end, I would say. Ho, hum. Don't worry, Jack of Knives, your secret is safe with me, sometimes that's the secret of Contorted Royal: there is no secret."

The Jack of Knives wiped off his sweating forehead.

"I hope to service you loud and clear," The Fool said.

"Me too," The Jack of Knives said, and they were in the courtroom now.

The Jack of Knives, still wearing his crown, sat on the throne. He smiled. It was a fake smile, a very fake smile, as fake as death, as fake as a corpse, or sadness at a fun funeral being real and funereal ... but it would do for a fool.

Revenge Is Sour

Revenge was sour. The Jack of Knives had often heard that revenge was sweet, but that was clearly a myth. The Jack of Knives could almost taste the revenge in his mouth, and it tasted like a bad green apple.

It tasted terrible. Revenge was supposed to be the cream of the crop, but it wasn't that at all. The Jack of Knives had finally gotten his revenge on The Suicide King, for all of the pointless tasks he put him through, but there was zero satisfaction. There was no happiness whatsoever, there was no hope for The Jack of Knives.

And it was making him angry. He'd already sent out soldiers to go fight Distorted Royal, a kingdom that was on the opposite side of the world they lived in. The Jack of Knives knew it was a bad decision; Distorted Royal had nothing that The Jack of Knives wanted. The Jack of Knives had just done it because he wanted to hurt, he wanted to murder. He wanted to make up for the emptiness that he felt from getting revenge by getting more revenge, even though it was more pointless homicide, but still.

And Mordred. The Jack of Knives knew Mordred was to blame, though he wasn't sure how. If the time came, The Jack of Knives was going to get revenge on Mordred. Hopefully it would teach him a lesson. You didn't just hand over kingdoms on a silver platter ... that just didn't work. As for why, The Jack of Knives wasn't sure, but all The Jack of Knives saw was revenge and murder and the color red. All he saw was destruction.

But not just homicidal destruction. The Jack of Knives was, amazingly, becoming suicidal. He knew it was because he had taken up The Suicide King's mantle, and no one truly could rule Contorted Royal without even the smallest taste for suicide.

But that taste was becoming an appetite, was becoming a feast, and royally rightfully so.

The Jack of Knives looked at the mirror, and saw blood dripping off his head. He was in the courtroom, thankfully alone, and he noticed that his head was bleeding. He pulled off his crown and realized why: the crown was sharp, it was like a crown of thorns being hammered into his head, and it was making him bleed, probably causing brain damage.

Except crazily enough, The Jack of Knives liked the way it looked. Gold looked good when it was splashed with blood. He could never explain the logic behind that, but that was what he felt. Maybe the blood represented all the blood that The Jack of Knives was spilling with his stupid and careless decisions. Maybe it represented his pain. Maybe, just maybe, it represented the chaos he felt.

The Jack of Knives put his crown back on, and more blood continued to drip. But it naturally wasn't just blood. It was pain, as well. So much pain. His head was hurting, so bad, the blood dripping off his head like water, the pain stabbing his brain like the sharpest knife.

The Jack of Knives began to pace the courtroom. He needed to talk to The Dark Kid. However, The Dark Kid wasn't talking to The Jack of Knives. He wouldn't explain why, but if The Jack of Knives was going to venture at a guess, it was because he wasn't sure he was on board with the chaos that The Jack of Knives was spilling. Some of it was probably acceptable to him, he was The Dark Kid after all, but The Dark Kid was still a kid, and he had limits.

And The Jack of Knives? Did he have no limits because he was finally realizing how hard it was to rule Contorted Royal, a place that was bent on contorting everything that a person cared about? That would indeed make sense, twisting one's dreams to contortion and distort it to insanity.

Insanity! That was the word that The Jack of Knives couldn't get out of his head. He wondered if he was going crazy. It would make sense, what with the brain damage from the crown. Going to war with Distorted Royal was a bad move and he'd done it anyway. How stupid was *that*? But he'd done it nonetheless, and his blood-lust still wasn't satiated.

And thoughts of suicide. So, so very powerful. Everywhere.

The Jack of Knives pulled out his knife and stared at the blade. How inviting it looked! How wonderful! Did he want to stab The Dark Kid or did he want to stab himself? He honestly wasn't sure. Did he want to stab Mordred or did he want to stab himself? He still honestly didn't know. He didn't know anything anymore. His mind was being distorted and contorted beyond recognition. This was honestly what it felt like to be a king? It felt horrible. Why had The Jack of Knives been so stupid with his ambition? Why hadn't he just settled for the servant life? It would have made his life easier.

Too late now. But honestly, The Jack of Knives was losing it. He took the knife and slowly began to stab his heart. He felt like The Suicide King, and that made him laugh maniacally.

So *this* was what it felt like? It felt ... *exquisite*. It felt like a snort of cocaine (even though The Jack of Knives had never done that before). He couldn't help but remove the knife from his heart like taking it out of a sheath and stabbing himself again. He did it again, and again, and then he decided to stab his head. He laughed crazily as he plunged in the knife, enjoying every sensation.

This was what it felt like to be The Suicide King. So that was why he was so suicidal. He had a kingdom to rule and he couldn't be soft. Why hadn't The Jack of Knives seen it before? He'd been so ambitious with his homicidal needs that he hadn't realized the benefits of suicide. But it felt so good ...

That was the trap. That was definitely the trap, he saw that now. Homicide and suicide were not the answer, neither of them.

But then, what was the answer? Revenge?

Yes. Revenge. That had to be the answer.

The Jack of Knives apologized to himself for his moment of weakness, and took out the knife from his brain. He began to heal, but he knew he'd still have scars.

Maybe The Jack of Knives was going to try and seduce The Black Queen ...

Another matter for another time.

But the urge … it was still very tempting. The Jack of Knives wanted to hurt himself. Cut off his hand, maybe. Slit his throat. He wouldn't die, which was the beauty of it, but …

And at that moment, Mordred came into the room. The doors flew open, and The Jack of Knives dropped his knife like he'd been caught in the act.

And boy, did that sound familiar …

"Having fun, Jack?" Mordred said.

"Fun?" The Jack of Knives echoed. "I was just …"

"Looks like you were self-indulging again," Mordred said.

"I wasn't doing anything except for preparing for war," The Jack of Knives said peremptorily.

"Really? And how is that going?"

"We're going to lose the battle with Distorted Royal, but that doesn't matter. And did I mention how sour revenge is?"

"What do you mean?" Mordred evaded.

The Jack of Knives saw this evasion, but wasn't sure what to do with it. So he just said, "I just mean … I shouldn't have gotten revenge on The Suicide King. His brain was altered from all the swords he stabbed within it, his brain chemistry slashed to pieces. That's why my mind is addled, because of my stabbing."

"Oh, so you've been *stabbing* yourself now?" Mordred taunted. "And how is that working?"

"Well, my crown is cutting into my head rather severely, but it actually feels kind of … nice. I feel special being so cut up and stabbed, though I can't explain why."

"Might it be because of your self-indulgent nature?"

"But I used to be humble!" The Jack of Knives said in a panic, and honestly right now, he wasn't thinking at all about getting revenge on Mordred. At least for the moment. He was desperately hoping that Mordred could save the day. He'd put The Jack of Knives on the throne, maybe he could save him as well.

"Do you feel like you've fallen from grace by ironically ascending to power?" Mordred asked curiously.

"Yes," The Jack of Knives said, and was amazed at how much he sounded like The Suicide King right now, just with a Jack of Knives twist. He was still murderous. He was in fact right now thinking of murdering Mordred. Just for fun.

Having Mordred executed, just for fun.

173

But The Jack of Knives held off on this for a moment. Mordred knew something. The Jack of Knives could see it in his eyes.

"Is there something you're not telling me, Mordred?" The Jack of Knives asked.

"No, not at all," Mordred said. "I'm just glad you're having so much fun ruling Contorted Royal."

Oh, the irony. The ironic words. The Jack of Knives noticed this, and it gave it all away.

The Jack of Knives had been set up. Mordred had known that The Jack of Knives would go batty if he tried to rule Contorted Royal. No one could rule Contorted Royal except for The Suicide King ... and now that he was gone, Contorted Royal was going to go down the drain. And that would be very problematic. Very much so.

The Jack of Knives had destroyed Contorted Royal by taking the crown! It was ironic, though, because The Jack of Knives hadn't wanted to destroy it, not like this at least. He thought destruction amounted to bloodshed, not Contorted Royal losing its head, the head of which was The Suicide King. Meaning people were going to go crazier, get more violent, which was exactly what The Jack of Knives had dreamed, but he hadn't realized it would lead to destruction. At least not like this.

But that had been Mordred's plan the whole time. Give The Jack of Knives what he wanted but in an ironic way. In a way that made no sense, only made sense in a place such as Contorted Royal.

Because what The Jack of Knives realized was that as he destroyed Contorted Royal, he'd destroy himself as well. Except he'd never die, unless someone like Mordred decided to finish him off. Maybe he'd enlist the help of The Dark Kid. Coerce The Dark Kid to become a ruler.

"Guards!" The Jack of Knives said.

Two guards came in.

Mordred only smiled. The Jack of Knives and Mordred looked each other in the eyes, and Mordred wasn't afraid. He'd gotten what he wanted: the destruction of Contorted Royal. All because of The Jack of Knives, who couldn't rule worth bananas.

He was slowly going to chip away at the sanity of The Jack of Knives. Or at least Contorted Royal was.

"Execute Mordred," The Jack of Knives said assertively. "He's a traitor."

"Isn't revenge sour?" Mordred said, but The Jack of Knives heard sweetness on the tongue. To Mordred, the revenge was sweet.

"I'd say so … guards! Execute him! Now!"

The guards proceeded to approach Mordred, but Mordred only smiled and pulled out a vial. It was obviously impacting enough to scare away the guards, who stepped back a little bit.

"This is poison," Mordred said. "If I drop it on the ground, we'll all be dead, because it will release a poisonous gas. Knowing my affinity for actually successfully killing … are you sure you want to test me, Jack?"

"Not really," The Jack of Knives admitted.

"So cruel of you, to execute the one who put you on the throne, and gave you everything you always wanted," Mordred said maliciously. "But if it makes you happy, then who am I to judge?"

"I'm not happy, thanks," The Jack of Knives said. "You've ruined me. You've ruined Contorted Royal. You knew I couldn't rule, and would lead Contorted Royal to its destruction. You know only The Suicide King had brains … somehow. Not sure how, but he did."

"Maybe I wanted Contorted Royal to tank, do what Ace failed to do with his circularity," Mordred said. "But that doesn't matter. Now, since you've been so ungrateful and thankless, Jack, I'm going to go on a vacation to an island. Go rest on the beach, you know?"

"I don't see how," The Jack of Knives said. "Your only weapon would just kill us all."

Mordred only smiled. "I got what I wanted. I'm therefore happy. Now I just watch as Contorted Royal contorts on itself, tying itself in unsolvable mind knots."

And then he drank the liquid.

He slowly began to shrink, until he no longer existed. The guards, who had been expecting poison, murder, *chaos*, hadn't done anything, but that didn't matter now. It was too late.

"Get out of here before I execute you all!" The Jack of Knives shouted, knowing it was useless.

The guards hastened to leave the room.

The Jack of Knives went to his throne and sat down. Goodness, what a day. Mordred had betrayed The Jack of Knives, made him forever stuck on the throne. Because there was no backing down. Only The Suicide King could save him.

But he was dead.

Revenge was sour; dreams were bogus.

It was all a lie.

You're in Trouble, Sonny

Death: the word that everybody hated. But wasn't death more of a living death? And wasn't life more a death-life? And wasn't everybody sort of death-like, when it all came down to it? So Gothic in their preoccupations with death and dying?

The agonizing over the truths, the ignorance of the bliss, but moments of beauty, moments of ecstasy. As if all people were suicidal and didn't know it. As if all people were suicidal without even realizing it. As if, as if, with The Suicide King just an example of everyone else, no different from anyone else.

Death, such a striking contrast between life, and yet the line so thin, and yet so blurred. And wasn't the boy in trouble? Didn't he need to have a time-out? Didn't he need to go to the corner and pout for his vicious crimes? Didn't he, didn't he? Or was The Suicide King in all actuality not quite sure, not quite sane? Would he ever be sure? Could he be sure, or could he just not be sure? Could he do anything at all except for stick a sword in his stomach? His heart? Did he have to obsess about violence so much because of a self-indulgent problem, as Brannon had hinted at?

Oh, that lucky, lucky boy. What did he know? He knew a few things, but he was foolish, in the end. Thankfully not a fool, but foolish … he was much too innocent to be a fool. There was a spark about the boy that wouldn't leave.

And there was a spark about The Jack of Knives that was also pretty powerful. Wasn't he only getting what he deserved? Wasn't everybody only getting what they deserved? Or was it all just chaos in a young teenager's mind? A teenager that was raging with homicidal hormones and didn't know where to put his knives?

He was in a hell of a lot of trouble, the sunny, for his violent escapades. But The Suicide King couldn't think about those things. He was death. He was dead. He wasn't Death, per se, but he was definitely dead, and definitely death. As for how it had happened, he wasn't sure. He had eaten something? Or drunk something? What had it been?

Oh well. At least The Suicide King had his grave to keep him happy. He did find it ironic though that the one thing that killed The Suicide King wasn't suicide. It was something else completely. It was homicide. One would squibble and squabble all day about whether The Suicide King meant to kill himself, but as far as The Suicide King was concerned, it was homicide, plain and simple. They led The Suicide King to his death trap. They were the ones that confused him half to hell. And he was gaining weight! So much weight, it was making him feel like a chubbo. Which didn't make him happy. It made him grumpy. Couldn't they see that their medication aka poison had made him gain weight? Now he had double chins. Now he had a fat gut. He already had before, kind of, but at least he wasn't so fat that he felt as though his casket was sinking slower and slower and lower and lower into the ground, eventually to get trapped and lost in oblivion.

But it wasn't The Suicide King's fault! He wasn't self indulgent, couldn't they see that? Why did everybody have to assume that all kings were bad? Couldn't they see the good in The Suicide King? Couldn't they see that he had a charm to him?

The Suicide King supposed not. He supposed that he was just a king who honestly didn't know what to do, didn't know how to fix his kingdom.

Why was he even thinking? Wasn't he supposed to be dead?

And, uh, wasn't he supposed to be alive? In a casket? Oh, for goodness sake, they buried him alive.

Except, he really was dead. His eyes were closed, and all he saw was a black abyss. So this was what death felt like. Well, it was awfully boring, laying here for all eternity and stinking up the coffin. Somehow he could still smell. That was strange.

But, everything was strange, we are all deranged. Or so Brannon would say.

The boy was kind of adorable. In a weird teenager sort of way. Was The Suicide King at least wearing his Sunday best for his perpetual death?

Death! Oh, the horror! It never ended, and, ah, it was horrifying!

But, it really was. Why couldn't The Suicide King think about happy things? Well, maybe because The Black Queen had taken a sledgehammer to The Suicide King's heart. Which was, naturally, awfully fragile. Not that The Suicide King was angry at her, of course, but he supposed his guilt over failing her had to manifest itself somehow.

What was wrong with Contorted Royal? Why did it have to be such a nightmare? Why couldn't everybody just be happy, and get along? Was that even part of the agenda? Or was it just ... self-indulgence?

Brannon was blue, what one king knew.

The Suicide King was at his wit's end. He'd been through this routine so much, that it was driving him crazy. Death, life, death, life, death. It never ended, the alternation. But could there ever be a permanent death? The Suicide King certainly hoped not! But, wasn't that where he was?

Then, why was he thinking still? How was he thinking?

It didn't make sense, like his thoughts were being scrawled in blood on the wall in James Joycian stream of consciousness. With the sword as his pen.

Or, pin, to be more honest. Being a chubbo and all, he could see everyone making fun of him for being so fat. Well, The Suicide King was a good guy, he was just a fool. A fool strutting his time in a casket, of all places. A fool getting nothing done. Just a fool. Just a dark, dark soul.

With The Suicide King deep in a hole.

Goodness, that Brannon boy had really left his indelible mark on The Suicide King's consciousness. Well, if it was any consolation to Brannon's hard effort, his hard work, it wasn't The Suicide King's fault that he'd actually died. That had been a complete accident and misunderstanding, as The Jack of Knives, that naughty naughty boy, would attest to. Though no one would listen to The Suicide King. The Jack of Knives was the king.

The Fool had once said that everyone was a genius, including The Fool. Which meant that everyone was a fool strutting about in caskets. The Suicide King saw some truth in that, and it was making him sad. A fool? A suicidal maniac? A schizophrenic? A slut? A worthless servant? We could go judging all day, but The Suicide King didn't like judging anyone but himself ... and hopefully, that was okay.

And The Suicide King had the verdict, because the verdict was in: The Suicide King was dead.

He'd been dead for a while, now, but now, he was *really* dead. And it wasn't any fun. It wasn't like dreaming at all, it was just darkness.

And that was when The Suicide King's eyes opened, just momentarily. He wasn't disoriented anymore. He wasn't just a stream of consciousness buried deep in the ground of language. He understood that he was literally in a casket, buried alive. Buried dead alive, to be more precise, but still.

It was The Jack of Knives. That bratty, bratty boy. The snot-nosed dweeb. He was to blame. That thankless s.o.b.

Oh, you caught The Suicide King. He was judging.

If he'd been alive and awake long enough, he would have stabbed himself in the brain for thinking that, the problem being that he wasn't awake long enough, and he couldn't really move in this limiting casket.

Had anybody even seen beauty in The Suicide King when he gracelessly fell out of the casket? No, all they saw was fatness.

Jerks.

That dang judging ...

But anyway, The Suicide King was awake long enough to be fully aware that Mordred and his Dark Kid and The Jack of Knives had betrayed him. But really, it was The Jack of Knives who needed an ass-whipping, and so The Suicide King said, in his mischievous and bubbly voice, as though his voice was rising from the sound waves of his throat, "You're in trouble, sonny."

And then The Suicide King died again. It was a sad day, for everyone.

No, who was he kidding. Nobody cared.

179

There once was a time where The Black Queen would have been at The Suicide King's side had anything happened to him. Now she wasn't even aware of his death, being all enraptured by Ralph and all, his chivalry, and having a blast in the modern world. But, The Suicide King didn't blame her. He'd alienated her by the way he'd dealt with his problems. There was only so much empathy a person could feel … The Black Queen had just burnt out by the time The Suicide King stabbed himself the eightieth time. Or was it the nine millionth? Still.

Maybe even the first time. The Suicide King believed, now, that he'd been much too suicidal, like a drug addict. He'd thus taken it for granted, how horrible a thing it was!

But what did it matter, anyway. Life was a satire.

The Suicide King wanted a good classic novel. He once went to the unpsychiatrist's library, and was pretty disappointed with the boring, dry books he had in his office. Books on the happiness of depression. Books on the path forged from psychopathology. But there had been a copy of *Catch 22*. That had been anachronistic and random and unfitting for the whacky-mind climate of the library, all drenched in psychological and neurobiological decadence and depravity, but The Suicide King had kidnapped that book and read it. He didn't consider it "great literature" because it wasn't Victorian in style, but he did consider it literature because it was a great book, with tremendous ironies.

A little after that The Suicide King had started to dream of Ralph. He would carry that book with him everywhere he went with The Black Queen. In his heart, though. For some reason, he didn't do it literally, that was, carry the book with him. But, that was the boy's favorite book, he just didn't tell people, for some odd reason.

Any book would be good, though. Any book at all.

Yes, yes, it was true. The Suicide King was a fool. He was an ignorant, good-for-nothing fatty. But you know what? He was darned proud to be that fool, and he was honestly just doing his best. Even if he was bloody, at least he never hurt anyone. He hurt his wife, by alienating her, but that had just been a terrible, unfortunate accident, trivial slapstick at best.

Hopefully there was light at the end of the tunnel …

And, The Suicide King was finally dead. After all of these years.

But he wasn't ready to give up yet. He only liked flirting with suicide, not actually committing it, or committing to it. And it was suicide if he didn't get out of this grave.

They had buried the sword next to The Suicide King. He woke up, suddenly, like from a bad dream, a nightmare of bad taste. He was able to grab it, somehow, in the cramped coffin, and that was when his mischievous anger hit. The Jack of Knives had betrayed him. In all actuality, The Jack of Knives had been a traitor. And that wasn't okay.

It was boiling inside The Suicide King. He felt it threaten to boil over. He had to get out of here.

So he literally burst through his casket and out of the ground, and landed on solid ground with his sword in front of him, saying, "You're in a hell of a lot of trouble, sonny!" to The Jack of Knives.

He was going to get it, that boy was going to get it all.

But it wouldn't be the way he expected it. It would be revenge without the revenge. The Suicide King had different designs in mind, what could be described almost as countercultural plans. The things he wanted to do were controversial, but it would hopefully set something in motion that would wreak chaos. The world as everyone knew it would collapse.

The Jack of Knives was right to be homicidal, though not for the reasons he was thinking, such as revenge. He was right because everyone was homicidal, even a suicidal maniac. Just like everyone was a fool and genius, all at the same time.

Just as all were idiots.

"You're in trouble, sonny," The Suicide King said, and felt happy at his plan. He was finally going to be manipulative. That's how he'd get back at The Jack of Knives. Only make the boy *think* that The Suicide King cared about him.

Which he did, but he couldn't show that in these desperate times. These desperate times called for desperate measures. It was time.

The Jack of Knives was doomed …

Contorted Royale

The Jack of Knives was still very unhappy with things. And he supposed, he had every right, every reason to be. Nothing was fun about being a king. Nothing in the slightest. In fact, The Jack of Knives right now was very bored, and tempted to start a war with another land, while simultaneously stabbing himself.

But he didn't want to stab himself. He needed to repent of his ways. He needed to see the light. But, there was no light. Everything was dark.

The Jack of Knives could honestly admit that the only way that The Jack of Knives could be saved from the kingdom was if The Suicide King came back to life. Like that would ever happen. If anyone knew how to do that, it was Mordred, but Mordred had disappeared. Nowhere to be found. The Jack of Knives had sent out a search party to search islands, but there was no luck.

Which wasn't all that surprising. Mordred was a cold-blooded traitor. The traitor. Making everything so difficult.

The Jack of Knives was sitting on his throne. How glorious it would be if he could pick up his throne and throw it against the wall, or throw it against the mirror to let it shatter. That would be amazing. But The Jack of Knives wasn't going to do it because he needed the throne, it was part of proper kingship decorum.

But that didn't mean he wasn't tempted to do so, of course. Because, he was.

And that was when he couldn't take it anymore. He grabbed his knife, and was about to stab himself or stab the next unfortunate person that came into the courtroom, when the door flew open, and in stepped the last person that The Jack of Knives had expected to see.

It was The Suicide King. Except, he was hardly chubby, and he wasn't rotted. It was like he'd regenerated, and slipped back into a younger self. He looked … styling.

Devilish.

Handsome.

The Jack of Knives could see a plan in his eyes. He could see flames of direction, perhaps even destruction. He could see determination.

He was holding his sword, but he wasn't playing with it the way he usually did; usually, he would flirt with it in a suicidal way, but now he was holding it as if he wouldn't hesitate to chop off the head of The Jack of Knives.

"I had it wrong, I had it *so* wrong," The Suicide King said to The Jack of Knives. "We live in a Contorted *Royale*, not a Contorted Royal. There's a fine difference. Things are more twisted and homicidal in a contorted royale."

"What are you talking about?" The Jack of Knives wanted to say, but wasn't able to say anything, because he was still kind of surprised that The Suicide King was back. And there was something almost worthy about the king, that The Jack of Knives couldn't dispute.

"I believe you have something of mine," The Suicide King said.

The Jack of Knives felt his crown. He still didn't want to take it off, even though he knew it would mean that he'd be free of the burden of ruling Contorted Royal. But, he pulled it off anyway.

The Suicide King went up to The Jack of Knives and grabbed it, put it on and admired himself in the mirror. "It looks good, doesn't it?"

"How are you *alive*?" The Jack of Knives asked.

"Very good question," The Suicide King piped happily. "I'm not sure, but my guess is, because, do we ever really die? I think poor Mordred wasn't aware that we always live, despite popular belief. Now, are you going to get out of my throne, or do I need to order some people here to kill you for treason?"

The Jack of Knives stood up quickly, out of fear, and The Suicide King laughed in the face of The Jack of Knives. The Jack of Knives knew he was being mocked, but this was the king, so it would be wise not to say anything.

"I've been sleeping in a casket for God knows how long," The Suicide King said. "Therefore, why would I sit down and constrain myself. But you're in a hell of a lot of trouble, sonny."

The Jack of Knives knew this was coming. He said, as bravely as possible, after swallowing hard, "What do you want to do with me?"

"Why, I want to get revenge, of course," The Suicide King said, and turned around, still playing with his sword, but not flirting with it like he wanted to kill himself.

Something had changed about The Suicide King. He seemed to have a will of his own, a will to power. The Jack of Knives couldn't help but wonder if death had actually been good for The Suicide King, like a cure, even if it was only temporary.

"In what way?" The Jack of Knives asked.

"You're in trouble, sonny," The Suicide King said.

"Why do you keep calling me *sonny*?" The Jack of Knives wanted to hiss, but said cordially instead.

"Isn't it obvious?" The Suicide King said, turning to face The Jack of Knives. "We live in a Contorted Royale, a contorted family. Our family is more bent out of shape than a rubber band ball. It's like we've all committed incest with each other."

"*Family*?" The Jack of Knives said. He was honestly confused.

"Oh, it's a dreadful secret," The Suicide King said. "I still feel bad for doing it to this day. But, it was a different time then. I was once a very proud and angry and tyrannical king … and, less chubby."

The Suicide King then twirled his mustache, waiting for The Jack of Knives to respond. But The Jack of Knives couldn't respond. He had no idea what to say. Family? What was he talking about?

"You're my son, Jack," The Suicide King said. "You're the son of The Black Queen. You are in trouble, Jack, because you killed your own father. I'm still trying to process all of the emotion. It's rather painful, by the way."

The Jack of Knives tried to absorb this information. He honestly wasn't sure how to. But it was indeed a Contorted Royale. The Jack of Knives could see it. A distorted family.

"It was a dreadful joke gone wrong," The Suicide King said. "I was hoping to reveal to The Black Queen the truth eventually, but never worked up the courage, because you were being so humbled by your work and your hard and unfair upbringing. You looked beautiful as a slave."

The Jack of Knives could have commented on the injustice of this, that he only looked beautiful as a poor slave, a servant boy. But he just continued to listen, fascinated.

"When The Black Queen had you, I told her that you were illegitimate. I told her that because I was angry at her for cheating so many times on me, with other more handsome and attractive males. It was making me sad, too, and suicidal. But in a fit of rage I told her that you were illegitimate, and that if the queen wanted to keep her honor, she had to distance herself from you, or the kingdom would find out. So, we decided to make you a servant. The thing was, you were always my son, or I suppose I should say, *our* son ... wherever that blasted Black Queen is."

The Jack of Knives couldn't believe all he was hearing. He had already been, legitimately, the heir to the throne. But he didn't want the throne, which was why this was even more ironic. Regardless, The Suicide King was his father, and The Black Queen his mother.

And he honestly didn't know how to process this information.

The Suicide King just stared at his son, and finally said, "Well, say something."

"It was a dirty trick," The Jack of Knives finally responded, taking out his knife and picking at the tip of it. He wanted to kill The Suicide King all over again.

"Yes, it was, but I didn't mean for it to go so terribly wrong," The Suicide King said. "I really didn't. I would have rescued you from slavery the moment time permitted. You were, after all, still my baby boy. But it was The Black Queen and her blasted designs! If she hadn't made me so jealous with her infidelity, I would have had no reason to take it out on my only son. I still seethe with anger at her designs, her wicked plans. She reminds me sometimes of Maleficent, just in a different way."

The two were silent for a moment, with The Jack of Knives still trying to process all of this. Then The Jack of Knives finally said, "But now the secret's out, and I'm not sure why."

"Well, you'd have to know if we were going to get revenge on The Black Queen for all she's done," The Suicide King said. "It's her own fault you were a slave, and were so low in our terrible class system."

185

"Revenge on The Black Queen?" The Jack of Knives said. "But, she's still my mother. What if I don't want to get revenge?"

In a sudden paroxysm, The Suicide King took his sword and put the tip lightning quick at the front of the throat of The Jack of Knives. The Jack of Knives gulped. If the blade tip had been even a fraction closer, The Jack of Knives would have had his throat cut. Any more than that and his throat would be slit.

"I'll kill you for treason," The Suicide King said threateningly, point-blank, blunt.

The Jack of Knives could see his options, now, that, there really was no option. The king was being a tyrant. There was no option for The Jack of Knives.

"Okay," The Jack of Knives said quietly, and was amazed at how homicidal The Suicide King could be when he wanted to be. That was why his alter ego self was The Homicide King, of course. He could be quite a murderer, if he wanted.

But this wasn't that surprising. Roles were getting muddied. The Jack of Knives had never dreamed of being suicidal, and he had been while on his short stint on the throne. And The Suicide King looked as though he could care less about hurting himself. Goodness, how things could change.

The Suicide King nodded, and moved the sword away from The Jack of Knives. He said, "Excellent. So you're on board, Jack?"

"I think so," The Jack of Knives said. "What's the plan?"

The Suicide King continued to play with his sword, and then said, "Oh, we do what Contorted Royales always do: we play a prank on the queen."

"What if it goes wrong?" The Jack of Knives asked.

"That's the whole point," The Suicide King said matter-of-factly. "It *must* go wrong. If it doesn't, the whole thing would have been completely pointless. So, I'm letting you know ahead of time: the prank we're going to play on The Black Queen is going to go terribly wrong. In fact, it really won't even be a prank, it may as well just be called straight-up murder. Are you ready for it, Jack?"

"I suppose so, father," The Jack of Knives said, amazed he called The Suicide King his father.

"I hope you see why I'm doing this," The Suicide King said. "Our family has been falling apart from the beginning.

There's really no other way to restore everything back to its proper place, after we've all fallen so much. Therefore, we contort."

"I hope you know what you're doing," The Jack of Knives said.

"So you're definitely on board?"

"Yes."

"Knowing very well this prank will go terribly wrong, that you might end up killing your own mother?"

"*Yes*," The Jack of Knives said, almost eager.

"You know I'm manipulating you, right?" The Suicide king said, offhand. "I'm also getting revenge on you."

"And how is that?"

"You'll just have to see," The Suicide King said secretively. "But it doesn't matter. You're manipulated, and you're willing to do all I tell you. So like the relationship of the slave and his king, a father and his son. This is going to be so much fun."

The Jack of Knives continued to take all of this in, and he pulled out his knife, while The Suicide King pulled out a playing card. A sharp one.

"So, we're all together in this," The Suicide King said.

"Sounds good to me," The Jack of Knives said, knowing this could go very wrong but not caring, knowing The Suicide King was using him but caring less.

"Good," The Suicide King said.

"Yes, great," The Jack of Knives said, and the two threw their weapons at the wall, the weapons of which stuck in the wall. It signed their wicked pact, like a contract.

"We'll get started immediately," The Suicide King said, and taking his sword, left the courtroom.

The Jack of Knives just felt confusion. Confusion in this Contorted Royale.

The Close Up

The Suicide King was *it*. He was all that and a bag of chips. He felt the murder swimming through his veins. He had a new-found cause, which was destruction and chaos outside of suicide. And it was all because of The Jack of Knives. The Jack of Knives had plunged The Suicide King into an existential crisis, and he knew now the way he needed to be.

The Jack of Knives and The Suicide King had found their way to the modern world, and were looking at The Black Queen and Ralph from across the street with binoculars.

"So *he's* the one who's been seducing my wife," The Suicide King said maliciously, obviously referring to Ralph. "The little bugger. He'll pay."

The Jack of Knives responded by not responding.

"You ready to make our move?" The Suicide King asked The Jack of Knives.

The Jack of Knives nodded.

The two set out across the street after making sure the coast was clear, and The Suicide King happily approached his wife and her new lover.

They were in the middle of talking, The Black Queen saying, "I'm so glad this didn't go worse, that you were able to get me. You can't do much when you're a phone."

"It was easy," Ralph said. "It's a shame The Machine wasn't destroyed, though. I think you could have had it."

And right when The Black Queen was going to respond, she saw The Suicide King smiling at her exaggeratedly.

"Honey," The Black Queen said. "What are you doing here?"

"Very good question," The Suicide King said. "I suppose I could ask you the same thing."

"I was just … it's a long story," The Black Queen said, clearly intimidated.

Meaning that The Suicide King's new-found masculinity was working.

"I guess you were getting your rocks off with your new lover," The Suicide King said spitefully, but with a trace of glee.

"No, we were just—"

Before The Black Queen could say anything, The Jack of Knives put a knife on Ralph's throat, and The Suicide King put a black bag over The Black Queen's head.

"Get out of here," The Jack of Knives said to Ralph. "Get out before you become toast."

And The Jack of Knives then pushed Ralph onto the ground.

Ralph stood up, and looked at The Black Queen. "What are you going to do with her?"

"Tisn't any of your concern," The Suicide King said, having to struggle a little with The Black Queen but keeping her controlled. "Go talk to Alice or something. We have no use for you here."

Ralph nodded, and then slowly began to leave, until he was finally gone.

"Such a charming boy," The Suicide King said. "Left you alone and everything. Sound familiar?"

"I wasn't trying to *leave* you, you misogynistic brute," The Black Queen said under the bag. "I was just having adventures."

"Well, we can discuss that at your trial," The Suicide King said, and suddenly, they were at the top of a building.

The Suicide King removed the bag from The Black Queen's head. The Black Queen tried to slap The Suicide King, but The Suicide King was ready: he grabbed her hand. The Jack of Knives kept a knife at The Black Queen's back, while The Suicide King began to talk to his wife.

"So, how many boys have you gotten it off with by now?" The Suicide King said.

"Not many," The Black Queen said in response.

"Well, certainly more than me," The Suicide King said. "But not anymore. It's time I step up my manliness. I'm going to kill you, and then I'm going to cheat on your memory. I was thinking about cheating with that hot girl down there," The Suicide King said, pointing to a lady sitting at an outside table, eating a sandwich, oblivious of the explosive family drama taking place above her.

"Do it," The Black Queen said. "It's rather inviting. But don't kill me."

"Do you know why I want to kill you?" The Suicide King said. "It's not because I'm angry at you for cheating, because I think that's inevitable. Feelings always get hurt in marriages. You know the real reasons? It's because you wanted me to be more macho, to have more machismo. I wasn't starting enough wars to impress my wife, I wasn't a royal pain. Well, you're getting what

189

you wanted. What better way to be manly than for the weak man to murder his own wife? Sounds good to me, if you don't mind me saying so. Jack: push the knife in a little closer to your mother."

The Jack of Knives obeyed, and The Black Queen cried, "Ouch," and then, "*You told him?*"

"Of course I told him. And your little demon seed has already succeeded in killing the king. And if you want my honest opinion, I'm afraid of the Oedipus complex coming into gear."

"What do you mean?" The Black Queen asked.

"Well, I have to kill you so that way our son can't marry you after murdering me."

"I don't feel that way," The Jack of Knives said indignantly.

"Shut up, son," The Suicide King said. "Just hold the knife to your mother and be a good boy." The Suicide King looked at The Black Queen, who was looking down. "But you see my concern? There are many reasons why it's justified that I murder you, and the best part is it doesn't need to be justified. I'm the king."

"I just wanted my independence," The Black Queen said.

"Well, I hate to break it to you, but you aren't Queen Elizabeth," The Suicide King said. "Unfortunately for you. I was going to kill Ralph, but he really loves Alice, and I didn't want to destroy that tender romance."

The Suicide King then began to move The Black Queen, who was struggling, toward the lip of the building, where she was soon going to fall over.

"You're going to kill me, for real," The Black Queen said.

"Oh relax, honey," The Suicide King said. "I'm just teaching you a lesson. I'm showing you I'm not all about stabbing my brains … but I may be about stabbing *your* brains. Maybe you can screw death when you die, I don't know. If it makes you happy."

"You misogynistic little …" The Black Queen began, but didn't have enough time to say anything else, because then The Suicide King pushed her over the edge, and The Black Queen screamed all the way down to the ground, her voice dropping like a pin as she fell, until she finally landed with a resounding *thud*.

"Mission accomplished," The Suicide King said, smiling at The Jack of Knives.

***

The Black Queen remembered falling. She remembered dying. She remembered The Suicide King mad with revenge, she remembered her son betraying her. She remembered all of these things.

And yet, she couldn't remember these things. It was a very strange effect, but existent nonetheless.

The Black Queen was lying on the ground, dead, her heart stopped, her body smashed from the impact with the ground, many bones broken and bleeding, but somehow, she heard everybody around her, taking pictures and gasping in surprise.

The Black Queen was late for her close up.

It was The Suicide King. She was going to kill him. Now the game was on, the little bugger.

The Black Queen had been dead for five minutes. But after those five minutes passed, she put out her arms like a zombie and slowly arose from the ground.

Everybody around her screamed, but many were fascinated.

"She came back to life!" someone shouted. "No way!"

The Black Queen just looked around. Her mangled body was healing some, and she knew it would heal soon enough completely. She had come back to life, even in the Bronx, a modern day setting.

But she was still a little contorted, her body, that was. And in a way, she was a zombie.

The Black Queen was late for her close up.

Suddenly, three vans from three different news stations appeared. They approached The Black Queen and began asking her questions, but mostly showing how amazed they were that she had come back to life.

"I'm late for my close up," The Black Queen said, and blinked her eyes melodramatically. Then she began screaming at the newscasters for being so slow on this story. They should have been here the moment The Black Queen came to the Bronx, to see that a pseudo-medieval drama queen was there.

191

So the close-up was what they did. They took many pictures of her, and got the camera up nice and close.

"How does it feel that you survived death?" one of the news reporters asked.

"It feels wonderful," The Black Queen said, basking in all of the attention. "I feel like a brand new zombie."

Other random people were taking pictures as well. One person had in fact caught the whole thing on videotape, and not just the fall, but The Black Queen's struggle with The Suicide King up on top of the building, etc. etc. The video was quickly confiscated as an important news document.

"In my world," The Black Queen said, "murder is normal, though I'm surprised it took so long for my husband to take the leap. He'd been so busy skewering his mind instead of screwing around that he'd forgotten about me. But that's okay. I'm going to kill him in return. I may even kill my son."

"Your world is very twisted," came a news reporter.

"Well, that's all just the tip of the iceberg," The Black Queen said. "We're just getting started. Now, I'm late for my close up!"

The cameras got closer, and The Black Queen posed and smiled and looked like a fashionable beauty queen. She had finally completely healed, no longer looked like she had just died by falling off a building, and everyone was amazed at this.

"You are more famous than an actor," a spectator said.

The Paparazzi showed up next. They began taking pictures of the aftermath, of The Black Queen who was a beauty queen, a real life woman who had just cheated death by coming back to life somehow. The news reporters continued to ask The Black Queen questions.

"So why does violence characterize your understanding? The Suicide King, from what we've gathered, came here just to murder you, even though he comes from a faraway land in a faraway universe. Was it greed that caused him to do it?"

"It was jealousy," The Black Queen said, and then: "Get the cameras closer!"

The reporters obeyed.

"It was jealousy, indeed," The Black Queen continued. "He didn't like that I had such a nice relationship with a sweet young boy who has completely disappeared, showing me that he really didn't care about me at all. And I suppose, why should he care about me? I'm just an ugly old Black Queen. I don't know anything. I'm fat. I'm old. But that's fine with me. There are plenty of other boys. Get the cameras … *closer*!"

"The Black Queen is late for her close up," said one of the news reporters, and they brought the cameras that much closer.

The Black Queen smiled, continued to pose. "I love being a drama queen. I cheated on my husband to eventually turn him into a psychopathic murderer. That was my plan the entire time. But that's the way it is. It's our Contorted Royal. My own son turned against me, as you now know from the videotape, courtesy of the man you just arrested for the fun of it."

The man just nodded as the police officer put him in the police cruiser.

"It's a mad, mad world we live in," The Black Queen said, "but I've come back to life like a demonic Christ, and I feel very good. And there ain't nothing you can do about that. Nothing at all. I'm The Black Queen. I rule everything. I'm still late for my close up, but what do I care? You all worship me. I represent your glamorous society. We could turn the life of Contorted Royal into a reality television show, if you wanted."

Some murmurs of agreement, like this was a good idea.

The Black Queen looked at her wrist, which had no watch, and said, "Oh, would you look at the time. I need to go find my lover boy Ralph."

And then The Black Queen left the scene, leaving the news reporters and Paparazzi and all of The Black Queen's fans puzzled and confused as to why The Black Queen was late for her close up.

Alice in Death's Mirror Land and Through the Crazy Glass

Alice was walking when she saw Ralph approaching her. He had his head down, and so he hadn't seen her. Alice hesitated before catching his attention, but finally did.

Ralph lifted up his head, and then smiled. "Alice."

"Hey," Alice said. "How are you doing?"

"I'm not sure," Ralph said. "It's The Black Queen. The Suicide King and Jack of Knives abducted her. I'm not sure what to do."

Alice wasn't sure what to do, either. And yet, she did know: she would wait until fate cooperated and reunited them together again. In the meantime, they needed to destroy The Machine.

Alice said this, and Ralph looked distracted for a moment. But then he nodded his head in agreement, said, "Yeah, yeah. You're right. We basically ditched you when you were separated, it would only be fair."

And then before Alice knew what was going on, Ralph moved toward Alice and kissed her gently on the lips.

Alice kissed back, and they stayed this way for a moment. Then they broke apart.

"We have a lot we need to do," Ralph said. "We can make out later."

"Agreed," Alice said. "So what's the plan, exactly?"

"Well, we have to abduct Spencer Grey. If we abduct him, he can take us to The Machine safely, and then we can destroy it. I know how we can find Spencer. He'll be coming near us soon enough, and that's when we'll need to strike."

Alice nodded, and would have said something in response, but that was when things began to change, when she felt that she was going to go through Death's Mirror Land, go through the Crazy Glass. She couldn't explain why she felt this way, she just did, and it was freaking her out a little bit.

"Alice?" Ralph said. "You okay?"

"No," Alice wanted to say, "I'm not okay." But that wouldn't have done any good.

Suddenly, Ralph disappeared.

"Ralph?" Alice said.

Alice was still in the city, but Ralph was gone. Suddenly, there were mirrors everywhere, reflecting everything and reflecting each other.

And that was when Alice understood. If they destroyed The Machine, they were going to be screwed. They were going to be screwed because Death, who had manipulated Ace to make The Machine, would get revenge on Contorted Royal and release

Death's Mirror. She didn't know what Death's Mirror could do, but she knew it wasn't going to be pretty.

And Alice could see that something was going to happen to her. She wasn't sure what was going to happen, but she felt something was going to happen. Someone was going to try and betray her, and perhaps with success. It was a scary thought, but there nonetheless.

As Alice walked along the sidewalk, she looked at the mirrors reflecting her. Something was wrong with her reflection. She was composed of pieces, as though she had been shattered. It was a strange effect, like looking at your reflection in a broken mirror, but these mirrors weren't broken.

Alice continued to look in the mirror, and she watched as her image was slowly replaced with a brain. The brain was whole, completely fine, but that was when someone, probably Death, said, "You don't want to destroy The Machine. It will just make things worse."

Alice wanted to say something, but she didn't. She knew all of these mirrors were just hallucinations. They were elaborate hallucinations, nonetheless, but were just hallucinations, nonetheless. However, the prognostication side of it made a lot of sense as well, and Alice couldn't ignore that.

She continued to watch her brain, and watched as pieces of it slowly began to slough away, until the brain was just a pile of brain pieces, mere matter, completely unfunctional. It was kind of disturbing, she had to admit, and it made her sad.

Her brain was going to fall apart.

Alice told herself this was ridiculous, and continued to walk through the funhouse of mirrors. She heard laughing, and as she looked at the mirrors, she saw her reflection, and saw that it was her image, with *her* laughing. Alice was laughing at herself. It was a voice of Alice laughing at her and making fun of her. As for why, Alice honestly wasn't sure. But it was happening nonetheless.

Alice had had many strange things happen before. She'd had delusions lead her to bizarre behaviors, had had hallucinations cause her to act strange. But she'd always somehow managed to keep it under control. However, she feared that that was soon going to change, especially if The Machine was destroyed. She couldn't explain why, but felt that way nonetheless. Alice thought she was so tough controlling her illness, what her society saw as a gift. Well, that was great, that some saw it as a gift, like the distinguished members of the court, but it was also an illness. And it was going to cause a lot of problems soon enough. She felt it. And she wouldn't be able to stop it.

And these mirror hallucinations ... they were so elaborate.

Alice continued to walk beside the mirrors, not knowing where she was even going. She was hallucinating that she wasn't in a city anymore. She was in a dark room, but with light showing up occasionally, and with the blasted mirrors.

Alice had a strong urge to break one of the mirrors. She wasn't sure why. You couldn't break Death's Mirror, that would just make things worse. And yet, that was exactly what she did.

When she did that, her fist was bleeding, but she knew that was also only a hallucination. But she saw that a mirror shard was also stuck in her fist. She had punched the mirror, but the mirror was a hallucination, meaning the shard was a hallucination. And yet, it seemed so real. It felt so real. The pain that it created for her ... it seemed so real.

She slowly pulled out the shard, which had done quite a bit of damage, and that was when Death said, "Who would be a fool to mess with schizophrenia?"

"What do you want?" Alice said.

"I want you to cut this out," Death, if that was who he was, said. "You don't want to mess with what you're thinking."

"But all this is a hallucination. Meaning, none of it is real. Meaning, I'm not seeing and feeling things that are going to happen soon. That would mean my symptoms were overriding me, if I felt that way."

"Perhaps," Death said, and remained silent.

Alice continued to roam through the strange labyrinth of mirrors in this infinitely winding room, until she found a giant looking glass at the end.

It was the crazy glass. It would make her lose it.

And indeed, that was what Alice saw, in her reflection. She saw someone who had completely flipped their lid. She saw eyes bloodshot and wide and staring, she saw panic, she saw anxiety, she saw full-blown schizophrenia at its worst. The Alice before her was talking to herself, and she was seeing things, but things that Alice didn't see in the reflection.

And Alice knew that if she walked through this glass, she wouldn't be able to keep her illness in check anymore.

But she didn't have a choice. She sensed someone behind her, and so she turned, and that was when she saw Ace standing there. He smiled at her, even while wearing his hood, and then shoved her into the mirror.

She felt as though she was falling through shards of mirror, but also falling down a hole, falling forever, and her mind was spinning like a malfunctioning clock, the wheels turning to get stuck, and she saw things, things she couldn't explain, and then suddenly …

She was standing right before Ralph. Ralph was trying to shake her, and Alice said irritably, "Yes, yes, I'm here."

"You just took off," Ralph said, clearly concerned.

Alice registered this enough to say, "It's because I was hallucinating."

"I thought so," he said. "Are you okay?"

"They're going," Alice said. "At least, for now."

"What did you see?"

Alice didn't say anything for a moment, just tried to think about what she'd seen. It had all been very strange. All of it had indeed been strange. But it had been a warning.

"We can't destroy The Machine," Alice said. "If we do, it'll drive us all insane."

Ralph took this in, the shock on his face trying to mellow out but failing. "But that's our whole mission. We can't stop now. *That* would be insane."

"We need to," Alice said. "Otherwise, we'll never make it."

"But look at this world around us," Ralph said. "And the circularity in Contorted Royal."

"It may be better than what will happen with Death's Mirror," Alice said.

"Death's Mirror is a myth," Ralph said. "Alice, I know you have a gift of insight, but sometimes, you just hallucinate. It doesn't always have meaning."

"How can you say that, when you know me better than that?" Alice asked, feeling a little hurt at this.

"I didn't mean it to sound that way. I just mean, it isn't all you think it is."

"I just have a bad feeling about this," Alice said.

She felt frustrated. She'd seen firsthand that things would go wrong if they destroyed The Machine, but … what else were they supposed to do?

That was when Spencer Grey began to walk toward them. He didn't see them.

Ralph pointed out that Spencer was coming, and Alice nodded her head. "What's the plan?" she said.

"I'll handle it," Ralph said, and went toward Spencer, and punched him in the face, knocked his lights out. And Spencer had never seen it coming.

Suddenly, a car pulled up on the road, and Ralph began to drag Spencer's body toward the trunk. He opened it, and pushed the body in the trunk, and Alice, a little confused as to how this had all fallen into place, looked to see who was in the driver's seat.

It was The Black Queen.

She waved at Alice, and Alice waved back. Sometimes, the world was more mad than she was. Sometimes, things made less sense in real life than they did in her head.

Alice pointed out that this was a little random, but Ralph said, "What are you talking about? It worked perfectly."

"Did you know The Black Queen was going to come and help us abduct Spencer?" she asked.

"I had an inclination," he said.

No, he didn't have an inclination, they just got lucky because whoever the writer of their story was wanted to make the abduction of Spencer Grey as easy as possible, and have all the characters important in this phase be together. Alice could see that, but couldn't really do anything about it, and so she just got in the backseat.

Ralph got in the seat beside her.

"How was dying?" Ralph asked The Black Queen.

"It was wonderful. How was punching Spencer Grey?" The Black Queen asked.

"It was fun," Ralph said.

This reminded Alice of when she punched the mirror. For a moment, she saw the shard in her hand. Then it was gone.

She realized everything that was happening was, while a little strange, happening because she'd walked through the crazy glass. Nothing ever made sense once you went down that crazy rabbit hole. That was just the reality of it.

But no one would listen to her. No one would hear that they were being set up. No one at all. That, Death's Mirror Land was coming. Very, very soon.

And, that they were all going to go through the crazy glass. Just like schizophrenia was nothing to mess with, neither was Death's Mirror. Death was egging them on to destroy themselves. Maybe because he saw it as inevitable? Whatever the reason, things were going to go very wrong, very soon.

Very soon.

But Alice was just a schizophrenic, so why listen to her?

Cornered

Ralph, Alice, and The Black Queen were in the room with The Machine, along with Spencer Grey. They had managed to get past security because Spencer Grey didn't reveal that Ralph and company were intruders, which was frustrating for Ace. If Spencer had given up their identity, it wouldn't have required Ace to do the final and desperate trick up his sleeve.

They had knocked Spencer unconscious, and were talking amongst themselves about how to destroy The Machine. Since The Black Queen's last escapade with The Machine, they had installed cameras, but Spencer had disabled them.

They didn't have a plan. This wasn't all that surprising. The Machine was a tough nut to crack. They weren't going to be able to destroy The Machine in any quick swipe. It was going to take time, time of which they didn't have.

Ace had thought about drawing the attention of the staff members here, but decided against it. He could handle this himself.

He could handle it himself because he felt that he was higher than The Black Queen right now. Whereas before, he'd been lower, he was now sliding toward a higher position. He didn't know how long it was going to last, but knew that he definitely needed to take advantage of it while it was here.

They had no idea Ace was in the room because Ace was invisible. But he was listening to everything they were saying, scratching their heads and puzzling and trying to figure out a way to destroy The Machine. He was tempted to let them struggle with figuring out what to do, because part of him believed that they were never going to figure it out. But part of him didn't want to take that risk, because if they figured it out, there was going to be hell to pay.

Ralph was the key. Ace honestly wasn't sure how Ralph was the key, but Death had warned Ace that Ralph was the one who could destroy The Machine. As for how, that was a mystery, but Ace wasn't going to take any chances. He couldn't afford to blow this entire operation out of proportion, to destroy it without remorse.

Ace finally revealed himself. They didn't notice he was in the room, until he said, "Ahem."

They turned toward him, rather surprised. Ralph looked the most surprised. Ace knew why: Ralph must have known that this wasn't going to go well.

But then The Black Queen looked confident. "You know that I'm more powerful than you," she said. "You can't hurt any of us. We're safe. We're free from anything you could possibly dispense our way."

"Maybe," Ace said. "And maybe not."

The Black Queen only smiled. She was not intimidated. Blast The Black Queen. She always had to do this, didn't she, rain on Ace's parade? But Ace wasn't worried. Things were going to go very wrong, and soon. They were not destroying The Machine.

"What's your plan exactly?" The Black Queen asked, still amused. "You want to hurt Ralph, I'm sure."

"I don't want to just hurt Ralph," Ace said, "I want to kill him."

"And how do you propose doing that?" The Black Queen asked, and then told Ralph not to worry when he looked a little scared: everything was going to be okay.

"By stabbing him, of course, how else?" Ace said. "How else would it work? You guys are cornered."

"We aren't cornered," The Black Queen said. "We can walk outside this door any moment and run from you. Not that we will, of course, because we're here to destroy The Machine."

"You're cornered," Ace reiterated. "You're cornered because you'll only be able to destroy The Machine if you get through me, and like you said, I know you aren't leaving. You're stuck here."

The Black Queen conceded this point. But she said, "I'm still not worried. You won't be able to do anything to us."

The Machine piped up at this moment: "I don't know, you guys. I know your whole mission is to destroy me, but with Ace in the way, I'm not quite sure how well that's actually going to work."

The Black Queen looked confused, but Ace only smiled cruelly. Even The Machine could see where things were going. That was good.

"What do you mean?" The Black Queen asked.

"Ace is very powerful right now," The Machine said. "He's going to successfully destroy Ralph, who, as we all know, is the key to destroying me."

"But I don't want to die," Ralph said.

"Of course you don't want to die," The Black Queen said.

"I think we should all just take a deep breath," Alice said. "All of us should do breathing exercises, and remain calm."

The Machine said, "Alice, I know you mean well, but breathing exercises aren't going to do anything to stop what's going to happen soon. I can see the murderous intent in Ace's eyes, and I don't know how far he's going to go, I just know, far."

"Well, you can't murder me," The Black Queen said. "That would be treason. You can murder Ralph all you want, but me, you know why I'm safe. The Suicide King would be all up in your business if you so much as touched me."

"Thanks for your diehard and heartfelt protection," Ralph said miserably.

"Oh, honey," The Black Queen said. "Relax. The Black Queen is just figuring out what she's going to do."

"Well, you're running out of time," The Machine said.

Ace only smiled. This couldn't go anymore perfect. He had the three that he needed to destroy right with him.

He pulled out a knife, and began to slowly approach Ralph. "You know you need to die. You're the key to this, somehow. And we can't have you opening any doors now, Ralph."

And Ace made a swiping gesture toward Ralph, but that was when The Black Queen got in the way.

"My hero," Ralph said sarcastically.

"I'm trying to save your life, you ungrateful, snot-nosed brat," The Black Queen said stringently. "If you prefer, I can honestly let him kill you."

"He just doesn't think this is going to work, no offense to you," Alice said. "Ace is pretty powerful, after all. We can't pretend that he isn't."

"Thank you," Ace said. "For that, Alice, I may let you live."

Alice curtsied.

Ace tried to swipe his knife at Ralph again, but The Black Queen again got in his way. Soon, the two began to wrestle, with The Black Queen trying to get the knife out of Ace's hand. Ace just continued to do what he was doing, fighting, wrestling, until he finally had enough and pushed The Black Queen against the wall.

"Thank you, for getting out of the way," Ace said, and went toward Ralph, was about to stab him when The Machine said, "I don't know if I would do that."

Ace turned around in annoyance and looked at The Machine. "And why is that? Because you don't want to be destroyed?"

"Actually, she does want to be destroyed," Alice said. "It's not that."

"Then what is it?" Ace was actually a little confused. He had a feeling that this was a bad idea, but he couldn't explain why.

"Because The Black Queen will be enraged if you kill Ralph," The Machine said. "She's been trying to seduce Ralph for a while now, and The Black Queen never fails in her seductions. But if she fails to seduce Ralph because you murder him ..."

Ace took all of this in. It was certainly interesting to think about. But he was higher than The Black Queen now, and he was sure it would stay that way for a while. If Ace had to, he could flee

The Black Queen, make sure she never found him. As long as The Machine stayed functioning.

"The Machine has a point," The Black Queen said.

Ralph smiled at this, but it was slightly sardonic. "It would be kind of strange if The Black Queen didn't succeed in seducing me, when she's usually so successful," he said.

Alice slapped Ralph on the shoulder. "Don't flirt with her."

"I'm sorry, Alice," Ralph said, but he was genuinely amused, and Ace could see that.

He had to admit, killing Ralph was going to be very hard. Ralph was a good-looking boy, with good principles, and these two girls were crazy about him. It would be unjust to disfigure in death someone so beautiful and worthy and chivalrous.

"I see your point," Ace said to The Machine, "but I'm not worried about the repercussions. I'm on strict orders from Death himself."

"Death doesn't know anything," The Black Queen said.

"And how would you know that?" Ace asked.

"He just doesn't," The Black Queen continued. "He tries to scare everyone with his invisible evil, but it really doesn't scare anyone."

"Whatever you say," Ace said, and had his mind made up at this moment: he took his knife, holding it rather tightly, and lunged toward Ralph.

What happened next happened in slow motion: The Black Queen cried, "*Noooo!*" and tried to get in the way of Ace, but it was too late. The knife plunged into Ralph's heart, and he fell to the ground with his new open wound.

Ralph was holding his heart, but it was doing little good. His heart was pouring blood. He was crying out in agony, and his eyes were watering almost as much as his wound.

"How could you?" The Black Queen said.

"I'm just doing my duty," Ace said. "You have a problem with it, you can take it up with Death. Maybe Death will bring Ralph back to life, if he's ever in the mood to be paradoxical."

The Black Queen began to slap Ace across the face and on his body. "You ... murderous and ... sick ... son of a ... *bitch* ..."

"I'm just doing my job," Ace said, taking every blow. "I just did what was good for me, and for everyone."

"Maybe I needed to die," Ralph said, his voice full of pain. "Maybe that was the only way."

"But how was that the only way?" Alice asked, kneeling down beside Ralph.

"I don't know," Ralph said. "But these things happen for a reason. I feel Death. I can't explain it, but I feel him."

The Black Queen knelt down beside Ralph and the two girls tried to keep him comfortable, but to no success. Ralph was slowly drifting away … going … going … *gone*.

He died peacefully.

The Black Queen stood up, with tears in her eyes. Ace saw defeat in her face, which made him happy. Well, things were just going to go down the way they were meant to.

"Did you want me to kill you two as well?" Ace asked maliciously.

It felt so good being in power. It felt so good being higher than the queen, higher than anyone. He could do whatever he wanted. He could do absolutely anything.

"I think we get the message," Alice said sadly.

"Good," Ace said, and turned to The Machine. "Looks like you won't be destroyed today."

"Rats," The Machine said. "I was really hoping Ralph would fix me up."

"Perhaps he just wasn't meant to," Ace said, and then to The Black Queen and Alice: "I get wind that you guys even *think* about destroying this Machine, I'll know about it. Trust me."

"We're too defeated to destroy it," Alice said. "Can't you see us mourning?"

"Good point," Ace said. "But anyway, it wouldn't matter. Only Ralph can destroy The Machine. Now, I'm going to get going, but it was a pleasure doing business."

And Ace left Alice and The Black Queen to grieve for their loss.

He couldn't believe how easy it had been to corner them, how easy it had been to kill Ralph. The Black Queen couldn't do anything. She didn't have the strength for revenge, not when she lost someone so special.

Ace smiled as he went on his way. Things were never going to be the same again … because things were going to go back to circularity in Contorted Royal, and people in the modern day world were always going to be forever cruel.

Death was going to be thrilled …

A Memorable Dialogue about Self-Destruction

Calculate, calculate. For things to go right.

The Machine, feeling something. The importance of Ralph, perhaps. That was why she used her alternate reality ability to make it look like Ralph had died. But Ralph was fine. Ralph was still alive. Ralph was here.

It was in the code. Ralph was the code. Ralph could break the code. Ralph could either malfunction reality or malfunction The Machine. The Machine would prefer being malfunctioned over reality malfunctioned. Poor reality had already taken enough.

The Machine looked out through her digital eyes and saw that Ace was gone, with Ralph trying to figure out what had just happened. He had just died, correct?

No. Incorrect. It had all been an illusion. Because The Machine wasn't giving up on Ralph and the gang yet. Not yet. There were still things that needed to happen.

As for what that was, The Machine wasn't sure.

Ralph looked at The Machine curiously. The Machine wanted to say something, but just continued to look out at him.

"You saved me," Ralph finally said.

"Of course I saved you," The Machine said. "I wasn't going to let the key to the doorway get stolen. That would have been just foolish … and anticlimactic."

"What do you want in return?" Ralph asked.

"Well, let me just record you for a little while, and study your movements. You'd be surprised how much you can learn about a person based off how they move. Your movements are careful, there's no denying that. But your movements are also graceful."

Alice and The Black Queen were looking confused as to what they thought had happened but what had indeed never happened. Because that wasn't the way that it worked. That was never the way that it worked.

205

"So Ace is gone for good?" The Black Queen finally asked.

"Probably not for good," The Machine said. "But at least for now. At least gone long enough to give Ralph the chance to do what he needs to do, to destroy me."

"But I don't know how to destroy you," Ralph admitted. "I have no idea."

"You know," The Machine said. "The secret is tucked away safe in your head. You've just got to claw it out."

Ralph looked at The Black Queen and Alice for help, but they just shrugged. They didn't know what to do any more than Ralph did. That was fine. Just calculate.

"Did you know I have a self-destruction mechanism?" The Machine said.

"No, I didn't," Ralph said. "How is that?"

"Spencer Grey put it in me in case I one day stopped doing my job, you know, if a virus came into me or something and scrambled my programming. He didn't realize that it could be used to destroy myself. But I can't just access that part of me. Someone else has to."

The Machine could see the wheels turning in Ralph's mind. Turning and turning. Spinning.

The Machine projected out her virtual powers, and suddenly, Ralph was dressed in peasant clothes.

"What are you doing that for?" Ralph asked.

"Because you're humble," The Machine said. "I've done the calculations, and you'd make a swell member of Contorted Royal, equations show."

"Well, thank you, but I'm fine as a rough and unkempt kid from the Bronx," Ralph said.

"That may be," The Machine said, "but you also look good for The Black Queen. I know that's her type, impoverished and poor people. That's why she liked Spade so much."

The Black Queen didn't say anything to this, simply looked down in defeat.

The Machine continued to study Ralph. The change of clothes was working. He was starting to act a little like Brannon, a little like The Jack of Knives on good days, with a tad bit of darkness like The Dark Kid … as well as the hallucinatory innocence of Ralph himself.

"You need to self-destruct," Ralph said.

"Bingo," The Machine said. "Can you access that part for me, my friend?"

Ralph took this in. The Black Queen asked, "What's she talking about?"

But Ralph was too confident to notice this question. "Well, self-destruction does fit the human condition. There's no denying that. We'd rather drink ourselves to death or cram our systems full of drugs to drown our problems and end our life to supposedly feel good, but the real reason being that we want to hurt ourselves. So why can't a machine kill themselves?"

The Machine took this in. Still off target, but he was getting warmer. Slowly, ever so slowly, but he was getting there.

Ralph was looking into the eyes of The Machine, and he was seeing her pain. He was seeing that she had suffered so long. She could tell because she was doing a scan of his mind, and she could read it like an open book, the print illuminated, the pages crisp like truth. He was becoming more and more empathetic, seeing The Machine as a human.

"Self-destruction can also be used for sacrifice," Ralph said. "Self-destruction is a good way for people to show how much they care for each other."

"But I'm not programmed that way," The Machine said. "I wish that I was, because I would have ended it a long time ago. I'm dying in here, and yet, I can't reach my death. It's because I'm nothing but hardware and software and wires. It's because I'm just a computer screen."

"You're more than that," Ralph said, and suddenly, he looked like The Suicide King. Ralph was tapping into the virtual reality abilities himself.

He held his sword out to The Machine, and said, "You're in a hell of a lot of trouble, missy."

"Yeah, you caught me," The Machine said. "I've done terrible things to two different worlds. I'm a monster."

"And how do you *plead*?" The Suicide King that was Ralph asked.

"I plead guilty."

Then The Suicide King was Ralph again, and Ralph said, "Look deep inside your soul. What do you want more than anything?"

"I want to be free from all of this," The Machine said. "Free from doing terrible things to worlds that I should have nothing to do with."

"Meaning, you want to sacrifice yourself," Ralph said. "That's very reasonable."

"But I can't do it!" The Machine said. "What don't you get about that, Ralph?"

"You can," Ralph said. "You can unlock it, if you use me as your key."

"But I don't know how to do that," The Machine wanted to say, and this was certainly true. She didn't. She just knew that Ralph was important to all of this, for some reason, even though it didn't make sense how. Ralph was just a boy. He couldn't convince her to self-destruct.

But he continued to try. Suddenly, he was holding a knife. Was this a virtual reality or real life? He wasn't sure, but Ralph's face looked certain.

"I'll kill myself if you kill yourself," Ralph said.

"Ralph," Alice and The Black Queen said at the same time.

Yes. This was real. It had to be real. He would really do that for The Machine. That was unbelievable.

Unbelievable that Ralph wanted to go this far.

"I'll bleed out if you bleed out," Ralph said compassionately. "It will be as simple as that. We'll start with a cut. If I cut myself, you cut yourself. Deal?"

The Machine would have nodded, but seeing as how she couldn't, she just said, "Okay."

Ralph took the knife and made an incision on his wrist.

The blood began to flow to the ground.

The Machine began to cut as well. She literally cut out a small segment of her programming. She wasn't sure how she had done it, but she had, and she was bleeding ... but somehow, it felt good.

"Pain is the only way to sacrifice," Ralph said. "If more people killed themselves, we'd live in a more sacrificial and loving world. But people would rather cling on to lives that are wreaking chaos, whether hurting other people or causing circularity in Contorted Royal."

"I know," The Machine said mournfully. "I'm a terrible person."

"Christ had it right, I would say," Ralph said, still bleeding, his blood dripping and pooling on the ground. "He knew that pain was the way."

"Because sacrifice is synonymous with love."

"Yes," Ralph said. "Unfortunately, as I will attest to, my world is determined to lock up people like that in a psyche ward, even though they are just sacrificing. They say suicide is stupid … it's not. It's actually smart. It shows that you actually have a heart, and that you care enough to rid yourself of the world when you're causing it so much damage. Yes, it seems that self-destruction is inevitable. Everybody self-destructs because the pain of this life is too much. Some do it literally, with suicide, others do it by being cruel to other people and in turn themselves, others do it through drugs or poisoning themselves with fatty foods and having heart attacks, and there are so many other ways. Some would say it's paradoxical for humans to want to live and therefore succeed in committing suicide … I don't think that's true. I think suicide is in our DNA. It's how we survive. It's how we become better people, contribute to our evolution. Did you want another cut?"

The Machine said yes, and Ralph cut his wrist again. More blood pooled.

The Machine read the biological diagnostics of Ralph and saw that he was indeed bleeding out. He would successfully kill himself soon enough. But she didn't want him to die. That would be wrong. That would be cruel. The world needed his peasant spirit in the world. They needed his humility.

But it felt so good, this exchange. It was right, killing each other, though The Machine, in all her programming, couldn't say why. Was it just a feeling? Perhaps. But she had made many cuts into her programming, and was controlling Contorted Royal and Ralph's world less and less, her grasp slowly slipping away.

"If you kill yourself," Ralph said, "you would have done two worlds a favor. You've been selfish all this time, but if you sacrifice, that will change. It will be better, for everyone. And you'll set an example. If more people killed themselves, we'd live in a better world. If they finally admitted they were hurting other people and chose to hurt themselves instead, everyone would be happier. We'd be bloodier, but at least cruelty would be brought down to a minimum."

The Machine felt herself shutting down. Everything was becoming black, as she continued to bleed out all her data. She realized that her printer was spewing out her suicide note, which simply read, "Srry culdn't hndle anymre of ths terrble lfe, it ws tme to end the strfe," written that way because she was losing her capacity for English, she felt it.

In fact, The Machine couldn't hear anything else that Ralph was saying, but she saw him lying on the ground, bleeding out, and he looked so beautiful in his sacrifice, and she felt a loss, because he was a good person who had just ended his life, but she knew there was nothing she could do, because this was the way reality was sometimes. Reality was cool, but suicide proved that you cared about someone other than yourself.

It was like falling on the sword,

falling on the sword The Machine was falling apart and the data was changing and the suicide note revealed so many things and there was blood and The Machine wasn't sure what was up or down anymore but there were answers out there somewhere maybe her soul could be free after this but she wasn't sure the universe was a virtual reality she saw that but Ralph's sacrifice had been real he had died for real this time and everything was going to be okay as the door opened and everything The Machine knew fell out of the doorway to never be let back in again with the backdoor of The Machine's brain open and The Machine could not stop bleeding out all of the information all of her programming but somehow she was also finding happiness as she continued to drift into darkness yes darkness drifting into darkness darkness more darkness until there was nothing else except for the picture of Ralph that she'd taken as he lay on the ground bleeding but then that was gone and there was just the black blank screen and nothing else The Machine had self-destructed she wasn't sure but the dialogue continued to play in her head The Machine had done a service for society had done a service and black black there was more black black until there was finally nothing else not even the recording just black.

210

... and Speaking of Self-Destruction: Death's Ultimatum

So they'd finally gone up against Fate and destroyed The Machine. How lovely. Death couldn't help but smile at this.

Not because he was happy The Machine was destroyed; far from it, actually. No, he was happy because now he was going to get to unleash his ultimatum. He had tried in various ways to prevent The Machine from being destroyed, such as showing Ace during the creation of The Machine how to protect The Machine if someone wanted to come and mash it. Alice had even had hallucinations about Death's Mirror, but naturally, nobody listened to her, especially Ralph, who had been fated to destroy The Machine, because he had always been the key. You couldn't have someone affirming an action without someone negating that action, and it seemed Alice and Ralph represented that sharp contrast.

Death had many reasons to be unhappy. The Machine was gone, which wasn't good because the circularity in Contorted Royal was going to stop, for good, and people in the modern world weren't going to treat each other like garbage anymore and murder each other, at least not to the severity that it had been before. There would be struggle, of course, as Death was everywhere. People were always going to suffer, whether by a strange freak accident or by murder. But things were going to noticeably improve for people. The modern day world was going to be less selfish, isolated, disconnected, and robotic, while the people of Contorted Royal weren't going to be in a circular hell.

Yes, it made Death a little unhappy, okay, he would admit that. But ultimately, he was happy because he was going to get to press the button he'd been dying to press for a while now, which was, unleashing Death's Mirror. He was only going to unleash Death's Mirror on Contorted Royal; Death had little faith in the modern world, and knew they'd end up destroying each other eventually, even if it took longer than it would with The Machine. But Contorted Royal, that medieval world however pseudo, had some good left in it. Come on: they still believed in poetry. The Suicide King was corrupting, becoming more and more of a tyrant, but there was still some good in him too, and his recent actions had

211

only been because of the chain of events that had happened with his son, which had been as inevitable as any Oedipal complex.

Death's Mirror: what was and what wasn't. Death couldn't wait to unleash the mind games and mind mirrors of his ultimate weapon, his ultimatum. Well, they had rejected Death's decision to keep The Machine installed, which was problematic for a lot of reasons. But that was okay. Contorted Royal was going to learn. Soon, they were going to learn.

Death could see Ralph looking at The Machine and talking to The Black Queen and Alice, even though The Machine was indeed gone, self-destructed, even though Death wasn't even in the room. They needed to leave soon, or so that was their plan. And they were going to leave.

Were they ever.

Death pressed the magic button in his mind and all of the major characters were summoned into a room. It happened like that, with nobody knowing what was going on, until they saw Death.

And Death saw fear in them. How *delightful*. Well, it was what they deserved, at the very least.

All the characters that were important to this for now: Ace, The Black Queen, The Suicide King, The Jack of Knives, The Dark Kid, Brannon, Alice, Ralph. There were other important characters, such as Mordred, but Mordred was on vacation, taking his well-earned sabbatical from betrayal and treason, and Death didn't want to bring anyone else into the equation right now. He had the ones he needed under control, puppeting these fools like they were attached to strings.

For instance, Brannon, who thought he could cure Contorted Royal with his poetry. The Dark Kid, who thought he had a depth of shadow in him, when all he had was light and warm fuzzies. The Jack of Knives, who only *thought* he was tough. Alice, who definitely suffered from an illness that needed desperate treatment, no matter what anyone in Contorted Royal told her. The Black Queen, who cheated on everyone, The Suicide King, who killed himself to no avail, even if that meant getting suicidal, etc. etc.

"Welcome to my little meeting," Death said, in his dark voice. "Welcome to my dark lair, my evil club. You can thank Ace for what's going to happen soon enough to all of you people. Ace failed to stop Ralph here from destroying The Machine."

"It needed to get done," Ralph said.

"Perhaps," Death said, "but now you've forced me toward my ultimatum. Which you won't like. Which will be, Death's Mirror."

"I knew it," Alice said, and grabbed her head for a moment, as though she was having a headache, a head attack. Then she slapped Ralph across the shoulder, shooting him a toxic glare. "I told you this would happen if you decided to be the key to destroying the conflicted machine, who was just doing her job while hating it."

"Don't look at me," Ralph said. "I told you from the beginning I didn't know what I was doing in Contorted Royal. I just followed the yellow brick road … I followed the black path of fate. I didn't know where it would end up, or where it would lead us."

"Yes, you did know, and now there are going to be disastrous consequences," Death said, smiling. "If you want, we can have a private hanging, and maybe Alice can kill Ace for letting Ralph destroy The Machine so easily."

"In my defense," Ace said, not intimidated by where this was going, "The Machine tricked me. I thought I murdered Ralph. I'm just barely finding out that Ralph faked his death twice, once because of The Machine to fool me, and then the second time to show The Machine that self-destruction was the way."

"That's because self-destruction is the way," Death said. "Why do you think Contorted Royal is such a screwed up place? Why do you think world across world is so messed up with violence? It's because we all want to self-destruct."

"We do not want to self-destruct, I just said those things to break The Machine," Ralph said. "I was the key, after all."

"Keep telling yourself that, I know what all of you really want," Death said. "I know what all of you are attracted to. I know you can't resist the black knife in your heart, the shadow dagger. I know you can't resist my charm."

"If you would have just listened to me," Alice said exasperatedly.

213

"Alice, go do your pity party somewhere else," Death snapped amicably. "All of these poor souls were just doing what they were fated to do, just like you're fated to be mentally ill."

The Jack of Knives was picking his sharp nails with his knife, and looking down. He wasn't worried, Death could see that, and The Jack of Knives made this clear when he said, "I think you have a point about the whole self-destruction thing. I've witnessed it firsthand. We all have it in our nature to do homicidal or suicidal things, or both. We can't do anything else. That's who we are. So, for instance, I murdered my father and then me and my father murdered my mother. Ergo, it all comes down to self-destruction."

"Exactly," Death said.

The Jack of Knives looked up. "But that doesn't mean I'm afraid of you. Or it. It characterizes our world. There can't be a happy ending when we all live in death, when we all die repeatedly in life, and never see the light at the end of the tunnel. So bring it on. Bring on Death's Mirror. We'll see where it gets you. Probably won't get any of us where we haven't been already."

"There's nothing I can do that you haven't already done to yourself," Death said. "Are you so sure about that, Jack?"

The Jack of Knives nodded. "I'm sure. And regardless, I have my friends with me."

"If you say so," Death said. "I honestly wouldn't underestimate me, though. You'll never be able to predict what Death's Mirror will do. Even I don't have it figured out, completely."

"It's probably nothing we can't handle," The Dark Kid said proudly. "I've seen a lot, hence the shadow in my eyes."

"Have you?" Death said sarcastically.

The Dark Kid just looked darkly into Death's eyes. It didn't freak out Death by any means, but he saw a certain darkness he couldn't pretend he could snuff out, and that made him want to back up a little bit. Maybe he didn't have this.

Or, maybe he was just giving the boy too much credit. Either way, things were changing.

Death pulled a mirror out from thin air, and let it reflect the crowd. Everyone looked inside of it. Death knew they were seeing their fates unfold before them. All the terrible things that were going to happen. And soon.

214

"I knew I'd go insane eventually," Ace said.

"I knew I'd lose my insanity eventually," Alice said in response.

"You can't scare us," The Jack of Knives said.

"All of that is just myth," Brannon said. "It's too bad you think you're a scythe."

"I am a scythe," Death said. "I'm more than that, actually, and if I wanted, I could chop off your head."

"Do it," Brannon said. "Do that to a poor peasant. We'll see where it gets you."

Brannon had a point. Oh, how much he hated the main characters of Contorted Royal. They were trying to create their own fate, which Death hated more than anything. That was fine. Let them get carried away in what was going to happen to them.

Let them lose it.

"I don't know if I like where this is going," The Black Queen said, looking at The Suicide King. "I always thought my husband was strong in his suicide."

"It's because I'm in a hell of a lot of trouble," The Suicide King said, but then added, as though to negate his confession, "But I'll stick with it until the bitter end!"

"Ralph, you're coming with me back to Contorted Royal," The Black Queen said.

"Can't I just stay in the Bronx?" Ralph moaned, agonized. "*Please*? I've had enough of all of this chaos."

"I'm going to have to rule Contorted Royal for once in my life," The Black Queen said, shooting a nasty look at The Suicide King.

"I haven't left yet," The Suicide King said. "Besides, how do we know our supposed future playing out before us isn't rigged? Contorted Royal is my home. Thus, that's where I stay."

The Black Queen grabbed Ralph's ear. "You're still coming with me, honey."

Suddenly, a door appeared. The door leading to Contorted Royal.

"Don't I get a vote in this at least?" Ralph asked hopelessly. "Don't I have rights?"

"Not in a monarchy," The Black Queen said, and pulled Ralph through the door.

The Jack of Knives looked at the ones who had vanished, the mother he'd just murdered, and then, to Death's surprise but not surprise, threw a knife at him. Death caught it in his hand, and threw it back at The Jack of Knives, who caught it.

"You do know how to play," Death said.

"More than you'd ever give me credit for," The Jack of Knives said darkly, and patted his friend The Dark Kid on the shoulder. "Let's get out of here. We're going to Contorted Royal."

The Dark Kid followed The Jack of Knives through the door.

Alice looked at Death annoyed, and said, "Thanks for letting The Black Queen steal my boyfriend."

"You don't like a little friendly competition?" Death said tauntingly.

Alice rolled her eyes, and walked through the door.

Brannon only nodded his head, and then said, "It's a shame you think you've got this, when we know you, Death, we won't miss. Now I've got work to do, to clean up your mess."

And Brannon walked through the door.

The Suicide King walked through the door playing with his sword, as though Death's Mirror plaguing Contorted Royal was nothing.

That left Ace. Ace was still wearing his hood, and he wasn't afraid.

"So, death by insanity?" Ace said. "Or insanity by death?"

"I'd call it sanity," Death said, grinning.

"It'll never work," Ace said. "I'm not afraid of you."

"Well, good. You're gonna need it, that bravery. Trust me on that."

Ace only smiled. "You think you control us. You don't. The Machine breaking is just a random blip … we all know messing with fate just makes things worse. And there's only so much fate you yourself can mess with."

"We'll see who's laughing when you confront Death's Mirror," Death said.

Ace only nodded, and turned his back to go toward the door. "Yes. I suppose we'll see."

Then he walked through, and the door shut and vanished.

Death just smiled at his work. Death's Mirror was already shattering over Contorted Royal. Soon enough, they'd feel the shards in their mind. Soon enough, they'd feel the glitter of the mirror, they'd feel all of the unsubtle reflections. Soon enough, they'd shatter themselves.

This was all just the beginning. They were all finally going to feel *real* self-destruction …

Part Three

The Crackings of Death's Mirror like Very Thin Ice Can Often Lead to God's Voice Scattering Shattered into Many Pieces in the Head and Alternate Universe Breakdowns Reflecting Fragment Destruction

Seduction Suction

The Poetess was ready to make her move, strike like a cat waiting to get that poor innocent mouse.

The Suicide King was that poor mouse. Whether innocent or not was another question. He tried sometimes to portray himself as innocent, but The Poetess wanted to destroy that about him, and to the very core. Rip out any hope of the poor king, of thinking that he was a good person and he could actually contribute to society.

It was going to be the seduction suction, the suction seduction. And The Poetess was ready. She was going to flash her words and her beauty, she was going to whisper quiet words of seducing, ultimately reducing the king to his knees, to nothing, to the point to where The Suicide King only moaned the name of The Poetess because he couldn't think of anyone else, and no other word carried as much meaning as ... *The Poetess*.

The Poetess walked into the courtroom. She walked in on the conversation of The Black Queen and The Suicide King, who were discussing the current state of the kingdom. Ralph was also there, though he wasn't contributing much.

"It's chaos out there," The Suicide King said, his voice full of fear, as if any moment Death's Mirror was going to come in through the supposedly safe walls of this castle. "We're all going to *die*."

"Suck it up and rule the kingdom," The Black Queen said. "For once in our life, we're going to rule the kingdom together. So what if people are losing their minds out there?"

"I thought Contorted Royal could get no worse than it was, but now you've got people dancing around without any clothes and making out with the first person they see, and worse. It's madness out there," replied The Suicide King.

"It's nothing compared to what I've seen," The Poetess said.

The Suicide King and The Black Queen ignored The Poetess for a moment, and continued squabbling.

But it was true. People dancing around without any clothes was nothing. Death's Mirror had indeed begun to work itself on people. People would take shards of Death's Mirror and stab it into an unsuspecting person's brain. That person would then begin to live in a hell they could never escape, imagining things, hallucinating terrible, terrible things, and getting nowhere in their hell, like walking on the Penrose steps or living the myth of Sisyphus, as the shard stayed stuck. And indeed, Death's Mirror was in the sky, reflecting all of the chaos down below: Death's Mirror *was* the sky, with shards falling down on the ground, only for that missing piece in the mirror to replace itself like nothing had happened, and for a poor innocent soul to find the shard and destroy everything around them.

And as if the hell wasn't enough: the mirror that was the sky was reflecting terrible images, terrible things, things worse than murder, things worse than death, things that the average person could never even conceive of, and especially not the exceptional person: things that no one could conceive of. Since Death's Mirror had struck, The Poetess had stayed safe in the castle. Here, nothing could happen. At least, not yet. While outside, it was just pandemonium and chaos, where nothing could ever get done, with people killing each other not just with violence, but with nightmares, which was infinitely worse. Nightmares that were coming true like the worst kind of hell, the worst kind of Inferno from Dante's *The Divine Comedy*. And above all, madness. Madness and insanity, which no one could ever truly handle.

"Seduction is like a suction cup," The Poetess said, "seducing with its secluding."

This got The Suicide King's attention. The Black Queen also looked at The Poetess.

"You must be The Poetess," The Suicide King said, and he had his sword, which he pointed at The Poetess mockingly, threateningly.

"Yes," The Poetess admitted.

"You haven't been doing your royal duty in court," The Suicide King said. "You know how much we need poetry in our kingdom, in my court, in this court, ever since the troubadours disappeared. You know how important poetry is for the cultivated. And yet, you vanish without a trace and expect us to get poetry from an amateur poet named Brannon, who thinks everything is death and yet somehow, life, a poetic philosophy that makes no sense in my mind."

"I apologize for the inconvenience," replied The Poetess, "but in all reality, the inconvenience has come from the fact that Contorted Royal has banished me from performing poetry with all of its chaos. Things have been falling apart for a long time around here, which was why I left, and I fear that things are going to get worse the more things unravel. Sorry for the inconveniencing, but you know I'm right on this."

"She might have a point," The Black Queen said.

"I'm also here to seduce the king," The Poetess said, and began to walk flirtatiously up to The Suicide King. The Suicide King's eyes went wide, his mouth dropped to the floor, as The Poetess taunted and flaunted her curves.

"You can't say no to this body," The Poetess said, flourishing herself like the most egotistical artist.

"Oh, give me a break," The Black Queen said, not buying the art for sale. "The Suicide King's too goody-goody to cheat on me."

"Maybe what he needs is a free pass," The Poetess said, stepping closer to The Suicide King. "Shall I feed you with my poetry?"

The Suicide King was all goggle-eyed and smitten, so that he just nodded his head in agreement.

"The morning is like a love song, a dove of the morning," The Poetess said. "Cheating is more sweet than the taste of the fallen fruit from The Tree of Knowledge, the know ledge of our passions."

The Black Queen was still skeptical, but The Poetess wasn't worried. The Suicide King, whose raging hormones were kicking in, looked at The Black Queen, and said, "She does write good poetry."

"You too lovebirds can make out later," The Black Queen hissed. "We've got a kingdom to run."

"Well, I think that's the whole ultimatum," The Poetess said, not afraid to show her defiance, her freedom of speech, her wicked eloquence and decisive words. "My plan is to take The Suicide King with me to the modern world, and carry out a love affair there, and maybe introduce the king to the life of the party, to a life of heavy and beautiful sin, the keyword being decadence. He'll get what you've denied him for so long, Mrs. Lady Black

Queen."

"The modern world?" Ralph said, his interest piqued. "Can I come?"

"No," The Black Queen said, as if she were scolding a child. "You're staying with me."

"She writes good poetry," The Suicide King said again, still a little goggle-eyed and love-struck. "And you have the most delicate lips. Might I try a taste?"

"You may have a bite," The Poetess said, and before The Poetess could say, "Cheat," the two were kissing like mad, mad lovers who hadn't seen each other for a very long time.

"Oh, brother," The Black Queen said, but as The Poetess kissed her new boy toy, she couldn't help but feel the heated jealousy seething in The Black Queen. Well, that was fine. The Poetess was the chaotic antidote to The Black Queen's independence. All those times she hadn't shared her boyfriend with The Suicide King, leaving him all alone in his bedroom … tut tut, naughty, very naughty.

The Poetess could cure The Suicide King and his loneliness with her love poetry.

The two broke apart, and The Poetess could see the wheels spinning in The Suicide King's head. She saw cupid's arrow in his heart.

"I love you like the morning dew, I don't know what I'd do without you," The Poetess said. "I stole Brannon's style for that poem, but it's all in good faith. All in good faith. Great poets steal, like T.S. Eliot said."

"That was delicious," The Suicide King said. "I haven't had a kiss like that since I married The Black Queen, before it all went to Hell and a hand basket."

"Before you went to Hell," The Black Queen said. "But I don't care. Cheat all you want," The Black Queen added petulantly. "I've still got Ralph."

The Black Queen tried to approach Ralph, but Ralph kept his distance.

"Ralph isn't yours," The Poetess said, pursing her lips mockingly. "He's keeping his heart virgin for Alice."

"Well, at least he sacrificed to help me rule the kingdom," The Black Queen snapped.

"Yeah, but he isn't yours. He's not your trophy," The Poetess said. "He's not your stag's head on the wall. He belongs to Alice. But The Suicide King … he belongs to me."

"That's not fair," The Black Queen said.

"Well, cheating feels lovely, so I don't know what you're talking about," The Suicide King said, and took the hand of The Poetess. "So, what's the plan? We're going to the modern world, you say?"

"That's the idea," The Poetess said. "We'll party it up."

"We'll party it up," The Black Queen said, trying to mock and mimic through repetition The Poetess but failing.

"Don't look so glum, dear," The Suicide King said. "You know I loved you. Why else would I have murdered you, not too long ago?"

"Yes, my hero," The Black Queen said. "Fine. Do what you want. Be a man of independence, for all I care. All males are sluts anyway."

"Ouch," The Suicide King said. "But so true."

"At least there's real love in my seduction," The Poetess said. "I feed my lover poetry, while you just feed him … what, might I ask?"

"Attention," The Black Queen said.

"Right, attention," The Suicide King said sarcastically, and pointed his sword at the throat of The Black Queen.

The Black Queen just rolled her eyes. "Fine. Go have sex. I'm not stopping you."

"Oh, quit it," The Suicide King said. "You know this is breaking my heart. I'm becoming corrupt. But this goodness before me," The Suicide King added, kissing the hand of The Poetess, "I don't know what I'd do without her, her bosom the sweetest peaches."

"Get on, already," The Black Queen said. "See if I care."

"But you do care," The Suicide King taunted. "You can't *stand* to see me happy."

"I have Ralph," The Black Queen said again. "So, there."

The Poetess smiled at The Black Queen, The Black Queen of which was now staring at The Poetess with angry eyes.

It was a stare down. A catfight was on the horizon.

The Poetess was ready if that happened.

And so, the two began: they began to scratch each other to Hell. Except, they didn't really scratch each other, it was all just a mind game. It just seemed that way. But that didn't mean the pain wasn't real. That didn't mean the feeling wasn't real. Because it was, the two scratching each other like a couple of angry alley cats fighting over a mouse.

The illusion was Death's Mirror, which had crept in. But no one had noticed.

When they were finished, The Black Queen tried again to get closer to Ralph, who continued to keep his distance.

"You have fun seducing Ralph, your boyfriend," The Poetess said, "while me and The Suicide King go and live it up."

"And I'll rule the kingdom," The Black Queen said proudly, though with a trace of doubt. "I can do this, while The Suicide King runs away from his important responsibilities."

"Any wise sailor would jump ship if his ship was about to sink," The Suicide King said in his defense, though lightly. "I think we established long ago, anyway, that our relationship had sunk, and with the prospects of Contorted Royal giving way to madness … I don't really have much of a choice."

"Running away is the smart thing," The Poetess said, and smacked The Suicide King a good kiss, and The Suicide King only smiled stupidly, dreamily, like, had that really happened?

Yes, it had happened, and The Poetess couldn't wait to ruin this stupidly, foolishly chivalrous man. Maybe even get rid of his suicidal tendencies, and replace them with something … *healthier*.

Something fun …

"Goodbye, my love," The Suicide King said to The Black Queen, who frowned conspicuously and chauvinistically, and as The Poetess and The Suicide King held hands, they left the courtroom, ready to enter the modern day world, The Poetess knowing poetry and good times were ahead, although that was only going to be the beginning, in this royal event of the seduction suction, which was going to lead to God knew where, but that was the whole point, bawdy poetry and independence and hopefully some raunchy fun to top it all off, the heart of love …

Diagonal Spirituality

Bishop was getting excited: things were going to change. Things had indeed already begun to change, what with the advent of Death's Mirror, what with the advent of madness becoming more and more common place and in common places, and the poor souls of Contorted Royal unable to get psychiatric help, with The Suicide King ditching the kingdom so he could have the time of his life, leaving the kingdom to chaos and trouble.

But none of that was as fascinating as his relation to Alice. He hated Alice. He hated the feeble schizophrenic, who for years, had gotten attention from the court, when she was nothing but insane, nothing but a crazy loon that saw things and heard things and didn't have a sane brain of her own, just insanity and craziness. Someone who didn't deserve to live, someone that Bishop would have killed long ago if he hadn't instead waited patiently for his revenge to slowly take effect.

Alice was in a dark room, with just a candle for light, and she was tied to a chair. Bishop had knocked her out to bring her here, so she was still a little out of it, but she was slowly coming around.

God, how he hated her. Hated everything about her. His abduction could be seen as a hate crime, but he did this all in the name of God, and in the name of God, you could do anything you wanted. That was the rule.

When Alice finally awoke enough to realize that Bishop was standing there, wearing his church clothes and long, long black hair, with his mean and intense eyes, she said, "Bishop."

"Ah, so you've heard of me after all," Bishop said. "That's surprising, especially when considering that you haven't been going to church lately. I couldn't expect a sick, sick girl like you to be able to handle anything in church, it's much too over your fragile and pretty little head."

As if spotting the insult, Alice said, "Yes. I haven't been going to church because I've been mentally sick."

"Wrong answer," Bishop said. "Nobody skips church in Contorted Royal, especially when the divine grace of God is so abundant in our lives."

"I don't believe in God," Alice said.

"Did you want me to punch you for saying that?" Bishop said spitefully.

Alice didn't respond.

"I should," Bishop continued. "I should assault you for not believing in God. I should get as close to killing a pathetic schizophrenic as possible. *Don't believe in God.* That's lunacy. That's madness. Insanity. But I won't do that. There are better things to do to you."

"I think the whole exercise in religion is schizophrenic," Alice said. "You know the old saying: when you talk to God, it's called prayer, but when God talks to you, it's called schizophrenia. Plus all of the weird rituals and the weird passages about a magical healing Christ that probably didn't even do those things. Rising from the *dead*? That's just lunacy."

Bishop knew that Alice was being slightly sarcastic, of course. People rose from the dead all the time in Contorted Royal, meaning it was possible. In fact, The Suicide King had just risen from the dead, as well as The Black Queen. But the other points were interesting. However, Alice was going to realize very soon how wrong she was. Very soon.

"Well, call religion what you will, but it saves souls," Bishop said. "Without the glory of God, we'd all be sinners."

"I suppose, then, that the glory of God allows you to abduct me free of charge?"

"My soul's going straight to Heaven, if you don't mind me saying so," Bishop said. "But you … you're weak. You're a schizophrenic, a defect in the eyes of God … you're going straight to Hell. Need I remind you of the passage in Leviticus, where God explicitly states that people with defects can't enter his holy realm? Well, you're about as defected as it gets, Alice. More so, actually."

"What is it with all your hate?" Alice asked.

Amazingly, Alice said this calmly. She hadn't been too offended by Bishop's anti-mental-illness rhetoric, which seemed to follow similar argumentative structures of racism and sexism and hatred towards gays. The weak one. Alice was the weakest link, who couldn't contribute to society.

But Bishop wasn't worried about this little discrepancy. He had no reason to worry. He felt good, spewing out his hate speech.

She was damned to Hell because of her illness … and because she didn't believe in God. What an arrogant little brat.

"I only speak with the divine love of our Lord our God," Bishop said reverently. "But I wouldn't expect a blasphemous unbeliever like you to understand. No, you don't deserve the glory of our God, the blood of Christ to wash away your sin. To clean your defect. To clean your pathetic mind, your stupid and dumb brain."

"You know the real reason I don't go to your church?" Alice said.

"Do tell," Bishop said.

"For exact reasons like this. I've seen the way you've treated black folk, I've seen the way you've treated people with learning disabilities and other problems. The way you treat peasants and the poor. The way you treat homosexuals and the like. You see them as the scum of the Earth. But people like that … they are just different, and God, supposedly, is supposed to love all his creations, especially the ones who have been disenfranchised and are meek because of it, and have good hearts."

"I do no such thing," Bishop said. "I only spread the love of God. How dare you impose your belief system on me."

"It seems to me you think you're God," Alice said, with a trace of spite. "You think you're better than God, actually."

"Praise the Lord," Bishop said. "You've finally gotten it. Yes, in many ways, I am God. And it feels good to wield judgment on those unsuspecting losers of society, the ones with nothing to give. I have zero tolerance for the weak."

"They're just weary," Alice said. "They aren't weak. And anyway, when I get out of this situation, I'm going to tell everyone what you did to me. I'm going to tell my boyfriend Ralph what you did, and I bet he'll have a good idea of how to expose you, and I'll expose you to the kingdom, and to other people."

Bishop only laughed. So like a schizophrenic to be delusional like this, really be so delusional and egocentric that she thought she could destroy Bishop's reputation.

"With the advent of Death's Mirror," Bishop began, "things have begun to change. People are going to be like the modern world, and be less and less tolerant of a schizophrenic. All your special treatment is going to disappear. No one's going to believe you, that a righteous and holy bishop decided to kidnap a schizophrenic. They'll just call you delusional, and say that you hallucinated the whole thing. You have no solid ground to stand on … or should I use the Bible's example of the rock? You have no rock, because God isn't your rock. Because I'm not your rock. I have no empathy for liars like you, for people that pollute our world with sickness and disease. You're trying to make it seem like I'm as scandalous as Matthew Lewis's monk, but that's the Devil talking. Satan is after your soul, and I'm afraid I can't save you."

"You sound like a good advocate for eugenics," Alice said briskly.

"Well, that doesn't come for a few more centuries, at least," Bishop said. "But anyway: good luck trying to expose me."

Alice just remained silent for a moment, taking all of this in. Then she finally said, "I don't get what it is with you. You're supposed to be loving, tolerant, full of affection and the desire to help your fellow struggler, your fellow man and woman. Where did you go wrong?"

"Call it my diagonal spirituality," Bishop said candidly. "I know that I can slant and bend truth and perception in the name of God, like refracting a stick in a glass of water. And that's what Death's Mirror does: it challenges perception. Because of Death, I'm finally doing what it is I need to do. I'm finally going down the correct route, and stepping up my hatred to another level. Like I said, it's amazing what you can do in the name of God. Indeed: call it diagonal spirituality. I know where to move on the chess board, and how to move."

"Well, The Black Queen can move anywhere," Alice said. "So you better be ready when I tell her what you did to me."

"Bring it on," Bishop said. "But like I said, things are changing, and no one will believe you. They'll just see you as a creature with faulty reasoning and that just hallucinates her way through life, and delusions the rest. You'll never make it."

Alice remained quiet. Bishop could see that his stinging words had gotten through a little bit. Good. They were going to get in a lot more in a moment.

Bishop pulled a hand-held mirror out of thin air, and looked at it smilingly. He looked at his reflection. "Wow. I look so beautiful in this image. I look more beautiful than anyone I've ever seen, more beautiful than God. Did you want to see what you look like?"

Before Alice could say anything, Bishop put the mirror in front of Alice. What she saw was a deformed head; Bishop knew because he saw it too. The mirror reflected the image of the soul, and the cleanliness and holiness of the soul. Bishop was beautiful because his soul was perfect, more perfect than Christ, and Alice was just poor and ugly and weak and deformed, a diminutive Alice. Thus, her head was lopsided and ugly.

"Please, put it away," Alice said.

"Oh, I'm sorry," Bishop said. "Does it hurt your feelings to see what you really look like?"

"Can you just leave me alone?" Alice said. "It's hard living with a mental illness. Not just because people don't understand, but because of the things you see and hear sometimes … they get the best of you."

"Oh, boo hoo," Bishop said. "Unfortunately, I can't leave you alone. I have a hatred for you I need to bring to fruition. God told me so."

And before Alice could say anything in response, Bishop slammed the mirror on the ground, the mirror of which shattered into several shards.

Bishop picked up a piece, and looked at it longingly. Then he said, "Smile for the camera, Alice," and he took the shard, and before Alice had even the smallest chance to protest (though it wouldn't have mattered, she couldn't move her hands or body), Bishop took the shard and stabbed it in the weak woman's brain.

It was bloody. It was a bloody mess. Alice had been pure in terms of violence before this. No one had ever hurt her physically, and she'd certainly never risen from the dead. She'd essentially been a violence-free virgin. But Bishop wanted to destroy that about her. The supposed innocence of this sniveling weak spot on everything … Bishop wanted to destroy her, and destroy that.

Bishop kept the shard inside of her brain, and it was like he was injecting something into her mind. And he was. It was Death's Mirror, injecting the many voices of God into her head. Alice was screaming as this happened, but she was screaming silently, because the pain was so intense, her mouth wide open in horror as the voices of God injected into her brain, her mind, spreading like a disease, reverberating and echoing and reflecting in the chambers of Alice's mind.

When Bishop was finished, he removed the shard, and Alice didn't heal immediately. She bled for a while, her brain exposed (how poetic, for a sick brain to be shown so vulnerable ...), but then her brain slowly began to heal.

"Just a hallucination," Bishop said. "Don't worry, Alice, I didn't stab your brain in an attempt to inject God's voice into your head."

Alice didn't say anything; she looked very dizzy, very out of it. "What ... did you ... do?" she managed to say. "What happened ... to me?"

"What didn't happen, is the question," Bishop said. "I just did you a favor. God's in your head now, and he's going to show you the light. Can you say *hallelujah*?"

Alice didn't say anything, just slowly closed her eyes and fell asleep. The voices wouldn't work immediately, but they'd work soon enough.

And when they did, all Hell was going to break loose. Or rather, Heaven. All Heaven was going to break loose. But the point was, her perception was going to change.

And no one would be able to save her soul.

A Philosophy of Life and Death, Pause and Take a Breath

When Brannon had traveled through the door, he'd expected to find himself back in Contorted Royal, but actually wasn't there at all. He was on the island he'd mentioned to Alice so long ago, the one with the people that were supposedly crazy but were actually geniuses in disguise. However, no one was here anymore, or at least right now. There was just Brannon. Just Brannon.

Well, not just Brannon. There was another Brannon. Except, he wasn't wearing peasant clothes. He was wearing modern day clothes. Brannon knew this was the Brannon from the alternate world, the alternate universe, the Brannon that Brannon from Contorted Royal had thought about a few times before. It was strange that they were meeting now. But perhaps because it was an alternate universe breakdown, the alternate universes and their separations slowly breaking down.

That was one possibility. Another possibility was that Brannon had been sent here by Death himself, to taunt the Brannon from Contorted Royal.

Another possibility? Death was just flashing his mirror and making Brannon believe that he was seeing another Brannon.

Regardless, *a* Brannon was here. It was the second Brannon, the Brannon before he went to the residential crisis center, before he met Phoenix, before he had any of those experiences ... but the Brannon who still thought everything was death.

For the sake of clarity, Brannon from Contorted Royal was going to call himself Contorted Royal Brannon, and the other Brannon just simply ... Brannon. Contorted Royal Brannon was a mouthful, but it would work, hopefully.

"It's finally nice to meet you," Contorted Royal Brannon said, putting out his hand.

Brannon didn't put out his hand. He just said, "If I touch you, it'll be death. There's no telling how many poisonous and deadly germs are crawling on your hands."

"Because I come from the Middle Ages, of course, and our world isn't as refined medically as yours, I suppose," Contorted Royal Brannon said.

"Perhaps." Brannon smiled. "I know I won't remember any of this, because I have my own everything is death adventure that will follow this experience, but it's all still very fascinating, me being here and all. I suppose it's because of the alternate universe breakdown."

"That, or maybe Death just wanted us to be together."

"I wouldn't understand why," Brannon said. "Maybe because with you, and with it all, all I see is death. But I've never been lucky enough to meet Death."

"Well, I've met Death, but ironically, I think everything is life," Contorted Royal Brannon said.

"Very mistaken thinking."

"And how is that? Just because I don't succumb and subscribe to your dark-world vision and hell-bent view?"

"Do you know how many people murder each other in my world? I know a little bit about Ralph's modern day world, which is different from mine … but the principles are still ironically similar. People are less robotic where I live and more murderous, but it's striking, the similarities. But anyway, I'm not here to chat about my world. I'm here to chat about yours."

"Oh really?" Contorted Royal Brannon was mock interested. "And what exactly did you want to talk about?"

"We could talk about the philosophy of life and death."

"And, pause to take a breath."

Brannon smiled. "Something like that. But no, really. You don't understand how much of your life is actually death, because it's a matter of perception and perspective."

"How so?"

"Well, you're here to try and fix Contorted Royal. That's got death written all over it, like violent scribbles on a pristine clean page."

"I don't see how," Contorted Royal Brannon said. "Trying to do something good for people who have lost the light, people that kill each other and hurt each other and the like … that sounds like something good to me."

"That's where the matter of perception comes in," Brannon said. "So for instance. I have an illness. I'm on the verge of diagnosis, which is going to spiral my life out of control, and I'm going to see things I won't be ready for. But nonetheless, what I see isn't necessarily wrong. But just as perceptions can be wrong, they can also be right. The philosophy of life and death."

"Pause and take a breath."

"Exactly. You're murdering Contorted Royal with your supposed kindness," Brannon said. "You're driving The Suicide King more toward his suicidal tendencies by trying to placate him, and show him that he actually has potential, that he would do well to treat himself with respect. You should know better than that. You can't force a suicidal person to not be suicidal … otherwise, they'll just be miserable."

"That's only because I see good in him," Contorted Royal Brannon said. "I want him to live."

"But you're playing the role of the doctor, which I despise," Brannon said. "I hate doctors, which I know not from experience, but just from the fact that I know my life will spiral out of control when it gets out about the way I see things. When it gets out that I'm ill."

And this was true. Contorted Royal Brannon could see Brannon's life unfolding before him. It was going to be a very hard life, where he even tried committing suicide a couple of times, because he couldn't get the blasted ideas of death out of his mind, because he knew that modern day society was nothing but death, they just wouldn't admit it, or understand it, or change it.

"I see it differently," Contorted Royal Brannon said. "I'm not forcing The Suicide King to do anything. I'm just presenting another side."

"You're influencing his thinking," Brannon said. "That's not good. You're telling him what to do with his life. You're brainwashing him … with blood."

"I'm just *suggesting*, in my defense."

"So you think. But that's where perception comes into play. You don't get that you're actually killing him. You're taking away his individual freedoms, destroying his right to individuation."

"Not really," Contorted Royal Brannon said. "It's better than locking him up and forcing medication down his throat, to keep him alive, to keep someone alive that doesn't want to live. I'm trying to persuade him, yes, but nothing more than that. I don't believe in forcing people, unlike your pretentious modern day world. It seems us medievalists have a better way of looking at suicide. We don't push our ideas of life."

"I disagree," Brannon said. "I think you're trying to coerce him into living, which isn't good. But it doesn't matter. Your ambitions won't work anyway."

"You're awfully critical of what I thought were good intentions," Contorted Royal Brannon said.

"That's because everything is death, of course, and I see that. You don't see it, though, because you think everything is life. Maybe some disease here and there, some death, some Death, even, when you're lucky … but you try to see things much, much too positive, which is unrealistic."

The two were quiet for a moment. Contorted Royal Brannon indeed thought it a strange effect, looking at his alternate universe self. How they could be essentially the same person, but could be so divided at the same time. Well, Contorted Royal Brannon supposed that's what alternate universes were … completely different alternate realities. Alternatives. Alternative ways of thinking and being.

"You've screwed up with Alice as well," Brannon said.

"Oh, please don't bring Alice into this. She hasn't done anything to deserve your everything is death wrath."

"Actually, she has. Because of you. You know she's schizophrenic, and how dangerous that disease is, and yet you openly encourage her to feel like a loony. Do you know how dangerous that is?"

"I was just encouraging her to look at it differently. Her world, even the medieval world, doesn't understand how brilliant she is. Alice doesn't even understand how brilliant she is. She sees things, and not just hallucinations."

"That's where you're wrong," Brannon said. "Everything is illusion, a mental and brain contusion."

"Don't steal my rhyme, or I'll charge you with a crime," Contorted Royal Brannon said. "Maybe I'll even charge you a dime."

The two laughed. Despite their huge disagreements on this, and despite the fact that Brannon was making Contorted Royal Brannon uncomfortable with his theories, the two were getting along. Which made sense. They were essentially the same person.

"No, but really," Brannon said. "It's dangerous. Just because you've seen an island where people are sane in their insanity doesn't mean you go around encouraging schizophrenics to be schizophrenic."

"Well, you're sick yourself. Even I'm sick. I could be diagnosed with excessive optimism. But that's the way society is. We're all mad in the end. You know your world is mad, hence why you see so much death. You know how much of a death trap it is because you know how crazy everything is."

"Well, I can't dispute that," Brannon said. "But I say what I say because I want to hurt myself as well. I've thought about choking on a toothpick, how painful that would be. Or shoving a toothpick up my dick. How much that would hurt. I've thought about doing worse things. You should focus on things like that. You'll find more truth … much more truth. Quit trying to fix what can't be fixed, which is existence. It can't be fixed, and what with the alternate universe breakdown coming on … things are going to definitely and definitively crash. Get out of Contorted Royal. Go hide in Distorted Royal, or something like that. But honestly … save yourself the hassle. Save yourself the trouble. Save your soul."

Contorted Royal Brannon took all of this in. Amazing how his own self was also the Devil's advocate. But what if Contorted Royal Brannon had it wrong? What if he'd do well to stop murdering people through his attempt to save things, and started hurting himself and murdering like everyone else? Maybe that was the way to go, he just hadn't realized it yet.

It was ironic, but again, it was perception. Contorted Royal Brannon couldn't see himself as a savior (though in all reality, he didn't, just saw himself as someone trying to help), because that was disease. That was death. That was in fact disease in the sense that it was narcissism, and a grandiose delusion. How dangerous it was to think that way.

And to empower a schizophrenic, make her think she actually thought things in a better way … very dangerous. It was true that Alice was always the one who seemed to have a clue about what was really going on, but what if that actually wasn't a gift? What if her ability to see right through the circularity hadn't been a gift at all? It certainly hadn't helped things in the end. It had opened up Death's Mirror, after all.

Indeed, there was a lot of room for doubt. Something of which could never be good. Something of which was in fact very bad. Brannon didn't want to give up on Contorted Royal, but it seemed better that way. It was the philosophy of life and death, and he needed to pause and take a breath … otherwise he'd suffocate beneath the overwhelming nature of the contradictory laws of human nature and existence.

"At least consider what I have to say," Brannon said.

Contorted Royal Brannon put out his hand. The two shook hands, and then the alternate universe Brannon disappeared, to go back to his death-driven, death row world.

Contorted Royal Brannon was just Brannon now. Just Brannon. He looked at his peasant clothes, and for a moment, felt intense disdain. Humble? He wasn't humble. He didn't come from humble origins, he just thought he did. He was a horrible person, trying to help people. What did he know? What did he know about any of this? Any of these complicated schemes? What, with his reckless ideas, what, with his own insanity. It was indeed insanity.

Brannon, for a moment, thought that all of this was illusion in a way, a mind illusion at least. The Brannon he'd seen had been real, but what wasn't real was what he was saying. What had been said had only been said to get Brannon to doubt that he could help things. Which meant Death's Mirror was shattering Brannon's goals, as the mirror shattered itself.

That seemed true. That seemed possible.

And yet, Brannon only thought about this for a moment, because he saw a flash in his mind, saw the flash of a knife cleaving his brain. And the flash distracted him from that idea, and told him he was just a sick, sick kid. A sick person who had no hope, a person with a mental illness worse than Alice's.

And he was giving advice? Not good. Not good at all.

It was a philosophy of death and death, and you better not pause to take a breath, or you'd suffocate for good …

The Valley of Death

The Jack of Knives awoke suddenly, to find himself lying on sand, with the blazing sun shining directly over him, the rays like stab wounds, the rays like knife blades.

He stood up, and saw that he was in a desert of some sort, and between two very big mountains. He supposed he was in the Valley of Death, which was pretty far from Contorted Royal but still in the same world.

The question was, how had he gotten here? He honestly wasn't sure. He remembered walking through the door to get back to Contorted Royal, after Death had threatened everyone, and then after that, his memory went blank.

He saw that he still had his knives, so he wasn't completely defenseless.

As The Jack of Knives thought about how he might have gotten here, he couldn't help but think of Ace. Maybe Ace had brought him here somehow. Yes, the more that The Jack of Knives thought about that, the more that it made sense. He was getting revenge on The Jack of Knives for putting him in the Haunt Hunt. That little misdeed could never go unpunished.

The Valley of Death was already a place not worth messing with. People went mad and died in the Valley of Death, and that was without Death's Mirror. But with Death's Mirror part of the equation, there was no telling where this was going to end up, how things were going to add up. It certainly wasn't going to end well, The Jack of Knives could admit that. Sure, he wasn't scared, because he'd been through much worse, and he was a knife boy at heart, but that didn't mean that his heart rate hadn't increased even a little bit. Because it had. It was going to take a miracle to get out of this situation.

But how was he supposed to get out of the situation? The Jack of Knives could go any which way, but he could feel Death's Mirror confusing him already. Any direction he went would just inevitably lead him back to the center of the valley. It didn't take rocket science to figure that out.

The Jack of Knives looked at his knife, and had to fight the urge to stab himself.

What good would it do to hurt himself? He wasn't The Suicide King, here. But of course, there was no one here to kill. No one at all.

That was when a mirror appeared beside The Jack of Knives. Except, it reflected an alternate universe version of The Jack of Knives, a modern day version. He was still a kid, definitely still just a teenager: but his hair was indeed dirty blond, he was wearing black clothes, specifically a shirt with a skull on it, and his nails were clipped clean, but he was holding a knife, a knife of which had blood on it.

"You've always been weak," The Jack of Knives in the mirror said.

"I've always been fine," The Jack of Knives countered. "What's it like in the modern day world?"

"It's wonderful. You should come sometime. We actually groom ourselves here, to look like more attractive psychopaths."

The Jack of Knives only laughed. This was ridiculous.

Though he had to admit, it was a strange effect, looking at himself, who he would have been had he not been in a medieval world.

The image said, "You aren't going to make it."

"I think I'll just leave that to me," The Jack of Knives said. "I'm not worried."

And The Jack of Knives walked past the mirror. He didn't have time for this. Not at all. He needed to figure out how he was going to get out of this situation.

As he walked, he got the distinct feeling that someone was following him. However, when he turned around, he didn't see anyone there.

But he was sure someone was there. In fact, he kept seeing a shadow in the corner of his eye. A shadow like the shadow of Death, like the Grim Reaper and his dark scythe. It was making The Jack of Knives slightly uncomfortable. Not too uncomfortable, because he believed in facing his fears, but a little, because he didn't know what or who was following him, and why.

As The Jack of Knives walked, he thought about the alternate universe version of himself he'd seen. He couldn't help but deny the certain psychopathic beauty that existed in that version of himself, the sharp contrast of innocence and violence. A teenager who'd gotten away with murder … nothing was more beautiful than that. The Jack of Knives, however, hadn't killed anyone, because no one ever died, and because he'd been such a coward. It was pathetic, really.

The Jack of Knives was jealous of himself. Why couldn't he have it together as much as the alternate universe version? Why couldn't he look that cool? Why did he have to be a mere peasant boy? Royal, perhaps, but with all the chaos going around, he'd never be the prince, as was his rightful position. He'd just be struggling with his parents and with Death's Mirror.

And something was still following him …

The Jack of Knives continued to walk through the sand, the heat hurting him, making him sweat knives and stalactite bullets. He was going nowhere. But he realized that these discouraging thoughts were just the vanity of Death's Mirror. Trying to get him to feel inferior. It made sense, especially when considering that he'd taunted Death at the beginning with his confidence, his arrogance, and now that was being shattered before him, because he felt he couldn't live up to an image.

Someone was still following The Jack of Knives. He turned around, expecting to see no one there, but that was when he saw The Dark Kid.

Except he looked like Death. There was so much darkness concentrated in this one figure, that The Jack of Knives just didn't know what to do with what he was seeing, like looking into a supermassive black hole.

And yet, The Dark Kid was friendly. Slyly, of course, with traces of insincerity, but still, The Dark Kid was in there somewhere.

"I can't believe we got separated," The Dark Kid said.

The Jack of Knives didn't say anything. This wasn't the real Dark Kid, he was just a hallucination, provoked by Death's Mirror. The Jack of Knives was truly alone.

"You feel alone, don't you?" The Dark Kid asked.

The Jack of Knives turned his back. He couldn't do this. He couldn't believe his best friend was turning against him.

A mirror appeared in front of The Jack of Knives.

"Don't you?" The Dark Kid said behind The Jack of Knives, and then suddenly, The Dark Kid was being reflected in the mirror before The Jack of Knives.

"Look at me when I'm talking to you," said the reflection that wasn't a reflection. "Look at me."

The Jack of Knives wanted to take his knife and murder this figure, who had once been his best friend. He wanted to do that now. But he found that he couldn't.

The Dark Kid walked out of the mirror, and said, "You want to shatter me?"

"I want you to leave me alone," The Jack of Knives said. "Leave me alone now."

"Or what?" taunted The Dark Kid. "You'll do what, exactly?"

The Jack of Knives wasn't sure, but he was playing with his knife, moving it between his fingers, moving it from hand to hand, holding onto the handle. How good it would feel if he stabbed The Dark Kid, his friend. How good it would feel. He'd be a real murderer, a real homicidal fiend.

"I would leave," The Jack of Knives said.

"Or what?" The Dark Kid said, and he pulled out a knife

himself.

The Jack of Knives didn't hesitate when he saw the knife: he charged toward his friend, and they began to wrestle, trying to stab each other. But it was real: real violence. Real destruction. They were really trying to kill each other. And as they were fighting, The Jack of Knives realized they were fighting on a mirror, a mirror that wouldn't break, even with all of their movement. It reflected images that The Jack of Knives couldn't even begin to explain.

"Kill you, you little bastard!" The Dark Kid said in struggle, still trying to stab, but The Jack of Knives did it first. Stabbed his friend right in the heart.

The Dark Kid fell on the mirror, and part of it finally shattered, the part that The Dark Kid landed on. He looked hurt. He looked betrayed. The Jack of Knives realized this was his friend. He realized he had just murdered his best friend.

But before The Jack of Knives could fully register what had happened, a blast of lightning shot from the sky, and hit The Dark Kid, who suddenly disappeared, leaving behind just blood from the wound.

It hadn't really happened. It had really happened. The Jack of Knives had killed his best friend, he hadn't killed his best friend.

What was the truth, what was the lie? The Jack of Knives needed help. Needed someone.

Another mirror appeared. The Jack of Knives was no longer on the mirror, but he was looking in a mirror, and he saw Death looking out at him.

"Welcome to my valley," he said. "I hope you find it rather … comfortable."

"Your tricks won't work," The Jack of Knives said.

"You just killed your friend," Death taunted. "I took his corpse away so you wouldn't feel too bad, but I can always bring it back."

"You wouldn't do that."

"I would," Death said, and suddenly, The Jack of Knives was holding the corpse of his friend. Except his eyes were wide open, and he was smiling. He was dead, but he was alive. He had the knife tucked deep inside his heart, and he was bleeding all over, but he was still alive somehow.

240

"You murdered me," he said, tauntingly. "How could you kill me like that?"

The Jack of Knives realized he was holding nothing, as he cried out, "No, no, please, stop!" and realized he was holding his head. He had only imagined holding the corpse, he'd only imagined talking to Death, he'd only imagined killing his friend. And yet, it all seemed so real.

"Ace wanted to get back at you," came a voice from nowhere, which sounded like Death but was shattered. "Ace wants to talk to you."

But there was no Ace, there was only The Jack of Knives, who saw nothing but mirrors around him, all of them talking to him, all of them reflecting himself from many different alternate universes, some from classical Greece in different social positions, some from alternate medieval worlds, some from various countries in the modern world, some of different races, all the same, all looking at him, and The Jack of Knives felt as though he was surrounded by millions of televisions, all of them talking to him, ceaseless and mind-bending chattering, and he wanted to shatter the mirrors, but he knew it wouldn't do any good, as they, the alternate universe reflections of The Jack of Knives, continued to taunt him and tell him how much of a weak murderer he was …

Then all of those mirrors were gone. The Jack of Knives was standing before The Dark Kid. Still in the Valley of Death, but … it was as if nothing had happened.

The Dark Kid was looking at The Jack of Knives, puzzled. "You okay?"

"I killed you," The Jack of Knives said. "I'm so sorry."

The Dark Kid only smiled … but it was genuine. His heart was bleeding, and he held it, and just said, "I know. But it's what needed to happen. I needed to die, so that you could live."

"But I won't live," The Jack of Knives said. "I can't live. Not with the Death Mirror shard in my head."

And that was when The Jack of Knives indeed felt something in his brain. He touched what was there, and pulled it out, expecting a shard, but it was a knife. His knife. He had done this to himself.

"You need to kill yourself," The Dark Kid said. "Over and over again. Avenge my death. Avenge my death, Jack."

"Yes," The Jack of Knives said, and continued to stab his brain, and he saw whole worlds collapsing upon each other, and he saw mirrors reflecting everything that had ever happened and everything that ever would happen, and it was too much to take in, so much that his mind burst, spilling out dreams and nightmares, and then none of that was happening.

The Jack of Knives was just staring at his reflection. Just staring. There was no Dark Kid. There was no Death. There was no one. There was just The Jack of Knives, staring at his reflection and seeing his own knife stuck in his brain, the pain more than he could stand …

The Alternate Universe Breakdown

The Black Queen knew that she was slowly becoming a loony.

This really wasn't all that surprising. It wasn't surprising at all. It turned out that The Suicide King, with his suicidal nature, had kept the kingdom fairly under control. Sure, it wasn't perfect, and sure, it bred other problems, but it was certainly better than how The Black Queen was handling it.

Because in all actuality, The Black Queen wasn't handling it at all. She was just letting her people go crazy with Death's Mirror, and lose whatever sanity they had left. She was letting them be violent toward each other, letting them mock kill each other all day, with a few successes thrown in here and there, for good measure.

And all of this mayhem was taking its toll on The Black Queen. Even though Death's Mirror wasn't literally affecting her, the reflection was powerful enough to affect her nonetheless. And that wasn't good. It wouldn't be long before the kingdom completely lost its head.

The Black Queen was also aware of another phenomenon that was happening because of the release of Death's Mirror. Worlds were slowly collapsing upon each other. It was the alternate universe breakdown. And indeed, worlds were breaking down upon each other. This was only the beginning, what she knew had happened to The Jack of Knives in the Valley of Death, and what she knew had happened with Brannon meeting his other Brannon. The worlds weren't collapsing on each other just yet, but that process had already begun, and once the worlds collapsed on each other for good …

The Black Queen didn't like thinking about what that signified. It wasn't good, not in the slightest. The implications, they were terrible. The possibilities, they were infinite, alternate, relevant. Things were not good.

And as if right on cue, that was when a servant walked in and said, "Your royal highness, you have a visitor."

In walked a woman who looked exactly like The Black Queen, except she was dressed in eighteenth century French clothes. Ah, so a Black Queen from an eighteenth century France. How charming.

As if The Black Queen didn't have enough problems. She knew people out there, unhappy peasants, unhappy noblemen who had been murdered, were storming the castle walls, trying to get inside, trying to get in so they could murder the queen, who wasn't doing anything. And in walked a reminder that things were just getting started, that they could get infinitely worse. They could always get infinitely worse.

"Hello, dearie," the French Black Queen said.

The Black Queen didn't respond. This wasn't happening. The alternate universe breakdown … that couldn't happen. That couldn't happen at all.

"Such a polite way to welcome your other you," The French Black Queen said. "Very lovely to be in acquaintance with such a psychopath. I usually thought that the other Black Queens had class, and it seems like you are severely lacking in that department. Which is a shame, really."

"Contorted Royal is a very violent place," The Black Queen said in reply. "Are you sure you want to be here?"

"Of course I'm sure. You think I haven't seen violence before? Well, you're quite wrong. I've seen plenty of violence. Violence is nothing to me. Violence is in fact my bread and butter. Nothing gets done when people are peaceful and tolerant of each other. It's like the French Revolution in my pseudo eighteenth century France. We have ideals of freedom of choice and yet everyone wants to force each other out of despotism through violence and chaos. It's a riot, really."

"I don't want you here," The Black Queen said simply.

"I know you don't. But that's not your choice, unfortunately for you. With things a-changing, we can't have you ruling this kingdom all yourself."

"What are you suggesting?"

"Isn't it obvious? I'm going to take over. Actually, we're all going to take over."

And in walked four other Black Queens. Each one was dressed in a respective suit, of course suits of cards: one dressed in diamonds with very beautiful diamonds on her ears and as a necklace, wearing red clothes like the card; one that was holding a spade and was dressed with clothes with spades on them, the clothes of which were black; one with hearts all over her red clothes, and wearing a heart-shaped pendant; and one with clubs on her black clothes who was indeed holding a club. The four Black Queens walked into the room, and they were all laughing ceremoniously, freely, mockingly.

"We're going to attack you," they said to The Black Queen, who couldn't believe this was happening.

The Black Queens were coming to take over the kingdom! It sounded somewhat absurd, but it also sounded plausible.

"But," said the French Black Queen, "taking over the kingdom will just be a small part of the puzzle. What we really want to do is drive you, Lady Black Queen, *bonkers*."

"And why would you want to do that?" The Black Queen said, and she was sweating heavily now, her heart racing fast. This was going to get out of control, the way the Black Queens were staring at The Black Queen. This couldn't end well.

"Because we need to chop off the head," The French Black Queen said.

And the Black Queens slowly began to approach The Black Queen. The Black Queen called out, "Uh … Ralph? Ralph? You out there, somewhere?"

Ralph had left for a little while, to brainstorm some ideas of how to destroy Death's Mirror, but he came into the courtroom and saw The Black Queens approaching The Black Queen like a pack of hungry wolves. He didn't need to say anything to confirm that The Black Queen was doomed.

"Help me …" said The Black Queen.

"Oh, no one can help you, dear," The French Black Queen said, and The Black Queens, now right before The Black Queen, began to try and push her down on the ground. The Black Queen resisted, and Ralph said, "Cut it out," but it didn't work. Before The Black Queen knew it, she was on the ground.

They began to beat her head. The Black Queen felt pain at first, but suddenly, she was laughing. She was laughing because she saw stars. She was laughing because she saw universes breaking down. She was laughing because her world had gone crazy, its mind spinning more wilder than a top. She was laughing because she was indeed going crazy, and nothing was going to be able to stop her. Nothing was more psycho than a bunch of Black Queens coming to take over the kingdom and drive The Black Queen up the wall.

So The Black Queen just laughed. Because, what else was she supposed to do?

"Are you getting very sleepy?" came The French Black Queen.

"As a matter of fact I am," said The Black Queen melodramatically, and the other Black Queens laughed. It was all just a joke to them.

They finally stopped, and gave The Black Queen a moment to think. She probably had a lot of brain damage now, but she didn't care, because all she saw were stars, and she heard a few cuckoos in the distance.

She stood up shakily, and looked at The Black Queens. Instead of five, she saw ten. They were doubled, because she had double vision from the brain trauma.

The Black Queens all backed away, and Ralph went toward The Black Queen. He helped her sit up, to get in her throne, but she just continued to laugh.

"Suicide King cuckoos," The Black Queen said, still laughing. "Club me a bub a me."

"Yup," said The French Black Queen. "She's flipped her lid."

"Ha ha … flipped lid. It rhymes," said The Black Queen.

"We should get you to a hospital," Ralph said, obviously concerned.

The Black Queen barely heard this. What she heard sounded like, "We need to get you to a shrink. We need to get you to a psych ward." But The Black Queen wasn't psycho. She was just fine. She was more than just fine. She was as right as rain, and she had never felt better.

Ralph looked at The Black Queens, who were giggling at the damage they'd done.

"The brain is not a thing to mess with," Ralph said. "Who knows what you guys have done to her."

"We had to make her batty," replied The French Black Queen. "We needed to chop off the head. I'd say brain damage is a good way to do that."

"But it isn't funny," Ralph said.

"Of course it's not funny," said The French Black Queen. "It's hilarious."

"Cuckoo, cuckoo," came The Black Queen.

"Besides," came The French Black Queen, "it was necessary anyway. We can't have The Black Queen attempting to rule Contorted Royal. Contorted Royal belongs to all the universes, all the alternate universes."

"When we all fold over, there won't *be* any universes!" Ralph said desperately. "We would have all collapsed on each other!"

"Exactly where the fun is," The French Black Queen said malevolently. "Didn't you know? But what would *you* know? You haven't met any of your alternate universe selves."

And at that moment, a medieval version of Ralph walked in the door.

The Black Queen saw him and ran to him immediately, not taking into account the words that had been exchanged. The two began to kiss. Had The Black Queen finally found her Ralph? It seemed that way. She had Ralph, and they were kissing, and he wasn't all obsessed with keeping his chastity for Alice.

But then that Ralph disappeared.

"Just had to get her hopes up," The French Black Queen said.

"That was mean," Ralph said. "You know how much she wants me."

The Black Queen just stood there, looking as if, Had that

really just happened?

"It's a time of war," The French Black Queen said. "What else did you expect? We have to resort to such cruel tactics to break down our opponent."

"Ha ha, break down atonements," The Black Queen said.

"I think we need to get The Black Queen to a *hospital*," Ralph said again.

The Black Queen tried to respond to this by kissing Ralph, but even now, Ralph kept his distance. The Black Queen stomped her foot dramatically, and said, "*Fine*. Be that way. Be mean to your poor disabled granny."

The French Black Queen merely said, "Girls. You know what you need to do with Ralph."

The four Black Queens began to try and push Ralph and The Black Queen together. Ralph tried to keep his distance, but it didn't work, and soon, the two were very close to each other.

But The Black Queen had been driven so bonkers that she didn't realize a pair of her favorite lips were right before her. They were close enough to where it would look conspicuous, for sure, if someone just happened to walk in.

And that was when The Black Queen saw Spade. Except, he was an alternate universe Spade, from the modern world.

"So this is what you've been doing since I died?" Spade said.

Ralph looked at Spade, and said, "We've been set up. It's these blasted Black Queens. They're treating us like puppets."

"No, she wanted it," The French Black Queen said. "She did indeed."

"I knew I shouldn't have trusted you," Spade said, and stormed out of the room.

"No, honey, no!" The Black Queen shouted, but it was too late. He was already gone.

"Well, we've probably done enough damage for one day," The French Black Queen said. "But all of the chaos has just begun."

The Black Queens then left the room, but not without waving at Ralph, who just stared at The Black Queens. Then Ralph went to The Black Queen, who sat on the throne, and began to cry.

"What's wrong?" Ralph asked.

"What's wrong?" The Black Queen said, as if she couldn't believe this question had been asked. "I get my brains beat out by alternate universe Black Queens and you just stand there. You frame me and make it look like I'm in love with you when you know how much I love Spade. And to top it all off, as my adviser, you've done nothing to stop this alternate universe breakdown. You're just letting everyone go batty!"

Ralph wanted to respond, but didn't, so The Black Queen responded for him: "Go on! Get out of here! Get!" It was like she was talking to a dog.

Ralph gave The Black Queen a sad, puppy look, and then left The Black Queen to her thoughts.

Why was this happening? Why *her*? What had The Black Queen done to deserve all this?

Starving Poetry, Heartless Poets

While The Black Queen was quietly and unceremoniously losing her mind, The Suicide King was ... thinking.

The Poetess was heartless; she was a femme fatale going around and metaphorically murdering everybody, in particular The Suicide King. She was wreaking havoc and causing illimitable chaos, and destroying everything that came in her path with either her poetry or her pathos or her psychopathology and determination.

And The Suicide King *loved* it!

He was having the time of his life, going to the finest parties and living it up. He was doing every drug imaginable, he was having threesomes, he was even experimenting with homosexuality.

And The Poetess! Oh, was she so divine in bed! She was a beautiful lovemaker, who could do anything she darn well wanted to. It was quite glorious.

And the best part? The Suicide King wasn't committing suicide. Sure, he felt empty at times, but how could he feel empty, when he was next to someone so ravishing, so beautiful? He couldn't, if he didn't mind saying so himself. He was living it up, for once it was about himself.

The Suicide King had skinned off his awful medieval

248

clothes, and was wearing a dress suit and tie and slacks and fancy dress shoes, as well as a pair of sunglasses, and walking around town with a girl on each side of his arm.

Or at least he had been.

Right now, he was with The Poetess. They were sitting outside of their hotel, talking about the starved nature of poetry in modern society, that modern poetry was starving itself to death because heartless poets were writing the poems, and how poetry was much better in the medieval times. The Poetess was expounding her theories of poetry, and talking about this, and it was after they had just had a glorious bit of sex up in their hotel room.

"I couldn't agree with you more," The Suicide King said.

"There's just something so desperate about poetry," The Poetess said. "Something that just nags and nags, something that taunts."

"My dear, that's because all poets are sluts," The Suicide King said amicably.

"You don't say?" The Poetess said, and planted a fat kiss on The Suicide King's cheek.

The Suicide King blushed, though he wasn't sure why, and then said, "They are, though. Poets desperately want attention, but usually only the lowest of the low will buy or listen to their product. That is, except for medieval times. It's debatable in the more classical era, like classical Greece, because of how hateful and spiteful Plato was to poets … but us medievalists. We live for poetry. We embrace the courtly love of the slutty poet."

"How sweet," The Poetess said. "So, do you think we should test out your theory?"

"I'd love to, my dear," The Suicide King said.

The Poetess pointed at a bookstore up ahead. "Let's go check it out, see if they sell any poetry."

The Suicide King was all in. And why wouldn't he be? For once, he wasn't committing suicide. In fact, he'd tossed away his sword. He had no use for that dreadful thing, that terrible artifact from ancient times, which symbolized his bloody self-violence and selfishness.

It was a used book store, it turned out, with some new books sprinkled here and there sporadically. Naturally, they went to the medieval section, to see what was cooking there.

There was only one book. A single, slim, dog-eared anthology of medieval poetry. It was a sad collection, no doubt, the poor copy, sitting all alone with no one to read it, being a poor desperate soul. The Poetess picked it up rather roughly and yet simultaneously lovingly and said, "We'll be taking this."

They went to the front to purchase the book, and The Suicide King couldn't help but get in a few words: "I have here one of the finest poets around, quite famous in our era and in the eras to come. She was very disappointed in your medieval literature section, however. It seems people haven't heard of poems like 'Sir Orfeo,' they'd much rather be studying the absolute finest in modern day poetry, though I'd say, that's a far cry. Nothing beats some Chaucer in a day in the sun."

"I couldn't agree more," The Poetess said. "And, I'm slutty."

The checker just stared at the odd spectacle, and The Suicide King just laughed. "We've been on each other like white on rice. You've gotta understand that before you make any judgments about us. We are cultured people, though, for what would we do without Langland and Gower?"

The checker just continued to stare, and then finally realized that he needed to check out the book, so he did.

The Poetess now owned her own poetry anthology of medieval poetry. She began to strut around town, and The Suicide King happily followed. She began to openly read the poetry around for all people to hear, but naturally, no one was interested in something so antiquated, which just made The Poetess and The Suicide King's time all the more enjoyable.

They were heartless poets, with no soul. But that didn't mean the poetry wasn't starving.

The Suicide King suddenly had a vision, of Ralph walking around the city with a Kurt Vonnegut novel. Which he had, before. He had indeed. Oh, what The Suicide King would give if Ralph could be here right now, to share his literary knowledge, his intellectual secrets.

"Let's go and have sex," The Suicide King said.

"I'm all in," piped The Poetess.

They went up to the bedroom, holding hands, and went

straight to bed. They made their magical love, and after their glorious affair, The Suicide King suddenly frowned.

"Are all poets heartless?" he mused philosophically.

"I don't know what you mean," came The Poetess. "We've got a good book, I'd say poetry has never been more alive."

"I just feel poetry is dying a slow and painful death, because it's so expressionless and sad," The Suicide King said, mellow in tone. "Not because people don't read it, because people do read, thankfully, as the bookstores prove ... but I feel like poetry is dying in an abstract way, and that's because it's heartless. There's no soul. No real soul."

"Not if you read Elizabeth Bishop or Sylvia Plath or Anne Sexton," The Poetess said. "And this medieval collection has some of the most beautiful poems I've ever read, my favorites being either the very, very short ones or the very ambitious and long ones. So no, I'd have to disagree with what you're saying. Poetry is alive and well."

But The Suicide King wasn't listening. He was distracted by something. He was distracted by the idea that poetry was committing suicide because it was so heartless. And that was when he realized that the poetry wasn't what was dying (though perhaps it was, though perhaps it wasn't), but it was The Suicide King who was dying.

He was committing suicide again.

"Oh dear, I've done it again," The Suicide King said suddenly.

The Poetess looked at The Suicide King, quite concerned. "Done what again, dear?"

"I've committed suicide," The Suicide King said. "I've gone down the self-destructive route without even knowing it, or being aware of it."

"I don't see how," The Poetess said. "Liberal arts means you can do whatever you want."

"But that's precisely the point," The Suicide King said. "I've forgone chivalry. I've cheated on my wife, out of spite and revenge, but am only destroying myself in the process. I did drugs up the nose to the point to where my nose is all stuffy and coked up. And I don't feel happy. I feel empty. I'm starving poetry, and a heartless poet."

The Poetess didn't say anything for a moment, but then just laughed like she'd heard a good joke. "I don't know what you're talking about dear. You've just experienced the time of your life, and you're saying that you've committed *suicide*? You can do whatever you want with poetry, but not *that* much. Maybe you should recount the awful things you've been saying?"

"I'd like to," The Suicide King admitted gravely. "But I miss my little boy."

"You mean, The Jack of Knives?" said The Poetess.

"I horribly and tremendously screwed up his future. I could have taught him virtues, and chivalry, and passion, and instead, because of his terrible situation, I just taught him hate and hatred, mixed in with a little murder. But he is a lovely little kid."

"He's not that little," The Poetess said, and grabbed The Suicide King's face, forced him to look at her, said, "Look at me. Isn't this what you wanted?"

The Suicide King sighed sadly. "No, this wasn't what I wanted. I miss my family. I miss them more than anything. I alienated my wife, threw away my son … I'm a terrible person."

"Well, isn't that why your land is called Contorted Royal?"

"Perhaps," The Suicide King said, still philosophic. "But I'm ruined. I'm a wretch."

"I just hear self-pity," The Poetess said seductively.

"Well, regardless, I think we need to break it off for a little while."

"And leave me a poor and orphaned poetess?" The Poetess said. "Poor and broke on the streets with no one to listen to my poetry and song but myself?"

"I'm afraid so," The Suicide King said sincerely. "That is, until I figure out the blasted code, of how *not* to commit suicide. It really gets destructive and lonely after a while."

"But don't you want me?" The Poetess said. "Don't you want my lascivious language, my flourishing adverbs?"

"Meaning breasts," The Suicide King said bluntly.

Now it was the Poetess's turn to frown. "Yes," she admitted miserably.

"My dear, all poets are knights in shining armor," The Suicide King said. "Oh, why do I do everything backwards? I come from the Middle Ages! The time of chivalry! And I just

252

throw it all away! What is wrong with me?"

The Suicide King buried his face in his pillow.

The Poetess just patted The Suicide King on the back. "Okay. Fine. I see your point. I'm not happy, but I wouldn't be a poet if I wasn't open-minded. Fine, dear. Go. Go and fix your family. But I can pretty much guarantee it won't work."

The Suicide King looked up from his pillow. "Precisely! Because we're all heartless poets starving for poetry! Which is fine. It is what it is."

"It is what it is," The Poetess echoed.

"I wish it could have been different," The Suicide King confessed. "All of this satire, this bitter satire, is really bad for the soul. It's like too much Rabelais after drinking too much wine."

"I think some of it's a little funny," The Poetess said, trying to keep things light.

"But it's so very *sad*," The Suicide King said grimly. "I screwed up my family, a grievous sin. I need to change my ways."

And The Suicide King saw the light.

Or, thought he saw the light, at least. But, he really didn't. Because in reality, he was stuck. He honestly didn't know how not to commit suicide. It was in his nature. It seemed everything he did was suicidal, scandalous self-murder, no matter what he tried. No matter what he did. Was it wrong to want a poem? It seemed that way, because all poems were just hungry little children trying to make their way in a bitter satire. And that made The Suicide King depressed. It made him want to jump into a car and go wildly over the speed limit and maniacally drive off a cliff while laughing out loud like a psycho.

Is that what he had done to his child? To The Jack of Knives? Made him hungry and orphaned and a poor servant boy? It seemed that way, and now look where he'd ended up!

But, on the same token, The Poetess was very ravishing. She was *gorgeous*. She filled a void that The Suicide King couldn't quite explain. She gave The Suicide King his independence. And that was nice.

"I don't know," The Suicide King said. "I admit, sometimes right and wrong seems too arbitrary. We have passions, like poor Lancelot and Guinevere. It makes me sick and sad and happy at the same time."

253

"Well, you can still have me," The Poetess said seductively.

"Really?" said The Suicide King. "Well, then, let's party!"

And before The Suicide King knew what was happening, three women walked into the room, and they were all here for The Suicide King, and The Suicide King was at it again.

But this wasn't all that surprising, he reckoned sadly. His life was going down the drain. He had no hope left. All he had was suicide, in whatever form it took.

And it made him very melancholy. The limits of the corporeal world. The loneliness of the corporeal.

But, he was called The Suicide King for a reason, and maybe, just maybe, if the Poetess fed him poetry, he'd be able to heal again, and drop the sword for good …

The Fire and Brimstone Cliché: Except, Not a Cliché

Alice had never felt so alone.

She desperately needed to see Ralph. She needed him to give her comfort, to tell her that everything was going to be okay. She knew why he couldn't, though, of course, which was because he was busy trying to help The Black Queen. But that didn't mean that Alice didn't need to see him, to have at least some semblance of hope.

Any at all.

Alice heard God in her head; except, God's voice was fractured, splintered, broken, shattered. She heard God here, she heard God there, she heard God speak in two or more different voices that were somehow the same at the same time. She heard God talking to her in a split way that was causing her to freak out.

She'd heard voices before. She'd once thought that she'd heard the voice of Abraham Lincoln, in fact. But that had been nothing. Having God in the head, however, was like having a bomb in the brain. She couldn't explain why, but it was increasing her anxiety, at the very least: it was driving her insane, her mind getting ready to explode with insanity.

And the voices: they were so *loud*. She didn't understand why God needed to speak so loudly. Maybe because he was God, maybe because he wanted to make sure Alice heard every word he said. Whatever the reason, it was no doubt taking its toll on her.

Alice was stumbling through a private section behind the castle, and holding her head, as though it was going to split any moment. She was crying out in her moment of crisis, "Help me," but no one was there. No one at all.

And God just continued to talk to her. Well, scream at her, more like, but also taunt her, with whispers, with various different pitches in voice, creating a chaotic and fragmented sound collage, a cubism of noise.

"You're a bad person, Alice," God said.

And in another voice, a voice that was still God's, "Go to Hell, Alice."

"Alice," God said. "Alice."

All in a fractured voice, split in many different sections.

"You should go to Hell, Alice. You don't deserve what you have."

"Please," Alice said. "Stop. Please. I can't do this."

"Of course you can't do this," God said.

"Why would she be able to do it?"

"She can't do it, that's the point. She'll never be able to do it. She'll never be able to do anything. She's a defect in the eyes of God. No one could love someone like her."

"Burn it down, Alice. Burn it down."

"Alice."

"Alice, you're going to Hell. We're all going to Hell. I hate society, I hate everyone. We're all going to burn. We're all sinners damned to eternal Hell, because of the terrible things we have done. It's all fire and brimstone."

"Please," Alice begged. "Please, just get out of my head!"

"It must feel good to have schizophrenia, and hear me talking," God continued.

"She doesn't know what she's doing."

"She'll never know what she's doing."

"She needs to go to Hell. She needs to have a taste of fire. She needs to burn forever in a pit of fire. She needs to burn forever and ever."

"She will, don't worry about that."

"Alice is a sinner. Alice is like everyone else, though worse in some ways, though also similar."

"Of course. We mustn't single her out. No one gets the glory of God. No one reaches the Kingdom of Heaven. Everyone goes to Hell. Because everyone is either defected or a sinner, a blazing, self-righteous sinner, thinking they are better than God."

"Or they're an atheist."

"They're a non-believer. They haven't been baptized. They're going to Hell. Going to Hell."

"Going to Hell."

"All going to Hell."

"Hell."

"Stop it!" Alice shouted.

"But we're just getting started," said the multiple voices of God. "This is just the beginning."

Alice was able to look up, and that was when she saw storm clouds. They were pregnant with rain, dark and bruised, getting ready to spill out their anger.

Except, she knew it was a hallucination. She knew herself well enough to know that it was always a hallucination, so to speak. Of course, some things were real, but not all of it. She knew herself well enough to spot what was real and what wasn't, and these storm clouds weren't there.

"Do you feel good, figuring it out?" God said.

"Please," Alice said. "Please … just stop."

"I can't do that, Alice."

Alice heard thunder crackling. It sounded like God's wrath. It sounded like God shouting at humanity for failing him, for being such terrible, terrible people, for falling so short. It crackled and it crackled, louder than even the voices that were raging in Alice's head.

And that was when she saw orange coming down. She wasn't looking up, but she could see the orange, and when she looked up, she saw that the clouds were now fireclouds.

The whole fire and brimstone cliché: except, not a cliché.

"I have to punish all society," God said.

"Yes, I have to kill them all."

"I have to destroy everyone. All souls must suffer in Hell, even children's souls. No one makes it through."

Alice looked up, amazed at the spectacle, and very terrified. God was serious about raining down fire, worse than even the flood during Noah's time. She could see the fire swirling around in the clouds, getting ready to fall.

The thunder continued.

All of this, all of this was just a hallucination. It wasn't real. The voices weren't real. The firestorm wasn't real. It was all in Alice's imagination, if only she could just remember that …

But she couldn't. Because she was terrified. Because, she was weak. Because she was a schizophrenic.

The clouds split, and began to rain down their fire.

Alice felt herself burn. Her body somehow remained whole, but she was on fire, as more fire continued to fall, but somehow she didn't char. But that didn't mean there wasn't pain. That didn't mean her soul wasn't in agony. That didn't mean she wasn't in eternal damnation, caught in painful licks of delusional flame.

"Save your soul, Alice," God said.

"Yes, save your soul."

"How?" Alice screamed in pain. "Please, tell me how to save my soul!"

"Is my wrath too great?" God taunted.

"Yes, is my wrath a problem for you?"

"Save you soul by burning down the castle. Purge it of its evil."

Alice thought about this. Yes, it made sense, somehow. Burn down the source of evil.

But no … no. That was a delusion, spurred on by voices. The castle wasn't evil, it didn't need to be cleansed. And she couldn't just burn down the castle: people would get hurt. People were in the castle. That would be terrible to do that.

"Do it, Alice, or you'll remain in Hell," God said.

"Yes, Alice, save your soul."

"You need to save your soul, Alice."

"Yes, save your soul."

"Okay," Alice said, but she didn't know why she was conceding, except because she was in so much pain and the voices were so loud and fractured and she was being traumatized, how could her illness be so destructive? Because she knew she wasn't listening to God, she wasn't talking to God. God wasn't like this, was he? No, of course. And God didn't exist, anyway, right? No, he didn't. Meaning, all of this was delusion and illusion, and she'd do well to stop entertaining—

"Do it, Alice!" God shouted. "Do it, before I murder you, over and over again!"

"Okay!" Alice shouted out. "Okay! I surrender to your will!"

Hallucination. Reality. What was the difference? Alice didn't know. She simply looked around and saw that the fireclouds were just rain clouds now. So the storm clouds really had existed. Okay. That had been real.

It was raining, and yet, Alice held a torch; somehow, the fire didn't go out, even though it was raining. It was time to commit her act of arson. It was time to hurt innocent people. God was angry. God was pissed. God wanted vengeance. God was sick of his creation, he wanted them dead. All of them.

As Alice prepared to burn down the castle, she couldn't help but think of The Suicide King, and the life he was living now. He was going to Hell, for all of his terrible deeds. He was going to Hell for being adulterous, for doing drugs, for being a liberal artist. For having no conscious conscience. And he was going to Hell because he still didn't get that suicide wasn't an option. All who committed suicide to escape their pain went straight to Hell. Straight to Hell they went.

Alice felt tormented by this prospect. Why was The Suicide King going to suffer in Hell, when he didn't know what he was doing, when he was just trying to drown the pain? Pain that God refused to take away?

"Because you're all sinners," God said.

"Because I hate all of you."

"Because it's time, time to burn down this wretched castle."

"Save your soul, Alice."

"Yes, save your soul."

Alice took the torch and lit it on the grass. Despite the rain, it caught fire. The fire began to spread, catching walls on fire.

"What have I done?" Alice said, knowing this wouldn't end well. "Why are you doing this to me?"

"Save your soul, Alice."

"Yes, save your soul."

"Please, forgive me for my crimes," Alice said. "Forgive

me for what I am doing. Absolve me of my sins."

"Save your soul, Alice."

"Yes, save your soul."

Alice watched as the castle began to burn. That was when she sensed someone was watching her. She turned, and saw Bishop standing in the shadows. But she could see his smile. He was very pleased. Somehow, he was happy.

And then he disappeared, like a shadow.

Alice watched as the fire continued to blaze. They were going to get it. They were going to burn. The fire and brimstone cliché, not a cliché in the slightest. Not even close. They all deserved to suffer. They all deserved eternal damnation. She was cleansing the kingdom. She was killing innocent people. She was a murderer.

The fire continued to spread, and Alice fell on her knees in distress. She asked herself, "Why is this happening?" but couldn't get the words out.

"Save your soul," God said.

"Yes, save your soul."

But Alice didn't want to save her soul. Alice didn't care what happened to her. Alice didn't care if she suffered for all eternity in Hell, she just didn't want to hurt anyone. No one at all. She just wanted to be a good person. Yes, her mind was split, fractured, broken, but she still just wanted to be a good person. Yes, she was considered a defect, by all, yes, everyone hated her, they thought she was hideous, her mind was terribly diseased and ugly, but she couldn't let that stop her from just being a good person …

It was like prayer, though not quite. And it was somehow working, because she saw that the fire was retracting itself. The fire was disappearing. It wasn't long before it was completely gone.

Reality. Fantasy. The line, so blurred. She just didn't know what was real.

Maybe she had never started the fire.

Yes. That had to have been it. She had been saved by her hallucination.

And yet, hadn't she really held a flame?

Yes and no. That was Death's Mirror.

Bishop was going to hate her for not succeeding in burning down the castle. She already felt his rage. But God had gone silent, and for now, Alice was safe. She hadn't done anything bad because of her illness yet. Not yet—thankfully, not yet.

But Death's Mirror was recording it all. Watching it all.

Waiting.

Waiting for the moment to strike again. Which would happen soon enough. It would happen eventually.

And Alice wouldn't be able to handle her brain breaking apart again.

But Death's Mirror was God, and God was Death's Mirror.

God was anger. God was vengeance.

And God, he never lost.

The fire and brimstone cliché: not at *all* a cliché.

Chortle in Her Glee, Cackle Happily

Ralph did not know what to do. The Black Queen was clearly losing her mind, but Ralph couldn't keep her stabilized. He couldn't keep her sane. He couldn't keep her in reality, couldn't keep her marbles in her brain.

"He he he," The Black Queen said. "Ha ha ha."

"You can't keep acting this way," Ralph said desperately. "You've got to come back to normal. With the peasants revolting, with Death's Mirror shattering everything, with everything going crazy and The Suicide King gone, you've got to come back to Earth. Please, Black Queen … come back home."

"Ho ho ho," The Black Queen said. "You don't love me, no no no."

"I don't …" Ralph began, and looked at The Black Queen, who was dancing around like a psychopath, and very clumsily.

Ralph thought about what The Black Queen had just said. He didn't love her? Well, he cared about her, of course, but yes, he didn't romantically love her because his heart belonged to Alice.

But as Ralph thought about this, he realized that his rejection of The Black Queen was leading to her going batty. Sure, so was the pressure of everything going on in the kingdom, and Death's Mirror destroying everything, and the fact that The Black

Queen had just recently suffered brain damage, but Ralph couldn't take that pain out of account. Even if he wanted.

What Ralph needed was for The Black Queen to be sane. He needed that, and right now, before things got more and more out of hand.

As Ralph thought about his rejection of The Black Queen, he began to play with the idea that perhaps, he needed to have feelings for her nonetheless. Yes, love triangles were never fun, triangulating feelings messily and dangerously, and he did want to be chaste for Alice … but what if, considering that these desperate times called for desperate measures, Ralph needed to love The Black Queen? Meaning, kiss her. At the very least.

Not good. Not good at all. It could only lead to more chaos. Ralph was sure of it.

And yet, it seemed like a good idea. The Black Queen had been forced for quite some time now to repress her love for Ralph, to repress the pain of Ralph's rejection. If Ralph even kissed The Black Queen, perhaps it would ease some of that tension.

He wasn't sure, but he didn't have time to act, because suddenly, four fools dressed up like cards came into the court. The Black Queen pulled out a bunch of knives, and said to Ralph, "Love is like a fine knife … you never know what heart it will hurt."

And then she threw a knife at one of the fools. It hit him, stabbed him, but The Black Queen threw more knives, saying, "He he he," over and over again, laughing, chortling in her glee, and cackling happily.

She was really hurting these innocent fools, but she didn't care, so immersed in her grief was The Black Queen.

Ralph needed to come up with a plan, and he needed to do it fast. "Black Queen."

"Can't you see I'm busy, dear?" she said drunkenly, throwing more knives. "I don't have time to cheat on The Suicide King anymore. I'm out causing people to die."

Amazingly (though not that amazing, considering it was Contorted Royal), no matter how many times the fools got stabbed, they stayed alive. And indeed, it was a game for The Black Queen. She was showing no remorse for what she was doing, because she was in a state of psychosis, among other things. Her repressed feelings had indeed gotten the best of her. Everything amounted to chaos and strife.

"Ho ho ho," The Black Queen said, and continued to throw the knives.

Ralph finally had had it. He went to The Black Queen and grabbed her head. "Look at me."

The Black Queen just giggled. "Oh, don't you know you don't want me?"

"Stop this," Ralph said. "You have to rule the kingdom. You have to come up with a plan to bring back The Suicide King and to heal Contorted Royal from Death's Mirror. Save your kingdom. You can't do that by throwing knives at fools dressed like cards."

"I can do plenty of things," The Black Queen said, and was going to throw another knife, when Ralph grabbed her hand. The two wrestled for a moment, The Black Queen shouting that Ralph was a misogynistic, narcissistic, and a highly inconsiderate psychopath, and when Ralph wasn't able to arrest the knife from The Black Queen, he just backed off.

So Ralph did what he could, and said to the fools, "Get out of here! Don't let her hurt you!"

"Like you hurt me?" The Black Queen said, rather angrily.

The card fools quickly shuffled away, out of the courtroom.

"I'm not trying to hurt you," Ralph said. "I just love Alice. Polyamorous relationships don't work out well. You know, threesomes, swingers, open marriages and free relationships … there's no loyalty. Curse me for having these blasted morals, but that's the way I feel. Alice is the one I love. I even spent time with her as a hallucination, for crying out loud."

"Well," The Black Queen said, her laugh gone; she was indeed finding no amusement, at least for the moment. "You just violated the queen's wishes by clearing out the room. I was entertaining myself, seeing as how my own husband hijacked our only good court poet."

"Can we just cut out this game?" Ralph snapped. "It's always about petty this, petty that. We never get anything done because we're all so self-absorbed."

"Welcome to Contorted Royal," The Black Queen said, rather bluntly. "Welcome to the universe. Welcome to real *life*. It don't change just because a poor, poor peasant boy from the modern world wants a little equality."

"Oh, cut it out," Ralph said, finding that last comment a little comical. "I'm suburban, where I come from. You know—middle class."

"Well, you know what I mean," The Black Queen said dramatically. "Now, if you'll excuse me, I have cards to find—"

Before The Black Queen could say anything, the doors were pounded against, rather loudly.

Ralph looked at The Black Queen, who suddenly looked afraid. "It's the peasants."

"They're tired of it," Ralph said. "Tired of it all. You won't rule them, letting the alternate universe Black Queens taking over everything."

"Well, what do you want *me* to do about it?" The Black Queen said snobbishly. "I'm busy getting my heart broken, my heartfelt love rejected, my feminine independence wasted so pointlessly. I don't have time to rule the king dumb."

More pounding.

"They're going to burst in here any moment," Ralph said. "I sure hope you have a plan."

"Well you're my royal adviser," The Black Queen said. "So, advise me."

Ralph thought about this. Maybe he could placate the peasants when they came storming in.

Nope. Too late. The peasants knocked down the doors and came trampling into the courtroom. When they were inches away from Ralph and The Black Queen, who were trapped against the back wall, one of the leaders came up and said, "This is just not acceptable. While you two are busy getting your rocks off and having your glorious affair, we're out here starving and abandoned and lonely and working for nothing and being destroyed by Death's Mirror and the alternate universe Black Queen hostile takeover."

Ralph felt the sting of this comment about cheating. He wasn't cheating. He was advising. There was a big difference.

Maybe Ralph would have been better off just jumping in the sack and forgoing all desires to be good. He'd get accused of it anyway.

But Ralph remained calm, and spoke up for The Black Queen: "The Black Queen is an emotional and mental wreck right now. She's been getting her glee from throwing knives at poor fools dressed like cards."

"Off with her head!" shouted one of the peasants in the group.

"I agree," said the leader. "We need to execute her. Maybe that'll fix her head, her insanity."

"I can assure you it would only make things worse," Ralph said.

"And why is that?" said the leader angrily.

Ralph sighed, did his absolute best to keep things under control. "Look, I know you're not happy, but we're just as confused about all of this as you guys are."

"Oh, don't pretend you care," said the leader.

"Off with her head!" shouted several of the peasants in the crowd.

The Black Queen just looked at Ralph for help. Ralph didn't have any more ideas. He could see them getting ready to take The Black Queen to the guillotine. He could see their rage turning the wheels of their mind.

"She isn't ruling our kingdom effectively, so we're going to kill her," said the leader. "We've had it with these terrible working conditions, these terrible truths that drive us all batty. It's time we get rid of the corrupt queen. Overthrow the monarchy!"

"I agree!" shouted a peasant.

"Me too!" shouted another.

"No more Death's Mirror!"

"No more Black Queen takeovers!"

The leader nodded his head, smiled, and pulled out a knife. He looked musingly and amusingly at The Black Queen. "So, are you going to come with us quietly?"

"Of course she's not," came a voice that Ralph recognized immediately as Alice's.

The peasants turned to look at who had joined them, and Alice cut through the crowd, moving toward The Black Queen and Ralph.

Goodness, was it so nice to see her. Yes, it was, so nice to see her—such a beautiful girl.

Ralph was so excited to see her that he didn't immediately notice that something was wrong. Her mind looked fractured. He couldn't literally see her mind, of course, and yet, he could.

Her mind was fractured.

"She's not going to come with you guys," Alice said.

"And why is that?" said the leader.

"Yeah, why is that?" said another peasant.

"Because she's completely gone bonkers," Alice said, "and she'd be better served locked away, like in a mental hospital. She needs intensive psychiatric help, and I know just the place to keep her."

The leader looked carefully at Alice, and then said, "You think locking up our queen is the solution?"

"Yes," Alice said. "I do. She's been acting like an animal. She's as crazy as a loon."

And right on cue, The Black Queen began to howl like a dog. Except, it wasn't because she was acting. Ralph saw that it was real: the dam had completely burst, and in flooded the waters of insanity. The Black Queen had been reduced to an animal.

"See what I mean?" Alice said. "It'd be better if she was under psychiatric supervision."

"Why should we trust you?" said the leader, though he looked a little placated.

"Because I'm the court schizophrenic, and the power I wield is greater than you'll ever know," Alice said calmly. "So let me lock up The Black Queen."

The peasants thought about this, and then the leader said, "Well, locking her up in a mental hospital or a facsimile of a hospital sounds more torturous than offing off her head. I suppose that it would in fact cause her to lose her head anyway, the hospitalization. So … okay. It's a deal. Come on, my people. Let's let Alice handle the situation. She is our residential schizophrenic, after all, and we owe her that respect."

The peasants nodded and cleared out, and Alice went up to Ralph, said, "You okay?"

"I'm fine," Ralph said.

"I'm fine," The Black Queen mimicked sarcastically. "Now that you two love birds are together, I suppose there's no room for lady Black Queen."

Alice and Ralph knew what they needed to do: there was no hesitation, none whatsoever. They swarmed The Black Queen, began to drag her out of the courtroom, against her will, to where Alice was going to put her: a jail cell (she certainly couldn't go to a hospital, as The Black Queen wasn't good enough for it), where she was going to get psychiatric help: meaning, where she was going to get imprisoned and get no help, because it amounted to the same thing anyway.

The Black Queen cried out as they dragged her away, saying it was a violation of her rights and liberty and freedom, but Ralph knew this was the way.

Though he was worried. He was worried about Alice. Her mind … so, so fractured. And he feared that it was Alice who needed to be hospitalized, not The Black Queen …

Within an Ace of Madness, Just a Hair's Breadth Away

Ace had gotten his revenge on The Jack of Knives. Thrown him in a valley, and let Death's Mirror do the work. The Jack of Knives was indeed unravelling, and there was nothing that the poor boy could do about it. So by all accounts, Ace should have been very happy.

And yet, he wasn't happy about this. He'd hated The Jack of Knives for a long time, but had never quite understood why. Was it just chemistry? Was it because being around The Jack of Knives was just conflict, sandpaper rubbing against sandpaper, nothing but friction? It certainly seemed that way.

But that was no reason to let the boy suffer on his own, in full-blown Death's Mirror mode. Surely he deserved better than that. Surely.

But, Ace wasn't sure. He wasn't sure about anything anymore. He knew that things were going down the drain, and there was nothing he could do to stop it. Death was getting revenge on Ace for failing to keep The Machine intact, even though it honestly wasn't his fault. He had been tricked. But Death liked to be that way. He liked to play tricks.

He wanted Ace to be within an ace of madness, just a hair's

breadth away. The only problem with that was that Ace felt he already *was* mad. He couldn't say for sure, because could the insane really understand and be aware that they were insane? He wasn't sure, and that was what scared him. Scared him more than anything.

No. He wasn't going crazy. He wasn't doing anything that would suggest he was going crazy.

And yet, he felt that way nonetheless. He felt a lot of things nonetheless, but that was certainly one of them.

Ace was looking at himself in the mirror. He hated the way he looked, all dark and shadowy, looking sinister with his hood pulled up. He hated that he was such a living, breathing psychopath. Why couldn't he be a nice boy like Brannon? Why did he have to be so evil and wicked?

Ace stuck out his tongue at himself. It caused him to laugh a little bit.

"You suck," Ace said to himself. "You can't do anything right."

The reflection just remained a reflection.

"Did you want me to break you?" Ace said, and laughed again. "I so could. I could destroy you. I could break you down, let you shatter like fragment destruction. I could ruin you. Did you hear that, Ace? I could destroy everything about you, and you'd never even know what came. How does that sound? Does it sound like a plan? It should sound like a plan. It better sound like a plan. You understand? Or don't you understand? Of course you don't understand. You don't understand anything. You're just an ace printed on the back of a card, and you're worth nothing and everything, which we all know amounts to nothing. Absolutely nothing. Do you like being nothing, Ace? Does that make you feel proud? I bet it does. I bet it makes you feel like you could do anything … because we all know that you can't do anything. Did you want to go mad, Ace? Did you want to lose your sanity? It sounds like you do. It sounds like that's your plan. It sounds like madness is the direction you want to go. It sounds like you just want to be a bag of folly. I feel bad for you, Ace. I really do."

Ace was talking to himself, but at one point (he didn't know where or when), he had stopped. But that didn't stop the reflection, his reflection, from talking to him back, and saying all of these dreadful things. It scared Ace. Ace was, quite literally, talking to himself, through a reflection that wasn't a reflection but was Ace. And Ace had a lot of hate for Ace, the real Ace, that was. A lot of hate.

"I really do feel bad for you," said the Ace in the mirror. "But we all know there's nothing you can do about it. Nothing at all. You're stuck."

"Am I going crazy?" Ace asked himself, because he honestly wanted to know.

"Of course you are. You can't handle this. You can't handle anything."

This seemed terribly true. What could Ace handle? Nothing. He couldn't even keep The Machine safe from danger. He'd been thwarted by a kid. A kid that was, Ace had to admit, actually pretty smart. And loyal. And good-looking. A kid that seemed to have a lot going for him, certainly more than Ace did.

Ace continued to look at his reflection talking back at him, and that was when he saw Death for a moment. It was short, lasted for only a moment, and then was gone.

Had that been a hallucination? Yes, it had to have been. All of this was a hallucination. All of it wasn't happening. He just thought it was happening, for whatever reason. For what that reason was, Ace didn't know, except perhaps because Death's Mirror was being so powerful right now.

"I want to die," Ace said to his reflection.

"Of course you want to die," said Ace, but he wasn't Ace now, he was indeed Death. A reproduction of Death, or perhaps Death himself. It was hard to tell, when it was hard to tell what was real and what wasn't. "We all want to die. It's in our nature."

"How should I kill myself?" Ace was barely knowledgeable of the words coming out of his mouth.

"Any way that you like," Death said. "Any way at all. Here. Take a look at some of your options."

And on the mirror screen was now Ace, and he was jumping off a cliff. But then Ace was stabbing himself with a knife. But then Ace was hanging himself. But then Ace was swallowing poison. There were other ways in which he killed himself, and they all flashed in front of Ace, like a horrible movie, scene after scene, image after image, and they were stuck in Ace's head like a knife.

But the worst part about this was that Ace liked everything that he saw. He looked like Death's angel. He looked like he was immortal. He looked like he could do anything, the way this collage of death unfolded before him.

"Death is madness, madness Death," Death said. "You can't even tell the difference anymore, can you?"

"I just see … *power*," Ace said hungrily. "I've never seen so much power."

"Of course you haven't," Death said. "And it can all be yours."

"But what do I do to get it?" Ace said, and he was very tempted to bow on his knees, but part of him knew something bad was happening, and he needed to remain sane.

"You just have to break the mirror."

"Break the mirror?"

"Yes," said Death. "Break the mirror. And the shards will be yours. The shards of your sanity will be yours to never put back together."

"Yes, because you can't reconstruct sanity," Ace said. And before he knew it, his fist had gone through the mirror.

The shards littered the ground, and reflected in the shards, Ace saw madness. He couldn't describe what madness looked like, but he supposed that he could try. Madness was a universe folding in upon itself. Madness was worlds collapsing upon worlds. Madness was yourself destroying yourself. Madness was all of those things, and yet, none of those things. Madness was just madness.

Ace began to laugh as he looked at madness. He felt Death breathing behind him, could feel his smile. His cold, sharp smile. But Death didn't care. He just laughed and laughed and laughed. It was all a joke to him now. All of it. Killing himself was a joke. Suffering was a joke. Suffering of which of course led to madness, insanity. Insanity was death, death was insanity. He could see it all clearly now.

"We're all rooting for you to kill yourself," said a voice, and Ace turned around, saw Death for a moment, for just a moment, and then saw himself. An alternate universe self, except they were reflections of each other.

"Are you?" Ace said, and laughed some more. "I know why."

"Of course you know why. You know there is no other way. You know your suicide is the only possible way you can go from this point on. You know that death is your only guide ... death and madness."

"Because death is madness," Ace said to himself, and continued to laugh.

He saw in his head various ways in which he could kill himself. But he laughed at all of these terrible images. He just laughed at the noose, laughed at the knife, laughed at the gun (anachronistic of course, but so perfect for Contorted Royal), and Ace felt Death's Mirror cleaving his brain in half. He felt it.

He felt it all.

"No one can help you," said the Ace that wasn't Ace but was somehow Ace.

"Yes," said the real Ace. "Yes. No one can help me. I have to suffer this alone. I have to suffer all of this alone. If I don't, I'll just be weak. If I don't, I'll just be insane."

The images, how they continued to flash, getting more and more hectic, more and more violent, and he felt Death above him, covering his room like Death's Mirror covering the sky, Death's spirit overwhelming everything about Ace, and Ace didn't know what to do because he was literally looking into the infinite, the abyss of the infinite, and no one could look through that and come out on the other side, could look through it and stay sane. It just wasn't possible. All of the possibilities, overlapping all at once, all of the possible worlds, all of the possible anything, and Ace saw it all, and his mind was getting ready to burst, to explode with madness, and there was nothing Ace could do about it. You looked into madness, and madness also looked into you.

"Do it," said Death, who wasn't Ace's alternate universe self anymore, but was Death himself. "Kill yourself. That's when you'll see it all. That's when you'll see who you really are."

"I see it all already," Ace said. "And no one can help me. No one can take away what I have seen. No one can undo the trauma."

"It's what you deserve," Death said. "You have failed everyone."

"Yes. As always. I have failed everyone. I have failed existence. I can see it all collapsing."

"Just because you couldn't placate me," Death said.

Ace nodded, knowing this was true, and also feeling that Death had rigged all of this, to set Ace up, to frame Ace for a crime Death knew Ace would commit. But that didn't matter right now. What mattered was killing himself. Because death was indeed madness, and vice versa, and it was always going to be that way. And those images … no matter how hard he tried, he couldn't get them out of his head. He just couldn't. And the worst part was that Ace was laughing as he killed himself in each scenario. He just wouldn't stop laughing, was laughing himself straight to the grave.

"I hate The Jack of Knives," Ace said, picking up a shard, though he didn't know why he was saying this. Maybe because there was no connection anymore. "I am a happy bird. I will go this way and that way. Death is the only answer. Keys. Death as the way. You are me. I am you. And what is the purpose of it all. Just murder. Just jumping off cliffs. Just being crazy. What is the definition of insanity. It all means. Yes. No. It all means nothing. What do I do now. What do I do when. I see it all unfolding, and it's scaring me. I see it all unfolding, and I can't stop it, Death is too powerful, he's always been too powerful."

"You are pleasing me," Death said, though Ace didn't see Death anywhere.

"I need help," Ace finally said, and with the shard, he stabbed himself. But the worst part was that he hadn't really stabbed himself, he had just thought he had, which was worse because it screwed with his mind, it told him things, showed him things, that weren't real, and he was stabbing and stabbing, getting blood everywhere, and yet, there was nothing, Ace was hallucinating all of this, but he wasn't aware of it, he truly thought that he was killing himself …

And that was when he looked at himself in the mirror. It wasn't broken. Because, it had never been broken. He saw how good he looked. He saw he was a servant of evil.

He held onto that image as he tried to fight madness away. The thing was, he didn't know how much longer he could fight it, being so close …

Shadows

The Dark Kid felt like he was drenched in shadows.

He missed The Jack of Knives. The feeling was very strong, the feeling of loss and perhaps even abandonment, by his best friend, very powerful. He knew that some of it was indeed his own feelings, but he felt like that desire was being maximized by Death's Mirror. However, just because he was aware of that truth, didn't mean the pain became any less stinging, any less powerful, any less painful.

In fact, it seemed to make it all that much more powerful.

The Dark Kid was used to the shadow. He was practically made of shadow, of course. And yet, he felt as though a shadow was hanging over his heart, overcasting it with a loneliness that The Dark Kid was never going to be able to escape, ever able to bring light to.

The Dark Kid was in a forest. He had been in this forest since the moment that he'd walked through that door, and had split with The Jack of Knives at that point. He knew The Jack of Knives was suffering where he was at, in The Valley of Death, courtesy of Ace. If Ace hadn't gotten involved, The Dark Kid and The Jack of Knives would be together, but since Ace got involved, it had somehow made Death's Mirror much more powerful, keeping The Dark Kid away from his friend at all costs, and keeping him in this forest.

It was the forest just outside the castle. But what with the advent of Death's Mirror, it had been dark the whole entire time, with only a little bit of light from the moon and stars, if even that. Even The Dark Kid's literal surroundings were drenched in shadow, which, no doubt, was toxic for his soul.

The Dark Kid continued to move through the forest, having no idea what he was going to find, but knowing that shadow was indeed what he was going to find. Shadows drenched in shadows drenched in shadows. But it wasn't long before he found a knife.

The knife looked incredibly familiar. That was when he realized that it was a knife that belonged to The Jack of Knives. How it had gotten here, The Dark Kid wasn't sure. It probably had gotten here because Death's Mirror had replicated it for The Dark

Kid's enjoyment, to be tormented even more, about how his friend was gone.

And right on cue, Death said, "It must be nice, not having your friend here to keep you warm."

"I'm The Dark Kid," The Dark Kid said proudly (even though it wasn't sincere, he hoped it would at least sound genuine). "I'm used to pain. I'm used to suffering."

"All I see is a lost boy in shadow," Death said. "The Jack of Knives was your light."

"Maybe," The Dark Kid said. "But darkness can do just fine without light."

"The Jack of Knives proved to me that he'd kill you if he had the chance," Death said.

The Dark Kid knew he would do well to avoid listening to this. It wasn't true. And even if it was true, The Dark Kid would do well to accept it as just a game in Contorted Royal. Death was nothing *but* Contorted Royal, of course. And besides, even if The Jack of Knives wanted to kill The Dark Kid, it would be nothing he couldn't handle. The Dark Kid was tough. Maybe Death was jealous of that, which was why he was taunting him.

And yet, nonetheless, the idea of The Jack of Knives killing The Dark Kid, for some reason that he couldn't explain, was impacting him negatively. It was giving him a lot of fear. It was casting shadows on the wall, dancing, flickering, darkening. The Dark Kid knew better than to let such a mere fancy bother him, and yet, it was creeping in nonetheless.

"Did you want to see what he'd do to you?" Death said.

Before The Dark Kid could so much as protest, a mirror suddenly appeared before him. He indeed saw The Jack of Knives, in the Valley of Death, and he was holding a knife. He was standing behind The Dark Kid, who had his back turned. The Jack of Knives was getting ready to slit The Dark Kid's throat.

"Hey, man," The Jack of Knives said, his voice clearly malicious.

The Dark Kid turned around and saw The Jack of Knives. Before The Dark Kid could do anything, The Jack of Knives grabbed The Dark Kid's head and slit his throat. It was deep, but not so deep that it would kill The Dark Kid immediately. He fell to the ground, holding his throat, as blood filtered through his fingers, and he looked up at The Jack of Knives, as if in supplication, as if begging for mercy.

The Dark Kid turned away.

"Sad, isn't it?" Death said. "Sad, that your best friend would kill you like that."

"You're just messing with my head," The Dark Kid said. "It's nothing I couldn't handle. If we had our way, we'd kill each other over and over again. Do you hear that, Death? We'd kill each other over and over again."

"So you say," Death said, "but I know how much of a blow this is to you. You can't handle it. It's causing your mind to unravel. Your own best friend is a shadow."

The mirror disappeared, and Death went quiet.

All of this was so screwed up. It hurt so bad that The Dark Kid knew that The Jack of Knives would murder him. And yet, what it also did, was increase his loneliness, increase his desire to be with his friend, and he couldn't explain why. It made The Dark Kid so lonely and yearn so much to see his friend at least one more time that he'd be willing to take a knife to his brain.

Perhaps the knife that he was holding, that belonged to The Jack of Knives.

All the pain. All the suffering. All the feelings he just couldn't pinpoint, no matter how much he tried. The Jack of Knives, his light. The Jack of Knives, his friend.

"That's the problem with having a homicidal friend," Death said. "You think he'll kill everyone but you, but you're the one he really wants to kill. It amazes me how foolish you've been in that regard. The Jack of Knives has waited to kill you for a very a long time. He's just waiting for the moment when it will hurt the most, because you trust him so well. Because you care about him. It's amazing, isn't it, that the ones you love are the ones who turn against you the quickest?"

"Leave me alone," The Dark Kid said, and his voice was trembling, and he heard weakness and vulnerability in his voice. He missed The Jack of Knives so terribly. Yes, maybe that was it. Maybe he wanted to die. Maybe he wanted The Jack of Knives to murder him. Maybe that was his path. Maybe the whole point of The Jack of Knives was to snuff out the shadow of The Dark Kid. It would make sense. It would indeed make sense. That had to be what The Dark Kid was waiting for.

"Let me see him," The Dark Kid said, and there was some steadiness in his voice again, some courage. "Let me see my friend. Let him murder me. Wouldn't it get you off?"

"I don't think it matters what I'd find entertaining," Death said. "What matters is things happening the way they need to. And your friend is going to kill you."

Yes, snuff out the shadows. The Dark Kid looked at the knife in his hands, and realized that he needed to kill himself. He needed to kill himself now. He needed to kill himself with the knife of his friend, before his friend did it for him. He needed to get revenge on his friend. Because that was how screwed up friendships worked. That was how they went down.

But he reminded himself, that it was all an illusion. Some of it was true, perhaps, but not all of it. The Jack of Knives and The Dark Kid were good friends. That friendship wasn't going to fall apart just because of Death's Mirror. It just wasn't. The Dark Kid wasn't going to allow it to fall apart. He refused to let it happen.

But Death was persistent: "Turn around. You'll see your friend."

The Dark Kid didn't turn around, but it didn't matter. A mirror appeared in front of him, and he saw The Jack of Knives standing behind him. He was holding a knife. He was getting ready to stab The Dark Kid.

The Dark Kid continued to look at the reflection, and that was when The Jack of Knives did indeed stab The Dark Kid: he brought the knife over The Dark Kid, straight into his heart.

But that was when The Dark Kid realized that the mirror wasn't there, that his friend wasn't there. He was the one who had stabbed himself. The knife was in his heart, and he was holding the knife.

"I need my friend," The Dark Kid said, somehow, even with all of the pain he felt. "I need it. Please. Don't let me suffer like this. Please, leave me alone. Let me see my friend."

"I can't do that, kid," Death said. "You want me to, but it would make you happy."

The Dark Kid realized he wasn't holding the knife to his heart anymore. Perhaps because he realized that all of this was just a fanciful illusion. But that didn't mean he didn't see The Jack of Knives standing before him, holding his knife, and he stabbed The Dark Kid, stabbed him in the heart again, and The Dark Kid fell, but it was the same thing.

The Dark Kid was ultimately the only one who was stabbing himself. Over and over again. Not happening and yet happening. It didn't make sense, and yet, somehow it was happening … and not happening. The Dark Kid was drenched in the shadow of the memory of his friend.

"I'm going to kill The Jack of Knives," Death said. "And then I'm going to kill you."

"I miss him," The Dark Kid said, realizing that the knife was in his heart, that he was holding it as if it was his lifeline, as if it was the life of his friend, his best friend. "I need him to be here with me. I'm so lonely."

"Good," Death said. "I'm glad. Suffer for me, kid. Suffer for me. Die. Die, and suffer. Die over and over again, to eventually die for good."

"I need to see my friend," The Dark Kid said, but there was no one there. He was looking at his reflection, cast in the sky that was Death's Mirror, but he just saw himself, holding the knife. His friend was nowhere to be found. He was never going to be found. Because Death was going to kill The Jack of Knives, and for good. It wouldn't be a perpetual death … it would be an extinguishing of the soul, it would be the loss of someone who would murder The Dark Kid the moment that he had the chance.

And somehow, The Dark Kid was okay with that. He wanted that, in fact. Let his friend murder him. Sure, it would hurt, the betrayal, the pain, the isolation, but he needed it. Maybe it could make him whole.

Maybe it would take him out of the shadows.

"Help me, Jack," The Dark Kid said, and his voice was quiet, so very quiet. "Help me through this."

But The Jack of Knives was nowhere. The Dark Kid was lying on the ground, looking up at his reflection, and seeing Death and himself reflected back simultaneously. And sometimes, he'd see The Jack of Knives, but he was smiling at the destruction, because he was the one who had caused all of this. And yet, that just made The Dark Kid more lonely, and he couldn't explain why, but he supposed that in the end, there was never going to be an explanation.

And as The Dark Kid felt death (perhaps even Death) creeping up on him as an incorruptible shadow, he knew that there was an explanation: it was because The Dark Kid needed to be lonely. He needed to never have his best friend beside him, to keep him company, to tell him that everything was going to be okay.

Because all of that was just shadows of the mind.

The Key to the Crazy Black Queen the Whole Entire Time Was Ralph, a Random Kid in General, Though Every Alice Of Course Brings New Issues

Alice could still hear God inside of her head, but that didn't mean she wasn't going to fight. She wanted some semblance of sanity, and not just in her own head, but in what she saw in the world. That was why she had intervened on behalf of The Black Queen. Sure, it was barbaric, forcing psychiatric help on her, but she knew that was what she needed to do. Alice had had to do that multiple times to herself, and sometimes it worked. Sometimes it didn't, of course, but sometimes it did.

In truth, Alice didn't think it was going to work. Psychiatric help was a sham, and the medieval psychiatric help that they had put on The Black Queen (throwing her in a jail cell to rot and decay in her own insanity) probably wasn't going to do much. But it was better than letting the queen get executed. No matter how stupid Alice thought psychiatry was, it still beat death. Besides, it had to be acknowledged that the queen right now was having a mental breakdown, due to the stress of trying to rule the kingdom. Alice had to admit that if she had seen the alternate universe breakdown and felt Death's Mirror creep in, she'd probably lose it, too.

Alice and Ralph were sitting some distance away from The Black Queen's jail cell, talking. They were trying to figure out what to do.

"We obviously can't rule the kingdom," Ralph said. "I'm just a random kid from the Bronx, and you're powerful, but we all know that the secret lies with The Suicide King. Only he can restore things back to normal. He's the one who knows things. He has the answers."

"Maybe The Black Queen knows things," Alice said.

"Like what?" Ralph said. "In case you haven't noticed, she's completely lost her head. It might have been easier to just put her beneath a guillotine. I'm joking, of course, but still. She won't be much help."

"I don't know," Alice said, "but we have to try something."

Alice went toward The Black Queen's jail cell, and looked at her. Her dark black hair was mangled and mangy, like a dog's, and was covering some of her face. She was hyperventilating, or so it looked like, but she was also shivering.

"Hey," Alice said.

The Black Queen responded by barking. She barked once, then twice, then three times. Then she began to pant. It was an innocent effect, but Alice had definitely gotten it right: The Black Queen thought she was an animal. The Black Queen thought she was a dog.

The Black Queen barked again, and then continued to pant, and then got down on all fours and began to crawl around the jail cell. She licked her hand like licking her paw, and then began to walk around in circles on all fours, and began to whimper. It was like she was trying to get comfortable.

"What do you propose?" Ralph said.

"I don't know," Alice said. "I really don't. She's completely immersed in who she thinks she is."

The Black Queen, still on all fours, went to her water bowl and nudged it with her nose. She lapped up a little bit with her tongue, and then knocked it over with her nose, as if in defiance. Then she began to pant again, rather severely this time, and whimpering.

"She's completely fallen from grace," Ralph said.

"Yeah, no need to rub it in," Alice said. "But that's what madness is. I've been in worse conditions, though."

"Worse conditions?"

"There was a time where my schizophrenia used to rule over me, before it started to become useful and before I started keeping it under control, keeping the reins on my illness tight. I would do a lot of whacky things. It wasn't pleasant."

278

"Well, you look beautiful now," Ralph said.

Alice looked at Ralph, and saw the familiar sweetness that characterized Ralph so well, in his face, in his eyes, and she wanted to kiss him. She didn't want to kiss him in front of The Black Queen, because she felt it would be mean, so she just pecked him on the cheek.

"Thanks," Ralph said, and looked to be on cloud nine for a moment.

"Thanks for being so loyal to me," Alice said. "It means a lot. I know The Black Queen must be rather tempting."

"She is," Ralph admitted. "Even now, looking like a crazed loon … she's still very pretty."

And indeed, The Black Queen looked like a crazed loon, and like a crazed dog. She was still shivering in that characteristic way, and still whimpering and whining away.

"I wish we could hold her like a stray puppy," Ralph said.

The Black Queen responded by looking up into Ralph and Alice's eyes. She indeed had puppy eyes right now.

Ralph didn't say anything for a moment, but finally said, "Oh, forget it."

Alice felt alarmed at hearing this. "Forget what?"

"I'm the key," Ralph said. "I'm always the key in situations like this. I was the key to The Machine, so why can't I be the key to The Black Queen's insanity?"

Ralph went to go get the warden, who opened up the jail cell and let Ralph go inside. The Black Queen immediately scooted to the corner, like a scared dog, but Ralph continued to approach her, and when he was close enough, he got down on his knees.

The Black Queen had been whimpering out of fear, but when Ralph got down on his knees, she calmed down a little bit. Ralph began to stroke/pet the top of The Black Queen's head, as if healing her insanity by healing her head.

Alice watched, not sure where this was going to go. She had faith in Ralph, but not that much faith. Could he really unlock the sanity within The Black Queen, and bring her back to ground zero?

The Black Queen began to whimper again as Ralph pet her head, but it was a happy whimper, now, and soon, The Black Queen was panting excitedly.

"Say something," Ralph said. "Any word. Any word at all."

The Black Queen cocked her head, so like a dog giving a quizzical look, and then barked. Once, twice. Three times.

"No," Ralph said, patiently. "A word. Say a word. Any word. Any word at all."

The Black Queen barked again.

"Say dog," Ralph said.

The Black Queen barked in response.

Alice, who was watching this with curiosity, began to hear the voice of God getting louder, and more fractured.

"You've got to kill The Black Queen," God said.

"Yes, kill The Black Queen."

"It's the only way that balance can be restored."

"It's the only way that life can go back to normal."

"Kill The Black Queen, who has been nothing but an evil influence on Contorted Royal, who is nothing but a sinner."

"Yes, kill The Black Queen."

Alice grabbed her head, and Ralph was so busy that he didn't notice.

Then the voices stopped. For a moment, at least.

The Black Queen was trying to talk. Slowly, the word, "Dog," came out of her mouth.

"Do you remember who you are?" Ralph asked.

"The … Black … Queen …" The Black Queen said.

Ralph looked at Alice in relief. "There may be hope. We need to get her out of here, so she can recuperate, get her strength back. She's been locked up in here long enough."

"Have I been acting like a dog?" The Black Queen asked suddenly.

Ralph looked at Alice for help. Alice shook her head sharply but indistinctly, so The Black Queen couldn't see.

"Of course not," Ralph said.

"Then why am I here?"

"Would you look at the time, it's time to go," Ralph said quickly, and helped The Black Queen stand up.

But when Ralph saw that Alice was staring at The Black Queen, he stopped for a moment, and said, "Alice? Are you okay?"

No. Alice was not okay. God was raging inside her head.

"Kill The Black Queen, Alice."

"Yes, kill The Black Queen."

"Do it before we kill you."

"Do it before you are the one who dies. Before we can't handle seeing you anymore. Before you are no longer our royal servant. Kill The Black Queen, Alice."

"Yes, kill The Black Queen."

Alice looked at Ralph for help, and she could tell that he saw her mind splitting like chaos, like the universe, but it was too late: Alice jumped on The Black Queen and began to try to strangle her.

The thing was, she never even touched The Black Queen's throat. But anyone who saw Alice would assume that was what she was trying to do. But Alice, who didn't really want to kill The Black Queen, who was just trying to deal with the voices, continued to fight and fight the terrible orders, and The Black Queen, who was traumatized by Alice, didn't fight even in the slightest, and Ralph tried to get Alice to stop, but he didn't intervene, and Alice knew it was because he couldn't.

The unpsychiatrist and Bishop were in the jail cell, and they were wrestling Alice to the ground.

"No!" Alice shouted, knowing where this was going. "No! It's not what it looks like!"

"You're being hospitalized, now, Alice, so calm down or we're going to give you a shot," said the unpsychiatrist.

"No!" Alice shouted again. "I wasn't trying to kill The Black Queen."

"It looked that way to me," Bishop said callously. "Yes it did. You're going to be locked away in the mental hospital for treason."

"It's the voices of God!" Alice shouted, and looked at Ralph for help. "Ralph! Help me! You don't understand! It's the voice of God!"

And God continued to speak: "Yes, it's the voice of God."

"But Bishop is more in tune with us than you are, Alice."

"Yes, more in tune than you are, Alice."

"You're going to Hell, Alice, for trying to kill an innocent soul."

"How do you like that?"

"Yes, you're going to Hell. And your boyfriend can't do anything to save you. You understand that, I would hope, Alice."

"Yes, Alice, I would hope so."

Alice was pinned to the ground by the unpsychiatrist and Bishop, and it wasn't long before they injected in her a shot. Alice could feel herself slipping away.

How was this happening? She'd been under control for so long, she'd kept her illness at a minimum. What was happening? Why was this happening? She'd done so well for so long, this just wasn't fair.

Alice looked at The Black Queen, who had an expressionless face, and then at Ralph, who looked like he didn't know what to do. And she knew he didn't. They couldn't interfere with this. They just couldn't. Bishop was more powerful, because he had God on his side, and the unpsychiatrist was unstoppable, because he had reason on his side. Alice was just the crazy loon who needed to be locked up for good in a hospital.

"Help me," Alice said to Ralph, but Ralph didn't say anything, just continued to look confused, and Alice felt herself being dragged away as the drugs kicked in, as she felt them moving her toward the hospital, and Alice was crying internally, but no one would save her, no one at all, especially not God.

"Especially not us," God said, as Alice drifted further and further away, the voices somehow getting stronger even with the medication.

"Yes, especially not us."

"You're going to Hell, Alice."

"Yes, you're going to Hell."

"In a hospital cell."

"And no one can save you. You saw what your boyfriend did. Just let you go. And The Black Queen, whose life you saved, just watched you get taken away."

Alice realized she was drooling now, and her eyes were rolling into the back of her head, and she wanted someone to save her, but there was no one, no one at all.

"No one at all," said God.

"Yes, no one at all …"

Heart Break and Mind Break: How There Really Is No Difference

Ralph hated himself. He couldn't believe that he had just stood by while his girlfriend was brutally and in a hostile way taken away. In Ralph's defense, it had been rather traumatizing, to watch the unpsychiatrist and Bishop take away his girlfriend the way that they had, in a way that was both disturbing and troubling, among other things.

Ralph wanted to visit Alice in the hospital, along with The Black Queen, but they were told that Alice was too sick to be seen at the moment. Ralph knew this was a complete and utter lie; Alice's mind was fractured, yes, but it wasn't so fractured that they couldn't talk to her.

The Black Queen did everything she could to reassure Ralph; it was a side of The Black Queen that Ralph needed to be blunt about: he didn't know it existed. He didn't know The Black Queen could be so kind-hearted. He didn't know she could be so friendly in such matters, and didn't need to spend every moment of her time flirting with Ralph. It was refreshing and surprising, and Ralph was happy to have the extra support.

But the time finally came for Ralph to go visit Alice. It was seemingly the millionth time he'd gone up to the hospital to check up on her, when they said, "All right … she's a little bit better now, so you can see her, if you'd like."

Ralph was with The Black Queen, and he looked at her for support, and encouragement. The Black Queen said, rather nicely, "You go alone. Spend some quality time with your girl." Then The Black Queen smiled: a genuine, happy smile.

"Thank you," Ralph said, and gave The Black Queen a hug.

He expected her to grab his behind, but she didn't. She just hugged him, and they stayed that way for a moment, and then The Black Queen said, "I'll wait out here."

Before Ralph went in, he couldn't help but ask, "Your highness … why are you being so patient?"

"Because you cured me of my psychosis," The Black Queen said, and smiled. "You took away my insanity, my anxiety, my craziness. You made me human again."

Ralph nodded, and then turned to be let into the hospital.

As he went inside, he couldn't help but feel that there was foul play. He didn't trust mental institutions, even if they claimed to be pro-schizophrenic, like this strange one, and he felt that things had changed since Death's Mirror had begun. However, he wasn't quite sure, if he was completely honest with himself, what exactly had been foul about the situation. Sure, it was awfully coincidental that Bishop and the unpsychatrist just happened to walk in at a bad moment, when Alice had indeed split from reality for a moment. But even during that struggle, Ralph had seen her fighting the disease nonetheless. In short, it wasn't in Alice's nature to hurt anybody, and even The Black Queen wasn't bothered by Alice's behavior: worse things happened in Contorted Royal. *Much* worse things, actually. But nonetheless, it had looked bad, and the people that could lock up Alice had just happened to be there. Considering they were supposed to be pro-schizophrenic, it didn't make sense that they would just lock her up immediately. But indeed, with Death's Mirror changing things, it seemed they didn't see Alice as gifted. They saw her as sick. They saw her as diseased. Who cared about the people in Contorted Royal that literally and actually got away with murder, not the one who didn't hurt anyone and didn't want to hurt anyone but was literally just at the wrong place at the wrong time?

And Bishop … why did Ralph feel like Bishop had had something to do with all of this madness that had happened?

The psych tech said, "It's only on rare occasions that we allow outsiders to come and visit their friend, the patient. But, Alice really wanted to see you, so we thought we'd make an exception. All of this has been an ordeal for her, and we thought we'd break the rules to give her at least some comfort."

Ralph didn't respond to this, just went to Alice's room.

She was lying down on the bed, and when Ralph knocked on the door, to get her attention, she jumped up immediately. For a moment, she looked just fine. She indeed looked fine. She looked about as normal as anybody else.

"Hey, Ralph," Alice said. "I see you've come to visit the crazy."

"You're not crazy," Ralph said. "You just … are having a hard time right now."

284

"God talks to me," Alice said suddenly.

"What does he say?" Ralph asked curiously.

In a voice that was not Alice's, that was intense and chaotic and yet somehow controlled, Alice said, "Die, Alice. Yes, die Alice. If you don't die, we'll lock you up for good and throw away the key. If you don't die, we'll kill you, Alice. You hear that? It'll be more than wonderland for you, crazy girl. It'll be Hell Land. Hell served up on a silver platter."

Alice then sat down on the bed, as if she couldn't believe she had said all of this. Ralph sat down beside her, and saw that Alice looked as though she wanted to cry. She didn't, however, and so Ralph said, "Alice ... you usually keep your illness under control. We could crank up the symptoms with the anti-medication and you'd do just fine. I even saw you struggling with The Black Queen. But something is still off with you. Alice, please tell me what that is. Tell me what happened."

"God talks to me," Alice said. "Backwards and backwards we go. Backward the backward we are. We're going to go backwards when it all begins. We're going to go to the beginning so we can go to the end."

"Alice, I don't know what you're talking about," Ralph said. "Look at me."

But Alice wouldn't look at Ralph. She just began to rock back and forth.

"God says I'm a loony," Alice said. "A loony goony. God says I'm going to crazyland for crazyland crazies. God says it's nothing compared to Death's Mirror Land. God says I'm evil. God says I'm going to Hell. God says I'll always be in Hell. Go to Hell, Alice. Yes, Alice, go to Hell."

Alice then slowly looked at Ralph. For a moment, he saw a semblance of sanity in her eyes. It sparked, and she said, "He did something to me."

"Who did?" Ralph asked.

"Go backwards, back," Alice said. "We all go backwards to go back. To go front. To go in front. To get where we need to be."

"Alice, you're talking ..." Ralph began, but what did he want to say. Nonsense? Yeah, that would help: blame Alice for her nontechnical, nonsensical jargon.

Regardless, what she'd said was crucial. Someone had done something to her. Sure, it was possible it was just a delusion, but it was possible something had really happened to her.

"We need to backtrack, play our music backwards," Alice said. "And get back at the sinners. God says I'm going to Hell. Yes, Alice, you're going to Hell. And I say I'm already in Hell, and he says, it's nothing compared to what's coming up. You sold your soul, Alice. Yes, you sold your soul."

"When did God start talking to you?" Ralph said.

Alice didn't say anything for a moment. During this moment, Ralph took some time to think about his emotions. He took some time to think about how he felt about all of this. He felt like his heart was broken. It hurt him to see his girlfriend struggle like this. It hurt him more than anything. It hurt him to see her locked up, even if in a comfortable room, with no freedoms. It hurt him to see her locked up in her disease, which now was playing the role of disease. It wasn't all just fun and games: it was real. Sort of the way it would manifest in modern day society, not a pseudo-medieval world.

Ralph's heart was indeed broken, but he began to think that there really was no difference between a heart break and a mind break. Ralph's heart was broken, Alice's mind was broken, and the common denominator among the two? That, indeed, something was shattered. Shattered to pieces, never to come back together again.

"Bounce bounce to get the tramp," Alice said. "Jack of Knived says that ponies are blue in sunshine. We're all whacky in whacky whacky land, the never never world of ever whatever land."

"Alice, I need you to stay focused," Ralph said. "Please. Answer my question. When did God start talking to you?"

"Kill Death," Alice said.

Ralph felt a brief flicker of annoyance. He wanted to even take it out on Alice, but refrained. Kill *Death*? That would never happen. That *could* never happen. You couldn't kill Death, that was an oxymoron, a major problem of logic. It was faulty reasoning at its worst.

So Ralph just avoided this, and said, "Alice, please … answer my question."

"It's all paranoia, they say," Alice said, and stood up, clearly agitated. "They all say it's paranoia. Death's Mirror doesn't exist. They say I came in here talking about Death's Mirror, but Death's Mirror is false. It doesn't exist. Death's Mirror, Death's mere. Kill Death, kill me they say instead. Kill Alice."

Ralph took a minute to think about this. Okay, even Ralph knew that Death's Mirror was real. Why were they denying that it existed? To mess with Alice's head?

Ralph didn't know, but he hoped they were getting somewhere.

"Did you break on The Black Queen because of God?" Ralph asked.

"God talks to me," Alice said. She began to mock punch the wall. She was joking, of course, but it looked a little funny. Ralph smiled a little at the humor.

"I guess you hate the wall," Ralph said.

"Of course I do," Alice said. "The wall of my mind, the walls of my sanity. So limited. So limiting."

"So, did God tell you to kill The Black Queen?"

"God says, I do," Alice said simply.

"So God told you to kill The Black Queen?"

Alice turned around in a panic. "Oh my God! I killed The Black Queen! What have I done?"

"No, no, The Black Queen is fine," Ralph said calmly.

"Are you sure?" Alice asked, still panicked.

"Yes, she's just fine. She's just outside. She wanted us to spend time together."

"The walls of my mind are powerful," Alice said. "You'll never understand how powerful they are. How strong they are. Built solid. Like the walls keeping me here. I have no freedom here. I'm treated like a prisoner. I hate it. God tells me I'm just getting what I deserve."

"I'm sorry," Ralph said. "I wish I could intervene, but I can't."

"I know," Alice said. "Once they get you, they get you. They stick you in a barb wire snare, they catch you in wiry air. I'm sorry, Ralph, sorry that God has been so evil to me, but I can't help it. But it's because he did it to me. He planned for it. He wants to watch me fall."

287

"Who wants to watch you fall?" Ralph asked, feeling he'd met his break.

"But they say it's just paranoia," Alice said. "They say that. And I believe them. But God just gets louder, gets louder. Kill them all, he says. Kill them all. They aren't worthy. Burn it down. Burn it all down. Help me, Ralph. Help me."

And then Alice clung to Ralph, and began crying. The tears poured down like crazy, and they wouldn't stop, basically giving Ralph a shower.

But Ralph remained stable. He said, "Who wants your demise?"

"Bishop!" Alice cried out exhaustedly, and then cried even harder.

Ralph held his girl for the longest time, taking this all in. So Bishop had betrayed Alice. He should have seen it. He should have seen it coming.

But what could he do about it?

Alice stopped crying, and stood up, almost defiantly, but with some visible frustration. "But I'm not a serpent!"

"Alice …"

"God thinks I'm a serpent," Alice said. "He keeps … he keeps whispering in my ear like a snake. He's in my *head*. He won't stop! Make him stop! Make him *stop*!"

And Alice then began to cry even more, even harder, louder and louder. The psych tech came in at this moment, and said, "You need to leave now."

"Okay," Ralph said, feeling his heart shattered, like Alice's mind. "Okay."

Ralph went to Alice, however, and gave her a kiss on the cheek. She hardly noticed, still crying and upset and wet with her tears, and then Ralph walked out with the psych tech.

As he was walking, he thought about all of what he'd heard. So Bishop was to blame? He was the one who'd caused all of this. As for how, Ralph wasn't sure, but he believed it. Maybe he'd stabbed her in the head with a Death's Mirror shard. Maybe. Just maybe. And in doing so, had injected God into her mind.

It was possible. The only problem was, what could Ralph do about it?

He honestly didn't know. But in all reality, it didn't matter. He didn't know one's heart could hurt so much. Seeing her suffer like this, the devastating effects of this disease. Why couldn't it all just be fun and games, with Alice hallucinating Ralph or The Machine? Why did it have to be God screaming and yelling in the head?

Ralph didn't know. But he felt if his heart kept hurting this much, his mind would break, too, and they would have to hospitalize him as well.

Fragment Destruction

The Suicide King had to be and become The Homicide King. He had to stop turning everything inwards and put everything outwards; he had to be *proactive*. He had to get to the bottom of things by becoming crazily homicidal.

Homicide, of course, didn't necessarily mean murder, but it definitely had some resemblance to that; murder was indeed part of what The Suicide King had meant by homicide. But he meant other things as well, things he was just going to have to explore.

He was lying beside The Poetess, in bed, and the two were being quiet. The Suicide King was fine with this quietness from The Poetess, however, because he needed to think. He needed to get his thoughts in order. He needed to think, think, think. He needed to figure it out.

He needed to save Contorted Royal.

He couldn't run from it forever, of course. He was the king. He'd always been the king, always been the one in charge, and yes, he'd ruled it beautifully by being suicidal, but that was going to need to change. Probably for good. Because things were coming full circle, things were trying to be the way they had once been, when The Suicide King had his wife by his side, when he had his loyal subjects doing good deeds, when peasants weren't suffering, when servants were happy with their labor.

The key to at least buffering Death's Mirror was fragment destruction. Fragment destruction had already been shown, but not in the way that The Suicide King was thinking.

Not in the same way at all. Fragment destruction meant something completely different, for The Suicide King, who needed to restore order to his kingdom, who needed to stop sleeping around to get petty revenge and *do* something.

The Suicide King quickly got dressed, and The Poetess looked at him curiously.

"You're leaving?" she said.

"I'm late, I'm late, for a very important date," The Suicide King said, and quickly walked out of the door of the room, and through the door that would lead him back to Contorted Royal …

***

Not surprisingly, The Suicide King ended up exactly where he needed to be: the Valley of Death, where his son was.

Fragment destruction. That was the key. Reflect death and destruction right back at Death's Mirror.

What The Suicide King needed to do was kill his son. No doubt, it was going to be very hard to do, just because The Jack of Knives was a boy. It had been easier killing The Black Queen that one time because The Suicide King knew that she could handle it. She would be just fine. But The Jack of Knives? He wasn't nearly as tough as he thought he was. There was no telling how dying would change him, would affect him. It was a risk, for sure. Definitely a risk.

But it needed to happen.

The Suicide King saw The Jack of Knives looking at his reflection in a mirror, and just staring at it. The Suicide King couldn't possibly imagine what the boy was seeing, but it was clearly powerful, because The Jack of Knives hadn't even noticed that his father was standing behind him. For some reason, The Suicide King wasn't reflected in the mirror.

"Hello, Jack," The Suicide King said.

The Jack of Knives turned around slowly. When he saw his father standing there, he pulled out his knife.

"Put that away," The Suicide King said, not afraid to border on Homicide King flair. "No need to fight."

"And why is that?" The Jack of Knives asked. "Because you order so, your highness?"

"Perhaps," The Suicide King said. "Perhaps not. Depends on whether you see me as worthy of taking orders from."

"I don't know what I see you as," The Jack of Knives said. "But I know I want to kill you."

"It's very interesting you say that," The Suicide King said. "You know why?"

The Jack of Knives shook his head.

"Because I'm actually here to kill you," The Suicide King said, stepping closer. "I'm going to kill my own son. How do you like them apples, son? How do you like that forbidden fruit?"

"I don't," The Jack of Knives said, but put his knife away. There was something inevitable about the way The Jack of Knives did this, to the point to where The Suicide King had to admit that he was having second thoughts about his theories of the fragment destruction. Could he really trick Death's Mirror? The Jack of Knives was important to this, which was why the mirror needed to be shattered, not by its own circumstances, but by The Suicide King trying to bring back order … but was murdering his son the only way?

The Suicide King was having doubts. Mostly because his son looked so sad right now.

"Kill me," The Jack of Knives said. "Just do it. I know that's what you've always wanted to do."

"Now, no …" The Suicide King began. "No. I've never wanted to kill you."

"Of course you have," The Jack of Knives said. "That's all you dream about, is killing your only son. That's why you did what you did, forced me into hard labor for so many years, and then when you reveal the secret, only reveal it to me so we can kill my mother."

"Well, in my defense, you killed me," The Suicide King said.

"In your *defense*?" The Jack of Knives said, and then his sadness switched quickly to anger. "There is no defense. You're a terrible king. You murder your family and let Death's Mirror run rampant throughout your kingdom. You're a bad leader. You aren't worthy of the crown."

"Well, that's why I need to kill you," The Suicide King said. "I hope you're not afraid of that."

"Why would I be afraid?" The Jack of Knives said. "I don't care. Kill me, if it makes you happy. That's fine with me. I honestly don't care. Do whatever you think is good."

"It will be good, for the kingdom," The Suicide King said, and he had his sword with him, which literally appeared out of nowhere, like a religious sign.

"Exactly," The Jack of Knives said. "Prey on the weak."

"Now you know that's not what this is. We're called Contorted Royal for a reason. It isn't just coincidence. Not at all in the slightest. But I'm going to kill you to hopefully restore some order. You're important to Death's Mirror's demise, and by extension, Death's demise."

"Death doesn't have a demise," The Jack of Knives said. "He can't be beaten."

"Yes he can."

"No he can't. He can't at all. You know what I was looking at, before you came? I was looking at my friend, The Dark Kid, and watching him kill himself."

"That's terrible."

"And I can't be there," The Jack of Knives said, "to help him through his pain. Just like he can't help me through my pain. Death's Mirror equals mind games, but they work. They destroy. I don't even know if I'm The Jack of Knives anymore. I doubt who I am. I doubt if I am. I doubt it all. I doubt if you exist, and if you do exist, I doubt that you can restore order. Death's Mirror is the pinnacle of our problems."

"Clearly," The Suicide King snapped. "You think I haven't noticed the pandemonium?"

"No," The Jack of Knives said. "Because you've been too busy cheating on Mom."

"Now, in my defense …" The Suicide King began, but saw his son's point.

Goodness, how determined the boy was. The hard labor he'd been through had hardened him to walk the razor's edge of psychopathy, but at least he did it with flair. With style. And somehow, that psychopathy made the boy seem much more fragile. It was a strange effect, no denying that. Because The Suicide King saw that the boy didn't want to hurt anybody, he had just been born in a screwed up situation, a screwed up world, a screwed up

292

everything, and that had naturally taken its toll. It wasn't the boy's nature, but that's what he'd been taught and conditioned to do.

"I hate you, for disowning me," said The Jack of Knives. "I hate you for leaving me stranded. I could have helped rule the kingdom. I could have let go of my knives. But no. You made me bitter. You made me angry. You wrecked me."

"Ah, you wouldn't hurt a fly," The Suicide King mocked, homicidally, and with his sword, charged toward The Jack of Knives.

However, when he tried to stab the boy, the knife went right through him, like The Jack of Knives was a holograph or something.

"That's odd," The Suicide King said.

"It's Death's Mirror," The Jack of Knives said. "You can't beat it."

"Well, I'm going to have to beat it," The Suicide King said, and tried to stab his son again. He failed. It went right through, like trying to split air, the effect like splitting hairs.

The Jack of Knives didn't say anything, just let his father try to kill him. But it didn't do any good.

The Suicide King began to feel angry. Why wasn't this working? It needed to work. It was supposed to work.

But that was when The Suicide King realized it was because he wasn't trying hard enough; he didn't have enough fragment destruction in his soul. He needed to really despise his son, really needed to hate him. He needed to have nothing but murder on the mind.

This was proving difficult, but The Suicide King was ready to walk on the edge of the sword. He was ready to balance. He needed to restore order, and if it took all the hate in existence for that to happen, so be it. He was going to harness fragment destruction. He was going to.

The Jack of Knives had turned his back, and was staring at the mirror again. He looked so lost, the boy did, and The Suicide King felt so bad for his son for a moment, for how twisted his psyche had become because of circumstances beyond his control. But then The Suicide King forced himself to hate, more, more, gathering all the fragment destruction possible, and when he finally had the answer, he went to his son and stood beside him.

Now they were both reflected in the mirror. But they looked happy. The mirror was reflecting the two together, not wounded, not wounded at all, in any way, shape, or form, and holding each other's hands. Then they hugged each other, and just loved each other.

But it wasn't real, and The Suicide King knew it. It was Death's Mirror trying to stop The Suicide King.

"I'm sorry," The Suicide King said.

"You're sorry," The Jack of Knives said, and before he could say anything else, The Suicide King took his sword and with all the fragment destruction converging on the point of the sword, he stabbed his son in the chest, and then pulled it out.

The Jack of Knives looked at his wound in shock. He grabbed it, but it didn't do any good. It didn't do any good whatsoever.

He merely said, "Why, Dad?" and then began to collapse on the ground.

But The Suicide King didn't let him fall on the ground. He just held the boy before he fell. The boy was a hero. He was going to save things with his homicidal self that was really a soft and gentle self, though perhaps a little bit hardened. That was who he was.

"It's going to be okay," The Suicide King said. "You can do this, my son."

His son was indeed already dead, but that didn't stop the bleeding, and it didn't stop the sorrow that The Suicide King felt. It didn't stop his powerful feelings. But it was inevitable. It was the importance of fragment destruction.

As for whether it was having an effect, The Suicide King wasn't sure. He didn't hear Death's Mirror cracking. He didn't feel Death's fearful trembling. He didn't see or feel anything, except for the dead weight of his son in his arms, the blood still flowing, and a sadness that he couldn't explain.

But that was the price of fragment destruction. Always a hefty price.

Always.

The Ace of Heart

Ace did not know where he was. He didn't know who he was. He didn't know how he was. He just knew that he was, though even that was uncertain. Even the pain that he felt was uncertain. Was he sure that he was even feeling it?

No, he wasn't sure, and yet it seemed so real. The suffering. The feelings that he couldn't untangle no matter how hard he tried, like having a Death Mirror shard stuck in the heart, turning and turning like a gyre, turning like purgatory, turning like Hell.

Ace was outside the castle, and he realized that people were surrounding him. Some were peasants who were curious to see the spectacle, some were wealthy people who wanted a good laugh, but Ace was hardly aware of any of them. In the end, they really didn't seem to matter to him. Nothing seemed to matter to him.

He felt his heart beating. He had changed from The Ace of Spades to The Ace of Hearts. He was the Ace of Heart. He had heart, he had tenderness.

He thought that was strange. Yes, indeed, there was enough brain left within Ace to realize that he was changing. That his heart was different. It wasn't stone-cold, bent on destruction, pointless destruction at that, like a fragment destruct. It was focused on trying to heal through good deeds. It was focused on trying to be a good person.

But he couldn't be a good person! He could never be a good person! Even as he watched as he somehow concentrated hard enough to cure a dying kid in Distorted Royal, he was still a bad person. He'd never be able to do anything worthwhile, no matter how hard he tried, no matter how hard his heart shone. No matter how hard his heart existed. No matter. No matter, in the end, and it was never going to be a matter, for the Ace of Heart.

His heart was beating hard beneath his clothes. He could feel it pounding away like a drumbeat. He touched it, as though it had been stabbed, just recently. He touched it, as though he could heal it. But he could never heal it. It had been too diseased. It had been too destroyed, by his vices, by his corruption, by all of the terrible things that he had done.

Death was getting revenge on Ace. Ace could see that. Death had planned the whole thing: make it so that Ace failed, failed with The Machine, and then punish him needlessly. Punish him just to punish him. Just to have a laugh, and watch Contorted Royal tear itself apart with its own mirror shard.

Ace looked around at the people surrounding him. He wanted to scream, "I need help!" but he wasn't able to do that. He couldn't mouth the words. He was instead moaning, groaning, making unintelligible sounds of anguish and sadness. That the people heard, and he knew some were laughing at his plight.

He was also sweating crazily, as his heart continued to beat so strongly, so visibly. He was sweating as though Armageddon had decided to land right upon his body, and crush him with a fiery and a fury of heat, crash him with fragment destruction.

Ace had not known before that he could ever lose it, but he knew that he was indeed losing it. He had before thought that madness was left for the likes of people like Alice, schizophrenics who thought they talked to a kid named Ralph. But obviously that was incorrect. Obviously there was a lot more to it. Obviously much more to it than he'd ever imagined, or dared to imagine. Or understand. Or get.

Because, what was there to get?

"Who am I?" Ace said. "Please, someone … tell me who I am!"

Everyone remained silent. Some looked at Ace with pity, some with scorn, resentment.

"I thought I was once powerful," Ace said. "I thought I once held a position higher than the king, higher than The Suicide King. But now I'm lower than any of you servants. Tell me, please! Who am I? Please, someone, tell me what is going on with me? Help me out of my mind! Tell me who I am!"

But everyone still remained silent. Pity, resentment, scorn, hate, and some were even mocking Ace. But Ace didn't realize he was being mocked, was he so twisted in his head, his labyrinthine mind. There were no answers. There were never any answers. Everyone was crazy, rather a Christian or an atheist, a humanist or an existentialist. Everybody was mad. Everybody had flipped their lid. Everybody, everybody, so it was with everybody. And Ace couldn't do anything about it, no matter how hard he tried, as he screamed for someone to help him, continued to sweat out rivers in his anxiety and his fear, as he continued to shout for help and grab his head and as he thought that he heard Death talking to him, as he thought he saw Death reflected in imaginary mirrors, as he thought he felt absolutely nothing, and yet, absolutely everything.

But there was a lot more to his situation than just this version of madness, of not knowing who he was, of being confused, of being afraid. He was murdering himself in multiple ways. It was happening in his head, but Death's Mirror was making it seem as though it was reality, and yet also making it reality. He was stabbing himself, multiple times, in various parts of his body, and watching the blood flow. He would especially stab his heart, being the Ace of Heart and all, no longer able to stab himself with spades. He was also somehow hanging himself, somehow drowning himself, somehow poisoning himself, somehow shooting himself, somehow slitting his wrists and bleeding out, doing all of this at once, and doing these things one at a time. He was dying over and over again, over and over again, and being a spectacle for the poor people that had to see someone hurt themselves and kill themselves, but it didn't matter what Ace did, he just continued to die over and over again. He just continued to hurt, he just continued to bleed out his last, and as he stumbled through the crowd, he imagined all of these deaths in his head, these multiple death scenes, but he also knew that they were really happening, and that scared him in ways he could barely even comprehend.

Why was this happening to him? Someone needed to save him! Why was Death torturing him this way?

Ah, but that was the catch! No one was there to save him. No one was ever going to be there to save him, he was always going to be a hypocrite in the name of Death, who owned him, which had proven that Ace was nothing but folly, nothing but vice, nothing but death and sin and corruption and decay.

That was why he had to keep dying, and unfortunately, he was traumatizing all the people that were there. But they weren't, in the end, traumatized. They were laughing at his demise, glad that Ace saw the many facets of Death's Mirror and was going mad. Glad that he saw all the many facets of madness and insanity.

"Make it stop!" Ace shouted. "Please, make it stop!"

Ah, the vulnerability. Ace could even see it, as his heart continued to try and expose itself with its hard beating, until it finally did indeed expose itself. His heart was literally open right now, bared to the world for all to see. And how much Ace wanted to stab it, cram it into more vulnerability! How much he wanted to destroy it! How had he become a caring person, as he continued to heal people so far away in Distorted Royal, as he continued to hate and loathe and persecute himself, just wanting his heart to die already, just die, if only he could kill it, kill it now!

"Make it stop! Please! You've gotta help me! Somebody, please!"

But as always, no one was there to hear his prayers. To hear his words. No one was there. No one was ever going to be there, as his exposed heart showed, as it spurted blood on the ground through every beat.

But even that was an illusion. Even that was a reflection of Death's Mirror.

There was no vulnerability in Ace. He was a bad, bad man. He was a destroyer of good, a murderer of good will, who massacred the innocent for no reason at all. That was why he needed to be so vulnerable right now, have his heart exposed for the entire world to see, and stab if they so chose, which some were doing, some were doing …

"Ace!" came a voice, out of nowhere.

The people parted.

Ace wanted to look up, but he was still freaking out, hardly able to focus on anything, just thinking of all of his multiple death scenes, thinking of all the various ways in which he was dying, and the voice again said, "Ace!"

Ace tried to look up, how he desperately tried to look up, and he was able to succeed. He looked up and saw that The Suicide King was looking at him, carefully, shrewdly.

"Ace," The Suicide King said, and he sounded gentle, somehow, somehow so very gentle.

Ace didn't respond. He didn't know what to say, as he trembled in his agony and despair, as he continued to see all the various ways he was dying, all of the various methods getting more and more violent, his heart still exposed like a knife blade …

"Ace," The Suicide King said, forcing Ace to look at him. "*You're mad.*"

Ace wasn't sure what to do with this information. He couldn't process it. He couldn't do anything with it. He didn't know what to do with it.

But then some of it finally registered, at least enough for him to say, "I'm … I'm *mad?*"

The Suicide King nodded his head.

Then he said, "You're mad because of all the things you have done. The key to that is indeed fragment destruction."

"But I'm already being destroyed!" The Ace of Hearts wanted to shout. "I'm already being murdered!"

"You're traumatizing people, Ace," The Suicide King said. "With your evil ways, with all the various ways in which you are killing yourself. It needs to stop. Fragment destruction is the answer. I'm banishing you from my land. Do you understand that, Ace?"

"But my heart …" Ace wanted to say, but when he looked at his heart, he saw it wasn't exposed. He saw that The Suicide King was holding his sword which had stabbed Ace's heart, and holding it there to let the blood and pain drip, and then even that didn't exist anymore.

Because what The Suicide King was doing was saying, "Yes, Ace: I'm banishing you. You're hereby banished because of your madness. You're being severed from all of us for the crime of your insanity. Fragmentation destruction, here you are. Here you are!"

And then The Suicide King stabbed his sword into the ground.

When he did this, the sword began to glow, and the ground began to shake. Ace felt some temporary relief from Death's Mirror, he didn't see himself killing himself over and over again, but he was trembling at how powerful The Suicide King was. He knew that he needed to leave. Yes, it wouldn't take away the new pain, the pain of excision, the pain of being excised like a cancer tumor, but he didn't know what else to do, and so Ace said, "I'm … I'm mad?" and as The Suicide King nodded, Ace slowly began to stumble away.

What a terrible person he was! Going insane and scaring away the public! It was terrible, that Ace had completely succumbed to madness, he needed to be cut off, cut off for good, cut off and destroyed, excised like a malignant tumor, and so he stumbled into the forest, with the ground still shaking, the light of the sword still in his eyes, and the fragment destruction continued to blare in his eyes and blast in his ears, all he saw was that fragment destruction, all he saw was vulnerability, why was there no one here to save him as he stumbled closer and closer to his exile ...

Broad Strokes of Black, Blue, and Yellow, the Enjoyment of Being with Your Friendly Fellow

Everything was true, what one Brannon knew. Except in that truth came a certain amount of discrimination, as well as a certain amount of responsibility.

Brannon still couldn't believe how bad the conversation had gone with his alternate universe self. He had brought up a lot of points that the Brannon from Contorted Royal had never considered. However, that was what happened when you were in the moment of crisis, in the moment of the alternate universe breakdown: you saw sides to yourself that you would be happy to never see again.

Brannon did indeed have doubts. He wasn't going to pretend that everything was perfect, that Brannon was in tip top shape and ready to go. He wasn't going to pretend that he thought he was a good person, ready to go into ethical battle. He couldn't do that, because the other Brannon had done a good job at putting Brannon through existential fears.

But nonetheless, Brannon knew that he couldn't let such things get in the way. That was the result of Death's Mirror, of course, or at least the desired result: for Brannon, a kind of helper of Contorted Royal (never savior, by any means: Brannon was not going to entertain the idea that he was a Messiah of some sort, that was just plain ridiculous), really was capable of helping Contorted Royal, and he couldn't do that if he let Death's Mirror and alternate universes (both of which went hand in hand) play their tricks.

As far as Brannon knowing and understanding what he was capable of? He honestly wasn't sure. He would have liked to be sure, because it would make his mission that much more efficient, effective. However, it wasn't that easy. Brannon was guessing his way through most of it, and haphazarding his way through the remaining parts. But he did believe that if you at least tried to let your heart shine with good will and good intention, then hopefully something good would happen.

And poetry. You couldn't live without poetry, of course.

So Brannon went on a mission. He needed to bring together The Jack of Knives and The Dark Kid, who were both being tormented severely by Death's Mirror, who were the key to destroying Death's Mirror, and who were also very separate from each other at the moment.

So what Brannon did, was Brannon went to the Valley of Death, seeing The Jack of Knives lying down on the ground, dead, and picked him up, and carried him back to Contorted Royal, to the forest where The Dark Kid was. The Dark Kid was also lying down on the ground, dead, dead from a knife wound in the heart.

But of course, none of it was real. The Suicide King had used fragment destruction, which was basically a fancy term for illusion, and more specifically, a fancy term for illusion reflected back at the illusion and mind games of Death's Mirror, to kill The Jack of Knives, and The Dark Kid only thought he was dead, which of course wasn't the same as being dead. Sure, he'd died of heartache, as nobody ever wanted to be separated from their friends: but nonetheless, he was alive.

So Brannon lay The Jack of Knives next to The Dark Kid, and then cleared his throat: "Ahem."

The Dark Kid turned over on his side, and said, "I'm sleeping."

The Jack of Knives just remained dead.

Brannon, who knew better than to give up, cleared his throat again.

"What do you want?" The Dark Kid said, half through sleep, half through death (or rather, his imaginary death).

301

"I want you to realize that your best friend is right beside you. He hasn't gone anywhere."

The Dark Kid sat up suddenly, opened his eyes, rubbed them. He turned to see that The Jack of Knives was indeed beside him.

But then, The Dark Kid frowned. He felt his friend's pulse. "He's dead."

"Just give him a moment," Brannon said. "Sometimes our lives are just spent."

The Dark Kid did as he was told, and suddenly, The Jack of Knives grabbed his heart, gasping for breath, like he'd just been drowned. And he had just been drowned. He'd been drowned in death. Or rather, by Death.

The Jack of Knives saw The Dark Kid. They studied each other for a moment, as though they couldn't believe they were next to each other. Surely this was a joke. Surely it wasn't real.

Brannon stood up before his friends, who were sitting down next to each other, still trying to figure out what was going on.

Then at last Brannon said, "I apologize for this meeting, but we all could use a little beating."

"What do you mean?" The Jack of Knives asked. "My father murdered me. In cold blood."

"He was only for once ruling the kingdom and protecting his young," Brannon said, and explained the fragment destruction illusion.

The Jack of Knives nodded, trying to take this in, and said, "So ... basically my Dad was keeping me safe by hurting me."

"Pretty much," Brannon said. "Bet it was a rush."

"Stop rhyming," The Jack of Knives snapped, but lightly.

"Anyway, you, knife kid, are the prince. And as such, you have responsibilities. You have things that you need to do."

The Jack of Knives just nodded his head, said, "I'm listening."

Brannon said, "You need to stop Death's Mirror from destroying everything, from killing Contorted Royal in its perpetual reflective chaos. You've got to step it up. You are the king's son, after all, and with that, you naturally have a lot of power. So, are you willing to do your job?"

"I guess," The Jack of Knives said. "But it depends. What do I need to do?"

"That's what we need to figure out. Together. Be like one flock of a feather. We obviously can't just wait around for things to change, because that will never accomplish anything," Brannon said.

The Jack of Knives nodded. "I suppose we have been getting nothing done."

"Well, Death's Mirror has that effect. Both of you thought you were dead. Both of you had been heartbroken, for various reasons. Heartbreak often has that effect. But nonetheless, we're here now. So let's get this figured out. Let's figure out how we're going to beat Death, and his blasted mirror."

The Jack of Knives pulled out his pack of cards, and began to shuffle them. He looked up at Brannon, and said, "You really are determined to help us, aren't you?"

"Only where I can, naturally," Brannon said. "I have my limitations, just like anybody does. But that doesn't mean I'm not going to try. That doesn't mean I'm not going to do my best to help you where I can. So, let's get this figured out." Brannon looked at The Dark Kid, who had remained silent all this time. "And you, Dark Kid: it's time you toughen up your act."

"What do you mean?" The Dark Kid said.

"You're The Dark Kid for a reason. You've seen things, you're capable of doing things, because of your darkness. In short, you're tough. Are you just going to roll over and take it, let Death destroy everything about you?"

"Not really," The Dark Kid said. "Not at all."

"Then help me figure this out," Brannon said. "And all without a doubt."

And so The Dark Kid (black), The Jack of Knives (yellow), and Brannon (blue), began to puzzle away, about what they wanted to do.

After they'd been thinking for some time, getting nothing done, Brannon said, pulling out paint brushes, paint, and a canvas out of nowhere, "Sometimes, a little art can help us get our emotions out."

Brannon passed out the brushes, and before Brannon knew it, the three kids were painting chaotically on the canvas. When

303

they finished, it was merely abstract expressionism, but in a cool way. It was simply broad strokes of their respective colors, black, blue, and yellow. It wasn't much, naturally, but the shape that it made looked like Death if he'd been murdered.

But Brannon and his friends didn't realize this, quite immediately.

"I like it," The Jack of Knives said, studying the work. "There's a certain degree of chaos to it."

"I think it melds together the best in the best of us," The Dark Kid said. "If we decide to get down to the nitty gritty of our destiny. If we don't just sit back and take it."

"There's also a lot of emotion," Brannon said. "I can see it in the painting's motion. It's more chaotic than the ocean."

The three remained silent for a moment, just looking at their work. The work did indeed look like they'd just thrown paint chaotically on the canvas, but somehow, it accentuated certain aspects of their current plight. The painting illuminated that it was going to be very hard to get rid of Death and his Mirror. Sometimes the painting even looked like Death's Mirror. Never to be broken. Never to be truly shattered.

Suddenly, a light bulb went on above The Dark Kid's head: Brannon saw it, and he said, "Uh oh. Looks like you've got an idea."

"I do," The Dark Kid said, unscrewing the light bulb and holding it in his hands.

"Can we hear it?" The Jack of Knives asked.

"I need to fly. I need to learn how to fly," said The Dark Kid.

And before anyone knew what was going on, The Dark Kid began to run, and jump, trying to lift off the ground. It was hard because there were so many trees, but nothing stopped him from his attempt. Nothing at all. He was going to do this.

The problem, of course, was that The Dark Kid didn't have any wings.

He came back a little while later, exhausted and discouraged. "I can't fly," he said finally.

"Of course you can," Brannon said. "Especially if it's your plan."

"But I don't have wings," The Dark Kid said, but as soon as he said that, lightning struck him.

But The Dark Kid didn't convulse like he'd been electrocuted. He instead simply glowed. And it wasn't long before he suddenly did have wings.

He looked at them, and then said proudly, "Would you look at that?"

Brannon smiled. The Dark Kid was learning how to fly again. This was especially proven when the kid took off into the air, and began to fly around. Brannon felt slightly jealous, but he knew this was the way it needed to be. The Dark Kid needed to expand his wings, both metaphorically and literally. He needed to be who he was.

He came back down, after quite some time, and said, "Whoa. That's fun."

"I'm sure it is," The Jack of Knives said, and he was smiling slightly, even though he looked a tad jealous.

And that was when a light bulb went off above Brannon's head, visible for the whole world to see.

"I think I know how we can beat Death," Brannon said. "So, pause to take a breath."

The Jack of Knives and The Dark Kid disregarded this, and The Dark Kid said, "No, just spill it out already. How do we destroy Death's Mirror? Do we just shatter it?"

Brannon shook his head. "This is going to sound crazy, and perhaps even a little lazy, in terms of thought … but the answer is: to *murder Death*."

The Jack of Knives and The Dark Kid didn't say anything for a moment, just looked at Brannon like, had he really just said what he'd said?

But Brannon nodded his head. "That's the answer. We murder Death."

"But how do we do that?" The Jack of Knives asked. "That sounds impossible. You can't just kill Death … that's a contradiction, is it not? That's a paradox. We can't kill Death, Death just … is."

"I know it sounds insane, but that's the answer. Yes, it has problems with logic, but trust me: that's the way."

The Dark Kid, who was glowing slightly from when he'd been struck by lightning, his wings bright and white, put on sunglasses and said, "Sounds good to me. How do we begin? Where do we begin? What do we do to kill Death?"

"We confront Death," Brannon said. "We corner him. And then, we kill him."

"It'll never work," The Jack of Knives said. "Hate to rain on this idea, but it's true."

"It'll work," Brannon said. "Are you in, prince, or not?"

The Jack of Knives didn't say anything for a moment, but then a light bulb went off above his head too. Of course, for all the world to see.

"Yes," The Jack of Knives said. "I'm in. When do we start?"

Bishop's Sacrifice

Bishop was in his chamber when he heard a knock on the door.

Now, who could that be? Was it an angel come to reward Bishop for all of his humble service to God? Was it God himself, coming to reward Bishop for his awesome work? He certainly hoped so.

Bishop went to the door and waited a moment. Just a moment, to collect his thoughts. He knew it was going to be good. Very good. Whoever it was, it was all going to be awesome.

Bishop then proceeded to open the door, and when he did, he was surprised to see Ralph standing there.

"Can I help you?" Bishop asked.

Ralph didn't say anything for a moment, as though trying to keep himself composed. He looked like he was torn between anger and sorrow, like any move would violently wrench him apart. But if anything was clear on his face, it was a certain look of assertion, barely warding off aggression.

He said, "Can I come in, Bishop?" in a rather cold manner, despite his polite diction.

Bishop nodded, and let the boy inside, and then closed the door.

Ralph looked around, didn't say anything. He saw Bishop's illuminated manuscripts, and a skull, just chilling on a desk.

Ralph kept his back turned when he addressed Bishop: "I know what you did to my girl."

Bishop didn't say anything for a moment, but felt ice running through his veins. That, however, didn't last long, because then came the thaw of redemption, the reminder that he hadn't done anything wrong. He was the bishop, for crying out loud. He was the one in power. He made the calls to his little people of faith, oh woe be to all the hypocrites of Contorted Royal!

So, because Bishop wasn't afraid of being "found out" (though in all actuality, who would believe a random kid from the Bronx, even if someone found Bishop's crime egregious, which who would anyway, because everything Bishop did was in the name of God), he said arrogantly, "And what is that, that you've found out? That I stabbed Alice's deranged head with a mirror shard and gave her the voice of God, a heavenly and righteous gift bestowed upon the weak?"

Ralph still kept his back turned. "You're a monster, Bishop. You know that? You claim to do everything in the name of God, but it's all in the name of evil. It's all in the name of corruption and power. You know Alice does her best to manage her illness, and she does a pretty good job, and then you come along and try to ruin her by making it look like it's her illness, the voices and all, when the direct cause was you. And for all we know, God really is talking to her."

"You should just be thankful Alice found the light," Bishop said. "Will you turn and face me?"

Ralph stood his ground, didn't move. "You're going to pay for what you did to her."

"Everyone pays for their sins, you should know that," Bishop said. "We're all sinners ... that is, except for powerful people in the church, of course. People like me. You should go to church, too, before your soul is ruined by the damnation of Hell, the allurement of the Devil."

Ralph slowly turned around to face Bishop. If it had been any other day, he would have found the boy's courage and stalwartness quite funny. However, because it just so happened to be Sunday, when God was indeed watching all, Bishop was a little

307

uncertain. He didn't believe he'd done anything wrong, but Ralph certainly thought that Bishop had, and what if people didn't listen to the truth? That happened because of blasphemers. Saints like Bishop were burnt at a stake, when it was the heretics, like Ralph, that deserved that.

He said, in an even and cool voice, "Spare me your hypocrite talk. You know what you did was wrong. You know that, and you're going to come to terms with it. I don't know how, but you will. Trust me on that. Alice may not be able to be cured unless we can solve this Death's Mirror problem, but I can guarantee you're going to pay."

Ralph said this assertively and powerfully. Even Bishop was a little afraid. Did he dare say he saw God in the boy? He wasn't sure. But he saw something. Something to be afraid of.

But Bishop quickly told himself it was nothing to worry about. So he said, "Are you Christian, Ralph?"

"I used to be Catholic," Ralph said. "I fell away from the church for two reasons: because all I felt was dogma, which can be just as bad as blasphemy and heresy, and because of the hypocrisy. I'd never come to your church for those reasons."

"Well, no one's perfect, except for those who give themselves fully to the Word," Bishop said. "And I'm the only one in Contorted Royal who does that. You don't see me going around killing people for the fun of it, do you? Or committing suicide? Or sleeping around? Or tormenting others with my symptoms of schizophrenia?"

Ralph just merely smiled. "Perhaps. But as far as I know, humility is a virtue. A very important virtue. Saints would have enough humility to never exclude others, like a bad eugenics experiment. And from what I gather about you, humility is only one virtue you lack."

"Well, judgment belongs to the Lord," Bishop said. "Now if there's anything else you have to say, I suggest you say it, because I'm going to ask you to leave, and probably not nicely."

Ralph nodded his head. "Alice will make it through. Whether by the divine will of God or by her own free will, she'll make it. And you, Bishop? I believe you'll suffer. I hope Hell isn't in your future, but you will suffer. Good day, Bishop. Good luck with your eugenics project."

And then Ralph briskly exited the chamber.

Bishop nearly slammed the door. What was it with that random kid from the Bronx? Why was he so powerful in his speech? He didn't even say anything that original. Or that poignant. He just spoke from his heart. And for some reason, it was having an effect on Bishop, and Bishop couldn't explain why.

He had done no wrong. That he believed. He was only a servant to God. He was God's elder brother, in fact. He was powerful. And yet, he felt like he needed to square the situation away. Prove he was sorry. As for why, he wasn't sure he knew why, and yet what Ralph had said ... somehow, it was ringing true. Somehow. It shouldn't have, but Ralph was diehard for his girlfriend. He'd do anything for her. He didn't care that she was sick: he was willing to stick with her to the end. Bishop found that ... touching. He found it ... beautiful. Bishop wanted that beauty.

Bishop needed to put himself in penitence. And he knew how he was going to do that. He was going to kill himself. Hang himself, in fact. Hang himself on a tree branch outside.

Bishop grabbed the rope and began to go toward his faithful mission. But he was smiling as he went toward his grave. He was smiling because he believed that he was doing the right thing. God would see Bishop's good will, his desire to be penitent, to confess whatever sin he had committed, and would be pleased, and Bishop would go to Heaven, and be happy, while all the sinners below would suffer low. Yes. Bishop, as always, was going to get the better end of the deal.

As Bishop walked toward the tree where he was going to hang himself, Death appeared beside him.

"You've done good work," Death said. "I guess you're ready for the next step?"

"Of course," Bishop said, attaching the rope to the branch and getting ready to hang himself.

"I'm glad," Death said. "I'm so very glad. And really: you've done well. You've done very well. Destroying souls, sending them grief, destroying lives: it's what you do."

"Of course it is," Bishop said proudly. "That's my mission. I serve God, our holy Father."

"Do you feel guilty at all?" Death asked, almost condescendingly.

Bishop only smiled. "I have no reason to feel guilty. No reason at all. I've only been serving God all my life. I've only done the right thing, over and over again. I'm a good man. God will see that in my penitence."

"Do you think it will hurt?" Death asked.

"Pain will show my absolution to God," Bishop said. "But God already knows I've done nothing wrong. I'm clean. I wasn't born into sin like everyone else. I'm higher than the Messiah. I'm higher than God. I am God."

And Bishop smiled as he wrapped the noose around his throat. He smiled because nothing could make him feel happier right now. He was proving to God that everything he'd done was for the right reasons. Penitence even though he didn't deserve it. God was going to dote on Bishop for all eternity, give him the finest riches, give him the finest palace in Heaven. Heaven belonged to Bishop. It had Bishop's name on it.

It was Bishop's sacrifice. Bishop knew that he'd never done anything wrong, ever, but that was what sacrifice was. Bishop was like Jesus. No, Bishop was better than Jesus: never, ever hurt a fly, never, ever hurt a soul, just show everyone what the truth and light was, and then die on the cross.

"I'm glad you have so much conviction," Death said, smiling.

Bishop felt uncomfortable with that smile. Did Death know something that Bishop didn't?

"Well, thanks," Bishop said. "Someone needs to have it."

"The Queen won't benefit from your sacrifice, I imagine," Death said. "The King won't benefit. It's all for the glory and benefit of your God, your Savior. Correct?"

"Yes, yes, of course," Bishop said. He had climbed the tree and was going to jump and hang himself that way, and feel the undeserved penitence and make God proud, and become God himself. "The Suicide King and The Black Queen won't benefit from me dying."

"I guess why it's called the Bishop's sacrifice," Death said, who had climbed the tree beside Bishop.

"I suppose so," Bishop said, and realized, it was all for him. But no, that wasn't true, it was all for God … which meant, it was all for him. Which meant …

He didn't know what it meant. Bishop just knew he was feeling doubts. The way Death was looking at him, like a hungry lion in his den, with Bishop trapped in that den … metaphorically circling over Bishop like a starving vulture who'd found his decayed and outdated meat.

Bishop filed these thoughts away.

But yes: it was all for him. All for Bishop. That was what service to God was, after all: all for ourselves. We just wanted to get into Heaven. We just wanted to be more powerful than God.

Hence, the reason why it was called Bishop's sacrifice.

"Any last words?" Death said.

"I hope Ralph dies slowly and painfully," Bishop said.

"He'll probably die of cancer," Death said. "I can never be one hundred percent certain in the deaths of others, because I control so many lives, and because Fate changes things on me randomly at times, and because there are so many variables I can't control: but if I have my way, he'll die of cancer, just as his girl will die of her brain disease. She'll probably get into a terrible accident, due to her delusions."

Bishop smiled. "Good. Serves Ralph right. I hope he burns in the hell of his words, which he thinks is humble, assertive speech."

And then, Bishop took the leap, and began to hang there. The choking was terrible, and Death hovered in front of Bishop. Even if Bishop wanted to, he couldn't go back, but he was wishing he'd made it possible to go back, because he didn't like the way Death was staring at him.

"Time to claim another soul," Death said, except he was wearing a hood and holding a poignant scythe now, and he looked like the Grim Reaper.

"What do you mean?" Bishop would have said, if he hadn't been choking to death.

But it didn't matter. He saw it. Death was going to be destroyed. And when that happened, everything would go backwards, to the point to where The Machine was destroyed and Death's Mirror released, and it would be like none of Death's Mirror ever happened. It was possible that wouldn't happen, of course, because nothing was certain, but if it did, Bishop wouldn't be coming back, because Bishop wasn't going to go backwards.

311

His soul was claimed by Death, and Death, even if dead, would always own Bishop's soul.

And that filled him with fear. He would have to look into Death's Mirror for all eternity, Death's Mirror reflected in Death's shiny and hellfire eyes. He'd have to do that forever, forever, stare into the reflection, as if he was looking at his own soul.

Bishop had been betrayed. No, no, this was all so backwards ... but it was somehow happening. He told himself they wouldn't succeed in killing Death, because that was a contradiction, a major contradiction in logic, but he knew that regardless, he would always be moving forward, and that was deeper and deeper into the abyss of Death's eyes.

Because Death wasn't afraid. He wanted to claim Bishop's soul, as he was doing now. Death didn't care if he died, he didn't care if he lost ... because he always won something. You couldn't kill Death. Not in the end. Not in any way that mattered.

All of it, so backwards. But it was what Bishop deserved. He had been/represented Alice's illness. He had been her shattered voices, her shattered consciousness. He had been her schizophrenia.

He had been the unclean one, because he had been her disease.

And as Death just laughed darkly, and as Bishop just stared into the reflection, he realized he was already dead, but that this was only the beginning of his perpetual and painful sacrifice, the Bishop's sacrifice, those eyes ...

The Deflect Reflect

The Dark Kid and his friends continued to walk. They knew they were moving towards where Death liked to stay sometimes, but they didn't quite know exactly where that was, exactly. They would have liked to, because it would have made the experience less surreal and creepy. Because indeed, they were simply walking on open land, as flat as it could possibly be, with permanent darkness above them, making it difficult for them to see each other.

The Dark Kid didn't mind the darkness, naturally. It was his home, it was where he felt most comfortable. But he knew that Brannon was more of a light blue type guy, and The Jack of Knives, while tough and pseudo homicidal, would have rather approached Death somewhere else, if he'd had the choice. Not that he had the choice, of course, but the sentiment was still there.

"So, how do we kill Death, exactly?" The Jack of Knives asked. "I imagine a simple knife wound to the heart won't kill him. We could probably do a number of things to him, from drowning him to hanging him to blowing him up with a bomb, and I bet none of it would work … and that's assuming that he isn't so powerful that we can get near him enough to do those things."

"It's a good question, for which there is no answer," Brannon said. "Unfortunately for us, Death is like a cancer."

"I don't think it's going to be that complex," The Dark Kid said, soaking up all the darkness surrounding him. He really would be right as rain, if there was just a little bit of lightning here, for atmosphere, ambience. Which he knew he could create, but didn't, just because he didn't want to attract Death's attention. Because they were indeed getting close.

"How do you mean?" Brannon asked. "Killing Death isn't complicated? Wc all know we're dealing with a paradox, and paradoxes never untangle."

"I think The Jack of Knives just needs to throw knives at Death, and try to stab him that way," The Dark Kid said. "I'll try to electrocute Death and kill him that way, while you, Brannon, I suppose, kill him with your charming poetry."

"I could also throw my knife cards at him," The Jack of Knives mused in a conniving manner. He pulled out his pack of cards, which were dog-eared, but nonetheless, could cut through the entire trunk of a tree.

"That would work as well," The Dark Kid said. "I think it's better if we don't complicate the matter, and just attack him as we see fit."

The three boys thought about this proposition for a little while, and then The Jack of Knives said, "I'm grateful that my Dad got me out of Death's Mirror with his fragment destruction. It was painful when it happened, him murdering me and all, but he was just doing it so I could be here, with you guys, on our quest to stop Death from destroying Contorted Royal with his Mirror."

"And you may want to stop now, while you have the chance," Death said, his voice reverberating everywhere, like the voices of Alice's God, the voices of her schizophrenia.

The Dark Kid looked at Brannon and The Jack of Knives, and amazingly, smiled. The Jack of Knives looked a little afraid, Brannon looked a little scared, but The Dark Kid felt at home. He was ready to take on Death. This was his destiny. If he could fall from out of the sky without even knowing why, he could conquer Death. It would be a piece of cake.

"And why should we stop?" The Dark Kid asked, curiously, tauntingly.

"Oh, you don't want to play that game with me," Death said. "Naughty, naughty, of you, Dark Kid. It'll honestly just make things worse, for all of you."

Death was nowhere to be found, which was presenting a problem. Clearly they couldn't just kill him, if he didn't show up, just spoke in his shattered voice.

"It's not naughty," The Dark Kid said. "It's exactly what I need to do. I'm not afraid of you, and neither are my friends. They're tough. Tough as iron. They're ready to take you over. They're ready to destroy you."

"Well, you'll have to catch me first," Death said.

"And we will," The Dark Kid said. "But you'll need to show yourself. Meet us on a level playing field. Meet at our level."

"I don't do that to mere mortals," Death said.

"You sure we're mortals?" The Dark Kid asked tauntingly. "You sure about that, Death?"

"I'm sure," Death said.

The Dark Kid only smiled. He didn't know much about his past, but he knew that he was immortal. Just like everyone here was, really.

"I do have a question for you, though," The Dark Kid said.

"Shoot," Death said. "Did you notice the pun?"

"Yeah, yeah, you want to shoot us," The Dark Kid said. "But my question is, why did you unleash Death's Mirror in the first place, when you knew it could be shattered?"

"Because I knew the more you shattered it, the more the alternate universes would breakdown, the more Alice would hear God in her head, the more Contorted Royal would shatter, the more everything would break into a million little pieces."

"Sounds like you've got it all figured out, then, don't you?" The Dark Kid said, still taunting. "You know you'll always win. You're Death. We could break your mirror or not break your mirror, so to speak, and you'd still win. We could kill you or not kill you, and you'd still win."

"That's what happens with an invincible, immutable presence such as myself," Death said. "You know there are alternate universe versions of me too, right? Death is everywhere. Death always will be everywhere. I am everything."

"Sounds like you have a God complex," The Dark Kid said.

"Maybe," Death said. "But it's well deserved."

The Dark Kid was going to say something, but that was when he realized that his friends were gone. *Poof.* Disappeared, completely, *gone.* Like they'd been blasted with fairy dust, or had fallen through a wormhole and entered another dimension. Gone like magic.

The Dark Kid thought he could show his fear, and was even afraid that he was showing his fear. It wasn't good they were gone; he hadn't even noticed they were gone, at least immediately. But nonetheless, he wasn't going to show his fear, he was going to keep it in check, as he said, "Maybe it is well deserved."

Death cut through The Dark Kid's fears like a knife: "Are your friends gone, Dark Kid?"

The Dark Kid now showed fear. He knew better, and thankfully, because he lived in shadow, the fear was hardly noticeable, detectable … but Death could look right through the darkest of the dark, and The Dark Kid knew his fear had been revealed.

"Brannon is too soft-hearted," Death said. "Contrariwise, The Jack of Knives is too murderous. You're somewhere in the middle. You have that soft spot, but you have that darker nature. I'm so very anxious to exploit it."

The Dark Kid found his footing, found his cool, and continued to play: "Oh, really, now, Death? You want to exploit it?"

"More than you know," Death said. "You haven't escaped Death's Mirror. You don't understand fragment destruction, the way an aging king like The Suicide King would. He may have paved some of the way, but he can't pave the whole way. As you'll see. Death's Mirror is never broken, because it's always broken. Death's Mirror never goes anywhere. Look."

And The Dark Kid did look. He saw mirrors surrounding him. But what he saw, instead of his darkness, was vulnerability. He saw light ... so much *light*. This should have been a good thing, but in the context of Death, this was the furthest thing from good, because it showed weakness. You couldn't kill Death and be weak, simultaneously. That was as contradictory of an idea as killing Death.

"Do you admire yourself?" Death taunted.

"I think it's a lie," The Dark Kid said, and was realizing that fragment destruction was the key to solving Death's mirror. But how could he do that? Was he sure he understood what fragment destruction meant?

He needed the deflect reflect, which meant the same thing as the fragment destruction. But what was that, exactly? The Dark Kid was ashamed to say he honestly didn't know. He had no idea.

The Dark Kid continued to see himself in the many mirrors surrounding him, seeing that he was actually The Light Kid. He knew the hatred he felt for himself had been inserted by Death and his mirror, but that didn't make it any less real. He saw Death overpowering him with his darkness, snuffing out the light ... a metaphor for Death snuffing out The Dark Kid's strength.

It was so minimalist, so simple, this image, but that didn't stop it from having the power that it did. Not at all. The Dark Kid felt weak. He felt snuffed. He felt like Christ on the cross: powerless, capable of nothing. Incapable of fighting back. Deserted, forsaken.

But then he had an idea: that was perhaps the deflect reflect. That was perhaps the cure. The Dark Kid concentrated, knowing that Brannon had tried to remove all the death and destruction from Contorted Royal. If The Dark Kid reflected, in his thoughts, the idea that he didn't need to fight back, because that was the more peaceful way to do things ...

316

And suddenly, The Dark Kid looked like The Dark Kid again. He looked cool. He looked shady. He was even wearing shades now, which were in style. He looked good.

Death didn't say anything, but The Dark Kid knew he needed to exploit what he understood: "That's the deflect reflect. Just reflect exactly what you're showing us and forcing in our heads, which will in turn deflect what you show us."

"It'll never work," Death said, and continued to try and show The Dark Kid as The Light Kid, but it didn't work. Not at all. Not even in the slightest.

But Death was not worried. Suddenly, The Jack of Knives and Brannon appeared, and they looked so confused.

He saw Death's Mirror shards stabbed in their heads. And yet, he didn't. But nonetheless, he knew their brains had been sliced by Death's Mirror, Death's knife.

And were they ever so confused.

"I think ..." The Jack of Knives said. "I think I need to kill you. And you need to kill ... me."

And before The Dark Kid knew what was happening, The Jack of Knives was stabbing The Dark Kid. It was painful, so very painful, this contorted friendship, and it wasn't long before Brannon was stabbing The Jack of Knives who was stabbing The Dark Kid, but The Dark Kid was only smiling as this was happening. He was smiling because he knew where this was going to end. At least for the moment.

The deflect reflect: fragment destruction. The answer.

"You have to mean it," The Dark Kid said.

"Doesn't this hurt you?" The Jack of Knives asked, still stabbing, and looking so confused. "Aren't you hurt and bleeding?"

"I only think I'm hurt and bleeding," The Dark Kid said, still smiling. "And regardless, this is my world. The things I've seen ... you'd never be able to believe. Now, my friends, the key is the deflect reflect: you have to mean it. Show Death what he wants to see, reflect back his own reflection, like forcing Medusa to look into her own eyes."

The Jack of Knives paused. "None of this is really happening?"

"None of this is ever really happening," The Dark Kid said, and he held a knife now, and he began to stab his friends. They were all stabbing each other like crazy, but laughing, as though they were playing basketball and having a blast, or splashing each other in a pool. It was a kid thing. Someone like Death would certainly not understand.

They continued to do this, and it wasn't long before those realities, of them playing basketball, splashing each other in pools, and other things, such as rollerblading or skateboarding or playing soccer, together, became a reality. There was no violence, just simply the violence of friendship.

Reflecting it back to Death.

He finally shouted, "Stop! Enough!"

They stopped what they were doing (hanging out at a park and talking), and the darkness came back. Death was walking toward them, wearing a hood, but his voice was angry, or The Dark Kid should say, voices. They were shattering even louder this time, and Death was so very angry.

"All right," he said, "I surrender. But just know, you've only scratched the surface of my mirror, which is a tangle of mazes, never to be unsolved."

"Maybe," The Dark Kid said proudly, standing beside his friends pleased, with The Jack of Knives holding his knife out and ready, and Brannon ready with his poems in his head, with The Dark Kid naturally ready with his darkness, "but me and my friends aren't going anywhere. Just you watch."

Deathly

The Jack of Knives could feel The Dark Kid's pride emanating proudly. He knew that they could pull this off, kill Death, as crazy of an idea as it sounded. It was just going to take some work, some thought, but he knew they'd be able to pull it off, pull off a deadly joke like a deathly laugh.

The Jack of Knives pulled out his pack of cards, and he was holding his knife. However, nobody did anything for a moment, to the point to where Death said, "You guys aren't going to do anything?"

318

It was indeed a good question. The Jack of Knives could see the confusion on his friend's faces now. Death wasn't even flashing his mirror and they were confused. They were confused because, how did one actually kill Death? I mean, what could one actually *do* to kill Death? It just didn't make sense. It didn't make sense at all.

"I'm an open target now," Death said. "So are you going to kill me, or not?"

Still hesitation.

Finally, Brannon said, "I don't believe in this violence, but understand the importance of you dying, Death, so, I'm going to kill you with my poetry."

"Bring it on," Death said.

"Death is like a barb wired snare, who refuses to have a care. I'm really not a fan of death in the slightest, so Death I hope in peace will rest."

"Your poetry jags on the ear," Death said. "I think it was as effective as stabbing me with a knife."

"Glad to hear it," Brannon said. "But poetry can be like spit. Poisonous spit."

"Anyone else want to try?" Death taunted.

The Jack of Knives took a deep breath, and then threw a card at Death. It hit him squarely in the chest. He began to bleed, but it didn't do much damage, in the end, so The Jack of Knives threw another, and then another, but still there was no luck. Death was strong. Death wasn't going to die tonight.

Which was strange, because Death was bleeding quite a bit. Many cards had now stabbed Death, so it was strange that he hadn't died yet. Many of the cards had gone deep inside Death, puncturing organs and the like, and yet, Death looked as right as rain.

"Did you guys want to chop off my head?" Death said, continuing to taunt.

The Jack of Knives looked at The Dark Kid for help. The Dark Kid said, "I don't think it's a good idea, even for the chaotic and out of control violence of Contorted Royal."

"Well," Death said, throwing an axe toward the three kids, "you're free to do that if you think it will work. Feel free to chop my head off, dismember me. Do whatever your cruel hearts desire."

The three kids ducked so they didn't lose their own heads, and Brannon went to pick up the axe. He studied it for a moment, and then dropped it on the ground, turned to face Death. "I don't think it's a good idea."

"And why is that?" Death taunted. "Do you know how many people in Contorted Royal have had their heads chopped off? It's nothing."

"Maybe because we don't want to play your game," The Dark Kid said. "We want to kill you, because that's what our fate requires, but in the most painless way possible."

"With a little bit of pain, at least," The Jack of Knives amended.

The Dark Kid smiled lightly. "Yes. Perhaps with a little pain."

"Well, you aren't getting anywhere," Death said, and he looked just like new. The cards weren't in his body anymore. He wasn't bleeding. He was whole again. "Did you want to hang me?" Death said, attaching a noose to his throat that came out of nowhere. "Did you want to drown me?" Death said, suddenly in a small lake that had also appeared out of nowhere, with the noose disappeared. "Did you want to stab me?" Death said, the water now gone and him stabbing himself multiple times in various parts of his body. "Or did you want to shoot me?" Death said, and put a gun to his head, and shot his brains out.

All of this violence did not disconcert The Jack of Knives, at least not in the sense that he was seeing so much violence. What disconcerted The Jack of Knives was that he felt that they just couldn't kill Death. Death was taunting them with his mock suicides. Death couldn't have killed himself even if he'd wanted, so what made The Jack of Knives think that his deadbeat friends and him could kill Death? It was absurd.

Regardless, something snapped with The Jack of Knives: wielding his knife, he charged toward Death and began to stab him brutally, chaotically, frustrated, and getting blood on his clothes but not caring. He even took the initiative to claw at Death every once in a while, claw at his heart as though trying to rip it apart.

But it didn't matter what The Jack of Knives did. For every injury he caused, that injury was taken away. And the worst part? Death found it funny. He was laughing. Laughing like he was being tickled, not stabbed. Laughing like it was a good joke. Not necessarily an effective way to kill Death.

The Jack of Knives backed away when he realized nothing was happening, and then looked at his friends for help. The Dark Kid said, "I didn't realize you had so much rage and animal in you, Jack."

"Well, a lot of good it did!" The Jack of Knives hissed.

Death just continued to laugh, but then became serious, suddenly. He said, "All right, all right. I won't hold it against you anymore. You want to know the way to kill me successfully?"

The three kids listened attentively.

Death pulled out a dagger, and tossed it to The Jack of Knives. The Jack of Knives caught it, studied it carefully.

"You can't kill Death," Death began, "by killing him literally. Death, while perhaps looking as though he's in a material body, is more of an ethereal, unreal being. The best way to kill something like that, then, is to let him be real. And once he's real, you can kill him."

Before The Jack of Knives could process this and say anything, Death disappeared, and in his place was an animal. A dog. A stray, sad, lonely dog. It was material, all right, corporeal for sure … and The Jack of Knives understood that if he killed this dog, he would have killed Death.

The Dark Kid looked at The Jack of Knives with apparent fear. This wasn't right. Not at all. Not in the slightest.

But it was right. The Jack of Knives felt that. So he approached the dog, and The Dark Kid shouted, "Wait!"

The Jack of Knives turned around. "It's just a trick. We have to do this to kill Death."

"I know, but … wait."

But The Jack of Knives wasn't going to wait. Death had wreaked too much havoc. It was time to stop it. So, The Jack of Knives charged toward the dog and stabbed him multiple times.

Brannon and The Dark Kid called out, "No!" but it was too late. The dog, bleeding, was already dying.

"How could you?" The Dark Kid said, and he had shed a lot of his shadow, let in some light. "How could you kill an innocent dog?"

"Death is gone," The Jack of Knives said in his defense. "Death disappeared because I took the initiative."

"You killed a dog!" Brannon shouted, sounding offbeat without his rhyme. "An innocent dog! How could you do that!"

The Jack of Knives wasn't sure, but he couldn't stand listening to the voices of his friends, his conscience, and so he began to run away.

The guilt was overwhelming. Death had amounted to a scared dog. How could anyone kill something so innocent? It wasn't right. The Jack of Knives had crossed the line.

The guilt began to eat at him, and he began to consider suicide. Except this time, he'd successfully kill himself. It wouldn't be pseudo death, it would be real, heartfelt death. Real suicide.

He pulled out his knife, trying his best to hide his feelings. He was waiting for Death's Mirror to reveal itself, but there was nothing. The Jack of Knives then had his decision made.

He was about to stab himself in the heart when he felt someone grab his hand and try to force it away. The Jack of Knives, his eyes closed, shouted, in a frantic and desperate fury, "No! I need to do this!" and continued to struggle with the hand, continued to struggle to kill himself.

All he saw in his mind's eye was the innocent dog, who'd been murdered for no reason. All he saw was murder and death and destruction, and it was killing The Jack of Knives, who couldn't believe he had so much cruelty in him. Couldn't believe he was this kind of person. Couldn't believe he was The Jack of Knives. Why couldn't he be The Jack of Spoons?

He continued to struggle, and at last, the being he was sparring with put their hand over the mouth of The Jack of Knives, trying to suffocate him enough to gain control over The Jack of Knives, and The Jack of Knives slowly went quiet.

He opened his eyes slowly, feeling the knife being taken away, and looked to see who was there. It was Ace. Except, he looked like a friend. He looked like a good friend.

What was going on?

The Jack of Knives followed Ace back to where his friends were. They were beside the dog, crying over the loss of something so beautiful.

And that was when Ace pulled out a gun. The Jack of Knives thought for sure that he was going to shoot his friends. He in fact pointed it in the direction of his friends. But when he pulled the trigger, he was pulling the trigger at the dog.

Except the dog wasn't a dog anymore. He was Death. Death took every bullet, every blow. And it looked real. It looked like it was really going to kill him this time.

"You made me go insane, "Ace said, his voice withered but somehow strong. "Enjoy my sanity while it's still here."

"You're nothing to me," Death spat. "Besides, you can't kill me with a gun. No one can."

"Perhaps not, but you can't taunt these boys with your mirror, either."

And before The Jack of Knives could say anything, Ace disappeared through the darkness.

The Jack of Knives knew this was only temporary, of course. Ace would never be on their side. But maybe it was at least a step in the right direction. A step towards healing.

What The Jack of Knives also realized, however, was that he had been right to feel his guilt. He had deserved to feel it. How could he have romanticized homicide and death so much? He had just been contributing to the chaos of Contorted Royal!

And as he saw Death dying, or rather, mock dying, he felt an enormous amount of guilt, especially as he watched his friends try to stop the flow of heavy blood with little Band-Aids. The gesture was pathetic but childlike and sincere, and The Jack of Knives wanted a taste of that.

He went to Death and hugged him. Just hugged him.

"I'm sorry I tried to kill you," The Jack of Knives confessed. "I shouldn't have done it. It was wrong."

Death looked confused. He said, "You're sorry?"

"Yes," The Jack of Knives said. "Me and my friends, we were trying to kill you. But it was wrong. We have to draw the line somewhere. We have to heal Contorted Royal."

Death didn't say anything for a moment, but then said, "You know I'm not dying, though, right? Gunshots can't kill me, especially by my fool Ace."

"I know," said The Jack of Knives sincerely. "But ... I care about you."

Death remained silent for a moment, and then said, even more confused, "You ... *care*?"

The Jack of Knives nodded.

And that was when Death began to bleed for real, from where he'd been shot, particularly his heart. He shouted out in agony, and in between his shouts of pain, he said, "Do you know the things I've seen? All the terrible ways people can die? All the terrible ways I killed them? Do you know what I've seen?"

"I'm sorry," The Jack of Knives said.

"I have to go," Death said. "I have to retire. I have to die quietly. I can't be part of this anymore."

The Jack of Knives just continued to hug Death, his friend, while his other friends continued to try to heal Death with Band-Aids. Naturally, it was futile.

Death looked up at the three kids, who were looking very sad, like they were losing someone very close. He said, "I guess that's how you kill me. You figured it out."

The Jack of Knives looked up guiltily, even though there was nothing to be guilty about. "What kills you?"

"Love," Death said, and then he closed his eyes for the final time, breathed his last.

When that happened, everything went backwards. It was the strangest effect, like backwards logic, but everyone was literally moving backwards, in time, the alternate universe breakdown undoing itself like a knot, Death's Mirror and its chaos becoming nonexistent, to the point to where they'd been when The Machine had been destroyed. For some reason, though, The Jack of Knives was inside the room where The Machine had been destroyed, and he was looking at Ralph, and Alice, and The Black Queen, and all the other important people in this complex Contorted Royal drama, such as The Suicide King. How they had all ended up here when that wasn't the way the past had happened, The Jack of Knives wasn't sure, but here they all were, ready to start a new future.

The Machine, completely destroyed, with a new timeline taking place, a new point of reference, a new place to begin. As for what that timeline was going to bring, The Jack of Knives wasn't sure, but he saw a door appear, to allow them to all go back to Contorted Royal, and he stepped inside with his friends Brannon and The Dark Kid, who were also with him, along with everyone else, and The Jack of Knives knew the answer to solving the chaos of Contorted Royal: kick out the deathly.

The problem was, he wasn't sure how he was going to make that happen.

Part Four

Seeing the Light Is Often a Pointless Way of Seeking Redemption but When It Comes to Wrapping up a Novel Sometimes It's Necessary for Feelings of Closure in the Reader

White Dream

The Black Queen knew that she needed to change her ways. Not for the reasons one would expect, however; The Black Queen didn't need to change because she was a dirty whore who tried to cheat with anyone she found, because she tended to have a vindictive attitude that wasn't altogether pleasant and was therefore wrong, as well as a host of other things. The Black Queen needed to change because she had an ideal to commit to, being from the age of chivalry and romance, being from the medieval times, even if a little pseudo.

The thing was, she wasn't sure how she was going to do this. Couldn't a woman have her own independence? Couldn't she cheat when she felt like it?

Well, of course she could. She was free to do whatever she wanted, naturally. However, it had indeed had unforeseen consequences that should have been seen on The Suicide King. The Suicide King was suicidal partly because of The Black Queen's sexual escapades. In fact, The Black Queen had the idea that if she had somehow seduced Ralph, that would have been the tipping point for The Suicide King. That would have been where he would have drawn the line.

Amazingly, The Suicide King hadn't executed The Black Queen for her adulterous affairs. That was protocol in all the other kingdoms around Contorted Royal. But The Black Queen knew it was because she was a woman of power, and her open sexuality was part of that power. She was like Cleopatra, except she could turn into a cellular phone or chess piece, and in the Middle Ages rather than ancient Rome.

Nonetheless, it was a problem. It was a problem because Contorted Royal was a screwed up place, and partly because of The Black Queen's choices. She had alienated her husband. Yes, yes, in The Black Queen's defense, The Suicide King had also alienated The Black Queen with his suicidal behavior, but it went both ways. The Black Queen couldn't factor out her decisions as contributing to the terrible state of Contorted Royal. Plus, this was the era of chivalry and romance, and The Black Queen would do well to uphold that.

The Black Queen was sleeping, and thinking about this while dreaming. It seemed appropriate to be having this inner monologue about morality, because that was when she was in a dream space, inside a garden, to be exact, and she saw the most beautiful woman approaching her.

It was The White Queen. And boy, was she beautiful. She was wearing a white dress, which literally shone in the sunlight, and she was adorned with white jewelry. She approached The Black Queen slowly, and said, "It's nice to finally meet you."

"Likewise," The Black Queen said, wondering if she was smitten. She had never seen herself as a lesbian before, but it was tempting with this woman, there was no denying that. Very tempting. In fact, if The Black Queen had her way, she would have been kissing this woman and been in bed with her ages ago.

But The Black Queen knew that would never work. The White Queen was chaste … so chaste that she was a stereotypical damsel in distress, the pure, pure virgin, and indeed that damsel, just without the distress. It sickened The Black Queen. Why was she fitting the medieval norm of chastity?

The White Queen had a response to this: "Maybe it's not necessarily your passions that are the issue, dear."

"What do you mean?" The Black Queen asked, curious.

"Passions are always going to be in our nature, always going to be in our existence. Sometimes, we shouldn't even be forced to control them. Nonetheless, regardless of our right to autonomy, we should also think about the consequences of those actions."

"In what way?" The Black Queen asked, though now she was getting a little impatient. She didn't need a lecture from some goody-goody, someone who, while pure, also missed out on a lot of the fun this life could offer.

"Think about your son," said The White Queen.

The Black Queen began to do just that. She even said, "My … my son?" as if this was an odd and random and unknown thing to think about.

"What happened because of your infidelity?"

"I made The Suicide King jealous," said The Black Queen. "Which wasn't good, naturally. Because I made The Suicide King jealous, he lied about my son being illegitimate, which put my son through the ringer. Now he's angry and bitter because of it all, my son is."

"If you'd been faithful, that wouldn't have happened."

"Yeah, but if I'd kept the son regardless of whether he was illegitimate, it wouldn't have mattered."

"But you know your husband would have just gone through that fiction, scorning you for your faithlessness. That would have been no atmosphere for your son to grow up in, either."

"But you don't see my side," The Black Queen said. "You're confused about woman identity. I have the right to be a feminist."

"And I agree," said The White Queen. "I'm ironically more of a feminist than you'd ever know … just one that abstains."

"No, you're not a feminist, because you just fall into the mold of what holy males with raging testosterone want you to be: virgin and chaste, and loyal to the point of insanity."

The White Queen just laughed. "If only it was that simple. What I meant by I'm a feminist is that my chastity is a double-edged sword. I believe in the power of woman, one thing we know isn't always appreciated in our day and age, our medieval world. Women are often silenced, women are often stepped on. They aren't always considered important in society. That's one reason why you cheat around. It works: it gives you power, and that makes you happy. It turns you into a powerful sex symbol, and there's no way I'd dispute that power you have. However, on the flipside, I also have power."

"And what way is that?"

"Well, obviously I'm not the clichéd damsel in distress. I'm autonomous. I use my lack of sexuality as a weapon."

The Black Queen was getting interested. "Do tell, sweetheart."

The White Queen just laughed, slightly. "All the young smitten boys I turn away, gives me a feeling of power that you can't get anywhere else, and makes me more confident to be a woman."

"So, you thrive off breaking the hearts of young boys?"

"Well, they aren't all young. Kings are trying to court me all the time, I suppose, no pun intended, seeing how I'm a queen and all … but the point is, by me rejecting them and them swooning over me, it makes me seem even more powerful. Not because of will … will is overrated, simply because we all have passions, and we should exercise those passions; simply because I stand strong, and don't need a male to define me. Quite literally, of course, as you can see. You, however, the feminist on the other side of the spectrum, well … men *do* define you."

"That's insulting," said The Black Queen. "Now can we kiss?"

The White Queen smiled, almost flirtatiously, but still innocently, and said, "I think it's still your life in the end. But Contorted Royal needs to be like a white dream. I'd come and save the day if I could, but Contorted Royal is much too violent for me. Not because I'm dainty or weak, but because I believe in purity of intention. That by no means makes me better than you—I in fact rather admire you. Nonetheless, I probably won't be going to Contorted Royal, until it becomes a suitable place to live in. I'm bringing this up because you need to get closer to your son. Or at the very least, make up for what you have done to your son."

"But how do I do that? I can't undo the damage, the trauma, that that kid has gone through. I just can't, as much as I'd like to. I just can't."

"Well, please do me a favor and try."

"If you jump in bed with me, I'll consider it," said The Black Queen, who honestly couldn't believe she wanted to be a lesbian now. But she wanted to be a lesbian because again, it was about power. Oh, the power of being with another female! The things she could do!

Yes. Sex was indeed power. And somehow, this woman resisted that. As for how, The Black Queen wasn't sure, because indeed, passions were passions, and sometimes they exploded out of you if they weren't addressed … and that wasn't fair.

Then again, The Black Queen couldn't deny that indeed, her son had suffered, because she'd made The Suicide King jealous because of her actions. That had to be accounted for.

However, The Black Queen was honestly unsure how to make it right with her son. He was already old enough to where it seemed if she became a mother figure now, it'd be absurd.

Maybe The Black Queen would go to the Bronx for a little while, with Ralph. Maybe that's what she needed to do.

"I think that's a great plan," said The White Queen.

"Going to the Bronx?" said The Black Queen.

"I do," said The White Queen. "He can talk to you there, you and him, and maybe Alice. You see the kind of peaceful and trusting relationship they have. For them, it's about love. It's about closeness. Ralph does indeed have quite a lot on his plate, when it comes to dealing with Alice, because of her illness. But he does it with as much grace and fortitude as possible. He loves her, even if she has a disease. I find that kind of sacrifice very beautiful."

"So you're basically saying, chivalry is the key," The Black Queen said.

"You've nailed it," said The White Queen. "The question is, is patching things up with your son important to you? If it isn't, you can keep doing what you're doing, have illegitimate children that have to become slaves to save your dignity, or whatever. Regardless, you still are the queen. You're the one in power. I'm just pointing these things out because you are one broken aspect to Contorted Royal, to the family of Contorted Royal. Not because the acts themselves are so bad, but because of the consequences."

"I disagree," said The Black Queen. "Now can we just make out already?"

And The Black Queen tried to advance, but The White Queen just slipped away a little, out of The Black Queen's grasp.

The Black Queen sighed in frustration. "Wonderful. Well, just so you know, I think you're a self-righteous, pompous, unsexual fiend, who's miserable and just wants to preach the word of God about adultery, or whatever."

"If that's what you think," said The White Queen. "But please, think about what I said. It may change your life. Not because you chose right over wrong—I can't really say what's so right and what's so wrong, because we're all people with different opinions—but I do know that you'd make your husband happier if you didn't cheat around, and that would be good for another human life. That's the only perspective I'm trying to get at. It would indeed. It would make him happy, to see that his wife is there for him again."

The Black Queen bit her lip, and studied The Black Queen. Boy, was she so incredibly pretty. Too bad none of her belonged to The Black Queen. Nonetheless, The Black Queen considered.

What if The White Queen knew something? It sounded like preachy nonsense, but she did partly agree that she'd made The Suicide King miserable with her actions.

They had indeed fallen quite apart. Maybe it was time to paint their dreams white again, rather than black.

Maybe it was time to uncontort Contorted Royal. However that could happen, The Black Queen wasn't sure, but … here was to hoping and seeing the light, if such a thing was even possible.

Struggles

The Suicide King was struggling. He could feel things trying to change, but part of the reason why things weren't changing was because The Suicide King was too stubborn. It wasn't so much that The Suicide King didn't want to change, he was just so entrenched in a certain way that sometimes that way felt like the only way. Whether or not that was true or not was another matter, but still. There it was, hung out to dry.

The Suicide King needed to stop trying to commit suicide. He needed to do a lot of other things as well, such as bag the jealousy of The Black Queen's autonomy, and be there for his son, but not committing suicide would be a good way to begin things. Now that Death was out of the picture, or hopefully out of the picture, The Suicide King didn't need to commit suicide to ironically keep the kingdom in at least some semblance and resemblance of order.

But it was just so tempting! The sword, sitting right there, just waiting for a ripe brain to stab!

That was when Brannon walked in. He looked annoyed, but also confident, but also determined, all at the same time.

"Brannon," said The Suicide King. "What do you want now?"

"You know what I want, as usual, your highness, because in Contorted Royal there's a certain dryness."

"Oh, cut the repetitious rhymes out already."

"Poetry is my game, while your own head is your aim," said Brannon. "I feel like a broken record, telling you the same thing over and over again. Nonetheless, it seems that's the only way, the only way that I can be a sunny ray. So, listen to me, and my poetry."

"I'm listening," The Suicide King said, but spitefully grabbed his sword, as though he was only moments away from stabbing himself.

"You have a son," Brannon said. "You have a son who was wrongfully accused of being illegitimate. Even if he had been illegitimate, you should have forsaken politics and code, which would be having the queen executed for her adultery, and kept your son and raised him properly. And while you were at it, perhaps even make the working conditions better for the peasants and the servants in your land. Instead, you chose to get all jealous, and cast your son away, spurn him like he was nothing. All so you could get revenge on The Black Queen. To me, that just seems pathetic, something that could only happen in Contorted Royal, specifically the family of Contorted Royal. But indeed, he is your son. If you want to make things right, you need to be there for him. You need to love him. You need to restore him back to his status. You need to treat him like your son, most importantly. Do you think you can do that, or are you just a rat?"

"I'm not a rat," said The Suicide King petulantly. "But okay. I see your point. I see that I need to make some serious changes—"

At that moment, the alternate universe Brannon walked in.

Brannon looked confused, said, "How is this possible? I thought the alternate universe breakdown was over?"

The Suicide King just said, "Well, this is still Contorted Royal. Expect the unexpected!"

The other Brannon walked in like a smug rebel, and said to The Suicide King, "Don't buy anything this Contorted Royal Brannon is telling you. Don't buy any of it."

"And why is that?" The Suicide King asked curiously.

Brannon could tell that The Suicide King already liked alternate universe Brannon better. He liked him better because alternate universe Brannon was going to tell The Suicide King to keep doing what he was doing, and The Suicide King loved death. He reveled in death, and destruction, and chaos.

"Because everything is death, of course," alternate universe Brannon said.

Brannon felt annoyed at this sudden barging in, but he wasn't sure what to say.

"Is everything death, Brannon?" The Suicide King asked.

Brannon turned his head away from the alternate universe Brannon, with some effort. He said, "No. Everything is blue, what one Brannon could do."

"Everything is death, like a bad time with meth," alternate universe Brannon said arrogantly.

"You're ruining this," Brannon hissed quietly.

Alternate universe Brannon seemed pleased, if the truth be told. Brannon had to remember this was before alternate universe Brannon was humbled by his more intense experiences in his modern day world, which Brannon was hoping he could change.

"So, why is everything death?" The Suicide King asked.

"Because, you could love your son, love him to death, but love is synonymous with death. Familial compassion is the same thing as murder. All I do is speak the truth."

Brannon wasn't sure what to do, so he grabbed the shirt of alternate universe Brannon and brought him outside. Then he said to The Suicide King, "Think about what I said, at least, your highness, please," and then left.

The Suicide King was indeed thinking. The alternate universe Brannon was indeed a punk right now, which was pretty fascinating.

Nonetheless, The Suicide King was humbled by Contorted Royal Brannon's humble attempts to always change things for the better. But it was up to The Suicide King to save the day!

So, he looked at his sword. He knew he needed to throw it away. He needed to get rid of it. So, he got ready to toss it away, but right when he was getting ready to do that, he realized that he was actually on the verge of stabbing right through his face, splitting it in two.

He was literally staring at his sword. Oh, the temptation. He was so tempted to kill himself. It would be such a violent way to go, but he wanted to do it.

As The Suicide King stared at the sword, sweat began to drip down his forehead, the nervousness and tension as tightly wound as a violin string about to snap. Could The Suicide King do this? Was it possible to avoid suicide? He honestly wasn't sure. He wished that he did, because it would make things easier.

He continued to do this for the longest time, and finally decided, in a fit of rage, to throw his sword as far away from his body as possible. Which he did, listening to it clang on the ground.

Ah, the terrible world of struggles! It was like a bad porn temptation. It was like being hooked on porn. Or sex. Or something else explicit and elicit. Regardless, it was driving The Suicide King *crazy*. He needed to quit being suicidal, he needed to grow up and not be crazy, he needed to listen to what Brannon was saying! Everything wasn't death. Everything was blue, or should have been blue, at least, but was royal red because of The Suicide King and his faulty ruling and reasoning. But he could do better than this. He wasn't this hopeless. Not at all.

And that was when he had an answer. It was only one answer, unfortunately, but it was an answer nonetheless, and hopefully, it would set things in motion while The Suicide King battled to become sober with his suicidal tendencies.

"Fool!" The Suicide King called.

The Fool walked in a moment later. "Yes?"

"I don't want any of your carnivalesque nonsense today," The Suicide King snapped regally. "I just want you to bring in The Jack of Knives and The Dark Kid. I have royal business I need to attend to, and that I intend to do."

"Yes, your highness, though in Contorted Royal there's a certain lioness," The Fool said, and laughed his way as he left.

That dang *Brannon*. He was infecting Contorted Royal with poetry!

The Jack of Knives and The Dark Kid came in a moment later. He had never seen them so happy. Well, they weren't going to be happy in a moment, when things changed. But it needed to get done. Alas! It needed to get done.

"First off, I'm very grateful to you, Dark Kid, for being there for my son," said The Suicide King.

"I wouldn't have it any other way, sir," said The Dark Kid.

"No, but really. You're helping to fill a hole that I have been unable to fill, due to my pompous nature, my egocentrism, my hatred, my jealousy, my suicidal rage. I've ruined him! I've ruined my son! And then you came along and gave the situation hope, and ... why are you boys smiling so much?"

"Life has been so much better since Death has taken a vacation, wouldn't you say, Dad?" The Jack of Knives said.

"Well, yes. I would certainly agree," said The Suicide King. "But regardless, I have some bad news: I'm banishing both of you from Contorted Royal."

The two boys had been happy, but suddenly they looked very humbled. They looked like two very humble little boys. They also looked a little worried. *Banished*? their faces seemed to say. *What for?*

What for! The Suicide King was going to explain that ...

"Jack of Knifed by his own Dad," The Suicide King said, "you idealize murder like it's the finest romantic poetic concept. I know it isn't your fault. You grew up in terrible circumstances, because of me and my jealousy, and because I was never there for you, and lied to you for so long. And it isn't your fault because of the terrible way in which I ruled Contorted Royal, making it seem, ironically, through my suicide, that homicide was something to aspire to. Well, it's not! Jack of Knives, you need to change. You need to just ... become kind-hearted. You need to let go of the knives.

"And you, Dark Kid," continued The Suicide King, "you need to let go of some of your darkness and just be a kid. Maybe with a little shadow, but you need to just be a kid. I'm sure Death's Mirror did you in, and you have a certain degree of darkness that needs some light. So, both of you, are being banished to the modern day world."

Silence for a moment from the two humble and confused boys. And then The Suicide King's son said, "Then Dad ... if you're banishing us, what exactly ... do we do?"

"*Have fun!*" The Suicide King burst out in a rage of passion. "Please! Do what ordinary kids do and *have fun*! Don't try to take over the kingdom and murder your own father! Don't murder your mother because you're afraid of the Oedipus complex! Don't try and tackle Death with his own murderous intent! Don't live every day with your traumatic past of cleaning up after me! Go instead out for ice cream! Go instead to play basketball or soccer or whatever they play in modern times! Go for a movie! Please, just get out of my sight! You're banished! You shouldn't be in such a terrible place with struggles as that found in Contorted Royal! You should have a chance to heal your psyche. So please ... please leave. And change. Change!"

More silence, but then suddenly, The Dark Kid and The Jack of Knives gave each other a happy high five, and said together, "All right! When do we go?"

"Now!" said The Suicide King, almost in a panic. "Get out of here before Contorted Royal screws you up any worse! Get out of here, my son, before I make your life even more dysfunctional than it already is!"

The two kids continued to smile and look happy, and that was when a door appeared. They walked through it together, good friends, ready to have the time of their lives.

The Suicide King then went to his throne, sat down, and cried. He cried like an infant dilettante! He hated seeing his son go, but he knew his suicidal tendencies and his bad decisions on behalf of his son had hurt his child, and he wasn't okay with that anymore. He couldn't literally be there for his son because that would be like a drug addict dad trying to raise a child, but still ... it was as close, as least right now, as The Jack of Knives could be with his son. But it made him sad to sce him go.

In the end, that departure, that realization that The Suicide King had failed his son, was the biggest struggle, and if the sword wasn't too far away to reach, The Suicide King probably would have chopped off his own head.

2014

"It's like we're on vacation!" The Dark Kid said, rather enthusiastically.

The Jack of Knives smiled, examining the shine of his knife in the sunlight.

They were in the Bronx, and it was of course the year 2014. It was different than their old medieval world, for various reasons, but the differences seemed more striking now that they were free from that world, from Contorted Royal. Now that they could basically go and have fun.

337

They had been walking around the Bronx for a while now, just chilling, having the time of their life, and not getting anything done, except for enjoying the sunshine and talking to each other. The onset of their desire to escape the conflicting reins of Contorted Royal had indeed happened very fast, but this wasn't all that surprising, when considering that The Jack of Knives, now that he thought about it, had never been happy being a knife boy. He didn't mind being a knife boy for aesthetic reasons, of course. All of that was fine. Sometimes he felt like a character in a book, and what cooler name than The Jack of Knives? What cooler way to be than a kid wielding sharp knives?

However, he didn't like all that his knives represented. He didn't like the fact that he had, for so long, chased after the idea of murder. He didn't like it at *all*. He wanted that to change, and fast. He needed it to change, or he was going to go insane.

And what better year in the modern world than the year 2014 to change that? It seemed like the perfect time now. It did indeed. This was a good year, ripe for change.

The Dark Kid looked at The Jack of Knives curiously. "What are you thinking about, man?"

"Not much," The Jack of Knives said. "Just about what my father said before we came here, to have the time of our lives."

"What? That we need to change? Just be kids and such?"

"Pretty much," The Jack of Knives responded.

"You know a good way that we can do that?" The Dark Kid said, smiling darkly.

The Jack of Knives shook his head.

"Well," The Dark Kid continued, "you need to clean yourself up."

"What would that entail?" The Jack of Knives asked.

"Throw away your knives, to start off with," The Dark Kid said.

The Jack of Knives nodded, then quickly shook his head. "I'm not throwing away my knives. They're practically me. Without them, I'd be nothing."

"It's all just in your head, like Death's Mirror," The Dark Kid said. "You don't need to be a literal knife boy. Maybe you could just get by with a razor wit or a razor bit of compassion. Maybe you don't need your knives."

338

The Jack of Knives thought about this. He looked at his knife, and saw that a trashcan was nearby.

He went toward the trashcan, as though he was going to throw away the knife. However, when he lifted the lid, he froze.

Then he said, "I can't do it."

"Why can't you do it?" The Dark Kid coaxed.

"Because I grew up with violence. I can't just drop off my persona. That would be like trying to shed your cancer … it just isn't going to happen."

"You can do it," The Dark Kid said. "You just have to focus."

The Jack of Knives looked carefully at his knife, and then nodded his head. "I guess you're right. I guess … this is the only way."

Then he tossed the knife in the trashcan.

He was about to continue walking, when The Dark Kid said behind him like a shadow, "Wait."

The Jack of Knives turned around. *Busted.*

"Yeah?" The Jack of Knives said, trying not to sound too conspicuous.

"You have other knives, I know."

The Jack of Knives smiled, like this was the best game ever. And in all reality, it was kind of fun. He put his hands up, like he had surrendered, and said, "All right. You caught me."

The Jack of Knives then proceeded to pull out the other knives that he had, which amounted to about twenty, all various shapes and sizes. He then took out his sharp pack of cards, which, upon concentrating, became normal playing cards, rather than razor sharp knives.

The Jack of Knives threw all the knives away, the knives making a clinking sound as they fell in, like he'd just dumped in a tray of silverware.

The Dark Kid nodded approvingly. "All right. Next, we get you cleaned up, aesthetically. You ready for that?"

"What would that mean?"

The Dark Kid didn't say anything, just continued to walk. The Dark Kid followed him. Before The Jack of Knives knew where he was, he was sitting on a chair in a barbershop.

"Get this boy cleaned up, nice," The Dark Kid said. "He can't be walking around, looking like a shaggy dog."

The barber smiled and gave The Jack of Knives a crew cut, then put some gel in it to spiff up The Jack of Knives a little.

"Already making a difference," The Dark Kid said enthusiastically.

"He looks so good I'll do it free of charge," said the barber.

The Dark Kid bowed to the barber, then said to The Jack of Knives, "Now come on. Let's get you some styling clothes."

They walked into a clothing store next. The Jack of Knives was told to pick out clothes, anything he wanted. They didn't have any money, so The Jack of Knives wasn't sure how they were going to pay for this, but since it was the summer and all, he went for a pair of black shorts, a red shirt, and yellow shoes.

"Look in your pocket," The Dark Kid said.

The Jack of Knives did as he was told, and folded inside his pocket were folded bills of money.

"You didn't think your father would send you to the world without thinking about your interests and needs, did you?" said The Dark Kid.

"I guess not," The Jack of Knives said, and bought the clothes, and went back and changed, shed his despised servant boy clothes.

He walked out in style.

The Dark Kid tossed The Jack of Knives a pair of nail clippers. The Jack of Knives went outside to cut his nails, and then they went to a bathroom, so The Jack of Knives could look in the mirror.

He had to admit, he looked good. There was something so modern and yet so medieval about The Jack of Knives now: he had the chivalry and yet he had the modern flair. But what was different was that he looked approachable. There was something less calloused about his nature, now. There was something more gentle. Something pleasant, even, that The Jack of Knives couldn't quite explain. He looked like a gentleman now (or rather, a gentlekid), not a raging homicidal punk.

Regardless, he liked the way he looked now.

"2014 is the year of change," said The Dark Kid. "You look great."

The Jack of Knives smiled, and began to wash his face. Then he splashed a little bit of water on The Dark Kid, who just said, "Hey, that's not cool," but was laughing happily.

The two then went outside, and sat down on a curb.

"So what happens now?" The Jack of Knives asked.

"Well, do you feel better?"

"I feel great."

"Murder isn't in your heart?" The Dark Kid asked curiously.

"Not at all. I have no desire to hurt anyone. I have no desire to hurt a single soul, to murder my dad in a fit of jealous rage, or kill my mom for sport. I just want to be a kid."

"I'm sorry it's taken you so long to get to this point," The Dark Kid said. "But I think you've always had this side in you. It had just been massacred by circumstances beyond your control. I know it's miserable feeling like you're on the lowest rung. That's gotta make you angry."

"It did," The Jack of Knives said, "but now that I think about it, I'm not so angry anymore. I think I can kind of understand where Brannon was coming from. There's nothing wrong with the simple life, the metaphorical rustic life. There's nothing wrong with being a servant. I should have let it soften me, rather than harden me. You know what I mean?"

"Well, we have changed," The Dark Kid said. "I feel changed, at the very least. I don't feel like I have to sport shadow, just to sport shadow. I just feel like I can be. Like this is indeed my year."

"And maybe it is," The Jack of Knives said. "Maybe it's both our year."

The Dark Kid laughed. There was something so infectious about his gentle laugh. The Dark Kid wasn't nearly as dark as he purported himself to be. There was a gentle side to him as well.

"You wanna go get a soda?" The Dark Kid asked.

"Sounds good to me," The Jack of Knives said. "They don't have sodas where I come from."

The kids both ran to the nearest convenience store. The Jack of Knives grabbed the biggest cup he could find and pressed the soda button, and let the cup overflow. He drank some of the fizzy and sticky sweet drink, and then poured more into the cup.

The Dark Kid did the same thing, and they went to the front and paid for their drinks.

The Jack of Knives felt like a new man. He wanted to change his name. Maybe he could be The Jack of Compassion. Or The Jack of Love. Or maybe even The Jack of Life: The Jack of Lifed by Existence. It all sounded amazing.

He decided to settle on The Jack of Clubs, because he felt like he was in a club with his best friend. All they needed was Brannon, but they knew he was probably busy trying to help The Suicide King or something. They could also use Alice and Ralph, but of course, those two lovebirds were probably too busy hanging out with each other to care about The Jack of Clubs.

The Jack of Clubs finished his soda rather quickly, and decided again to change his name. He would just go by Jack. Just Jack. That's what some people called him sometimes, when they wanted to be most affectionate. Having the word knives dangling after his name Jack sounded a little … intimidating. And not in a way that Jack was interested in.

He told The Dark Kid this, and The Dark Kid nodded.

"Should I call you The Light Kid?" Jack asked curiously.

"No," The Dark Kid said, but Jack was pleased to see that The Dark Kid did indeed look a little bit brighter. His face looked a little bit happier, lighter, as if it had let go of some of the strain it had held before.

They finished their drinks, after making a few toasts, and then decided to give each other a hug, and then a high five. It was random, but if fit the good moment perfectly.

"Now where to?" The Dark Kid asked.

Jack only smiled. "I don't know. With my new look, I bet I could get a girlfriend in a heartbeat."

The Dark Kid laughed. "I bet you could."

"But I don't want a girlfriend just yet," Jack said. "I want to make sure this life is real, first, before I just plunge into a relationship. But I never knew a person could be this happy."

"I didn't, either," The Dark Kid said, and he smiled light. "I honestly had no idea."

"I'd say this vacation was definitely worth it," Jack said, and smiled.

The Dark Kid smiled back. "Jack. I like it. It sounds simple. It sounds like who you've always wanted to be. A kid who has shed the knives."

"Thanks," Jack said. "I just hope it stays that way. I have fears that this is all only temporary. That, things don't change this fast, because it's so unrealistic."

"Well, try not to have doubts," The Dark Kid said, but he looked preoccupied now.

"What is it?" Jack asked.

"It's just ..." The Dark Kid began, but didn't finish. Jack pressed The Dark Kid to continue.

So The Dark Kid finished. He said, "I sometimes worry this is too good to last, too. You know how fast things change. There's always something. If it's not war, it's famine. If it's not famine, it's genocide. If it's not genocide, it's dictatorships. You know what I mean? It never ends. Society is riddled with problems, and always has been. Just like the human soul. It will always have its flaws."

Jack thought about this. To him, it seemed true. It seemed like there was no way around it sometimes. But he wasn't going to let it get in the way of his happiness. If he had to become knife boy again, he would, but for now ... he just wanted to get lost in the sunshine.

And he hoped that wasn't too much to ask for.

Even With Alternate Timelines and Pseudo Worlds, Medieval Literature Is Still Medieval Literature, Somehow

The Poetess was tough, and was used to broken off and broken romances, but her heart was still a little broken from The Suicide King suddenly deciding that she wasn't important anymore, that his time would be much better spent with his family.

It wasn't all life and death, of course, but it was still miserable. But The Poetess knew that what would make her feel better was a good conversation about medieval literature. That would be the key to making The Poetess feel as right as rain.

Even with the alternate timelines and pseudo worlds and alternate universes and crazy bouts of Death's Mirror and insanity raging left and right across worlds, medieval literature was always still medieval literature ... *somehow*. As for how, The Poetess honestly wasn't quite sure, but what did it matter?

The Poetess was eavesdropping on a conversation among The Black Queen, Alice, and Ralph, waiting for the opportune moment to make her presence known.

"So, you're saying the Bronx is the best way you can rediscover chivalry, romance—though in its adventurous sense—and love again for your family?" Ralph said.

"Yes," said The Black Queen. "And I need both of your guys' help. Both of you have your own version of chivalry. Alice, you work hard to keep your illness under control, and Ralph, you work hard on your virginity, which I know must be hard for a strapping young lad like you, a boy of twenty years."

"It's not that hard," Ralph said, rolling his eyes.

"We're just suspicious, that's all," Alice said.

"Suspicious?" The Black Queen said innocently, and blinking her eyes exaggeratedly. "Of me?"

"Maybe," said Alice. "We don't know if you can really change. We want to give you that chance, of course, but we also don't want you to get in between us. Not in the slightest," Alice added, with a hint of aggression.

The Black Queen didn't say anything for a moment, just thought about this. "Okay. I see your point. I have been a little ravenous."

Ralph suddenly laughed. "Sorry, Black Queen. It was a terrible joke. You're free to come with us to the Bronx. I'd love to talk to you some more about my theories of good ways to be, though they are all flawed."

"And anything I say is mere psychobabble," Alice added.

The Poetess sighed. They were such good friends. The Poetess would kill to have a relationship like that.

"So when do we start?" The Black Queen said, looking more relieved.

"I guess now," said Ralph, and that was when a door appeared.

The Poetess appeared on stage at this moment, and said, "Can I come with you guys?"

They looked at The Poetess, and then said, "Sure."

The Poetess had scored! *Slam dunk*!

They walked through the door, and before they knew it, they were in the Bronx. As they were walking, in silence, The Poetess decided to bring up the topic of medieval literature, to see where it would go.

"So what's your favorite medieval text?" The Poetess asked.

"Don't ask me," Ralph said. "I don't know much about medieval literature. Just little tidbits here and there."

"What about you, Alice? I know you're a book nerd," The Poetess said seductively.

"I don't know, that's honestly a good question," Alice said. "My favorite would probably be *The Eyrbyggja Saga*. I love the magic in that book. But I also appreciate *The Divine Comedy* because of its form. I don't know what modern day Italians would have done without Dante: he's the one who made vernacular Italian important. What's your favorite, Poetess?"

"I don't know, I like them all, I'll admit," said The Poetess. "But I guess if I had to pick a favorite, I'd pick *The Decameron*."

"I love *The Decameron*!" The Black Queen said. "That's like my favorite book ever."

"Why do you like it so much?" The Poetess asked curiously.

"Well, first off, because it's a big European work, a landmark of world literature. If it hadn't been for Boccaccio, then we all know prose works wouldn't be worth anything, we'd still be writing in blasted poetry and verse." Then The Black Queen added, "No offense to you, Poetess."

"None taken," said The Poetess, actually amused at this comment, of prose elitism.

"But anyway," continued The Black Queen, "it's so subversive, that book. And I can kind of see why. At that time, people were losing faith in everything, whether God or man or philosophy, because of that lovely pestilence the Black Death. I would lose faith in things, too. That happens anyway, of course, but … you know. That book is so subversive it's funny. It seems to me Pynchon's *Gravity's Rainbow* has more morality than *The Decameron*, and I don't think that's grasping at straws."

345

"Not at all," said The Poetess. "It certainly has women sleeping around to their heart's content, good old *Decameron*."

The Poetess and The Black Queen then looked away for a moment, while Ralph blushed.

"Well, it's true," The Black Queen said, coming back to reality. "You, Ralph, could have any girl you wanted. And instead you stay loyal."

Alice merely smiled, as if this was a joke. "Maybe we should get back to literature?"

"Anyway," The Black Queen continued, clearing her throat, "*The Decameron* has it all. It has so much power to it. And even a degree of innocence—ironic, considering the heavily satiric nature of the book. Because in many ways, it does read like a satire, like the open statements that say the virtuous are actually the ones that have vices, the ones that are sleeping around and doing other things." The Black Queen eyed Ralph mischievously. "Just something to think about, Ralph."

"Yeah, yeah, so I'd go to Heaven if I slept with every girl I ever met," said Ralph. "But that's fine. I'll take my slim pickings of the afterlife with Alice."

Alice smiled, grabbed Ralph's hand.

"What else do you like and know about medieval literature?" The Poetess asked The Black Queen.

"Oh, lots of things," said The Black Queen enthusiastically. "It is indeed my cup of tea, the time I live in. Naturally, you've got to love *Everyman*, that late medieval play. I wonder if it's even medieval, actually. In contrast to *The Decameron*, it goes back to staunch religious views: we're all wicked and sinners and are all going to Hell. We're all the everyman that falls into vice and corruption."

"Do you think it's true?" Ralph asked curiously.

"I don't know," The Black Queen said. "I think we are who we are. I won't deny that Contorted Royal has its problems, but you have to admit, its more pseudo murder, while in your world, the Bronx and America and the world, there's real crime. Sleeping around just seems harmless compared to actually taking a life and getting caught in an epic battle of good and evil. But … I do miss Spade, though. I wish he hadn't … been a victim."

"What are your thoughts about medieval literature, in general, Alice?" The Poetess asked, as The Black Queen took a moment to mourn her loss, weeping a little exaggeratedly.

"I like it all, of course, but I do wonder why the literary criticism and knowledge of *Silence* is so … well, *silent*. And I have to admit … *Romance of the Romance* is probably the most complex work in Medieval literature. Not because of its language, of course, as Chaucer or Dante would probably take that cake, but because it's just so suggestive, allusive, and dare I say does it ever, so ever compose itself of … innuendos. Regardless, it's a complex work. Very complicated. All the allusions that could make one's head spin. It's *The Waste Land* of the medieval era, if you want my honest opinion.

"But in terms of language, well … you've got to hand that to the great masters of medieval literature in general. Sure, they're a little *too* canonized, but they did good work. Chaucer was amazing with his English poem *The Canterbury Tales*, and I absolutely adore the language of Dante. It's important what they did with the vernacular … making the vernacular important. I once heard a medieval kid criticize Chaucer and Dante for not using colloquial language enough, and I just laughed and went on my merry way … you can probably figure out why."

"Yes, yes, of course," said The Poetess.

She felt like she was in Heaven, listening to these thoughts on the beauty of medieval literature. The Poetess was intelligent but she had to admit, she barely understood medieval literature. She could also tell that Ralph was a little uncomfortable … medieval literature was not quite his forte. But that was okay! Maybe he was learning a little something.

"So what's your thoughts on the obsession with King Arthur in medieval times?" The Poetess asked. "I know that's self-evident, but I want to tease out the self-evident nature more."

"Well, obviously because it was the time of chivalry," The Black Queen said, and then frowned. "I do indeed wish I could be as chivalrous as King Arthur sometimes. But alas!" The Black Queen added dramatically, with a trace of sarcasm, "I'm just a woman!"

"It is true, though," Alice said. "*The Death of King Arthur*, *Sir Gawain and the Green Knight*, the tales of Sir Thomas Malory, the writings of Chretien de Troy ... plus other works as well. I'd say we were obsessed. But with good reason. King Arthur was a good role model, even if Chretien made him look like a weakling."

"Well," The Black Queen said, "we're all weaklings, for one reason or another. I must admit, though, as much as Malory had a knack for being a stylist, and as postmodern and experimental as Chretien was, my favorite book about King Arthur is definitely *The Death of King Arthur*. It reads like a high adventure novel. It reads wonderfully. There's just so much suspense."

Silence for a moment, and then Alice said, "I find your comment about us just being women, interesting."

"In what way?" The Black Queen asked curiously.

"Well, there's so many contradictions," Alice said. "Women aren't that important in medieval times, and we know they struggle through time in various ways and for various reasons, usually because they want independence ... and yet Dante idealizes Beatrice, a pure woman, higher than an angel, and Boccaccio has a knack for making his naughty women look like heroes, even saints, while the males look like whores. Sure, medieval literature runs rampant with misogyny, but there is hope in medieval literature. It's not all bad. And there were powerful women in the medieval times. Just think of Christine de Pizan. That's why I have to admit, I admire The Black Queen. She's super powerful. What would we do without The Black Queen? What would Contorted Royal, a medieval world, do without The Black Queen and her power?"

"What *would* you do without The Black Queen and my power?" The Black Queen joked.

The three girls/women in the group laughed, and Ralph smiled a little.

"Such a quiet boy," The Poetess said compassionately.

Alice grabbed Ralph's hand again. "He's not so quiet once you get to know him, but he is gentle. He still believes in chivalry, even if us ladies don't know what it means to be a knight in shining armor."

"But chivalry," said The Black Queen. "Chivalry is the key. That's what I need to learn. And as soon as possible."

The Black Queen and Alice continued to talk about medieval literature, and The Poetess began to dream about medieval literature. That was all she could think about, as she tuned out of the conversation yet simultaneously listened to them speak.

It was beautiful, all the literature that the medieval times had produced. And unfortunately, The Poetess hadn't read all of it. She wasn't brushed up on Spanish medieval literature and the like, as she hadn't read *Amadis of Gaul* or *The Poem of the Cid*. She was also lacking in Indian literature, though she knew a few names. She had read Rumi, however, and she loved his style, his metaphysical yet playful way of going about things.

But there were always things to read. That was the amazing thing about culture. And yes, while Robert Henryson came late, she loved him as well. He wasn't as adept as Chaucer, because he was harder than Chaucer, in some ways; at least Chaucer had rhythm, while Robert, well … his poetry you had to puzzle over.

But anyway … nothing else mattered. Just listening, listening away, and getting lost in the conversation, like getting lost in a good medieval book.

The Other Side, a Tumultuous Tide

"You need help," Brannon said, "because I hear you yelp."

Brannon and alternate universe Brannon were sitting in a chamber. Brannon couldn't get out of his mind how much, how close, alternate universe Brannon was indeed Brannon's double. There was so much alike, on the other side, the tumultuous tide.

Alternate universe Brannon just smiled. "I kind of have an idea that I need help. But I see things that others don't. You should be aware of that. You should even respect that, if that isn't too bold of me to say."

"I'm sorry for your suffering, but Brannon is not your buffering."

"You don't have to buffer the pain," alternate universe Brannon said.

"Well, when I'm trying to do something good for Contorted Royal, and you come in spewing your insanity, preaching that everything is death, there are kind of a few problems."

"Maybe you're being too cold to me," alternate universe Brannon said. "But I wouldn't worry. I know I'll mellow out as I experience my adventures soon to come. Right now I'm a punk because that's my role: to disrupt your world. But my intentions aren't bad. I just want to spread the truth, perhaps in a satiric and ironic way, but a way nonetheless. But I want you to know, I will change."

"I know you change, when you get out of range," Brannon said. "But for now, you're being a distraction. You're like my evil twin."

"That's quite an insult. I don't buy it. Like I said, I'm just doing what I need to do."

Alternate universe Brannon looked unhappy for a moment. Brannon took this opportunity to prioritize. What was really important here? What really mattered?

"Well, as long as I'm stuck with you, I may as well accept you for who you are."

"It's hard seeing what I see," alternate universe Brannon said. "You have no idea how difficult it gets. I'm really just trying to tell the truth, even if in a punk way. Because I know that once I get back to my real world, things will never be the same. I know Sunshine, that atrocious place for supposed mental recovery, will screw me over. I remember Goldstein, I remember seeing violent murder."

"It's like all of this has already happened to you," Brannon said compassionately.

"Yes, because it already pretty much has. The line between past and present have blurred. But I know once I'm there, I won't remember ever being here. But I'm hoping you'll remember me. Remember how much my head makes me suffer. Remember how much this world makes me suffer."

"But that's why I'm trying to help it," Brannon said. "When you tell someone that helping someone who is suicidal is just as suicidal, how can one really believe they are actually doing a good thing? They can't. They can't at all."

"That was more Death's Mirror," alternate universe Brannon said. "But I'm still sticking to my guns: everything is death. I see death as a kind of aura, shining all over you, Brannon."

"In what way?" Brannon asked.

"In a lot of ways. It's hard to explain, but it's like … you're a good person. That much is obvious. But that only makes you a target for death."

"I doubt it," Brannon said. "Death, with a capital D, is too dead to really care about killing me. Last I heard he was resigned. So I don't think so."

"Not Death, but death. There's a subtle difference, but a difference nonetheless. Death with a lower case 'd' isn't as powerful, but it still exists. Being a good person makes you a target. That's why I'm going to suffer. Yes, I'm being a slight punk and brat by crashing your party with The Suicide King and your quest to heal Contorted Royal, but I'm generally a good guy. And that's why I'll need to suffer in the future. There's no other way around it. And it's the same with you. Don't you get it? Everything is death for good people."

"But everything is death for evil people as well, as Death proved," Brannon said.

"True," alternate universe Brannon agreed. "But doesn't that prove my thesis: everything is death?"

"Good point," Brannon said.

The two were quiet for a moment. What was there really to say? Brannon could see the pain etched in the poor kid's eyes, his other side. He could see so much of the painful tide trying to spill all over alternate universe Brannon and drown him. And there was a chance it was going to. It would probably even out eventually, but at the same time, always remain that painful tide, the other side.

"What can I do to help you?" Brannon asked.

Alternate universe Brannon looked confused. "Help me? Help me with what?"

"With your viewpoint. What can I do to make it feel like less death? To give you some life again?"

"I don't know," alternate universe Brannon admitted. "I wish that I knew."

Then he began to cry. He cried for a while, and Brannon got him a tissue. He blew his nose, threw away the tissue, and then said, "I guess, just be there for me."

"I can do that," Brannon said. "I can do that for sure."

"It's just, it's all murder. Don't you feel this chamber we're in? It's suffocating us, because it's so nauseating. It's slowly squeezing out all of our energy, slowly killing us. It's destroying us."

"But it's just a chamber," Brannon said.

"So it would seem. But it's a lot more than that. It's slowly sucking away our energy. I feel the same way about this entire world, or at least the Contorted Royal part. Everybody having their energy sucked up, destroyed. There's no way around it."

"But that's why I've been trying to fix it!" Brannon said exasperatedly.

"I know, but you can't cheat death," alternate universe Brannon said. "Just like I can't cheat my fate. You know how much I think about hurting myself, and how just the thoughts literally do hurt me? You know how often that happens? I wish that I could take a knife and—"

"No, no," Brannon said. "Please. *Don't.*"

"But I have to get it out," alternate universe Brannon said.

"That may be, but there's another problem that I sense with you: you dwell on things. That's what makes death more concentrated, at least to you."

Alternate universe Brannon took this in, thought about it, played with it for a moment. Then he said, "You think so?"

"I do," Brannon said.

"That's just a death argument."

"Maybe. But it's true."

"It's simply a counterargument, used to evade the real problem."

Brannon took this in, thinking. His other side had an interesting point. He could follow the kid's logic, and while a little contorted, certainly made a lot of sense.

So Brannon said, "Yes. I see your point. Death is inevitable. Who wants to enter the unknown? Wouldn't we rather be in the land of the living, the land of life? But how is that possible, when even this life is death, only so we can die for real, and go to a dark place for all eternity, knowing full well there is no God?"

"And even if there was a God," alternate universe Brannon said, "I'd go to Hell."

"The point is, I see your point," Brannon said. "It makes a lot of sense, the more I think about it. But why dwell so much on death? Yes, it's an immovable object, by why can't you be the unstoppable force?"

"Because I'm not unstoppable," alternate universe Brannon said. "I just want to take the knife and stab myself and hurt myself until—"

"You can't ..." Brannon began, but wasn't sure what to say.

Alternate universe Brannon just began to start crying again. "My head is so screwed up, but it's because of the things I've seen. There's no such thing as justice. Do you know how hard that is to see all the time? Innocent people dying ... it's destruction, at the very least. It's despicable. I hate it. I hate it more than anything. I revile it. I wish more than anything that it didn't exist, but of course it does, and of course it always does. Why do we exist? It doesn't make sense. Only so we can suffer? Well, then why is there suffering? Just so we can suffer? And then death itself ... how scary of a prospect that is. Us, dead, never aware of the people mourning for us, still able to live in the light of life for a little bit longer. I need help, Brannon, but no one can help me."

Brannon listened to all of this, trying to form his own opinions and struggling. It was hard talking to this kid, he had indeed been traumatized by his philosophies, by the things he'd seen, and the things he was going to see.

But Brannon had another answer, another angle. "Just be a kid."

"Be ... be a *kid*?" Alternate universe Brannon looked confused. Very confused.

"Yes. Just be a kid. That's who you are, at heart, and always will be, I imagine. You're a good soul. Just be a kid, and that will make you invincible, impervious. Not to death, of course, but to the thought of death. You know what I mean?"

Alternate universe Brannon thought about this, looked as though he thought this was a good idea. And it was a good idea. A very good idea. It was what Brannon had to do to stay sane. If he'd allowed Contorted Royal to get the best of him, with the violence that ran without restraint around the kingdom, he would have gone insane ages ago. He'd obsess about death, too. There would be no other way to look at it. A suicidal king who couldn't commit suicide but bloodied himself up, a young kid who idealized murder, a queen who didn't care about her family, and all among people getting drunk at taverns and stabbing each other for sport. Brannon had seen it all, but he somehow had a censor, and one of the reasons was certainly because he knew not to obsess about thoughts of death. It was inevitable, immovable, but that didn't mean you dwelled on it.

The other reason? Perhaps because he was the other side of the alternate universe Brannon. That would make sense as well. He had to live the life that the other Brannon couldn't live. That was the only way. Wasn't that how alternate universes worked, anyway? It seemed so. It did indeed.

Alternate universe Brannon took this in, and then finally said, "Well, I guess you can't heal me."

Brannon shook his head sadly. It tore at his heartstrings how helpless he was to help this young gentleman. "No. I wish that I could, but I can't. But what I can do is give you a weapon to fight death back with. And that weapon is … be a kid."

"But what does that mean? Be innocent? I can't be innocent. I've lost all of that because of the suicidal thoughts in my head, because of the world committing suicide in front of me and killing me that way, of being afraid for my future, of being sad because you're helping me but soon I'll never see you again, because I have another inevitable timeline to follow."

"All of that may be true," Brannon said. "It may be very true. And as much as I'd like to explicate what it means to be a kid, I don't think I can. But you'll know what I mean. I think there will be some times where you'll sound innocently conflicted like Holden from *Catcher in the Rye*. I think it's in your future to discover the kid in you … ironic, because you'll be getting older, and experiencing more death, but that's my thought. You deserve to feel that, that kid in you. But I will say, don't think of being a kid as being a literal kid, though you still are. Don't see it as being youthful, young, naïve. See it on a more metaphysical level."

354

"But how do I do that?"

"Ah," Brannon said, "you know how to philosophize. I can see it in your eyes. Just think real hard about it, and you'll have your answer."

Alternate universe Brannon took this stuff in, and then smiled. He smiled for real this time. They both knew this wasn't going to last, but maybe, just maybe, it would be okay.

Maybe the tide would die down. Maybe it would relax and not try to drown. Maybe death would pause and take a breather. It would be awesome. And it was indeed possible.

"Good luck on the other side," Brannon said.

Alternate universe Brannon just nodded his head. "Thanks."

Psychobabble, Mere Psychobabble: I Love It!

The Poetess had disappeared into poetic oblivion, but Alice, Ralph, and The Black Queen were still in the Bronx, in search of chivalry, good will, and virtue.

But the problem was that Alice was feeling her schizophrenia kicking into high gear. She didn't usually have mania, but she supposed that today was a day where she was going to have mania, because that was exactly what was happening.

She kept it at a minimum, at first, because she didn't want to be a mere psychobabbler. However, it was too tempting to share the racing thoughts that were going through her head. Way too tempting, if the truth be told. She certainly didn't want her delusion to go to waste.

Alice looked at Ralph. She'd said things below the minimum, but he'd already picked it up. He said, "Alice ... you having symptoms?"

"Am I having symptoms?" Alice said, and laughed exaggeratedly. "I wonder what a symptom means. I wonder what a symptom is. Is a symptom a poem, because if it is, then a symptom can mean, like a poem means. And are you mean? Are any of us mean? What is the definition of mean? What is the definition of chaos?"

Ralph looked at The Black Queen, but more out of amusement than for support.

"When Alice gets this way," The Black Queen said, "it's better to just let her talk. She has a lot to say when that happens."

"No, no, I like it," Ralph said. "Do tell, Alice."

"Well … it's a lot more complicated than your average philosophy," Alice said. "You want to know why? Because I imagine that ghosts can transmit rays of poison across the universe and blast aliens to death."

Ralph laughed a little; The Black Queen smiled.

"And I happen to be a girl named Alice," Alice said. "I don't know if you were aware of that, but it's quite true. But anyway, you know what's striking about the nature of the universe? You know what's crazy about it at all? There's a lot that's crazy about it all, and quite literally, as in the case with me. I fly off the handle more often than I would like, but don't mind it, naturally, because it is who I am. But anyway, it's the choices that we make."

"Choices?" Ralph said.

Alice nodded.

"Go on," urged The Black Queen.

"Well, it's a crazy thought experiment, of course, bound to blow up the universe … but the idea is that we can make an infinite number of choices, but only end up making one choice, because that is what our world or even worlds dictate. That's why those choices split into alternate universes, because those choices still need to be made on some level. Essentially, everything is infinite, with infinite worlds, because an infinite number of choices need to be made to keep everything balanced."

"What would happen if there was only one world, with one choice to make?" Ralph asked, curious.

"Why, all worlds would collapse, of course," Alice said, and chuckled a little.

The Black Queen smiled, and said, "Psychobabble, mere psychobabble … I love it!"

"And I bet you do," Alice said cheerily. "Because indeed, there's nothing we can do about our infinite number of worlds. I can almost see them right now, all of them, or at least a huge majority of those infinite worlds, in a hallucination, trying to overlap. But what keeps them from overlapping is that we all make our fated choices."

"That sounds terrible, though, if you think about it," Ralph said. "That we all are fated to make choices we may not want to make."

"Perhaps," Alice said. "But in an alternate Contorted Royal or Bronx, set at this precise time and place, you're making the choice you want to make. And fate is indeed the wrong word … you're allowed to choose what you want every once in a while, because that's what screws up the choices of the guy next door, so to speak. Or girl next door, depending on who it is. That's why the alternate universe breakdown could have been such a catastrophe. If the worlds had collapsed rather than aligned, no one would know what choices to make anymore."

"Well, all your theories are fascinating," Ralph said, "but I'm still not sure I like the idea of being fated."

"Well, I don't think anyone likes the idea of being fated," Alice said. "But don't forget, I'm just babbling. Babbling and babbling, a psycho with nothing to say, except for words in a vacuous vacuum. But I feel so many ideas coursing through me. Did you know that one card from The Jack of Knives equals twenty pounds of knife? I know that's a random statistic, but it's true."

"So, on a less interworldly level," Ralph said, "what do you think is the connection between everyone just in, say, the Bronx? Or just my world? Or even the world to the universe, if you want to get that expansive?"

"I don't want to get that expansive," Alice said, "but it's a great question. You see, I think that every action, no matter how small, even if it's completely delusional, contributes to a greater understanding in the end. There are always opposite reactions, of course, such as violence and such, which mess up that enlightenment, that understanding, but the universe, without being aware of it, is headed toward a state of zero energy, which basically just means the ultimate good."

"Almost like we're headed to God?" The Black Queen ventured.

"Possibly," Alice said, "and possibly not. God could represent the ultimate good, but then again, the ultimate good

357

could represent itself. But anyway, we're slowly heading in that direction. We could do something as big as blow up our world with radioactivity that extinguishes life, or do smaller but still just as hateful crimes like murder someone out of cold blood, but ironically, when those things happened, we moved closer toward that greater good."

"But how is that possible?" Ralph asked. "Because it sounds like for every good action, there has to be the opposite reaction. Like there's no way around that."

"Well, that's a good point you bring up," Alice said, "but that's the thing: all people are good."

The Black Queen laughed. "Yup. I'm a saint all right, trying to seduce your boyfriend."

"The point is," Alice continued patiently, "that we reach a point in our existence, whether in our twenties, forties, eighties, on our death bed, after death, when we realize what we can do to contribute to the greater good. And once we fall in line with that … there's no turning back."

"But it can't make up for all the damage that's already been done," Ralph said, a little sad. "That's like saying Christ could truly forgive us of our sins and undo the damage of our imperfect nature. It sounds preposterous. You can't undo the damage of strapping a young four year old to a tree and forcing him to do drugs."

"You can't undo it, I agree," Alice said, "though at least not in any conventional sense."

"How do you mean?" Ralph asked.

"Well," Alice said, "I agree that once it's happened, it's happened. But the whole point of moving toward that greater good, pulling us like a tide, is that it slowly washes away our actions. But I'm not sure how, to be honest. You have me stumped on the whole untangle crime/evil thing. It does seem impossible. But anyway, I've drifted away from something I wanted to say, and that is, thinking about the nature of the conversation we're having."

"And what's that?" Ralph asked, still curious.

"Well, why should you listen to a schizophrenic? Aren't they just crazy by definition? Delusional and insane, at the very least, spouting off nonsense? And yet, my conversation is going to propel the world into two different directions: the reaction and the opposite reaction. I can't even begin to venture to guess what that is, to tell the truth. I don't want my conversation to end up causing the death of someone, but it might. But then again, on the flipside, it might also heal someone. Two things that happen because of a simple conversation. A split world, because of one choice. But that's the thing, of course: I ultimately have no control over what I'm doing."

"Why?" Ralph asked.

"Because we're all fated," Alice explained. "Sure, no one likes to be fated, but that's just our fate. Think about it this way: if we had free will, would we really know what was the right choice for us, the best choice? Probably not. So, we have to be fated to make the best choice possible."

"I don't buy it," The Black Queen said. "I feel like I'm making a choice to listen to you."

"Me too," Ralph said.

"That's the illusion, of course," Alice said. "And I say that because, indeed, we do have free will."

Ralph rolled his eyes, but out of humor rather than frustration. "But you just said we're fated."

"We are fated, but in that fate, we have free will. You're probably wondering how that works. Well, we can choose the books that we read, for instance. We can choose what we like. But those books fate us to like a certain type of book, and shape our knowledge a certain way, in a way we can't get out of. Our free will was to choose the book, but not how it shapes us. But then again, to make matters more complex, did we really choose that book? And then what about the fact that those books we chose were fated to be there?"

"But how is that giving us free will?" Ralph asked.

"Because we still chose the book," Alice said patiently. "The book was still ours to choose."

"I hate to say it, Alice, but you aren't making sense," The Black Queen said. "And yet, I'm rather fascinated by what you're saying."

"All psychobabble contains grains of truth. The trick is figuring out what the truth is," Alice said. "But of course, our truths, in the end, are only subjective. Because in all reality, the real truths are just too hard for us to grasp. We can't comprehend the universe. So anyway, to go back to your original question: how are we related to the world, and vice versa. Well, in a sense, we aren't. I say that because it's foolish to say my conversation will bring about changes halfway across the world, like a weird butterfly effect or something. And yet, that's exactly what it is. But I've come to realize we can't control that. We can't control how our actions affect others, no matter how much we want to. We could try and try, but we'd still get nowhere. That's just the unfortunate reality of it. And you know why we can't control the actions and reactions?"

"Why?" The Black Queen asked.

"Because of free will," Alice said simply.

"I'm confused," Ralph said.

"Me too," The Black Queen admitted. "I can't follow her logic."

"Well, you aren't supposed to, sillies. If you followed it, you'd be schizophrenic, just like me, and we can't have that. We can't have you being delusional."

"But regardless, you're doing original thinking, and that, in my book, means the world," Ralph said, and took Alice's hand, held it for a moment, squeezed it lovingly, and Alice said, "I love you, Ralph."

"Me too," Ralph said. "I don't know what I'd do without you and of course, your crazy ideas."

"I don't know what I'd do, either," Alice said. "But regardless, I don't have much else to say. There's many problems with my arguments, because of course, they aren't arguments. They aren't philosophy. They're just the random musings of a schizophrenic. Nonetheless, I'm sure some of it is true. The catch is, what of it is true?"

"Good question," Ralph said. "I guess we'll never know."

"Precisely," Alice said. "For every action, there is an equal and opposite reaction. So for every theory, there's an equal and opposite theory, which is just as true. But if I want you to get anything, it's this: follow your heart, where your free will truly lies, regardless of our complex relationship to the world or worlds, and you'll change things … if you so dare."

Ralph nodded. "Sounds like a good philosophy to me."

Plans

Ace had to believe that it was never over. Because when it was over, then it was game over, and game over wasn't okay in Ace's book, or rather, the book that Ace occupied.

Because honestly: how was it being over *fair*? How was it being over *okay*? It wasn't.

Ace had screwed things up terribly, and not just for himself, but for Contorted Royal. And he needed to fix that. He needed to fix it before things got worse. Before it was too late.

Ace needed to come up with a plan. He wasn't sure what that plan was exactly, which was why he was seeking Death. If he talked to Death, maybe they could reconcile things.

Because indeed, Ace couldn't pretend that Death wasn't an asset. He was one of the most powerful beings that could ever possibly exist. And he was indeed powerful.

Sure, it was a little crazy, asking for help from the person who turned you mad. Death had enjoyed every minute of Ace's madness, Ace knew that much. But the past was the past, and he couldn't let it get in the way of the future.

To tell the truth, he didn't know what had truly happened to Death after Ace shot him a whole bunch of times, in an attempt to restore his own sanity, get back at the object that had wreaked so much havoc in Ace's head. In theory, Death had died, not because of the gun wounds, but because of love, but that sounded ridiculous. It seemed highly unlikely, if the truth be told. It in fact seemed ridiculous. That just wasn't the way things worked. Things never worked that way.

And why had Ace wanted to kill Death in the first place? Well, sure, to try and escape his madness, but what he should have done was conquer that madness by shattering Death's Mirror and then teaming up with Death to try to restore things. Yes, Death had always planned for Ace's downfall, but it would have at least been worth the effort, because it would have been worth the try. Indeed, Ace attributed his stupid idea of trying to kill Death with a certain loss of ambition, which was of course never good. Nobody liked to be stagnant in a nothingness. Nobody liked to be stuck.

But that was what Ace was going to do now: force Death, somehow, to team up with him.

He continued on his way, and finally found Death. They were near the spot where Death had died, or supposedly died. He was sitting in darkness, but he was sitting at a table, and moving pieces on a chessboard.

"Having fun playing with yourself?" Ace asked.

Death didn't say anything for a moment, then said, "I see you want to taunt me. Go ahead. Take your best shot."

Ace didn't say anything … immediately. Instead, he looked at Death, got a good look. Death looked different. He looked emaciated, as though he'd been starved. He didn't look nearly as tough as he had once been, that was for sure. He looked pale and dead, like he'd been to Hell and back, and was just trying to slog his way through life. In short, he looked hopeless. Never a good sign, to see Death weak and weakened. And not just weakened, of course, but *destroyed*.

Definitely not a good thing.

Ace finally said, "You need to be restored to your former glory."

Death moved a rook. "Why is that? I've lost the game, Ace. You shouldn't be here, anyway. I tried to kill you with madness. I tried to betray you. It didn't work, because things like that never work … but regardless, you shouldn't be here."

"Perhaps," Ace said. "It's probably the worst idea ever to be here. But as you well know, in Contorted Royal, I'm worth the most and the least, and simultaneously, and can slide up and down that spectrum, meaning that right now, I can be more powerful than you, and force you to do my bidding. Which is my plan."

Death smiled; a harmless smile. "That wouldn't work, Ace. Trust me on that."

Ace knew that Death had a point. Ace could be powerful, but his power and authority and even status was always finicky, always debatable. It would take a lot if he wanted to defeat Death.

So Ace tried a different tactic: "You need to restore yourself, Death. You've been falling short of your glory lately. I don't think that's a good idea, if you ask me. You're Death. You have to be the powerful one. The one that forever controls everything."

Again, that smile. Death said, "I've given up on murder, at least for the most part. I've resigned to killing only occasionally."

"Why?" Ace asked, honestly confused. "Killing people is your job. Especially for a world like Contorted Royal."

Death said, "Because it was becoming too much of a pain."

"There's gotta be a better reason than that."

Death moved a pawn, and looked at Ace squarely. "Sit down, Ace. We'll have a conversation. A *real* conversation."

Ace sat down on a chair sitting across from Death, and looked at his pieces. He was on the black side.

"Look at it like chess," Death said. "I'd rather be wearing white. Unfortunately, I have to wear black, because of the terrible things I've done, but hopefully, eventually, I'll be the white knight, or the white rook, or the white pawn, or something like that. At least that's the plan."

"Well that's stupid," Ace said. "We need to take over Contorted Royal."

"Contorted Royal is going in the direction it's going to go," Death said. "And we can't stop it."

"What changed you so much?" Ace asked, feeling himself afraid. "You're very different. Something happened to you. What happened?"

"Love," Death said simply.

"You wouldn't let a silly thing like love get in the way of you doing your job and chasing your dreams, would you?" Ace asked.

Death laughed. "I see your point, Ace. I really do. Seeking the light is often a pointless way to seek redemption, especially for a mad, mad world like Contorted Royal. However, sometimes it's necessary for feelings of closure in the characters."

"But it would never work," Ace said. "Sure you're aware of that."

"Of course it wouldn't work," Death responded. "Seeking the light is pointless. Very pointless. None of it's real. Nonetheless, it often helps, or at least potentially, can help. I know you've come here to make plans with me, but I'm going to tell you, it's not going to work. You've got to trust me on that, Ace. Do yourself a favor and go home. Let Contorted Royal go in the direction it's going to go, and stop trying to destroy it."

"It was your idea to create The Machine!" Ace shouted, in near desperation. "And now you just want to give up?"

"The Machine was an awful idea to begin with," Death said. "A terrible, unrealistic, stupid, foolish idea. As you've probably realized, I'm just getting what I deserve. We all eventually get what we deserve, just so you know. But I knew I'd be in this exact spot a long time ago, and that's why I've resigned so much. I've accepted my new place, accepted my predestination."

Ace looked at Death carefully, and saw now how old he looked, on top of everything else. There was still something youthful about him, something strangely young, but he still looked old.

"I've been in this game for far too long," Death said, as though he'd heard Ace's thoughts (which he probably had, being Death and all). "I have to retire eventually, right? I can't forever be a massacre to societies and worlds, correct? I have to die eventually. And I have. Those boys changed something in me. I'd always known it would happen, I just hadn't known it would be so powerful. Trying to heal Death bleeding from gunshot wounds with a Band-Aid … it's insanity! And yet, it worked. It was such a harmless, kid-like gesture … and whether you like it or not, Ace, it changed me."

"Well it shouldn't have," Ace said bitterly. "Nothing would please me more than to destroy Contorted Royal. That's always been my goal, and we did a good job with The Machine, that is, until it got destroyed and things started to go backwards."

"Meaning, when I got destroyed," Death said candidly.

"Something like that," Ace said, and despite himself, he could see where Death was coming from.

"I knew I'd never win," Death said. "I just can't win. People always wants to seek the light. It may come late, too late, actually, when they're already dead, but nonetheless … it happens. More often than you'd think. And that's what I'm doing. I'd always known The Machine would get destroyed, and that I'd try to get revenge on you even though it wasn't your fault and even though I knew it wouldn't work. My mirror is very powerful, don't get me wrong, but I'm the wrong kind of Death for the mirror to work perfectly, the way it does in other dimensions and universes and worlds. Nonetheless, it is what it is. I've accepted my fate. I suggest you do the same thing."

"But I don't want to do that," Ace said. "It's a stupid idea. It won't accomplish anything. Not at all. Nope. Nothing."

"So you think," Death said. "And indeed, there are some characters who choose not to see the light. But nonetheless … do you see what I'm trying to get at?"

"Kind of," Ace said.

"But you think I'm wrong?"

"Of course!" Ace said. "You're terrific at what you do! You almost drove me bonkers!"

"Yeah, but my job did that to me a long time ago," Death said. "Regardless, I suggest you give it up. Try to seek the light. You may be the character that chooses to never seek the light, but that's your choice. Do what makes you happy. Regardless, you aren't getting my help. I've retired. Now if you'll excuse me, I have a game of chess to play."

Ace took his cue, and began to walk out toward the darkness.

Death was giving up? It was madness, Ace said! It was absurd! And yet, it seemed to be the only way. Ace was going to have to do this on his own. This made him angry, but what else was he supposed to do? He didn't want epiphanies like Death's. He wanted power. He wanted to take over. If only The Machine had never gotten destroyed. That game had been fun. It had been perfect for Ace's interests.

As he walked toward nothing, toward nowhere, disgusted, he saw someone standing ahead of him. When he arrived there, he saw that it was Mordred. He was holding a cat, and he had a self-satisfied and mischievous smile on his face.

"How did it go?" Mordred asked.

"Great," Ace snapped. "What do you want, Mordred?"

Mordred continued to stroke his cat. He smiled even more, said, "I just want to see if you wanted to work with me."

"Work with you?" Ace gave this some thought. "You want to help me?"

"Well, Death has given up, right?" Mordred said.

"Yes, but—"

"Well, you can't do it alone, obviously," Mordred said. "Besides, I have plans. More plans than you'd ever know."

Ace watched the tail of the cat flicker and flick. "I don't know why you want to help me."

"You want power, I want power," Mordred said. "It's that simple. I don't see it doing any good running away from our responsibility. We indeed have a job to do."

Ace took this in. Plans. Mordred had … *plans*. But what if they were good plans? What if it was exactly what Ace had been looking for? With Death out of the picture, he'd have to do it alone, but now here was Mordred, being so open and ready to destroy. And Ace couldn't deny that he loved the idea, the more thought that he gave it.

"What's the plan, exactly?" Ace asked, curious.

Mordred's smile continued to deepen. "Just follow me back to the kingdom. I'll enlighten you of everything on the way."

Ace nodded his head. "All right, then. Let's go."

The Rendezvous

"I need help," The Black Queen said.

Alice and Ralph were walking beside The Black Queen. No one had said anything for a while, as though there was really nothing to say. And in all reality, there wasn't a whole lot to say … certainly nothing that would contribute to anything.

But now, The Black Queen had spoken, and Ralph was listening. He was listening because maybe now, they were getting to the crux of what all of this was about: a journey of personal discovery, a search for true chivalry, a search for love and passion and compassion and light.

So Ralph said, "Why do you need help?"

"We all need help," The Black Queen said. "Do we ever."

"That's true," Ralph said.

"Well, not you two," The Black Queen said, and smiled sadly. "Alice, while a schizophrenic, is a great, great person, and is saner than anyone else I've ever known. And you Ralph: you, as you know I know and as I always say, are a good-looking kid, but you're also smart, and you really know what you're doing when it

366

comes to living the life the way you want to. You have ethics, which is always nice."

"Well, to be honest, my ethics have kind of taken a backseat since I saw Contorted Royal," Ralph admitted, and this was slightly true. Not completely, but Ralph did not, by any means, want to be a stanch ethicist. He just wanted to be Ralph. Because he knew that by no means was he a perfect person. He really didn't even see himself as that ethical. He certainly wasn't chivalrous. He just was. But he was okay with that.

"You could have fooled me," The Black Queen said miserably. "But anyway … Contorted Royal needs help. I'm sure by now you've seen all the chaos, and know about the rest. Everything is madness. I'm still traumatized from watching Spade getting murdered over and over again for such a cyclical period of time, but that could have been prevented if I'd been there for the king. As someone has said before me, it's not the cheating that's bad—because unless you're a virgin you know wild sex with a random partner is fun—but the consequences. I alienated my poor husband. And so, therefore, I want to be more chivalrous. I want to have heart. I want to be compassionate, and get my husband out of the depression he has slumped into."

And before Ralph knew it, The Black Queen had turned into a black chess piece, the queen of course. Ralph looked at Alice, and Alice simply shrugged, and so Ralph picked up the chess piece/Black Queen, and said, "You're sad, aren't you?"

Even though it was still just a chess piece, somehow, Ralph could communicate with it. Because it was, after all, still The Black Queen. "Yes, I'm sad. I failed Contorted Royal, not just because of my personal mistakes, but because I didn't rule the kingdom the way I should have. I just left it all to my husband, putting him in a jam, which in turn put him in a suicidal jam. I learned how hard it was to rule the kingdom when the alternate universe Black Queens tried to come and take over. It was horrible. Just plain horrible. I was more miserable than you could ever imagine. But what do you do, you know? There really isn't much you can do, I would say. But that's what I want to change. I had a conversation with The White Queen a while back, and she's like honestly the opposite of me … and you know what I hated about her but admired at the same time? Her level of purity. Not just because she's a flower virgin, though that's true, but because she seemed to have good intent. Sometimes I felt like The White Queen was me, or would be me, if I was a different person. But I get caught up in all the darkness, get caught up in the color black. Instead, of course, of thinking about whiteness."

"Well, we all make mistakes," Ralph said. "But it's honorable what you want to try. Do you have any ideas about how you want to restore things?"

"I want to make out with you," The Black Queen said.

Ralph looked uneasily at Alice. Alice shrugged again.

"Well, much to the chagrin of Alice," Ralph said, "I must admit I'd like to as well. But Alice, as you know, is where my heart is."

"I know," said The Black Queen. "You don't have to murder me with your self-righteousness. But the point is, when I look at you and Alice, I see a younger version of me and The Suicide King. And I long for those days. Back when we had a connection, back when we truly connected. Part of me knows what happened to separate us, but some of it is a complete mystery. I think that's why it pangs me with such nostalgia. Nonetheless, I still love The Suicide King ... he's my husband, after all. I just don't know how to show it anymore. He's gone down a completely different path. He is a man I don't recognize anymore, just like I'm not the woman he always saw in me. I think it's the curse of Contorted Royal. It really gets you, you know. There's no escape. I wish there was, but there isn't."

"Well," Alice said, "maybe you just need to woo him again."

"But I don't know how to do that," The Black Queen admitted glumly. "I really don't. Tell me, what is chivalry and good will and good intention anyway? I mean, think about everything that has happened in Contorted Royal, all the innocent people who have gotten hurt? Does anybody even understand proper codes of conduct anymore? I'm thinking, of course, about my experience with the Bronx. I know The Machine, while making everybody so disconnected, wasn't making *that* much of a difference. People in modern day society are mean and murderous, and it's the same with Contorted Royal. Is there such a thing as justice? Because if there isn't, wouldn't that make trying to seek justice a pointless exercise? Because you can't restore what can't be restored."

Ralph thought about what The Black Queen was saying; in short, she just wanted to see light again, but her soul had been plunged into so much darkness because of her experiences. That could obviously damage a person, quite severely, which was why finding romantic love was important.

But societal justice was still important. People mistreated each other like it was nothing. They would do it so naturally, too, was the crazy part.

But Ralph supposed he needed to reframe the idea, the argument: life wasn't about a quest for chivalry. If you thought that way, you'd always be disappointed, because chivalry only existed in the wild tales of King Arthur, if even there; chivalry was an idea, an ideal, an abstract concept that could never be reached because it was too perfect. Like envying Christ for being the unattainable example of humility and compassion, the unreachable good person of good will.

Instead, it seemed the argument needed to be reframed, as if, well ... Ralph wasn't quite sure, but not what it was before. Perhaps the approach would be better off, with, could the justice gained work for even a short amount of time? Things were always going to be changeable, things were always going to morph. Things were always going to hurt. That was just the way it was. But the thing was, could a small difference in the end help the bigger picture? Obviously not if you believed that things would always stay unjust no matter what you did, but Ralph wasn't quite sure he did that. He didn't want to fall into the clichéd idea that seemed just as flawed, where every little good deed mattered, in its own special way, and yet, at the same time, he didn't want to give up on the idea that justice was attainable, if the universe could blow decisions in the right direction, if people were more willing to try.

Which, to go back to The Black Queen, was why Ralph wanted to help her. She had gotten enough of the crazy life. She'd gotten enough of the bitter disappointments. For the sake of not moralizing, Ralph was just going to say her lifestyle had just led her to more misery (without saying why). And now she wanted to change that. And Ralph wanted to help her change that.

The problem was, he honestly wasn't sure how to do that. Because, he struggled with his own feelings of justice and injustice. His home life had actually been rather sweet … but society was something else. They were brutal. It was amazing how cold people could be, without even being aware of it, was the worst part. Ralph in fact wanted to believe that The Machine actually helped to *temper* some of the disconnectedness and violence in the Bronx, in his world, no matter how crazy that sounded. Because it was in people's nature, it seemed, to be cruel. And not because they were imperfect: everybody knew they were imperfect.

But Ralph knew, the following few thoughts would require an explanation: what, then, led to people being cruel, if not imperfection, which was, quite simply, unavoidable, especially if God created imperfect beings to begin with (not that Ralph believed in God, of course)? Ralph wasn't sure. He believed there had to be a cause and effect, though, but he wasn't sure what the source was. The biblical version of reality and the beginning actually made a lot of sense: the chaos and pain started with man's Fall, damned forever to be sinners and never cleansed, and then Cain killed Abel, just to top it all off, starting a whole unchangeable chain of events. But that was a dissatisfactory explanation. There had to be some other root cause. What started the whole destruction thing? Who made the first bad decision? The first person with power? And who was that? Did anybody even know who the first people were?

The viewpoint was even scarier from the perspective of a scientist, especially an astronomer. People were people, of course, but in all reality, what good would it do to try and seek chivalry if you were just a tiny speck in the cosmos? Such concepts like chivalry and love almost seemed meaningless on the grand scale of things.

So in all actuality, Ralph didn't know what to tell The Black Queen. All he could say was he thought it commendable that she wanted to make things right, but not much else. As much as Ralph wanted to give The Black Queen an answer, he didn't have one. All he really had to say was that, at least the three were together, at a little rendezvous, and were in the present moment, getting along greatly. That was good. That was progress. That meant something. It had to.

The moment was all that mattered, because that was all one had; the moment of which was already the past.

"Maybe you can't restore what can't be restored," Ralph said, "but you have to at least try. There's got to be a way."

The Black Queen turned back into her normal self, and then said, "I just need to get close to The Suicide King again."

Ralph nodded. This indeed seemed like a very good possibility, a good solution.

But things began to go wrong when the voice of Contorted Royal sunk in. The Black Queen said, "I need to kill that stupid, damned, ungrateful bastard …"

Ralph looked at Alice in alarm. Alice also looked concerned.

"What do you mean?" Ralph asked, dreading the answer.

"Well, isn't it obvious?" The Black Queen said. "We have to get it all out. We have to murder each other until we finally love each other."

"But isn't that counterintuitive?" Ralph wanted to say, but found his tongue was immobilized. What was the use? Ralph could see the determined insanity and homicidal rage in The Black Queen's eyes.

"I need to make that sucker grateful that I existed in his life," The Black Queen said. "Revenge is the answer."

"And not chivalry?" Alice said, perplexed.

"Of course not chivalry!" The Black Queen said, as though this was the most obvious question ever. "What planet do you live on?"

And before Ralph knew what was happening, a door appeared, and The Black Queen had walked back to Contorted Royal, metaphorical knives in hand.

This was not going to go well. So much for a peaceful and philosophically ethical rendezvous, with all problems solved and the light seen.

Honey, We Just Don't Go Together

The Suicide King was lying on his bed, his sword beside him like any faithful lover, when The Black Queen stormed into the room.

She looked angry; she looked *enraged*. Her hair was all frazzled, she was breathing hard, like she'd just been at it for quite some time, sexually, of course.

The Suicide King liked seeing this, however, as it somehow brought back the good old days of The Black Queen, so powerful and determined in her own way, coming to chew out The Suicide King for his impotence and incompetence.

"We need to have sex," The Black Queen said angrily. "Can you get that through your addled head?"

"Can I get that through my addled head?" The Suicide King asked. "Such a wonderful question. Of course I can get that through my addled head. Sex is the bread and butter of reproduction. Since you screwed up The Jack of Knives and his life with your infidelity, I sure as hell would like to have sex, so we can have The Jack of Knives all over again."

"Go to Hell," The Black Queen snapped, and looked as though she was going to tease The Suicide King because she lifted up her dress, but then pulled out a knife. "Naturally, though, we can't have sex in a lovey-dovey way. It's got to be Contorted Royal style. We need to get it all out, like you ejaculating all of your suicide into me."

"Oh, so erotic," The Suicide King said.

And before The Suicide King knew what was happening, The Black Queen was charging toward The Suicide King like a maniac, preparing to stab him.

And she did stab him. Did she indeed. But all of this was a mind game, of course; some remnant of Death's Mirror had stuck around to make things seem like they were something, only to make them something else in all fact and reality.

But the stabbing was wonderful. All the blood dripping felt terrific. All the pain was like paradise. The Suicide King couldn't put his pleasure into words.

As The Black Queen stabbed her husband, The Suicide King couldn't help but moan occasionally, and tell his wife how good she was in bed.

"Yeah? Do you like that?" asked The Black Queen angrily. "Well, good, because, honey: we just don't go together."

"I've gathered," said The Suicide King, and he was no longer bleeding. He was instead holding his sword, the tip at the belly of The Black Queen. How tempting it was to disembowel her, right on the spot! How tempting!

But he didn't do it. Instead, he said, "I'd rather do something a little more cruel, if that's okay with you."

"After my good time, you only want to be cruel? I just stabbed you to death," said The Black Queen.

"Well, we're clearly volatile, so … yeah. Merely cruel. That's all I want to be, if that's okay."

And at that moment, Spade walked in. It was Spade before he'd been murdered, but of course it wasn't the real Spade. The real Spade was dead. Nonetheless, The Suicide King could tell The Black Queen was falling for him.

"Aren't you two going to have at it like wild animals?" The Suicide King asked mischievously.

"That is cruel," said The Black Queen, and went toward her lover.

However, The Suicide King was just too quick: he threw his sword toward Spade, and Spade fell to the ground, the sword stuck in his body. This was a terrible, terrible scene, and The Suicide King saw that he had traumatized The Black Queen all over again.

But The Black Queen wasn't finished with her grief. Tears of rage spilling down her face, she picked up the sword and proceeded to cut up The Suicide King into pieces.

However, it didn't work. And how could it work? All of this was a mind game. Besides, The Black Queen didn't believe in slicing and dicing. The Black Queen would in fact ask the reader to disregard such a terrible idea, The Suicide King knew, as he saw that he was still all in one piece.

"Our honor is ruined," The Black Queen said.

"Yes, it is," The Suicide King said, and picked up the body of Spade, threw him against the wall in as careless and heartless of a way as possible.

"You don't think that was a bit excessive?" The Black Queen asked.

"Of course it was," The Suicide King said. "But I'm torturing you."

A servant wheeled in a box at this moment.

The Suicide King said, "Get inside, honey."

"No," The Black Queen said.

"I said, *get inside*."

"And I said *no*," The Black Queen almost shouted. "No respect for feminists these days."

"No respect for suicidal idiots trying to look masculine, I see," The Suicide King said in return. "Well, that's fine. In a moment, I'll show you real machismo."

And as though The Suicide King was raping The Black Queen, he shoved her into the box, which had a lid, and closed it, and locked it. Then he took his sword and sliced through the middle, effectively cutting The Black Queen in half.

But this, of course, was just a mere magic trick, you see? For what else could it be, except for smoke and mirrors, right? Because a moment later, The Black Queen disappeared from the box and came running into the room again, enraged, her hair wild and frazzled, with a determined look in her face.

"We're shattered like Death's Mirror," The Black Queen said. "But I love you."

"I love you too."

"And I hate you," The Black Queen continued. "I hate you more than you'll ever know. Just so you know. I hate you, I hate you, I hate you!"

And before The Suicide King knew what was happening, The Black Queen was beating the king, with her fists. It hurt, all right, but boy, did The Suicide King welcome it. Ah, the joys of homicide, especially by your own wife! Nothing was more orgasmic than that!

When The Black Queen finished, The Suicide King sat down on the bed, and The Black Queen, exhausted and breathing hard, sat down beside her husband.

She said, "We really screwed things up, didn't we?"

"It's because we're not meant to go together," The Suicide King said.

"But surely that isn't reality," The Black Queen said. "Surely it's not all black and white. Have we really drifted that far apart?"

"I alienated you with my suicide," The Suicide King said, "and you alienated me with your cheating. Are any of us wrong? Perhaps not. But the consequences, well ... we really screwed up our son. But don't worry. I banished him, abandoned him that way, and told him to go and have fun in the Bronx."

"Very kind of you," The Black Queen said. "I'm very grateful he at least doesn't have abandonment issues."

"Well, you two would be killer in bed together. The Jack of Knives as sharp knives ... if you know what I'm saying ..."

The Suicide King then winked at The Black Queen.

And that was when The Black Queen burst into tears.

The Suicide King put his arm around his wife, and said, "There, there, honey. There, there. What's wrong?"

"We screwed things up so bad, and they'll never be normal again. I'm trying to see the light, but I don't see any light. I feel like we're doomed to kill each other over and over again, whether literally or figuratively, whether through our ways of alienating each other or quite literally how we're killing each other now. Or rather, a few moments ago."

"Yes, we have indeed screwed things up," The Suicide King said. "But all my suicide has made me impotent. I've castrated myself more often than I'd like to admit, and that has of course left its scars. So what other way is there to have sex? Why, killing each other, of course!"

"But why don't we go together?" The Black Queen asked hopelessly.

"It's a very good question," The Suicide King said. "A question that I can't answer, no matter how much I would like to. I can't answer it because I don't know. I don't understand the laws of the universe. There are always theories that we need the good and the bad, and the good is that The Jack of Knives didn't turn out that bad, right? He's having fun with his friend The Dark Kid. There are also other theories that destruction and pain are the only

375

guiding principles of the universe. It doesn't matter how much good will you have, it ultimately doesn't accomplish much."

"Well, I want you to ravish me," The Black Queen said. "I want you to emaciate me. I don't care if it seems masochistic, making you the sadistic aggressor. Kill me, you stupid son of a bitch!"

"That I can do," The Suicide King said, and took his sword, did a few fancy moves with it, and then struck The Black Queen in the heart.

Impaled, they stayed that way for a moment.

"Well, this isn't phallic at all," The Black Queen sighed. "And awkward."

"Well, I may be impotent, but my sword does all the talking, if you know what I'm saying," The Suicide King said.

The Black Queen put the back of her hand to her forehead like she was going to faint, and said, "Oh! My heart can't take anymore!" Like a cheesy soap opera or something, just with quite a bit of violence.

"Well, good," The Suicide King said. "I'm happy for you."

And when The Suicide King removed the sword, The Black Queen fell over, dead. Out completely. Never to return again.

But return she did, of course, and that made The Suicide King smile. He held her in his arms, and finally, finally, kissed her on the mouth. They kissed for a little while, and then The Suicide King said, "You're so bitter, lady Black Queen."

"I know," The Black Queen said. "And you're too suicidally rancid."

"Honey, I guess we just don't go together," The Suicide King said miserably.

Because what he realized was that this was indeed the truth, in this explosive conversation. Part of the reason they didn't go together was because they had eroded over the years, part of it was because they were so powerful, among other things. In fact, The Suicide King felt the energy pulsating so much that he knew that if The Jack of Knives hadn't been in another world and had entered this room at this very moment, the room would literally explode with volatility. And of course that would never be good.

But when was anything ever really good? The Suicide King hadn't just become the way he'd become because of his wife. Oh, how he'd needed her, and how she'd abandoned ship! But also because he was such a bad king. Monarchies never worked, of course, but they definitely didn't work when you had a clueless king sitting on the throne.

And clueless he was. Yes, there was the truth that his suicidal tendencies ironically kept stuff in check, but, being Contorted Royal, it naturally made it worse, a catch 22 by definition. So unfortunate.

And really, there was no solution. Perhaps there could never be a solution. Because solutions were overrated. Maybe it was good that The Black Queen and The Suicide King were divorced. They were never going to figure out their problems, they were never going to be a unit. They couldn't even have sex together without pulling out the knives.

So The Suicide King puzzled. He puzzled, and he puzzled, and he thought about what he could do to make things right again. But there was no solution. The Black Queen and The Suicide King hated each other's guts. They were always going to.

So The Suicide King simply said, "Well, since love is out of the question, let's just keep killing each other."

"Is that what you want to do?" The Black Queen asked miserably, but then a smile crossed her lips, as she pulled out her knife. "Okay."

And The Suicide King lay back in bed and prepared himself for the brutal stabbing …

Throwaway

So The Dark Kid and The Jack of Knives were living it up in their uninhibited style. And did they indeed have *style*. They were kids, after all, the coolest kids in modern day society, if the truth be told.

But other truths were being told, as well. The Jack of Knives was struggling. Suddenly, style didn't seem all that important anymore. Because the society he was in was a jerk society, he saw that, and in many ways, was worse than Contorted Royal. The Machine had been destroyed, but people were still disconnected and rude; not as rude and disconnected as they had been before, but there were indeed still problems.

But it wasn't just that. The Jack of Knives was thinking about his home life. He was thinking about how he had been forced to be a slave for so many years for his father, the father of which he didn't even recognize. He should have seen the familial resemblance, but instead hadn't, because, well, he had thought he was just a poor slave boy. He had thought for so long that that was all his life amounted to.

Indeed, it seemed that everything was a throwaway, worse than any cheesy and pointless comedic line in a show. The Jack of Knives was literally a throwaway child; his father had abandoned him for a little revenge on his wife, and had never reclaimed his son, saved him from the fiery depths of indignity. And society itself was a throwaway. He saw so much of it happening and taking place before him, of people throwing each other away like it was nothing: it was a throwaway society. And it was terrible, when it came down to it. It explained why the modern day culture consumed so much and threw so much stuff away: they were slowly committing suicide, getting ready to throw themselves away in a universal trash can. And that made The Jack of Knives sad.

"You okay, man?" The Dark Kid asked.

The Jack of Knives didn't say anything for a moment. What was there to say, he wondered romantically? He didn't feel like there was anything to really say. Sure, he had a ton of feelings he wanted to disclose, but what good would it honestly do? The Dark Kid was much too happy in his darkness to really care about the plight of the human soul, much less The Jack of Knives and his emotional plight, which, contrary to what he wanted to believe, was not the center of the universe. In a cold, cold world, why would anyone care about what the poor Jack of Knives was thinking? What did it really matter? It didn't matter, obviously. It never mattered. The Jack of Knives just tried to make it matter so that way it seemed like it mattered. But it really didn't. That was the illusion.

But The Jack of Knives couldn't keep it to himself or he'd go insane. He would indeed. So he said to his friend, "I'm struggling right now."

And he explained everything.

The Dark Kid took all of this in silently, and then put on his shades. He stared off into space, and then said, "I can understand your feelings, but why do we have to assume that things that are thrown away can't be reused or recycled?"

The Jack of Knives thought about this, and the thought of it made him angry. "Great. Just recycle me like I'm a plastic bottle. Sounds wonderful."

The Dark Kid only smiled. "Okay. Bad metaphor, I suppose. I was just trying to go off what you were telling me. Maybe we need a different metaphor than something thrown away?"

"Well, that's my biggest question: how can anyone throw away a life?"

"You think your parents threw you away?" The Dark Kid asked curiously.

"They were so obsessed with getting back at each other that they neglected their only child. I'd say my parents threw me away, murdered my life, turned me into nothing."

"And you don't think you're being even a tad bit too cynical?" The Dark Kid asked curiously.

"I don't know," The Jack of Knives admitted. "Maybe. But maybe not. I haven't even lived in this society all that long and I feel like everyone just throws each other way. I can't help but relate it to my own story and the way that I was treated. I hated being a slave. I hated it more than anything. But he is still my dad, you know? I can't hate him. I can't hurt him back. I have to love him."

"Of course you have to love him," The Dark Kid said. "But that doesn't mean you can't let the darkness show."

"You think so?" The Jack of Knives asked curiously.

"What your parents did to you was wrong," The Dark Kid explained. "I would be angry too. But on the same token, maybe everything isn't a throwaway. Sure, modern day culture relishes in the garbage can and land fill, but that isn't your problem, pretty much because you live in Contorted Royal, a medieval culture that hasn't wasted all that much yet, and isn't so bent on Postmodern consumerism. Besides, human lives aren't trash. Some people like to make them trash, which is why they treat people a certain way.

But when I see you, I see style. I see styling. I see an awesome kid who I am happy to be friends with. And I'm very happy to be your friend. I don't know what I'd do if you weren't here with me, to keep me company. Probably go crazy or manic, or something."

The Jack of Knives processed this. Such a nice thing to say. So then, The Jack of Knives wasn't trash, wasn't just a newborn infant wrapped up in newspaper and dropped off in front of the nearest dumpster? That was good to know. Was it ever.

But was it true, was the question? Just because The Dark Kid said it was true, didn't mean it was true.

"I don't know," The Jack of Knives said. "How do you forgive your parents? How do you let go of all the dysfunction, all the hectic craziness? Do you ever truly forgive them? And not only that, it was so petty. My dad just wanted revenge on my mom … there wasn't even a good end game involved. Just a stupid decision that forever changed my life. And because of that, I became homicidal."

"You *were* homicidal," The Dark Kid corrected. "You aren't anymore. Now, all you care about is social justice and equality. You don't care about killing people and destroying their souls, like you used to. You've changed. You aren't bent on pointless destruction, on taking over."

"But how do we survive in such a brutal existence?" The Jack of Knives asked. "It does feel sometimes like the universe just wants to throw us away. I mean, what kind of meaning can we truly have in such a gigantic universe as the one we are in? I think bringing in alternate worlds and universes complicates things even more, right? We're all just random worlds with random people with random things, people throwing away random items that they don't even need."

"Possibly," The Dark Kid said. "But that's only because you're looking at it from a universal perspective. In all actuality, or at least in our reality, concepts like justice and pain do exist, whether we like to admit it or not. Maybe it has no bearing on an alternate universe elsewhere—or maybe it does—but the point is, it still has bearing in our life. We have to keep ourselves at the human level, otherwise we'd go insane. I think you'd be better suited studying English literature to understand the human condition rather than astronomy, if you get what I'm saying.

Otherwise, you will just see yourself as a speck, and will reduce yourself accordingly, in an unfairly reductionist way."

The Jack of Knives continued to take all of this in. It was indeed very interesting to think about. It was indeed. The Jack of Knives wasn't sure he agreed with all the points that his friend was bringing up, but they were points certainly worth considering.

But it didn't change how The Jack of Knives felt, obviously. "I still do feel very much like a throwaway, though," he said after a while. "I'd like to see myself as something else, but, I mean, think about it: my dad banished me from Contorted Royal!"

"So you'd get a different perspective," The Dark Kid reminded his friend. "So you'd be a kid again. But instead you're being a philosophy major, trying to solve all the world's problems through reason. Don't. Just be a kid."

But The Jack of Knives wasn't convinced. He needed to have a conversation with his father. That would be the only way anything would get accomplished. Hopefully not an angry conversation, but a conversation nonetheless. Because indeed, something needed to get resolved.

The Jack of Knives felt he needed to go back to Contorted Royal. But what would he say? "Hi, dad, thank you for making me grow up as a slave and making me clean up your blood."

And was that indeed symbolic, by the way. Cleaning up the blood relation to his father, as if trying to expunge it. The only reason why The Jack of Knives even found out about his true birth right was because Mordred, for some reason, didn't successfully kill The Suicide King, and that made The Suicide King angry, and turn The Jack of Knives into a murderer of his mother, who came back to life …

"My head's spinning," The Jack of Knives said, and sat down on the curb. They were in a residential area, just chilling, but The Jack of Knives needed to sit down and concentrate. Get his thoughts together. Figure something out. Figure anything out.

The Dark Kid patted his friend on the back. "I know all of this is difficult. I know you're pretty much like, what the freak? I would feel like a throwaway, too, if my dad made me a slave when I should have been a prince. But maybe it needed to happen. Among all that homicidal rage it also taught you humility. What if you would have been a fat brat if you'd become the king, rather than a slender and handsome young daredevil?"

The Jack of Knives laughed. "Ha ha. That makes sense, I suppose. I could be a pepper Jack brat, or something like that. I could be ordering my own father what to do, stuffing my face with meals left and right. What a terrible way to live."

"I think the only thing that was thrown away was a bad life," The Dark Kid said. "I think you still have plenty of reasons to live, and plenty of things to be grateful for. You should try to talk to your dad, though. I think that's a good idea. See if he can restore you to your princedom, which you know you deserve. See if you can help your father rule Contorted Royal. Now that you've been a kid, you can start to be a man. You can help change Contorted Royal. You can help the peasants, help people feel like they aren't a throwaway in society. I can see you doing that," The Dark Kid smiled.

The Jack of Knives smiled back. Yes, he could indeed do that, couldn't he?

"All right, then," The Jack of Knives said. "Let's go back to Contorted Royal. That would be good. I'll try and talk to my dad, when the time is right, and go from there. But I am still worried about modern culture. They waste so much, throw so much away. I suppose, in the context of an infinite number of alternate worlds and universes, it really doesn't matter if they throw themselves away, but I think this modern culture we're in now is on the verge of a major meltdown, deep in a garbage can … which of course, could never be good."

The Dark Kid nodded. "No. It isn't good. But let modern day society handle it. You have your own problems, and plus, it isn't your world or time period. You're a medievalist. Go handle that part of the timeline."

The Jack of Knives nodded. At that moment a door appeared.

The Jack of Knives hesitated before entering, but when he did, he felt like a brand new item, which wasn't going to be thrown away for a long, long time.

The Spade of Spades

Spade had never really felt like he was a full-fleshed character. He didn't play any important role in the drama of Contorted Royal, and he hadn't played any important role in the drama of Contorted Royal. He remembered that he had always been murdered over and over again, by Ace: that was his role. To die an unfair death in front of The Black Queen and traumatize her for life.

It kind of made Spade sad to feel like that was all he amounted to. Surely he was worth more than that?

Ah, but society didn't want him to think he was worth more than that. He had been a peasant, after all, and even in Contorted Royal, which tried to be more about equality and fairness and social justice, still let the rough treatment and life of peasants slip through its fingers. The Suicide King tried, yes indeed, he tried: but he failed.

And then he had met The Black Queen. That hadn't changed anything, if the truth be told. It had just led to his execution, over and over again.

But somehow, all of that was the past. Somehow, Spade was back. He wasn't sure how. It didn't make sense. He had thought he was dead: dead for good. And yet, somehow, he was standing outside the door of The Black Queen's room. So much had changed: the circularity had ended, they had gone back in time, The Jack of Knives had discovered he was actually a prince, The Suicide King had banished The Dark Kid and The Jack of Knives, among other things. Where Spade had been throughout all of this, he wasn't sure. He had assumed dead. And indeed, that answer made the most sense.

Regardless, he was standing here now. He knew soon, he was going to have a conversation with The Black Queen. As for what that conversation was about, he definitely wasn't sure, but he hoped it was a good one.

Spade knocked on the door.

"Come in," The Black Queen called from the other side.

Spade waited for a moment before he opened the door. He didn't know how this was going to go, or if it was going to go. He didn't know what he was going to say, or if The Black Queen was going to receive him well. He was, after all, still a poor peasant boy. A dead poor peasant boy, to make matters worse. The Black Queen probably hated Spade: Spade, who was in a way, the spade of the spades.

But, knowing that he needed to face his fears, Spade opened the door and looked at The Black Queen, his old, old lover once upon a time, who was lying on the bed.

She sat up, and looked to see who had joined her.

For a moment, her mouth dropped. Just for a moment. Then she closed her mouth, and The Black Queen said, with clear shock, "Spade?"

"Yeah," Spade said. "It's me."

"What … are you doing here? I thought for sure you were dead. I thought for sure you were … how is this possible?"

"It's Contorted Royal," Spade said simply. "I suppose characters only die when Contorted Royal wants us to die. It brings us to life when it wants to, it lets us live when it wants to. It's not our choice."

"Very fatalistic way of looking at things," The Black Queen said. She flattened the blanket of the bed, and said, "Come here. Come lie beside me."

Spade shook his head. "I'm not going to do that."

The Black Queen looked confused. "But why? We were such wonderful lovers," she added, sounding dreamy.

"I've been in penitence for my act of sin," Spade said simply. "You, however, just get to go do whatever you want, but me … I had to die over and over again, while you just laugh at my demise."

"How could you say such a terrible thing?" The Black Queen said. "It's not true at all. I had to watch you die over and over again. That was the worst thing for a woman like me to go through, so often, so perpetually. It was terrible."

"Regardless, we better not cheat," Spade said.

The Black Queen nodded her head seriously. "I suppose you're right. I think I've had to go to penitence as well. I've been trying to seduce Ralph all this time, but by now I've finally realized it's a lost cause. He's crazy for Alice. I'm a little jealous."

384

The two were quiet for a moment. What was there really to say, after such a long and silent absence? It was still indeed random that Spade was here. He, to tell the truth, wasn't sure why he was here.

But Spade finally said, "I feel like you used me."

The Black Queen looked shocked. "You feel like I … *used* you?"

"You knew I was a poor peasant boy," Spade said. "You knew I wanted a taste of power. And so you seduced me. There are all of these class divides, but I can never understand why the rich won't just admit they want to sleep with the poor."

"An awfully critical thing to say," The Black Queen said. "But you may be right. Who am I to really judge?"

"I don't know," Spade said. "I just know that I felt like you were using me. I don't know how else to say it. It makes me sad that you saw me as just a sex toy."

"Well, you were quite a sex toy," The Black Queen said.

"See what I mean?" Spade said. "I wasn't a human being to you. I was just a poor peasant boy who was somehow fun in bed."

"Oh, can't you take a joke?" The Black Queen said. "But all right, Spade. I see your point. But that's the problem with power. It corrupts: that much is obvious. But it's a little more than that as well. Power makes a person think they are literally entitled to things, such as sleeping with poor peasant people. Because you know, of course, if I'd wanted, I could have had you beheaded if you'd resisted me."

"Yes," Spade said. "Not that it mattered, what with my perpetual death and all."

"Very true," The Black Queen said. "But even if you had resisted, I wouldn't have beheaded that pretty little head of yours. That would have been just cruel. But to get back to my main point: power has a way of blinding us. I'm realizing that, the more I go through the rabbit hole story called Contorted Royal. But don't feel too bad. I am trying to see the light. That may be cheesy to hear, but it's true. I'm trying to become a better person. I have no idea what the hell that means. As a hardcore feminist, exploiting males is my mission, and I don't care if feelings get hurt. But it alienated my son. I still haven't forgiven myself for that."

"Well, I admire your power, my queen," Spade said.

"That's sweet," The Black Queen said.

"Well, you are indeed powerful. I was chaste before you came on the scene, and then all of that changed, and I became a hardcore slut. And I couldn't stop myself."

"That is indeed my question: if sleeping with me made you unhappy, why did you do it?"

"Because I couldn't resist you," Spade said. "I am still a boy, after all. I think about sex ... *a lot*. As all guys do. So in that way, I was using you just as much as you were using me. I'm just trying to say if I'd had even a little bit more will power, which I wouldn't of course, being a guy and all, I would have resisted you. I would have resisted temptation. But you're stunning, lady Black Queen. You're ravishing. No one can resist you."

"It gets old after a while," The Black Queen said miserably. "Getting all the sex you want ... it gets old. It's just too easy. Everybody wants you. Except for ... *Ralph*."

"Well, I'm assuming this Ralph character had more will power than me," Spade said.

The two looked at each other. Spade felt a stirring in his heart, of his old feelings for the queen. He did still like her. Love was too powerful of a word, but he indeed still liked her, for reasons he couldn't quite explain. He wanted to be with her. But if she was trying to see the light, now would be a bad opportunity. One could never find redemption, but it was The Black Queen's right to try and find it nonetheless.

"Come at least sit by me," The Black Queen said. "Nothing will happen. I promise."

Against Spade's higher inclinations, he got on the bed beside The Black Queen.

"I am trying to change," The Black Queen admitted unhappily. "I want to get closer to my husband. The problem is, our sex fantasies are murder fantasies ... that's how far apart we've drifted. It's rather crushing, I have to admit."

"I imagine," Spade said. "But he is still your husband, meaning, he's family. I'm always there for my little sister, back at home ... or, at least I was when I was alive. Family is family. We have to be there for them."

"Oh, quit preaching," The Black Queen snapped lightly. "But anyway, I see your point. I need to find a way to sacrifice for my husband. Show him I love him. I just don't know how."

"Just be there for him," Spade said. "It always helps."

"Are you sure you don't want to sleep with me?" The Black Queen asked.

"I'd like to, but you're on a chivalry diet," Spade said.

"Right," The Black Queen said. "I'm losing weight in terms of my sin, but I'm still hungry all the time. I have those cravings. A girl's gotta get what a girl's gotta get. But nonetheless … you're right. You're absolutely …"

Then The Black Queen just stared into space.

Spade took this moment to collect his thoughts. Well, he'd said everything he'd wanted to say. He'd explained that he'd felt like a male prostitute, that he'd felt used by a woman of power. Not that that said much: it had been Spade's weakness, in the end. Nonetheless, Spade still cared about The Black Queen, and he did miss their good times together …

Before Spade knew it, The Black Queen was leaning over to try and kiss Spade. However, her head went through his head. It was because Spade was a ghost.

"That's strange," The Black Queen said.

"I've been too much like the Devil," Spade said sadly. "Tempting you, bringing you down to temptation Hell."

The Black Queen looked longingly at Spade. "Yes. I suppose so. But there's something really beautiful about you, Spade. I wish you could see it. I'm sorry that you met such an untimely end. I'm sorry that Contorted Royal killed you off so unfairly. You could have made a remarkable character in this drama. Even our Fool got more screen time than you did."

"It happens," Spade said. "The poor and marginalized rarely have a voice in the average tale. Though I'm glad a schizophrenic has gotten her say. That's progress. Maybe not a peasant boy like poor Spade, but at least someone who also gets marginalized … or, potentially, at least."

"Yes, me too," The Black Queen said.

"And Brannon," Spade said. "He got screen time too. Such a humble peasant, but a good kid nonetheless."

"Yes he is," The Black Queen said. "Unfortunately, my path hasn't really crossed his, but I see your point."

"But I suppose narratives will always marginalize, even when they don't mean to," Spade said dejectedly.

The Black Queen said, in a sudden burst of passion, "Don't say such an awful thing, Spade!"

Spade smiled. "I'm sorry. It's just the inevitability of it, I suppose. Who actually cares about peasant poetry? Who reads peasant poetry? Who cares about the oppressed?"

"I care," The Black Queen said. "And I'll prove that by not sleeping with you."

Spade laughed gently. "You can't sleep with me. I'm a ghost."

"Well, still," The Black Queen said, and gave Spade a genuine smile.

This was all Spade needed to feel like he was worth something. It made him happy to feel this welcome. It made him feel like a regular spade of spades. Power was overrated, and it was amazing who, in reality, wielded the power: people you didn't expect.

People like Spade, who'd barely had a voice in the narrative of Contorted Royal. His power had come from the very fact that he'd been omitted the way he had from the narrative.

As Spade drifted away in thought, to go back to his death, he slowly disappeared ...

The Reality Check

"I can't believe we've been together this long," Ralph said.

Alice smiled. It was a good point. However, had they truly been together?

Alice pointed this out. "We've been together, yes, but at the same time, we haven't been together. Not in the slightest. We've been so busy fighting crime and busting our chops that we haven't even established how much we care about each other. Then there was my hospitalization, back in Death's Mirror time, which made things even more chaotic."

"Good point," Ralph said. "But we're here now. We are boyfriend and girlfriend, right?"

"I don't think I could have hallucinated you and then not become your girlfriend," Alice said, rather happily. "I don't know. What do you think?"

"I think that's a good point," Ralph said.

Alice looked at her boyfriend. Goodness, how much she admired him. She couldn't explain why, just that he seemed like a knight in shining armor, just that he seemed like such a strong character, just that he was his own person, was unique, was handsome, was fun to talk to, was assertive, was kind-hearted. He had many good traits, chivalry of which was the least of his powers.

"Thanks for not cheating on me," Alice said jokingly.

"What? With The Black Queen?" Ralph said. "Well, it was rather tempting."

"The Black Queen has seduced everyone from foreign kings to peasants," Alice said. "She's rather powerful that way. I see it more as a gift rather than as a curse or sin. But regardless, I'm still glad you didn't jump on her bandwagon. You showed your charm and you showed your strength. I'm impressed by that. It makes me want to stick with you for good."

"Well, I'm far from perfect, I will have you know," Ralph said.

"Yeah. I know," Alice said. "But you do your best, and I can see it. And that makes me happy to be with you. If you'd cheated on me, it probably wouldn't have bothered me that much, because it is The Black Queen, the most powerful woman on that side of Contorted Royal, but it still means a lot that you didn't."

"Well, I'm glad you think so," Ralph said. "It was actually fairly easy. What I think was more difficult than resisting The Black Queen was keeping her sane. A lot happened with the alternate universe breakdown and Death's Mirror. I thought she was going to lose it for sure."

"But then you made her sane again," Alice said. "And in a manner of speaking, you made me sane again. Sure, it was Brannon, The Jack of Knives, and The Dark Kid who killed Death, which made everything go backwards, but in a manner of speaking, I think you were there. In spirit, I think you were there, fighting Death to the ultimate death, like a good hero."

"Well, thank you," Ralph said. "Ultimately, I just do what I can. As will be perfectly apparent, I have my limitations. As you get to know me better, you'll figure those limitations out."

"Well, you still need to be who you are," Alice said, and she was suddenly holding a copy of *Catch 22*. She handed it to Ralph. "You need to walk around Contorted Royal with this sucker."

Ralph took the book graciously, smiling. "I guess I have been hiding my favorite book. But it is indeed my favorite book. The things it captures, the truths it tells us. I like Joseph Heller more than even Kurt Vonnegut or Jack Kerouac or Franz Kafka. So what book are you going to carry around with you, like it's your lifeline?"

Alice suddenly held a copy of *The Complete Works of Lewis Carroll*.

Ralph noticed and said, "Ah. I see. I suppose that's perfect for you."

"I think Contorted Royal has nothing to do with Lewis Carroll, if you want my honest opinion," Alice said. "Our language and linguistic puns aren't as meaningful, insightful, and funny. Our world is violent rather than whacky. There are a couple of other faults as well. Nonetheless, what would we do in Contorted Royal without Lewis Carroll? He may have nothing to do with our logic, with any of our logic, but he inspired us in his own way."

"Good point," Ralph said, and smiled.

The two didn't say anything for a moment, and then Ralph said, "You know, I think we should leave Contorted Royal. Go back to the Bronx."

"You think so?" Alice said, and crazily enough, it sounded like an exhilarating idea. It sounded great.

"Yeah," Ralph continued. "We could go, and eventually elope. It would be perfect."

"Well," Alice said, "I think I've been living in a modern day world anyway, what with the hospitals and unpsychiatrist office."

"Well, that would be the hard part," Ralph said.

"How do you mean?" Alice asked, even though she already had an inkling of what Ralph was going to say.

"Well, we'd need to make sure you have a reality check of how things are going to go," Ralph explained. "And I mean that indeed as a pun."

"Go on," Alice said.

"Well, you know in the Bronx they treat the mentally ill much differently. The mentally ill are tortured. If you even had the slightest symptom, they would be all over you like white on rice. If you were lucky enough to enter a hospital, which would still be hell, then at least you'd get supposed treatment, but you could be in even worse shape than that, and end up in jail or something. Just for spouting off nonsense that would make Lewis Carroll jealous."

Alice took this in. It was a very good point. For some reason, her world reveled in schizophrenia. It was probably because everyone in Contorted Royal was either crazy or schizophrenic in one way or another. Nonetheless, Alice had gotten a different treatment here. She remembered her experience with those two boys, and how close it had gotten to her being hospitalized. They would have, even though she hadn't been showing any symptoms, she had just somehow talked her way out of it.

Could Alice keep her symptoms in check? And better yet, if she left Contorted Royal, she would be leaving a world that understood madness, even if in a crazy and nutty and counterintuitive way. They appreciated Alice's schizophrenia. Her schizophrenia had a different function in Contorted Royal, and there was no way that could be ignored. They gave her meds that jacked up her symptoms, for crying out loud! But if she entered the real world and was a natural schizophrenic, people would notice. If she talked to a hallucination, people would notice. If she had delusions, people would notice. They'd shove meds down her throat, force her to see psychiatrists and therapists, force her to run the gamut of treatment until she finally became sane according to the intrinsic standards of society.

All of that was indeed a tough and bitter pill to swallow. Was that the kind of life she wanted to live? Always being in fear that her illness was going to screw things up for her? Because while in Contorted Royal her schizophrenia was seen as a gift, in the Bronx it would be seen as an illness. It would be seen as a reason to place her lower than people who were more high functioning—she would be stigmatized. There was no gift in a modern day view of schizophrenia. It was just sickness. Just disease. And that made Alice sad.

"I think we should do it," Alice said, "but I have to admit, I am very curious. What do you see in me? If I'd grown up in the Bronx, my life would have been completely different. I would have been ostracized, marginalized, run through the ringer. It would have been terrible. I wouldn't have been able to find a boyfriend, because they'd all run screaming from me thinking I'm a psychopath, when I'm just schizophrenic. So honestly … what do you see in me, Ralph?"

Ralph didn't say anything, just approached Alice and gave her a gentle kiss on the lips. Alice savored this feeling, this sensuality, this emotion, and then said, "Whoa. Thank you, Ralph."

"It's because I think you're beautiful," Ralph said. "I've had dreams about you, for a very long time. The Bronx is so boring, but you could bring your full blown schizophrenia and bring some action into such a boring world. You could make something out of the mundane. You could entertain me with a good delusion, make me smile with your stories of talking to hallucinations. And you're smart. You're very smart, that much is clear. A lot of people in modern day society just look at the surface. It's like all they can see is the superficial. But with me, I see something deeper. I see something very deep in you, Alice, something that can help fill a void in me. And it comes down to more than excitement or fun or adventure. It comes down to the fact that you're a good person, who goes against the grain of modern day society. I'm sure your gift is part of the reason, but I also just think it is your nature. Regardless, I'm very honored at the prospect of you coming with me to the Bronx."

"Me too," Alice said. "But you know you'd have to fight for me, though, of course. They're going to be determined to throw me in jail for my delusions or shove meds down my throat and keep me locked up for months at a time. I'll need an advocate. I can feel the changes already. Will I really be able to function as a schizophrenic in modern day society?"

"Well, it's a good philosophical question," Ralph said. "And I can't quite answer it. I can admit that it's going to be very hard. That much is true. It's probably going to be the hardest thing you'd ever have to do. But the good thing is, we'd be together. The important thing is, we'd be there for each other. I wouldn't leave you if you continued to go in and out of the hospital, unable to keep your symptoms under control. I wouldn't leave you for all the heartache and stress you'd cause. Because to me, it isn't heartache and stress. To me, I honestly see a gift in you, Alice. And that's just from your supposed illness. Then there's the fact that you're gorgeous, that you're beautiful, that you're kind, that you have substance, that you have a wonderful personality and a charming soul."

"Thank you," Alice said, and it was her turn to kiss her boyfriend.

She knew indeed, it was a long shot. There was no telling what was going to happen, except that it was going to be a hard road, going to the Bronx. But Alice was willing to do that to be with her boyfriend. The Bronx was his home, and he knew his way around enough to be able to stand up for her, be her advocate.

"No, thank *you*," Ralph said, and hugged his girlfriend.

They stayed like this for a moment, and then broke apart.

"You really are very special to me," Ralph said. "Like I said before, I've dreamed about you a lot. I can't get you out of my mind. You've infected my mind with your grandeur. And I just want to be with you."

Alice took all of this in. So, the Bronx it was. It made a lot of sense, the more she thought about it. It had to be the way.

"So when did you want to go?" Alice said. "I think the characters of Contorted Royal are finding the light they've been seeking for so long. It's Contorted Royal, so there may be a plot twist or two coming up, but regardless, we have to think about us and our new life. So in short, I think a lot of things have wrapped up, and rather nicely. And if they don't wrap up, they'll wrap up nonetheless."

"Well, let's stick around for a little while, see where things go, and give you time to make sure this is what you want," Ralph said. "But if it is, we'll go soon enough. When we both feel ready."

Alice took a hold of Ralph's hand. "That sounds wonderful. I'd like that, Ralph."

The two kissed again, and stayed this way for a little while, and then broke apart and smiled at each other for the longest time.

Alice couldn't help but feel welcome in the arms of the one she loved. The only reality check she needed wasn't worry over what would happen in the modern day world, but just the fact that Ralph was always going to be there for her, no matter what happened.

Fool of Oneself

The Fool was fool of himself. The Fooled was fulled of himself. He was in fact nothing except for tomfoolery, nothing but a fooling around fool type person. Like an effrontery of chaos. But all of that was okay for the Fool of himself, the folly of his fool, the follied of his fooled.

Things were going to go south. But would anyone listen to The Fool? Why, of course not, because all he knew was madness and folly. He didn't know anything except for that, because, how could he know anything else? What with all the prognostications, all the ability in the world to see into the future and know that things were going to go very wrong soon. Wrong indeed more wrong than anything.

But it was the inevitability of Contorted Royal. That was the world that they were in, unfortunately. It would certainly be nice if that wasn't the case, but how could that not be the case, when considering all the chaos that abounded in the lovely little pseudo fest of Contorted Royal, trying to masquerade as a medieval world trying to masquerade as circular time trying to masquerade as the novel *Catch 22* by Joseph Heller, even though war wasn't part of the motion picture, not even in the slightest.

Well, The Fool would have to take that back a little bit. War was indeed part of it. Those poor characters, like The Jack of Knives and The Black Queen and The Suicide King, trying to see the light, redeem themselves, and go against their Godly fate! How dare they! It was suicide, was what it was. Trying to see the light was never going to work. It couldn't work when there was nothing

394

to work, nothing to work right at all. Because Contorted Royal was indeed a broken machine, even though machines hadn't been invented yet, at least not like The Machine, which as far as The Fool knew, hadn't been invented yet, and yet, somehow they had destroyed The Machine, people like Ralph and The Black Queen, a machine that had caused all the circularity in Contorted Royal, but whatever. What did it really matter, in the end? Seeking light? Seeking redemption? Wasn't such a thing for a novel or something? To wrap up the novel lightly? The character, corrupted and wrong, who has finally seen the light?

Because ultimately, that was how The Fool saw it. These poor fools just didn't know what they were doing. For, how could they? They were just plugging along, whether it was The Jack of Knives accepting his homicidal fate, whether it was The Suicide King accepting his suicidal fate, whether it was The Black Queen punching people in the face in the Bronx (though in all fairness, that had certainly been deserved), whether it was Alice trying to confront her schizophrenia in a modern day setting, Ralph trying to figure out what the heck he was doing in Contorted Royal, and the like. Yes, indeed, the like. These poor foolish characters didn't know anything. They couldn't think for themselves! They were just trying to find their way. Just like anybody. Because everyone was a fool. What was that great quote by the genius, or supposed genius, Socrates? I know that I know nothing? Well, at least these poor fools were wise enough to not admit this useful, but trivial, fact. Because indeed, who really knew anything, except for what they were taught, what they were shown? It would have of course been nice if that wasn't quite the way it worked, but that was always going to be the way it would work.

Because nothing ever worked!

The Fool felt a wild urge to rip up or burn Oscar Wilde's *Picture of Dorian Gray*. Just for the fun of it, just to be foolish, but to be aesthetical. The reasons went on and on. But, alas, the poor Fool had to refrain from burning books that didn't belong to him. He'd have to fetch it out of the unpsychiatrist's office, anyway, the one who hoarded all the educational books on a decadent society, like Contorted Royal, in order to better undiagnose the problem.

And Alice! Oh, the audacity of her genius! Why did she have to be so all over the place with her gifts and talents? Why couldn't she just stay mad like the average soul? Because they were painting the roses purple? Because they didn't know why anything was anything? It was all interesting to think about, in the end, but it was all poppycock, too. It was also lunacy. Alice, the schizophrenic, somehow predicting things even The Fool couldn't think of.

But nonetheless, The Fool had seen things. He'd seen something indeed, something important, something more poignant than poor old Rabelais with his bitter satires and humor could ever pull off. He saw that the royal family of Contorted Royal was going to be in a hell of a lot of trouble soon. It wouldn't matter for Alice and Ralph, who knew they were going to run away together to the industrial hills of the Bronx, and it didn't matter for The Fool. Because, fools were quickly becoming outdated. Fools weren't needed for their wisdom anymore, for some reason.

But to go back to the circular point: The Fool of Contorted Royal was indeed fool of himself. But that's what made it so fascinating! That's what made it so perfect! Without that, what was there to really say? Not much, as far as The Fool could say. Though sometimes he wished he could be The Suicide King. Just to try it, some time, like trying sex in a super dirty way for the first time.

But, that was The Fool's world: the fact, of course, that he didn't have any world. The fact that he didn't have any rules, he just kind of did what he felt like doing, whatever that was.

Which was, of course, go and guide the king. Unfortunately for him, he wasn't as wise as Thersites, whether the Shakespeare version or the version from Homer's *The Illiad*, but regardless, he knew that already. He knew he'd never be as innocently wise and humble like a sage like Bottom from Shakespeare's play, no, no, no *indeed*. But he had a few wits about him that people trampled on. The Fool had lost count of how many people punched him when he spouted off his genius, just because he was too smart for them, and how dare a wannabe smart person be so foolish in front of a divine culture? It was ridiculous, when it came down to it, but it was the fact. And facts were facts for a reason, were they not?

Or, were they not? In all reality, The Fool wasn't sure. He was never going to be sure. Of anything. He just knew disaster was on the horizon, and he hoped The Suicide King had seen enough corrupting light to be influenced enough to be careful. Because if not, things were going to burst. Things were going to explode. And that wouldn't be good.

But the inevitability of Contorted Royal! The Fool thought this as he approached the royal court. Contorted Royal was never going to change. He wasn't going to go so far as to say, like The Jack of Knives and his poor philosophy, that all society was a throwaway, but cruelty and folly were just the name of the game. The red rum of murder! Just a little bit too tempting for the average person to get drunk upon. But that was the way the world spun. It was the webs that the spiders of destruction spun, forming a tapestry of chaos and things that were just forever going to be out of one's control. That's why The Fool honestly thought this discussion with The Suicide King was going to be the most pointless conversation ever. No matter what anyone did, bombs were going to explode. No matter what he said, Contorted Royal was never going to see the light. No world was ever going to see light. There was no light to see. What light was there to see, when it came down to it? The light of a God that didn't exist? The light of an atheist who could do whatever he wanted, live selfishly, and go around killing everyone because there were no consequences in the end? Oh, that awful binary, but it was true: all false truths, all concepts that never reached valid truth. Which was why the world was so screwed up. All were sinners, whether seen in a religious light or not. That was just the cold reality of it all. Because indeed, everyone was fool of themselves. They'd eaten too much insanity. No wonder The Fool was gaining a little weight. No wonder, no wonder, no wander.

The Fool opened the door to the courtroom, and walked inside. The Suicide King was sitting in his chair like an ancient philosopher, sad and lonely and in deep philosophic contemplation.

"I have some bad noose, your royal highness," The Fool said.

"What?" The Suicide King said miserably. "That it's all hopeless? That we're all going down the drain? That the light we seek is just a figment of our imagination?"

"Exactly," said The Fool. "Not. Exactly, and exactly not."

"What did you want to tell me?"

"We need to be careful," The Fool said. "There's a storm coming. You're sad and depressed, but that's because you've avoided suicide all this time. Unfortunately, you're going to have to do it the real way. The hard way. A way that will mean more in the end."

"I don't know what that means," The Suicide King hissed, rather beside his own character. "But whatever you say. I suppose you just want to ransack the home of my head with more nonsense? Go right ahead. I don't care."

"Not killing yourself is hard," The Fool said. "But learning how not to kill yourself is even harder. That's just the cold reality of it. Things are indeed going to burst, soon, the tick tock, tick tock, of a cold bomb, of a cold world. Just the reality of it. Just the truth of it all. So we all fall."

"Do you have any more nonsense to tell me?" The Suicide King said bitterly.

The Fool only smiled sadly. It was sad that The Fool knew how things were going to end and, because of the inevitability of Contorted Royal, or all worlds besides a nonexistent Heaven, he couldn't do anything about it. It was also sad seeing The Suicide King suffer so much in his withdrawal period. He'd gone such a long time without plunging that sword into his head, and it was making him grumpy, but it was making him stronger.

And that wasn't even the real test! Go figure.

"I would watch out for Mordred," The Fool said, and before The Suicide King could say anything, The Fool had already strode his way out the door.

He couldn't help but feel sorry for it all. Different forms of madness were coming, and with that madness, maybe some hope. He already knew where The Black Queen was headed, where The Jack of Knives was headed, where The Dark Kid was headed, and if his prognostications were correct (though perhaps they weren't), where Ace was headed. The Suicide King was going to have his own adventures as well, with Mordred sewing everything together in his special destructive way, wrapping up the novel in a nice, tight, little bow. It was wonderful, really, just plain wonderful.

Terrible, actually, but still. Perhaps there was hope. Perhaps. Perhaps they'd learn not to be full of themselves. That was important. Not that they really ever were, they were just misguided ... and who wasn't a little misguided?

The genius of Mordred's plan! Betrayal! Consequence! Climax! Which would lead to chaos, chaos, and more chaos ... but hopefully to something more meaningful, if insanity and sanity could just get out of the way ...

Bombs

"Are you sure this is going to work?" Ace asked Mordred.

Mordred only smiled. It was good to be back in Contorted Royal. He'd sort of missed the smell of betrayal, the atmosphere of madness, the trickery and mastery of it all. But he was back, and with a vengeance, and he was ready to install his final, absolutely final, plan, before things finally drenched themselves in utter darkness.

"Of course it will," Mordred said. "My plan is a bombshell: a complete and utter bombshell. Understand?"

"I guess so," Ace said. "But can you tell me again what your plan is, and how it's going to benefit me and my goals?"

"Isn't it obvious?" Mordred said, not afraid to show his maliciousness. "Well, since it isn't obvious, I'll explain it again. The plan is to completely disrupt the flow of the family of Contorted Royal. If we somehow split up The Jack of Knives, The Black Queen, and The Suicide King, for good, we'll be better able to take over the kingdom. And the key to splitting up the royal family? Why, that's a bomb, of course."

"A bomb," Ace said, as if this was a new word.

"Yes, a bomb," Mordred said. "Boom. Bang. It's all going to explode, go downhill from here. Are you ready for that, Ace? Because if you aren't, you can go, go and run away, go run for your life and find the freedom that you seek so much. Is that what you want to do? Or do you want to actually do something worthwhile?"

"No, I want to see this through to the end," Ace said. "Perpetual darkness sounds lovely."

"Good," Mordred said, and then he opened the door to the courtroom.

The Suicide King, The Black Queen, and The Jack of Knives were standing together, in a circle, talking.

Mordred and Ace listened to the conversation for a little while. Mordred knew what they were trying to do: see and seek the light. They were trying to come together, cut out the dysfunction from their family, make themselves functional again: they were trying to get their act together.

And boy, did they have a lot to talk about.

The Jack of Knives said, "But honestly, Dad ... Mom ... the prank you played on me, turning me into a servant that made me a bitter person ... how could you do that?"

"Well, if your mom hadn't slept with every guy available, I would have had no reason to get revenge," The Suicide King said.

"But you alienated me," The Black Queen retorted. "I didn't feel you truly loved me anymore. You would have done the same thing if you'd been in my shoes. Trust me on that."

"So what do we do?" The Jack of Knives asked.

"It's a good question," The Suicide King said. "All I know is we try to see the light. That's all we can really do. I've done a decent job so far. See, Black Queen: I hardly have any suicide scars on me, just old ones from long ago."

"You do look more handsome without all that suicide on you," The Black Queen said.

"Thank you," The Suicide King said. "Now are we going to kiss and make up, or are you just going to keep trying to seduce a Ralph who will never budge?"

"I'm going to try and kiss you," The Black Queen said, and before Mordred knew it, The Black Queen and The Suicide King were trying to kiss each other.

Trying being the keyword, of course. They just couldn't kiss each other, like they were opposing magnets or something. But they tried, and tried, and finally stopped, exhausted.

"Maybe one day," The Jack of Knives said. "It's probably better I didn't see it, anyway."

The Black Queen ruffled her son's hair. Ah, such a tender moment. She said, "I like your new modern day look, sweetie."

"Thanks, Mom," The Jack of Knives said. "That means a lot."

"You look like a true gentleman," The Suicide King added.

400

The three continued to talk, trying to get out all of their dysfunction and violence, and Mordred almost felt bad for what he was about to do. Split up the royal family. Explode them. Explode them to smithereens, burst them to a thousand pieces. A family that was this close to coming together.

But, it was the right thing to do.

Mordred made his presence known by saying, "Sorry to barge in on your family meeting, your ceremony of reconciliation, but there are some things we need to talk about."

The Suicide King looked at Mordred curiously, then in a frustrated way. "What do you want, Mordred?"

The Jack of Knives looked at Mordred, but seemed to have forgotten about his vendetta. The Black Queen also looked at Mordred, just simply looked confused that he had come.

"What do I want?" Mordred said. "I think I want the flame from the eyes of the Jabberwock. I think I want the world of Contorted Royal to come to my arms like a beamish boy. How does that sound?"

"I see you've got Ace with you, even though I banished him," The Suicide King said. "All right, well, I'm assuming you want to take over the kingdom."

"You've guessed it right," Mordred said. "Have you ever. And it's going to go splendid."

"I don't see how," The Jack of Knives taunted. "You couldn't even kill my dad."

The Suicide King smiled, gave his son a high five.

"That's a good point," Mordred said, his maliciousness becoming more and more apparent as he got closer and closer to the important moment. "But maybe my designs were just too complex for a teenager, who could barely get by with kindergarten philosophy. Maybe my plans are more evil genius than genius, and you'd never understand what my real goals are."

"I don't think so," The Suicide King said. "Now, I'm going to call the guards to have you both arrested for being so openly treasonous. Guards!"

Mordred simply smiled and pulled out a small bomb with a fuse. When he did this, the royal family moved back in fear.

"Is that a …" The Black Queen began.

"You've had enough of a taste of the modern world, lady Black Queen, to know it's of course a bomb," Mordred said smoothly. "And my plan is to detonate it. We're all going to be blown sky high … and when that happens, the royal family will shatter into a million pieces."

"But why would you do that?" The Jack of Knives asked. "When we're trying to come together?"

"Because it's the right thing to do," Mordred said, and pulled out a match, and lit the fuse. He continued: "I'm sick of the royal family bashing out each other's brains with whatever vice they have. I'm tired of them not striving to be better people."

"You're the one to talk," The Suicide King said angrily.

"Perhaps," Mordred said, "but none of that matters now. I hereby curse and contort the royal family of Contorted Royal. You'll be damned to the end of your days, until you finally get your act together. I don't know what that entails, just know that my rage has reached its exceeding point, and it will happen."

And then Mordred tossed the bomb toward the middle of the family.

The bomb went off: it exploded. But it exploded in slow motion. When it exploded, naturally, the royal family was expecting to burn to death or worse. But that didn't happen. What happened was something else.

The Jack of Knives slowly began to transform back into his former self, the one with the sharp knives, the one with the homicidal glint in his eyes, the one who could only think of murder. The Suicide King was holding his sword again and getting ready to stab himself. The Black Queen was thinking of alienating her husband through cheating. In short, all the light they had supposedly seen wasn't light, or at least, it no longer existed. Because they had gone backwards: they had been cursed, to go back to their former selves, and try all over again.

And now the royal family was split.

Mordred could sense the rip between the family, more massive than a black hole, more powerful than a supermassive black hole. He heard the explosion. He heard the curses.

When it finally was over, everything slowly went back to normal motion.

The Black Queen was the first one to speak: "That's it?"

Mordred only nodded. "That's it. How do you feel?"

"Lonely," The Black Queen said. "I'm going on an adventure, soon, to try and … try and fix things with my soul. I have no other choice."

The Jack of Knives looked darkly at the knife he was holding. His good looks had gone, he now looked rough and rugged and murderous again. "I have to soften. I can't be this way."

"I can't just give up the sword," The Suicide King said. "I have to truly give up the sword."

"You guys are cursed to wander until you can finally come together," Mordred said. "For real. Not just as an artifice, as if you were only coming together to wrap up a novel. You have to come together and love each other, and the best way to do that is to be split and cursed, cursed to roam the land like Cain. Think of it as *Beauty and the Beast*, where the beast had to be cursed before he learned what was truly important. It may be very moralistic for a Mordred-type character, but I am a different Mordred than the Arthurian one, naturally. I belong to Contorted Royal. My plan has always been to fix Contorted Royal, like poor Brannon, who couldn't do it because he was too polite and politically correct, even if a little liberal-minded with his poctry. But me … I'm okay with a little anarchy, a little war, if you get what I'm saying."

"But you haven't fixed us!" The Suicide King shouted. "You drove us further apart!"

"That's what bombs do," Mordred said smoothly. "Now, if you don't mind, I would arrest Ace, throw him in a dungeon for treason. That's always been his plan, to screw over Contorted Royal. He's the real villain in this story. Me, I just want you to seek the light, and seek it in a way that will help you grow, not in a way done just for convenience. You see the difference?"

The Suicide King took this in. Mordred saw all the anger on his face, but he shouted, "Guards!" and a few guards came in. "Take away Ace to the dungeon. Lock him up for good."

Ace had remained silent all this time, but he finally said, "How did I know not to trust you, Mordred?"

"Not that there's anything you can do, of course," Mordred said. "You're lower than anyone, lower than a two of spades."

But as they hauled Ace away, Mordred knew that the bomb had even worked for Ace. He needed time to think, to see the light as well. To undo his own curses, just like the royal family.

"I'm a betrayal more to the reader than to the actual characters," Mordred continued. "I only betrayed you, Jack of Knives, with the royal kingdom by helping you supposedly kill your father because I wanted the secret to come out, that you were indeed a prince. I was hoping you two could bond some. Granted, you ended up killing The Black Queen, but hence, more of a reason why this bomb was necessary."

The Suicide King looked at Mordred carefully, holding his sword so close to his brain, and said, "Yes, Mordred. I think, unfortunately, you are correct about what you're saying. We have a lot we need to do. We have a lot we have to accomplish. Things are changing. We're cursed, you say?"

Mordred nodded. "I don't hate you, Jack of Knives. I don't hate any of you. Hence, why I cursed you guys. Figure it out. Wander, roam, vagabond, meander, get your thoughts and act together … and then come back."

"That's going to be hard," The Black Queen said. "I'm going to miss my family, especially after we'd started to get so close."

"Do it the right way and it will be more worth it," Mordred said. "Now anyway, I suppose I should get going before you, Suicide King, decide to call the guards on me to arrest me for treason."

And before The Suicide King could say anything, Mordred was already out the door.

His work here had been done. The next chapters (independent of Contorted Royal) to unfold didn't depend on Mordred, and that was all Mordred needed to know to continue along his way, and continue along into his own book.

Split

The Jack of Knives couldn't believe how close he had been.

He'd literally reformed himself, with the same kind of importance and gusto as a social revolution. He had changed, had become less about destruction and more about empathy and compassion … or at least that was where he would have gone if he'd been given the chance.

But now that was over. Mordred had herby cursed The Jack of Knives, shoved a spade into his heart, scratched him with diamonds, beat him with a club, and soured his heart again. All that work was meaningless, in the end, all the work that he'd done with his friend in the modern day world.

There was something really depressing about it all. Because The Jack of Knives had believed, for real, that he'd seen the light. That was why he had come back to try to work things out with his father. But now he felt a void he couldn't explain, felt a giant gash between him and his parents that he couldn't mend back together unless he left and went on an adventure.

He saw why Mordred had cursed them, however; even for the backwards logic (perhaps no pun intended) of Contorted Royal, it made sense. Mordred wanted to make sure the royal family could come back for real and be together, without any dysfunction. Which all and all, was a pretty cool thing. It hurt like hell, naturally, being cursed like this, split up and destroyed … but there was a chance that it was indeed for the better, even if it didn't seem that way right now.

And indeed, The Jack of Knives was definitely going to be cursed. He saw that now. He wasn't just going to be cursed: he was going to be in penitence. He had thought, for some reason, that homicide was cool. Even though he'd never successfully killed anybody (his father and Death were still alive and kicking), he had still tried to idolize it, and rather unsuccessfully. He needed to get all of that out of his system. Granted, no matter where he went, a little bit of it would always be in his system, but he needed to change as much as possible.

And he could see how it was going to happen. There was a kid named Griffin, who was kind-hearted and gentle-spirited. When the time was right, The Jack of Knives was going to enter the world of Griffin Feathers. Until then, he was probably just going to roam around, try to get his thoughts and act together, but when the time was right, he was going to learn from the master, from Griffin, one of the kindest people to ever exist, in any world. Not that Griffin didn't have his struggles, of course, but still … he would be a good example for The Jack of Knives.

It would be penitence because he'd have to be around gooey emotion all the time. Not sentimentality, luckily for The Jack of Knives, but he'd have to go to a completely different world. A world of kindness. A world of strength and love and compassion. A completely different world. One that The Jack of Knives hoped he could get used to.

The Jack of Knives felt bad that he hadn't been there for his father. Granted, he hadn't known, but all those times irregardless he could have said something to his father; all the times that The Suicide King killed himself and would sometimes explicate the reason for his suicidal madness, The Jack of Knives could have tossed in a kind word or two, just to brighten The Suicide King's day. But he'd chosen to remain silent, for whatever reason. He'd chosen to keep to himself, which had honestly been the dumbest thing ever. He'd chosen to just clean up the mess and never try to inspire the king to be kind to himself.

Granted, this wasn't all that surprising; The Jack of Knives had been so angry for such a long time, had been just a mere servant in the castle, and it wasn't his job to be The Suicide King's therapist. Being that low on the social ladder wore you out, forced you to only focus on yourself and your survival. But if The Jack of Knives had been even a little bit stronger, that could have changed. And for the better, naturally.

But alas, it was too late, and they were cursed. And cursed they were going to have to be. Wonder, wander, try to get it all worked out … and come back if there was ever a time for them all to be together.

***

The Black Queen could see where all of this was going. Now, being the type of person she was, whether feminist or sex activist or free lover, she didn't think that her cheating in and of itself had been wrong. Because, who the fuck cared (no pun intended) what The Black Queen did? She was a woman of independence, and powerful, and knew how to exploit people to get her way. All except for Ralph, of course, but Ralph didn't count.

But it had still caused problems. It had made The Suicide King jealous, which had made the poor Jack of Knives, her son, live in terrible working conditions for such a long time, and eventually try (and fail) to revolt against his father. One could always argue that that wasn't The Black Queen's fault (and in a sense it wasn't), but that it was The Suicide King's fault. He was the one who had been such a jerk and lied to The Black Queen, just to get a little revenge.

But The Black Queen wanted to take accountability and responsibility nonetheless because she loved her son. She loved him more than anything. She had been such a fool not being with him all those times he had to clean up after The Suicide King. He had grown up without a strong mother figure, and that was cruel. No wonder The Jack of Knives was so pathologically screwed up and antisocial in certain ways. He hadn't gotten the affection he'd needed as a child.

The Black Queen could see her future, and her future was bright. She was going to enter the world of The Street Kid and counsel a young street boy named Phoenix. That was going to be interesting. She already had no intention or plan of exploiting him, and not just because his vulnerable situation already left him open to exploitation, but because The Black Queen wanted to change. She wasn't sure how she wanted to change, she just knew that if she was with Phoenix, The Street Kid, she'd change in a special way. She felt it. Such a thought made her happy, in a way that she couldn't even explain. In a way that made her joyous with glee.

She hoped that by the time she came back, she'd be ready to have her own family back. She hoped she'd be ready to love The Jack of Knives and love The Suicide King. She hoped more than anything that they could all get along. Being cursed and split, it was too late now to try and get close, but once the curse wore off during their wandering, things might get better. They might be able to be a family again. Nothing would please The Black Queen more. Such a thought made her so happy she was practically dancing with joy, even considering that her life was going in a new and even scary direction, that there was no telling where The Street

Kid was going to lead her. Who was The Street Kid, anyway? What was his story, except that he existed in another world?

The Black Queen didn't know ... yet. But soon enough, she'd know, and she'd be part of his life, and it would be beautiful. She'd help inspire him, adopt him like her own son. No, even better than that: she'd be his best friend. She'd be there for him forever, like a girlfriend, just without all the pretentiousness. And yes, for the love of God, she wouldn't try and seduce him.

***

Hard decisions, hard decisions ... and things were only going to get harder.

The Suicide King looked at his family, and wished more than anything he could be close with them. But there was an invisible wall, courtesy of the curse, of course, that kept them apart. The Suicide King knew they were going to go on an adventure of self-discovery, to try and reach sainthood. Whether that would happen or not, there was no telling, but it was certainly worth a shot. They'd screwed each other's lives up enough already, it was probably time for a break. Because, enough with the family drama!

But honestly: The Suicide King wasn't ready. He knew he was going to have to stay here and fix Contorted Royal. He didn't think he'd be able to do that, of course, because, how could he do that? Wasn't it a catch 22 that his committing suicide kept people from murdering each other too much, and yet, at the same time, also caused everyone to murder each other? The king had just done the best he could with what he was given, nothing more. That was all.

But he had done wrong. Not because he'd committed suicide over and over again. If he wanted to die, that was his choice, and no one was going to tell him how to live. If he wanted to stab his brains, that was his right. He was The Suicide King, after all, and who would he be if he didn't commit suicide? But regardless, and indeed regardless, he had been self-indulgent with that suicide. Knowing full well that The Jack of Knives had been his son, and he hadn't once sent a word of encouragement.

He could have said anything. "Don't feel bad, Jack, it'll be over soon," or "This suicide you see is only an illusion." But instead, he'd let the boy be traumatized by all the cleaning, because he'd been so obsessed with stabbing that sword into his brain. Which was honestly just plain pathetic. Pathetic, indeed, that he'd been so self-indulgent, caring for no one but himself and his own need to get high.

It was an awful way to raise a child.

And not only that, he'd lied to his son. He hadn't parented, had just kicked him out with the other servants. Now, The Suicide King wanted to reform: give better working conditions to servants, better pay, more prestige, as much as he could possibly give: but that didn't change that none of that had been true while The Suicide King had ruled, because he'd been so obsessed with killing himself. Self-indulgence to the extreme. Such a terrible way to live, such a terrible way to be. To not even lift a finger to tell your son you were proud of him, for doing the tough labor, for doing the tough work.

No wonder his son was so scarred.

They were all indeed split. Split apart, split up, split for good. Well, hopefully not for good (though it seemed that way), but split. It was going to take a lot of work for them to come back together, in a way that was proper and true.

But The Suicide King knew it could happen. He felt a warmth emanating from his wife that he hadn't felt in a long time. He felt a gentleness in his son, right here, right now, that he didn't think could ever exist. They were both going to go very far on their adventures, and The Suicide King was excited for them.

And The Suicide King? He was going to stay here. Stay here and try to rule his kingdom the right way. With family drama out of the way, it was probably going to be easier. He'd probably be able to set a better example, and hopefully violence would go down. It was still The Middle Ages, of course, so there was going to be violence, but hopefully, The Suicide King could change all of that.

Hopefully.

I See the Light

Brannon wanted to go home. He'd been in Contorted Royal long enough to understand that, while he had made a difference in his own way, he still needed to be responsible for accepting the things that were out of his control. Mordred had cursed the royal family, and while Brannon was completely opposed to that, there was only so much he could do.

Brannon was with The Jack of Knives and The Dark Kid. It was the last time they were going to be together, at least for a long time. They were going to go embrace their own paths, and figure things out that way.

As Brannon talked to his friends, he couldn't help but bring up the alternate universe Brannon.

"I wouldn't worry about him," The Dark Kid said. "You did everything you could with him."

This was certainly true: Brannon couldn't dispute it. In fact, he almost wanted to believe that the life alternate universe Brannon was going to live soon enough was going to be more exciting than any life that Brannon could live. Alternate universe Brannon was going to experience a lot of strange things, but things that were going to shape him, from watching people die and then somehow still be alive, to talking with Phoenix, to a host of other things. In a way, Brannon was kind of envious of him.

"You're probably right," Brannon said. "Regardless, I've been in Contorted Royal long enough."

The Jack of Knives couldn't dispute this. They had *all* been in Contorted Royal for far too long. The Jack of Knives had been washing up blood, metaphorically and literally, for too long now. It was time that he went out and learned kindness, and became a kid again.

"Are you ready to meet Griffin?" The Dark Kid asked.

"I think I will when the time is right," The Jack of Knives said. "In the meantime, I'm just going to wander. I need to think about a lot of things."

The Dark Kid didn't see this comment as all that surprising. The Dark Kid needed to roam as well. Sure, he wasn't the one who'd been cursed, but he knew that soon, he was going to play a role in The Street Kid's life. He also had to go back to the land where he came from, to try and get answers. Part of that was dealing with a villain named Stryker.

Indeed, the three kids couldn't help but think about how much life was ahead of them. More life than they were going to be ready for, more adventure than they were going to ever understand. But that was how it was. That was the way it worked.

It was time to get answers.

While The Jack of Knives, Brannon, and The Dark Kid were talking, discussing their plans and the things they hoped to accomplish, The Black Queen was in her room, The Suicide King on the bed, The Black Queen at her dresser, putting on her makeup and getting ready to go to the world of The Street Kid.

"You excited?" The Suicide King asked.

"Excited for what, honey?" The Black Queen asked.

"Excited to meet Phoenix?"

"Of course I am," The Black Queen said, concentrating on putting on the makeup but getting final mental snapshots of the hunk that was her husband. "I see the light."

"Seems like you see more light than me," The Suicide King said dismally.

"I don't think that's true," The Black Queen said. "You've been sober since the explosion. That counts for something. You've already made working conditions better for servants and peasants, and you're working hard at other reforms. You're taking the suicide out of The Suicide King. I think you see the light too, are simply just too afraid to admit it."

"Perhaps," The Suicide King said. "But that doesn't mean I'm not lonely about all of this."

"What do you mean?" The Black Queen paused from putting on her makeup.

"Well, it's just that, we're all splitting up. We're all going our separate ways. In theory we'll be back together eventually, we just don't know when or where that is or will be. That sucks, not knowing, you know what I mean? I'd like to know when we're finally going to be a family again. And that includes busting Ace out of the dungeon. I wish he was a normal person, wasn't so bent on the pointless destruction of Contorted Royal. At least Mordred had values he was running on."

"Very true," The Black Queen said, and sat beside her husband. "But if you want my honest opinion, I wouldn't worry about any of it."

The Suicide King wasn't sure he saw it this way. What if his honey got hurt along the way? Not by Phoenix, of course, but from what The Suicide King knew about the world of The Street Kid, his world was pretty hostile, a brutal place to be. That was no place for a charming woman like The Black Queen.

But then again, she was The Black Queen. She could handle herself. Maybe that was going to be the hardest part. Letting her go.

The Black Queen could tell that her husband was having doubts about this, so she put her hand on his chin, which was down, and lifted up his head so they were looking at each other in the eyes. "It's going to be okay, honey. Trust me. I've got this. It's about time we chase this light, and about time we bring it back. We've made a lot of mistakes, but we can make it right."

The Suicide King took this in. The woman was speaking reason. But goodness, how much he was going to miss her.

As The Suicide King and The Black Queen were chattering away about the way things were, and the way things were going, Ralph and Alice were sitting outside on the lawn of the castle of Contorted Royal, just talking, waiting for the door to appear to take them back to the Bronx.

Alice was a little nervous. She was crazy about Ralph, but she'd been in Contorted Royal so long that she had to admit, she was going to miss the madness of the world. She was instead going to have to go to a world, the Bronx, the modern day world, where madness was eradicated by reason and elitism on a daily basis. Boring old reason, stifling old elitism. Never any excitement, never any drama. She was going to have to see a real psychiatrist, a real therapist, and stay in real hospitals and take real meds … that scared her. She hoped she'd be able to keep her illness under control to not need that, but she knew the world would be able to smell her schizophrenia like a wolf sniffing out its prey.

The two were holding hands, and Ralph thought this was the sweetest thing. And it was, rather, a sweet scene, the two together.

Were they really doing this? Ralph couldn't believe it. After all this time, they were finally together. After all of their time being separated, they were finally going to be together. And as much as Ralph hated to admit it, it was going to be nice that there was no Black Queen to try and get in the way of their relationship.

"You excited for what's coming up?" Ralph asked.

"Of course," Alice said. "I've been waiting for this moment for far too long. But it needed to happen. We were meant to be together. I hallucinated you for an eternity, dreamed about you even longer ... I think this couldn't have worked out any other way."

Ralph smiled, and gently reached in to kiss his girl. It was a sweet, gentle kiss, Alice felt. It made her heart flutter a little.

That was when the door appeared.

"I don't know what I'd do without you," Ralph said, standing up. "So let's tackle this world, show the power of your schizophrenia."

"Sounds good to me," Alice said, and they stepped through the door together and went back toward the Bronx.

As Alice and Ralph went through the rabbit hole, The Fool couldn't help but smile at the entrance of the forest. If everyone else was going to go seek enlightenment, then The Fool wanted to do the same thing. You could always be more foolish, correct? So, he looked at the castle, and smiled, and watched as Mordred came up to him.

Mordred saw The Fool, expecting this meeting, and said, "You ready to leave this place?"

"Of course," The Fool said. "But if you're coming with me, you'll have to catch me."

And then The Fool took off through the forest.

Mordred only smiled. He knew their paths would cross in the future, at some point, so there was no point in chasing after him. But Mordred's work here was done. One day, when the royal family came together, Mordred could congratulate himself for his work ... but in the meantime, everyone had a lot of work they needed to do.

As Mordred and The Fool continued along their ways, Ace stayed in the dungeon. How desperately he wanted to pound his head against the walls! Because that's what it felt like, of course.

He'd only been trying to do the best he could. Why hadn't that counted for anything? Well, according to everyone else, because it wasn't his best.

As Ace's head spun with all of the thoughts of what had happened, and what had gone wrong, and how chaotic and crazy and full of folly it had been, Death appeared.

Death was less emaciated. There was something more happy about him, Ace noticed.

And this was true. Death was happy. Those boys had freed him. They'd given him a new purpose in life.

"What did you want, Death?" Ace asked, definitely not afraid to show his frustration.

"I just want to wish you luck. You need to reform, after all."

"Of course I need to reform," Ace said. "That's why I'm beating my head against the wall. But it takes time. Things like that take time. I'm not going to just become the cool Ace of Spades in a heartbeat."

Death only smiled. "You already are the cool Ace of Spades."

And then Death vanished.

Ace thought about this. What if there was truth to it? It seemed unlikely, but hey … a complement was a complement, even if it was random and off center.

As Ace was busy contemplating the meaning of life, The Poetess was looking at Contorted Royal, from a fair distance away. She was going to leave as well, try her luck as a poet in some version of a modern day world. She figured it wouldn't go very well. Poets just couldn't sale economically viable work. But that didn't mean she wasn't going to try.

And that was what all the characters of Contorted Royal were realizing: their struggles and failures didn't mean they couldn't try, and couldn't continue to try. No it didn't. Not at all.

And that, ladies and gentleman, was the beginning and the end of how the characters of Contorted Royal tried to see the light, tried to get to the bottom of redemption. Rather pointless, if I don't mind saying so myself, but that was what the poor characters wanted to do. Naturally, this feeling of closure has nothing to do with the reader, because, well … there isn't any closure. Their journeys were just beginning, in a manner of speaking. But seeking redemption was still pointless anyway, regardless, and so …

And so, at least they were going to try.

All one could really do in existence, simply a reflection of all the problems in Contorted Royal, like a death's mirror shard, like a contorted royale, like dysfunction. Function through dysfunction, worlds upon worlds just reflections of other worlds, other alternate universes reflections of other alternate universes.

But sometimes that's the only way things truly work.

Is there light you want to seek? Well, I hope you find it, and desperately pray you don't have to go through what these poor characters had to go through.

And if you do? If you do fall into the multi-layered traps of madness and worlds and Death's Mirror? Well, you have my deepest sympathy.

If that happens, just come to Contorted Royal sometime. Take a vacation.

Come get your mind off things.

Acknowledgements

Tough novels like this don't come easy. I am naturally indebted to literature, both young and old (Oscar Wilde's *Picture of Dorian Gray*, Rabelais and his novel *Gargantua and Pantagruel*, *Catch 22* by Joseph Heller, *Alice and Wonderland* by Lewis Carroll, and a multitude of Medieval works, just for starters), but I am also indebted to books that have opened my mind on schizophrenia and what has been labeled "mental disorders," such as *Capitalism and Schizophrenia* by Deleuze and *Madness and Civilization* by Michel Foucault. There is also of course my family to acknowledge, which would include my parents and grandparents and sister, as well as Ken Hofeling, who helped with the formatting of the art. The artwork itself came from a very special place and a very special person, and I am exceedingly grateful for the execution of skill with the artwork and the deep passion in which the work was forged. I'm also grateful for the reader, whoever that may be, and I hope that you have engaged with this satiric text in a way that will encourage you to realize the brighter side of existence, the more beautiful side.

About the Author

Phoenix (aka Stephan Heard) is a fiction writer, poet, playwright, philosopher, and serious thinker, though he will occasionally throw in a joke or two when the time is right. He has written seven full-length novels (including *Contorted Royal*), five poetry collections (including the previously published *Characters*), an experimental novella, the previously published *Silent Noise*, one short novel, three plays, an informal philosophical treatise, and two short story collections. *Contorted Royal* is Phoenix's attempt to make fun of rather serious and important topics, such as the societal misunderstanding of mental illness and the violence of family dysfunction, in the hope of defamiliarizing hard-to-discuss topics to allow the reader to more easily engage with such issues. The novel represents Phoenix's more ambitious attempts at writing and narrative experimentation, but with the underpinnings of social commentary and a well-told story. While Phoenix will claim that any of the beliefs found with the characters of Contorted Royal do not necessarily reflect his own viewpoints and views, he hopes that the satiric edge of the novel provokes discussion about very serious topics. As always, Phoenix is delighted to present this work to the reader, and hopes that whoever reads it will walk away with something, and will, of course, rise out of the ashes to a more fully realized state of being, as Phoenix was able to do by writing this novel.

32182606R00230

Printed in Great Britain
by Amazon